continued ...

"Hotter than hot."   —*All About Romance*

"This is a Wilde and delicious book! It will make you Wilde with desire . . . Get ready for a hot and bumpy ride into exquisite passion and desire."
                    —*Reader to Reader Reviews*

"Ms. Denison knows how to make a story more than a romance. She makes it sensual, electric, and with a plot that keeps readers turning the pages. With a talent such as this, readers will agree that she'll be around for a long time to come!"   —*The Road to Romance*

"Denison gives us another sensuous tale about the Wilde brothers that borders on erotic. Her men are sexy, charming, and gorgeous, and her heroines are strong yet vulnerable women who can hold their own with a Wilde man. *Wilde Thing* teases, entices, and seduces readers!"   —*The Word on Romance*

"Janelle Denison is a master at creating the perfect bad boy . . . Passion sizzles with each and every erotic encounter, and there are plenty of erotic scenes guaranteed to heat the room."   —*The Romance Reader's Connection*

Born to Be Wilde

JANELLE DENISON

B

BERKLEY SENSATION, NEW YORK

THE BERKLEY PUBLISHING GROUP
Published by the Penguin Group
Penguin Group (USA) Inc.
375 Hudson Street, New York, New York 10014, USA
Penguin Group (Canada), 90 Eglinton Avenue East, Suite 700, Toronto, Ontario M4P 2Y3, Canada
(a division of Pearson Penguin Canada Inc.)
Penguin Books Ltd., 80 Strand, London WC2R 0RL, England
Penguin Group Ireland, 25 St. Stephen's Green, Dublin 2, Ireland (a division of Penguin Books Ltd.)
Penguin Group (Australia), 250 Camberwell Road, Camberwell, Victoria 3124, Australia
(a division of Pearson Australia Group Pty. Ltd.)
Penguin Books India Pvt. Ltd., 11 Community Centre, Panchsheel Park, New Delhi—110 017, India
Penguin Group (NZ), 67 Apollo Drive, Rosedale, North Shore 0745, Auckland, New Zealand
(a division of Pearson New Zealand Ltd.)
Penguin Books (South Africa) (Pty.) Ltd., 24 Sturdee Avenue, Rosebank, Johannesburg 2196,
South Africa

Penguin Books Ltd., Registered Offices: 80 Strand, London WC2R 0RL, England

This is a work of fiction. Names, characters, places, and incidents either are the product of the author's imagination or are used fictitiously, and any resemblance to actual persons, living or dead, business establishments, events, or locales is entirely coincidental. The publisher does not have any control over and does not assume any responsibility for author or third-party websites or their content.

BORN TO BE WILDE

A Berkley Sensation Book / published by arrangement with the author

PRINTING HISTORY
Berkley Sensation mass-market edition / September 2007

Copyright © 2007 by Janelle Denison.
Interior text design by Stacy Irwin.

ISBN: 978-0-425-21082-6

BERKLEY® SENSATION
Berkley Sensation Books are published by The Berkley Publishing Group,
a division of Penguin Group (USA) Inc.,
375 Hudson Street, New York, New York 10014.
BERKLEY SENSATION and the "B" design are trademarks belonging to Penguin Group (USA) Inc.

PRINTED IN THE UNITED STATES OF AMERICA

10   9   8   7   6   5   4   3   2   1

Dear Readers,

The wait for Joel Wilde's story is finally over! Here he is, tough and lean and breathtakingly sexy. Thanks to all of you who've written to me asking for his story, and for hanging in there while I wrote it. I hope it's everything you've anticipated, and much more.

Joel is the last of the Wilde family. In past books, he's always come off as casual and laid back, and for the most part he is. He's served in the Marines, has seen and done things he'd rather forget, and just wants to live a simple, uncomplicated life as a bachelor. His main focus is his job as a security specialist, and when an old friend calls in a favor, Joel finds himself in way over his head with a woman who is sensual and determined, and has no qualms about discovering just who Joel really is beneath all that rough and tough military facade.

This story took many unexpected turns for me, especially with Joel's character. He was far more complex than he'd let on in previous books, and he had deeper emotional issues that explained so much about the life he'd chosen and why he swore he was better off being single and on his own. But Lora Marshall, the woman he'd promised to protect, refuses to let him be a slave to his past and to those fears that keep him from committing to any one person.

For those of you who might be reading about the Wilde family for the first time, I hope you enjoy this story enough to want to read about the rest of the Wilde gang. So far, there are seven stories in all, and those books can still be found at your favorite online book source, or at your local bookstore.

While the members of the Wilde gang have all found their happily ever afters, the wild and sexy fun doesn't stop here with Joel! In *Born to Be Wilde* you'll get to meet three of Joel's good friends, Ben, Jon, and Kevin, all ex-marines who now work for the same security firm, Elite Security Specialists. Each one of these men will be getting his own story, as well. Right now, I'm working on Ben's story, and *Wild for Him* is scheduled for release in summer 2008. I hope you'll find these friends of Joel's as fun and charming as I have.

For now, enjoy Joel and Lora's story, and be sure to visit my website at www.janelledenison.com to read more about the Wilde series, check out my upcoming releases, and enter my monthly giveaway contest. I also blog weekly at www.plotmonkeys.com, so please come and join the fun!

Happy Reading!

Janelle Denison

One

"I need your help."

Startled by the desperate request drifting through the phone line, Joel Wilde's fingers tightened around the cordless receiver pressed to his ear. It had been one helluva long time since he'd heard that voice, but he recognized it instantly. A friend. A comrade. The man who'd literally saved his life.

"Zach?" he asked incredulously.

"Yeah, buddy, it's me." Zach Marshall's forced chuckle fell flat. "It's been a while, huh?"

More than four years, to be exact, Joel thought as he sat down on one of the barstools in his kitchen. As marines they'd been assigned to the same Force Reconnaissance unit, and after serving their country for four and six years respectively, they'd both opted not to reenlist. Their last mission in Baghdad had been harrowing, and one that neither of them had been eager to repeat. In fact, most of the men who'd been a part of that assignment had walked away with either physical or emotional scars. And for some, both.

Joel was a man who'd always thrived on risk and adventure, but his tour of duty in Iraq had been much more than he'd ever bargained for. After watching good men die and nearly losing his own life, as well, Joel had wanted nothing more than to join the real world again and live a normal life, free from strict rules, from relentless, rigorous missions, and from being responsible for other men's lives.

He'd tried to keep in touch with Zach over the years, but Zach was a wanderer, always seeking action and adventure. He was a good guy at heart, but he was also a drinker and a gambler and usually found trouble instead. Which brought Joel back to the reason behind his friend's call.

"What's going on, Zach?" Joel was compelled to ask, but dreaded the answer.

"I'm in trouble. *Big* trouble." Zach's voice cracked with the faintest hint of despair. "I owe a bookie a shitload of money that I don't have."

Joel wasn't surprised, just disappointed that his friend hadn't changed his ways. Obviously Zach hadn't learned his lesson after one of their comrades, Bruno, had beaten the crap out of him when Zach had neglected to pay up the five hundred bucks he'd lost to the big, burly marine during a poker game.

Joel blew out a rough stream of breath. "How much?"

A noticeable pause ensued before Zach finally answered. "Over fifty grand."

Joel's mind reeled with disbelief, and a ripe curse escaped his lips before he could stop it. "Jesus, Zach, I don't have that kind of cash to give you."

"I know, and I swear I'm not asking you for it," Zach

tried to assure him. "But this situation involves more than just me. Remember my sister, Lora?"

They'd never met personally, but Joel did, indeed, remember bits and pieces about Lora Marshall. Zach had openly shared the amusing letters his sister had written to him on a weekly basis, and the occasional picture she'd sometimes include along with the correspondence.

It had been a very long time since Joel had seen any of those photos, or even thought of Lora Marshall, but as he closed his eyes, her features easily filled his mind. She'd possessed a lovely face with soft, pretty features, which was framed by rich, shoulder-length brown hair that looked shiny and silky to the touch. In a bleak, war-filled existence, he recalled being drawn to her laughing, inviting blue eyes, and a smile that was both sweet and sensual in an understated way.

Joel's gut clenched at the thought of Zach putting her life in jeopardy somehow. "What does your sister have to do with any of this?"

"I need you to make sure she's protected," Zach said on a quick rush of breath. "These people I'm dealing with . . . they might be looking for her."

Joel jammed his fingers through his too-long hair and frowned, not liking the direction this conversation was taking. "And why would they be looking for Lora?"

The silence that followed was deafening.

"Dammit, Zach," he bit out harshly, his own anger rising swiftly to the surface. "You can't just drop something like this on me and not tell me what the hell is going on. If your sister's life is at risk, in any way at all, I need details, *all of them*, in order to keep her safe."

"Okay, I'll tell you everything you need to know." Zach's tone was more subdued now. "Just promise me that no matter what, you'll look after her until I get this mess taken care of. She doesn't have anyone else, and I need to know that she's in good hands. You're the only one I trust to keep her safe from any harm."

Joel absently rubbed a hand over his jean-clad thigh, right where a puckered scar resided—an ugly, glaring reminder of how Zach had once risked his own life to save Joel's during a covert mission. Joel *owed* him, and while Zach hadn't come right out and said as much, Joel was certain that his friend was counting on that return favor now.

Keeping an eye on Zach's sister was the least Joel could do. "You have my word that I'll take care of her," he promised, then reached for the pad of paper and pen on the counter in front of him. "Now tell me why your sister's life is in danger."

Zach exhaled a long, deep breath, obviously stalling a few extra seconds. "The guy I owe the money to is demanding payment, which I don't have. Not yet anyway. I just need more time to get it."

Joel highly doubted that extra time would help Zach's situation in any way. Most likely, he'd use any respite to chase good money after bad in hopes of striking it rich in a bet based more on luck than skill. And that rarely paid off. After all, gambling cities were built on losers, not winners.

"How much time?" he asked Zach.

"A few weeks at the most. And in the meantime, the reason why I need you to watch Lora is because I did something incredibly stupid."

A noticeable pause ensued, and Joel waited not-so-patiently for his friend to continue, which Zach eventually did.

"Right before I enlisted in the Marines, my sister took out life insurance policies on both of us worth one hundred grand, just so we'd have something if anything should happen to either one of us, since we have no other family. It's a prepaid policy and it doesn't expire until we each turn thirty, and that's still another eight months away for Lora."

Joel swore beneath his breath. Certain he knew just how Zach had used that life insurance policy, his stomach cramped with a sense of apprehension, followed by a swift kick of anger. "Go on."

"I used the life insurance policy on Lora as collateral against the loan I took from a guy named Lanny Mendoza," Zach reluctantly explained, confirming Joel's suspicions. "I was desperate, and I honestly never thought he'd need to use that policy, but after a streak of bad luck, I've discovered just how ruthless Mendoza and his gang of men can be. His thugs beat the shit out of me and broke my arm and nose, and now they're threatening to go after Lora if I don't pay up, and soon."

Because with Lora dead, Zach could collect on that life insurance policy to pay back his loan, with interest. It was a chilling thought. While Joel was furious that his friend would drag his own sister into his sordid dealings, at least Zach was doing what he could to ensure that his sister was protected.

"I'm really afraid for Lora's safety," Zach said, his anxious tone backing up his fears. "You know I wouldn't ask you to do this if I had any other choice."

"Yeah, I know." Joel tapped the end of his pen on the notepad. "Where can I find your sister?"

"About four years ago she moved from Springfield to Chicago. She's living in a small one-bedroom apartment by herself."

Joel jotted down the name of the complex Zach gave to him, along with Lora's home phone number, surprised to learn that she'd moved clear across the state and lived so close to him. Especially since he distinctly remembered from one of the letters she'd written to Zach during their time in the service that her boyfriend had proposed, and she'd accepted. So why was she living alone?

Curious, Joel said, "I thought she was engaged to get married."

"She left the jerk two years ago." Zach didn't offer details, and Joel didn't ask for them, since that personal information wasn't pertinent to the case. "She works full time during the day at the St. Claire Hotel as a masseuse and part time at night at The Electric Blue. Her best friend, Sydney, owns the place, and it's relatively new. Have you heard of it?"

"Yeah. Actually, I've been there . . ." Joel's voice trailed off as a sense of recognition washed over him. It had been months ago that he and his friends had gone to The Electric Blue to check out Chicago's hottest new bar, but what he remembered most about that night was how distracted he'd been by one of the bar waitresses that had looked so familiar to him. Not to mention the awareness that had been evident between the two of them at first glance.

At the time, he couldn't place where he'd seen her before. Now, as Joel thought back to the pictures Zach had shared with him of his sister, he knew. The woman he'd been intrigued by and attracted to had been Lora Marshall.

What a small world it was.

"Hey, Joel. Are you okay?"

Zach's urgent tone pulled Joel back to the present. "Yeah, I'm fine."

"Look, I don't have much more time before I need to get off the phone," Zach said. "If I can't get the money, Mendoza's guys will probably come looking for Lora in about a week, which gives you plenty of time to insinuate yourself in her life in an inconspicuous way."

"In an inconspicuous way?" Joel repeated, not bothering to hide his irritation over Zach's suggestion. "What's wrong with the straightforward approach? Just tell her the truth and that I'll be around to protect her until you get your shit together?"

Silence reigned on the other end of the phone line, and Joel imagined that he'd made Zach cringe with his honest expression of the situation. Tough shit, he thought, and shoved his fingers once again through his hair in growing agitation. Zach had gotten himself into this mess, and Joel wasn't about to make any of this easy on him. His friend needed someone to give him a reality check about his addictions and how they were affecting not only his life, but now his sister's.

Finally, Zach spoke. "I know I royally fucked up, and I'm the worst kind of bastard for doing what I did. But I love my sister, and if you tell her the truth . . ."

Zach's voice cracked with raw emotion, and he cleared his throat before continuing. "This isn't the first time I've gotten myself into this kind of trouble, and if Lora finds out what I've done with her insurance policy, I'm afraid she'll never forgive me. Or worse, she'll disown me as her brother. She's the only family I've got, Joel."

The other man's sincere appeal struck Joel right where he was most susceptible, because family was one of the most important things in his life. The support. The camaraderie. And knowing you could count on someone for anything. His brothers and sister were close, along with their cousins, so Joel could understand why his friend didn't want to risk his relationship with his sister.

"Whatever you do, please promise me you won't tell her what I've done," Zach pleaded.

Blatantly deceiving someone went against Joel's character, yet there were many times when his profession as a
security agent required him to take on a new or different
persona in order to do his job. This case would have to be
no different, because Joel knew he wouldn't, and couldn't,
turn down his friend's request.

Resigned, Joel rubbed a hand along the stubble on his
jaw. "I'll do it," he finally said.

"Thank you." The relief and gratitude in Zach's voice
was palpable. "I owe you, buddy."

"You don't owe me anything." Especially since Zach
had saved his ass in Baghdad. In comparison, this was a
small favor to grant. "But I do need a promise from you in
return."

"Anything," Zach said willingly. "Anything at all."

Joel stated the one thing weighing heavily on his
mind. "You need professional help, Zach. You're out of
control. When you start gambling with other people's
lives, you've gone too far."

"I know." Zach turned somber. "I swear I'll put myself
into a rehab program once this is over."

"I'm going to hold you to that." If there was one good
thing that came out of this disaster, it would be finally
getting Zach's life straightened out.

"Hey, I heard you went into business with Jon, Kevin,
and Ben," Zach said, changing the subject for a moment.
"Some kind of security firm, right?"

"Yeah, Elite Security Specialists," Joel said of the
company he'd started with three of his fellow ex-marines
and good friends. "We're doing pretty well."

"That's great to hear," Zach replied sincerely. "I know
it's been years, but I've missed hanging out with you guys."

The melancholy in Zach's voice was unmistakable, and
Joel couldn't help but wonder how lonely the past years

must have been for his friend. He wondered, too, if Zach was still desperately trying to escape the horrors they'd lived through in the war.

Once their term in the Marines had ended, he and Zach had spent two weeks together living it up and trying to forget what they'd endured. They'd caroused and partied with a bevy of willing women, and made up for all the wild, frivolous fun they'd missed out on during their time in Iraq. Then they'd gone their separate ways. Zach had driven off to Atlantic City with his wallet filled with the savings he'd accumulated during his time in the service, and Joel headed back to Chicago, where he'd grown up, to figure out what he was going to do with his life now that he was no longer a part of the United States Marine Corps.

He'd spent nearly two years doing oddball jobs before going into business with three fellow ex-marines as security agents. They'd formed ESS Group, and were hired to do everything from setting up security at venues and special events to protecting high-profile clients to undercover work when it was warranted. In just a few years' time, the company was well on its way to becoming one of Chicago's top security firms.

Joel had managed to make a life for himself outside of the service with a job he enjoyed. Unfortunately, Zach hadn't been able to put his time in the Marines behind him and was still living like a nomad.

"You know where to find us, Zach," Joel said, extending an invitation he hoped his friend would someday accept. "By the way, where are you?"

"I'd rather not say. The less you know right now, the better."

"Fair enough," Joel conceded. "Is there a way I can at least get a hold of you if I need to?"

"My cell phone." Zach gave him the number, and Joel added it to his notes on the pad of paper.

"I've got to go," Zach said reluctanctly. "Semper fi, Wilde Man."

Joel couldn't help the smile that formed on his lips. It had been a long time since he'd heard the nickname the guys had given him in the service. "Semper fi." *Always faithful.* And that code applied to his fellow marine and friend.

"GOD, he's so hot, I'm about to melt into a puddle right here and now."

Lora Marshall smiled in amusement at her co-worker Monique as they waited at the end of the bar for their drink orders. Sydney, Lora's best friend and the owner of The Electric Blue, stood on the other side of the mahogany and brass bar, mixing an array of cocktails and popping the caps off chilled beer bottles with an ease and rhythm that came from years of experience. Despite how busy Sydney was, she didn't stop from joining in on the conversation.

"Who's hot?" she asked over the loud music. There were dozens of good-looking guys in the place, and she gave the crowded bar area a quick glance in search of the mystery man Monique seemed so enthralled with.

"Lora's guy," Monique said as she set two beers, a mai tai, and a cosmopolitan on her tray. "Table sixteen. The one dressed all in black."

Lora rolled her eyes. She didn't need to look in that direction to know who was sitting at the designated table, especially after hearing Monique's description. "He's not *my* guy." But she had to agree that he was definitely *hot.*

"Oh, yum." This bit of interest came from Sydney,

who'd spied the dark-haired guy and found him to be just her type. "Well, *I'll* certainly take one of him."

"Sorry, boss." Monique added a pineapple wedge to the mai tai and pressed a lime into the long neck of a bottle of Corona. "He wants Lora. He *always* asks for Lora." With that, she picked up her loaded tray and made her way through the throng of customers to deliver her drinks.

Lora couldn't deny Monique's claim. Yes, he did always ask that she take his order. This was the third night he'd come into The Electric Blue, each time with a friend. If the past two evenings were any indication, he'd order one beer, maybe two, and nurse them for the next few hours until the place closed. Even though he didn't lack for female interest, he never danced with anyone, though his friends seemed to enjoy the singles scene.

"Well, well, well," Sydney drawled. With a sly grin curving her lips, she expertly flipped a bóttle of Ketel One vodka in her hand and poured two shots of the liquor into a tumbler for an apple martini. "It appears you have yourself an admirer. He looks like the kind of bad boy who would be perfect to end your two-year dry spell."

It was a familiar conversation between the two of them. While Sydney enjoyed all kinds of male attention, in the bedroom and out, Lora was far more particular and didn't do one-night stands.

"I've dated since my breakup with Brent," she said in defense. Unfortunately, none of those too-conservative men had aroused anything more than amicable feelings. There hadn't been any kind of zing or real attraction to make Lora want anything more than a casual friendship with those guys.

Sydney served the martini to the woman standing at the bar in front of her and rang up the sale before saying over her shoulder to Lora, "Sure, you've dated here and there, but I'm talking about sleeping with a guy. You know, mutual physical pleasure, orgasms, and all that fun stuff. It's just not normal for a woman your age to go that long without sex."

Lora laughed, grateful for the loud music that helped to drown out her friend's frank observation. "I've done just fine on my own." Refusing to elaborate on that comment, she went on, "Besides, if you haven't noticed, between my day job and working here in the evenings for you until closing, it's not like I have a lot of free time to pursue any guy."

Sydney cast a quick glance at her watch while pouring another drink. "You know what? You're absolutely right. You're getting off at ten tonight. I'll keep Monique until closing. Use the time wisely." She winked at Lora.

Lora shook her head as she placed the Long Island iced tea on her tray. "I don't mind staying."

"You're off at ten," Sydney said adamantly. "I certainly don't want to be responsible for your lack of a social and sex life."

"Fine." Lora added a mudslide to her orders to deliver. "I could use the extra sleep." Even over the noise in the bar, Lora heard Sydney's sound of disgust and had to bite her bottom lip to keep from grinning.

"Please do *not* waste the extra time on sleep," her friend said. "Not with a perfectly hot and sexy man eyeing you like he wants to eat you up in one big bite."

What a delicious, decadent thought. A light shiver coursed through Lora, and her Electric Blue T-shirt suddenly felt too tight across her breasts. Instinctively, she glanced toward *him*. Sure enough, he was watching her, and even from across the crowded room their gazes met.

Always dressed in black—T-shirt, jeans, and shoes—he

looked a little dangerous, and a whole lot like a rebel. A daring rule-breaker. A man who thrived on risk and adventure. His too-long, tousled black hair and the dark stubble shadowing his lean jaw only added to that tantalizing image. Then there were those stunning, piercing blue eyes of his that had the ability to tempt a woman to sin. With him. In many different, erotic ways.

Lora sighed, and as if he knew exactly where her thoughts had traveled, a slow, disarming smile tipped up the corners of his sensual mouth, bringing to life an instantaneous awareness that coiled low and deep in her belly. Her attraction to this man was undeniable, like nothing she'd ever experienced before.

"Oh, for God's sake, take him into the storeroom and do him already," Sydney teased. "I'll have Monique cover for you."

Her friend was absolutely outrageous. But then again, Sydney had always been bold and brazen—the exact opposite of Lora's more cautious, reserved nature. "I'm so *not* that kind of girl," she said primly.

"Maybe you ought to be." Sydney passed a shot of tequila Lora's way, which completed her drink order. "Bad girls have more fun. Trust me, I should know."

Yes, Lora was very aware that Sydney had worked hard to cultivate her wild and unabashed reputation over the years—with much success. It helped that Sydney had the body of a *Playboy* centerfold, wore tight, revealing outfits to flaunt those curves, and wasn't afraid to use her sexuality to get exactly what she wanted. Being a "bad girl" had served Sydney well—in business *and* pleasure.

Lora had known Sydney since their freshman year of high school, and even though the two of them were so different, in so many ways, they'd forged a tentative acquaintanceship that ended up blossoming into a strong and lasting friendship. They'd been together through the years, in good times and bad, and even through Sydney's unexpected pregnancy at the age of fourteen—always supportive of each other and never judging one another. Only Lora knew that Sydney's gutsy, assertive personality was all a facade to hide a very painful childhood that had left deep emotional scars.

Lora double-checked her order pad against the drinks on her tray to make sure she had everything. Then she went ahead and added one more item. "Can you give me a bottle of Sam Adams?"

Sydney arched an auburn brow as she uncapped the beer and slid it down the counter to Lora. "His choice of drink?"

"Yes, and his name is Joel."

"Ahhh, you're already on a first-name basis." Sydney grinned.

"He introduced himself the first night." Lora shrugged and added a stack of cocktail napkins to her tray.

"A first name is all you need to do the deed," Sydney said with a naughty inflection in her voice. "Now go and make those deliveries. The crowd's getting restless and they're looking for some action."

Knowing that meant Sydney was going to ring the loud cowbell behind the bar in the next few minutes, which would announce the employee entertainment that The Electric Blue was known for, Lora picked up her tray and passed out the drinks to her customers, then headed over to Joel's table.

"Hi there," she said, and set the chilled bottle of beer on a napkin. "Sam Adams, right?"

Up close, that slow, lazy grin of his was even more potent and disarming. "Am I that predictable?"

There wasn't anything about the man that struck her as

tame or boring. "I'm just going on past drink orders, and you're becoming a regular."

He leaned back in his chair, and even that slight movement exuded an abundance of male confidence and sex appeal that should have been deemed illegal. "What can I say? I like the atmosphere here."

He liked *her*. The sentiment glimmered in his vibrant blue eyes and infused her with a pleasurable, sensual warmth. There was no ignoring the truth making itself known . . . she really liked him, too. She was very attracted to him, but there was something else about this man, beyond the physical, that drew her. She supposed it was his easygoing charm and affability that made her feel so comfortable around him.

As he continued to smile at her, a flash of familiarity swept over her. It was as if she'd seen him before, but she couldn't pinpoint when or where. It wasn't the first time she'd felt that connection, but it was one of those feelings that remained too elusive and indefinable for her to fully grasp.

She redirected her attention to the other man sitting at the table, who was obviously a friend of Joel's. "What can I get you to drink?"

"I'll take a Sam Adams, too," he replied easily. "By the way, I'm Jon."

He was a good-looking guy, and his grin was very warm and friendly. "Nice to meet you. I'm Lora."

"So, what time do you get off work tonight?" Joel cut in smoothly.

Lora was used to the question, since it was one he asked every evening. The past few nights she'd helped close down the bar, but Sydney had just given her strict orders to take off early. "My shift is over at ten."

"Ahhh, my lucky night," he said, looking very pleased.

"Would you like to go somewhere after work and have a drink with me?"

She automatically shook her head. She might work part-time as a cocktail waitress, but hanging out at a bar other than The Electric Blue on her off hours really wasn't her thing. "I don't drink."

"Anything?" The amusement in his voice was unmistakable.

"No alcohol," she clarified, certain she'd just effectively pegged herself as too much of a Goody Two-Shoes, as Sydney often called her, for Joel to pursue her further. Which was probably just as well.

"How about coffee?" he asked as he stroked his long fingers down the condensation gathering on his bottle of beer. "I know a great coffee place down the street from here. It's even within walking distance."

"I have to go to work early in the morning." It was an automatic response, one she used on men she had no interest in going out with. But with Joel, she was beginning to wonder why she was resisting when the attraction between them was so strong. So arousing. So tempting.

"I promise not to keep you out late." He placed his right hand over the left side of his chest and glanced up at her with a hopeful look that transformed his edgy good looks into a more boyish appearance. "Please don't break my heart by saying no."

She laughed, certain that *he* was the heart-breaker in this scenario. That was a good enough reason for her to keep her distance from him, since she'd been on the receiving end of that kind of emotional upheaval before. But despite all that, there was something irresistible and charismatic about him.

Jon leaned forward in his seat and spoke loud in order to be heard over the music. "If it makes you feel any better, I can vouch for the fact that he's an honorable, trustworthy guy." Then he graced her with an engaging grin that had no doubt worked magic on many women.

She believed Jon, and most importantly she trusted her instincts. She thought about everything Sydney had just said to her and came to the conclusion that her friend was right. She did need more of a social life. Besides, just because she had a cup of coffee with Joel didn't mean they'd end up in bed together.

"So, what do you say?" Joel asked. "One coffee drink of your choice, and we'll call it a night."

This time, she didn't hesitate with an answer. "Sure."

He blinked, drawing her attention to those long, sooty lashes and his vivid blue eyes. "Excuse me?"

She almost laughed at his startled expression. After all her previous excuses, he obviously thought he'd heard her wrong. "Yes, I'll go and have a cup of coffee with you."

"Well I'll be damned," he drawled in a deep, satisfied tone of voice. "It *is* my lucky night."

At that moment, Sydney rang the loud cowbell behind the bar, signaling that it was time for the waiters and waitresses to give the crowd the kind of entertainment and sexy fun they'd come to expect at The Electric Blue.

When she'd first agreed to work for Sydney when her friend was shorthanded, Lora had had reservations about this part of the job description. She wasn't the type to get up in front of a group of men and women and strut her stuff like all the younger, college-aged employees so effortlessly, and eagerly, did. In fact, it had taken her a few weeks to gather up the nerve to participate, then another solid week to get used to dancing in front of so many people.

But now, many months later, she'd learned to enjoy the nightly ritual. Not because she was an exhibitionist, but rather because it had become a fun, harmless escape for her. A time and place where she could indulge her sensual side while keeping her emotions under wraps.

"Work calls," she said to Joel, then glanced at Jon as the crowd behind her started cheering and chanting for the revelry to begin. "And I'll be back soon with your beer."

She headed for the nearest platform and set her tray on a shelf. As she hopped up onto the stage and the strobe lights flashed and the music took on a seductive beat, she decided that tonight she was suddenly feeling very daring and uninhibited.

And *he* was the reason.

Two

WATCHING Lora dance was Joel's favorite part of the nights he'd spent so far at The Electric Blue. While jumping up on the nearest platform or stage and enticing the crowd with a provocative shimmy and shake was all part of the bar's entertainment, the only cocktail waitress that captured his complete attention was Lora.

Many of the other girls were outrageously provocative with their dance moves, which the younger twentysomething crowd seemed to love and cheered on enthusiastically. Lora's rhythm was far more subtle, like a slow, deliberate tease, which made watching her much more appealing to him than the in-your-face bump and grind action. Joel was a man who appreciated maturity—intellectually and physically. And Lora possessed brains as well as a body that was soft, lush, and womanly.

He was a big guy all over—from his wide shoulders to his large hands and long fingers to his taller-than-average frame. And because of his size, he liked his women amply proportioned to handle and complement a man of his stature. There was no doubt in his mind that Lora would be a perfect fit for him, in every way.

Despite his resolve to keep his relationship with Zach's sister strictly platonic, Lora was the epitome of his fantasy woman. She wore the same tight, cropped T-shirt as all the other employees—except while the other girls displayed more concave stomachs, Lora's exposed belly looked soft and supple, and there was a helluva lot more cleavage peeking from the deep V down the front. Her faded jeans sat low on her curvaceous hips and hugged the rest of her shapely figure, and her smooth, rounded ass was a fine example of how that particular part of a woman's anatomy should look.

She captivated him with the graceful sway of her hips. Fascinated him as she swung her long, dark brown hair over her shoulders. The strands looked silky and shiny beneath the overhead lights, and the rich color accentuated her beautiful, and striking, green eyes. A slight smile curved her lips as she glanced his way, and there was just enough come-hither in her gaze to make a slow, simmering heat settle deep between his legs.

Undoubtedly, he wanted this woman, but acting on his desires wasn't an option. Instead, using their attraction to lure her in and keep her close so he could protect her was his ultimate goal. And having her finally agree to see him outside of work was a huge step in that direction.

"You're finally in," Jon said, his loud voice rising above the music and mayhem in the bar.

His friend made it sound like a mission, which Joel supposed this assignment kind of was. And Lora had been tougher than most to crack. More reserved. More cautious. The opposite of her brother, who acted first, then thought about the consequences later when it was too late to do anything about his poor judgment.

"Here's hoping I can stay *in* and keep her close on a regular basis." One night out together for coffee didn't guarantee him anything where Lora was concerned. He took a drink of his beer, then leaned his forearms on the table. "I know the other guys are getting tired of taking turns watching her place at night." Until Zach was in the clear, he had Lora under twenty-four-hour surveillance.

Jon grinned. "Hey, you gotta sleep sometime."

"Well, I appreciate the help." And the time off from ESS he'd been able to take in order to watch over Lora. Everyone understood that this was a personal issue for Joel, and something he felt compelled to see through because he owed Zach at least that much.

"We're all a team, Wilde Man," Jon said. "And we were all friends with Zach in the service. He might have asked you to watch over his sister, but we're all in this together, in whatever way you need us."

Joel nodded, knowing he'd do the same for Jon, Ben, or Kevin. They might have all started Elite Security Specialists together, but they were more like brothers than co-workers. They'd watched each other's backs in the Marines, and they still did, even now.

Jon pushed his chair back and stood. "That said, I've got a blond beauty sitting at the bar who's been eyeing me for the past half hour, and I'm not about to let a hot babe like her go to waste."

Joel chuckled and tipped his beer toward his friend. "Have fun."

"Oh, I intend to," he drawled, then headed off in the direction of his evening's pursuit.

Joel spent the next hour nursing his beer while waiting

for Lora to finish her shift. He kept a keen eye on everyone she came into contact with, knowing that a customer could easily be a potential threat sent by Zach's bookie. The evening passed without incident, until Lora was finally off the clock and he was escorting her toward the front entrance of The Electric Blue.

Once they were outside, Lora visibly shivered as the cold night air washed over them. "You can certainly tell it's mid-October," she said, and slipped into her light-weight coat as they walked along the sidewalk. "The temperature keeps getting cooler and cooler."

He reached out to smooth down the collar of her coat, which was flipped up in the back, and his fingers brushed against the side of her neck. Her skin was incredibly soft to the touch, and he could have sworn he heard her suck in a quick, startled breath at his unintentional caress.

Dropping his hand back to his side, he made as if that brief contact hadn't affected him, too. "Then a cup of coffee is just the thing to warm you up."

Smiling, she adjusted her purse strap over her shoulder and pushed her hands into her jacket pockets. "I'm looking forward to it, actually."

Even though it was after ten in the evening, there were still plenty of people on the streets, though no one paid them any attention. A block later they reached The Daily Grind, and Joel opened the door for Lora to walk in, then followed behind her.

"Hey, Joel," a young, pretty girl behind the counter greeted him enthusiastically. "It's been awhile since you've been by."

"I was in the neighborhood tonight, and I thought I'd bring a friend in for a drink." He glanced at Lora, who wore an amused expression, and he knew why. The girl, who was barely out of high school, obviously had a crush on him. "What would you like, Lora?"

She perused the menu for a quick moment. "I think I'm going to splurge and have a café mocha, with whipped cream."

"And I'll have a cappuccino." He pulled out his wallet and paid for the drinks.

Once their orders were up, he grabbed both large paper cups and led the way toward a vacant table against a large window overlooking the street outside. Considering the chilly weather, The Daily Grind was busy and there were only a few available places to sit. He would have preferred one of the more comfortable couch setups where he could talk to Lora with more privacy, but at this point he wasn't about to be choosy.

"Hi, Joel," another worker called from across the place, loud enough that he had no choice but to acknowledge the perky café manager.

"Hi, Kate," he said with a friendly smile. "Is Liz around tonight?"

"No, she left a few hours ago with Steve," the cute girl replied.

"That's good to hear. Steve needs to be sure she doesn't overdo now that she's pregnant again." Joel placed their drinks on the table, then shrugged out of his black leather jacket before helping Lora out of her coat—this time without touching any bare skin.

The humorous glimmer in her eyes and the fanciful smile curving her lips was unmistakable. "What's with that grin on your face?" he asked, already suspecting he knew the answer.

Shrugging lightly, she sat down at the table. "Judging

by the enthusiastic reception you just received, I'm thinking that you must come here frequently."

"It's been a few weeks, but I do stop by when I get the chance," he said, and settled into the seat across from her, which also gave him a clear view of the front door and anyone who walked through. "Not only does The Daily Grind make some of the best coffee drinks in Chicago, the owner, Liz, is married to my cousin Steve."

She took a sip of her coffee. Her lashes fell to half-mast, and an appreciative moan escaped her as she savored the warmth and flavor. "I have to agree with your assessment of the drinks. This is the best café mocha I've had in a long time."

He watched her lick a dollop of whipped cream off her upper lip, and felt his entire body tighten with the urge to taste her for himself. Clearing his throat, he shifted in his seat and focused on business, with the pretense of getting to know her—which would hopefully lead to yet another date between them. Time was of the essence since he had no idea when Mendoza's men planned to show up and follow through on their threats against Lora, and getting as close to her as possible, and quickly, was his top priority.

"So tell me something. You mentioned having to work in the morning. I know the bar isn't open during the day, so I'm guessing you have a second job?"

"My day job, which is my main source of employment, is at the St. Claire Hotel." She wrapped both her hands around her cup, as if to absorb the warmth of the drink. "I'm a masseuse at the spa."

He stretched back in his seat and let a lazy smile tip up the corners of his mouth. "Which means you must be very good with your hands," he teased, then took a drink of his cappuccino, which was strong and rich, just how he liked it.

She rolled her eyes at the double entendre encompassing his comment. "Oh, please."

He chuckled. "Okay, I'll admit, that was cheesy."

"Definitely cheesy," she agreed wholeheartedly, though she was smiling in amusement. "It's a pick-up line I hear much too often from the businessmen that stay at the hotel and are interested in after-hour, off-the-clock company, if you know what I mean."

He dropped his gaze to the slender fingers holding her cup of coffee. "Well, your hands do look incredibly soft and smooth." Reaching across the table, he gently grasped one of her hands and caressed his thumb along her silky palm. "They feel that way, too. Not at all like a cocktail waitress who has her hands in water all the time and spends her evenings cleaning up after customers."

Heat and awareness kindled in her gaze as he continued to stroke his fingers along her hand and fingers, but she didn't pull away. "It's the lotions and oils I use all day long. I suppose that outweighs the manual labor of working at The Electric Blue at night."

"Your work schedule is awfully busy." Reluctantly, he let her hand go, but he couldn't help but wonder if her skin felt as velvety soft everywhere else. Like her breasts. Her stomach. The inside of her thighs. "What do you do in your free time?"

"Sleep." She laughed, the sound light and carefree. "Seriously, I really don't mind all the work. It keeps me out of trouble and helps out my girlfriend Sydney when she's shorthanded at the bar."

Joel knew she spoke the truth. Not only had Zach told him about her heavy workload, Joel had done some investigating on his own and it appeared that Lora hadn't had much of a social life since she'd broken things off with her fiancé two years earlier. Basically, all work and no play had become her motto.

"Enough about me." She tucked her hair behind her ear and studied him curiously. "What do you do for a living?"

"I'm a partner in a security firm here in Chicago, along with Jon, whom you met back at the bar, and a few other friends. The company is Elite Security Specialists." He gave up the information easily, since he wasn't keeping his background or his personal life a secret. No, the only secret he was protecting was Zach's.

He went on. "We deal with intelligence issues, investigations, setting up surveillance, search and recovery, and we even travel internationally if requested." He deliberately left out the very basic "undercover protection" scenario, which reflected his current assignment with her.

She swirled the last of the liquid in her cup, her features full of fascinated interest. "Do you travel often for business?"

"As often as I can. I prefer the international assignments, actually. I like to travel and I'm known for taking on the edgier, more controversial gigs. It's something I enjoy."

Something in her expression changed. "So, your job is risky and dangerous."

"It can be, depending on the case," he said with a shrug. He'd spent most of his life pursuing a good challenge and adventure, so he rarely gave it a second thought. Being a risk-taker was who and what he was. "And other times my job is boring as hell. Security threat assessments, venue security, surveillance, that kind of stuff."

She tipped her head thoughtfully. "What you do sounds very high-tech."

"No, not really." A group of people walked into the café, and he gave them a quick glance before returning his attention to Lora. "A stint in the Marines in Special Ops does a lot to prepare a guy for all kinds of security assignments."

She appeared taken aback for a moment, and her brows creased in a slight, contemplative frown. "The Marines?"

"Yes, I served in the Marine Corps. Six years, actually." He watched her expression change and knew that things were clicking in her mind, just as he'd intended. He'd deliberately mentioned his time in the service, knowing where it could possibly lead. "Is something wrong?"

She studied his face intently. "What's your last name?"

"Wilde," he said, preparing himself for the snowball effect, when she realized exactly who he was. But it needed to be done in order to get at least one pretense out of the way.

Sure enough, realization dawned, and her green eyes widened in a combination of shock and surprise. "Joel Wilde," she said as a genuine smile appeared. "Oh my God. I thought you looked familiar when I first saw you at The Electric Blue, but I couldn't figure out where I'd seen you before. Your hair is much longer now than in the pictures I saw of you when you were in the Marines. You had a standard military crew cut then."

He pretended confusion, even as he inwardly winced at the recollection of having his hair shaved off when he'd enlisted. "Excuse me?"

Her grin blossomed full-fledge, and her eyes danced with amazement. "You served with my brother in the

Marines and you were in the same unit. Zach Marshall?"

"Well I'll be damned," he drawled with just the right amount of astonishment. "You're Lora Marshall, Zach's sister."

She nodded enthusiastically. "That's right. Zach sent me pictures of the two of you and some of the other guys in his unit. He wrote me letters and mentioned your name all the time. You two were really good friends back then."

"I still consider Zach a good friend, though I have to admit that I haven't heard from him in years. How's he doing?" he asked, curious to find out what Lora knew of her brother's habits and current way of life.

She inhaled a deep breath and averted her gaze to her coffee cup. "The last I heard he was doing okay."

Obviously, Zach was a painful subject for her. "The last you heard?"

She glanced back up at him, and didn't bother to try and hide the heartache reflected in her eyes. "Honestly, it's been a while since we've talked, and months since I last saw him. I'm not even sure where he's living anymore."

"Don't you have any way of contacting Zach?" Surely her brother hadn't completely extricated himself from her life.

"I have his cell phone number, but he never picks up, so I just leave him messages. And he always seems to call me when I'm not home and uses the answering machine to let me know he's okay." She sighed softly and crossed her arms in front of her on the table. "I really miss him, and I wish he'd come home."

The honest emotion reverberating in her voice grabbed at Joel, forcing him to keep a tight rein on the rising anger he once again experienced toward Zach. For hurting his sister who cared so much about him. For using his sister as a pawn in his addictions. For letting alcohol and gambling ruin his life, and possibly Lora's.

"Oh, wow," she said with a shake of her head, which caused her thick, rich-looking hair to settle around her shoulders like a cloud of sable silk. "I didn't mean to get so melancholy on you. It's just that Zach hasn't been the same since he left the service, and I constantly worry about him."

"That's completely understandable." She had good reason to be concerned about her brother, and she didn't even know the half of the kind of trouble Zach was in.

She finished the last of her drink. "It's getting late and I really should get going," she said, regret in her tone.

Figuring they'd covered enough ground for one evening together, he didn't push her to stay longer. Instead, he stood and slipped into his leather jacket while she did the same with her coat. "Come on, I'll walk you back to your car," he said.

"I can't believe that you and I met," Lora mused as they strolled side by side toward The Electric Blue's parking lot. "I mean, what are the chances of that?"

If she only knew. "Very slim, I suppose." Unless a meeting was deliberate, as theirs had been.

They reached her car, a compact red Volkswagen Jetta, and she unlocked the vehicle with a press of her remote. She opened the door before turning back around to face him. "Where's your car?" she asked.

"My ride is right over there." He hooked a thumb back toward the front of The Electric Blue, where he'd parked his Ducati Multistrada, a badass bike that was built for power, speed, and a whole lotta fun.

"Ahhh, a big, black motorcycle. I should have guessed." She gave his appearance a quick, sultry once-over before meeting his gaze once again. "I have to admit, the bike suits you."

Grinning, he rested a hand on the door frame and braced his other arm on the roof of her car, caging her between the open door of the vehicle, and him. Then, he leaned in a bit closer. "Wanna go for a ride sometime?"

She arched a brow, amused by his flirtatious and tempting question. "Is that what you ask all the girls?"

"No, just you. I've never asked another girl to go for a ride on my bike." Without thinking, he reached out and gently wound a strand of her hair around his finger, feeling ensnared by this alluring woman, in more ways than one. And that was a very dangerous thing, he knew. "I promise I'll go slow and easy with you, so long as you hang on tight for the ride."

The innuendo in his reply didn't so much as fluster her. If anything, she rose to the challenge. "What if I like it fast and intense?"

His grin broadened with shameless intent. "Then I'd say that you sound like just my kind of girl." His voice dropped to a low, husky pitch, and a slow hum of arousal infused his veins.

He couldn't help his response to her. He always did enjoy indulging in playful, provocative banter with a woman, and the attraction and sexual tension between he and Lora made it all the more exciting.

Releasing her hair, he dragged his fingers along her jaw and caressed them down the side of her neck. Her skin *was* silky soft to the touch. So sweet. So tempting.

"I also aim to please, sweetheart," he murmured as his gaze dropped to her captivating, kiss-me mouth. "If you like it fast and fierce, then that's exactly what you'll get."

The parking lot lights illuminated those deep green eyes

of hers, which had darkened with heat and acute awareness. He brushed his fingers over the rapid pulse beating at the base of her throat. Her soft lips parted in unmistakable invitation, and her breathing deepened, causing her chest to rise and fall in a way that beckoned him to look and appreciate those fine feminine curves. Her coat was open, enabling him to see her tight nipples pressing against her T-shirt—from the night chill or their provocative exchange, he wasn't certain. Either way, he ached to take those lovely breasts in his hands just to see how well she fit into his large palms.

He curbed the impulse. Just barely. "So, if I give you what you want, does that mean you'll go for a ride with me?" At the moment, it wasn't straddling a motorcycle that he had in mind, but rather having her soft, slender thighs wrapped tight around his hips as he took her on a fast and wild ride of a whole different kind. The erotic thought made his cock twitch and ache between his thighs.

Oh, man. He was in deep, deep trouble with her.

She caught her full lower lip between her teeth as she seemed to consider the implications of his question. Just as he had. "I'm not that easy," she said, her tone light and playful. "But I'll think about your offer and let you know."

He chuckled at her sassy and very unexpected reply. Her ability to make him laugh was yet another thing he enjoyed about her. "You be sure to do that, but don't make me wait for long."

The humorous moment gradually faded, and in its place something more intimate and sensual simmered between them. Her eyes softened with desire, and he knew without a doubt that he could have easily kissed her. Knew she'd let him take her mouth and give them both a small sampling of the kind of carnal pleasure that promised so much more.

He'd always been a man who took what he wanted, especially when it came to women and what was so freely offered. But this time, kissing Lora would be a huge, monumental mistake, because he was certain one taste of her wouldn't be enough to satisfy the gut-level craving he was beginning to develop for her. Not to mention he'd be overstepping boundaries he had no business crossing.

He'd agreed to protect Zach's sister, not dive into a hot and heavy affair with her just to appease their attraction. Because of his job and his carefree way of life that didn't include being tied down to anyone, a short, temporary relationship was all he was willing to offer any woman. And knowing Lora's past history from many conversations with Zach during their time together, he got the distinct impression that she was the kind of woman who'd need a stable, secure man in her life.

So, as difficult as it was, he took a huge step back and shoved the tips of his fingers into the front pockets of his jeans—just as an added precaution.

A flicker of disappointment passed over her features, then she covered it up with a smile. "Well, I guess this is good night, then."

He gave her a nod. "Good night, Lora."

She slipped into her car, and once he heard her lock the door he headed over to his motorcycle, trying to shake off the light buzz of arousal with every step he took. She headed toward home, and as he followed behind at a discreet distance, he wondered how in the hell he was going to spend the next few weeks around Lora, courting her in order to stay close to her, without touching her. Without kissing her. Without taking her exactly where those eyes had all but begged him to go back in the parking lot.

His ripe curse was drowned out by the rumbling of his bike's engine. He was in for a long couple of weeks of excruciating sexual tension with no relief in sight.

At least not with the woman he wanted the most.

Three

"'MORNING, Syd," Lora called out cheerfully, announcing her presence as she walked into her best friend's two-bedroom apartment, which was located right down the hall from her own place. "I brought doughnuts, so come and get 'em while they're good and fresh."

Lora headed into the kitchen, but no one was there. Figuring Sydney and her fifteen-year-old daughter, Cassie, were still in their bedrooms getting ready for the day, Lora went ahead and poured herself a cup of coffee and rummaged through the refrigerator for the cream. She and Sydney had an open-door policy for the most part, and keys to each other's apartments. Most mornings they met for breakfast before Sydney had to take Cassie to school and Lora had to head off to the St. Claire Hotel for work.

"I heard your chipper greeting all the way in my bathroom," Sydney grumbled as she entered the kitchen, wearing a pair of form-fitting jeans and an equally form-fitting blue sweater top. Her naturally wavy auburn hair, which reached the middle of her back, was still damp from her morning shower.

After letting out a loud, obnoxious yawn, she narrowed her gaze at Lora and asked, "Why are you in such a good mood this morning?"

Sydney was so *not* a morning person and couldn't understand how Lora could wake up so early and be bright-eyed, rested, and ready to face the day. Sydney would sleep in until noon, given the chance, but she had a daughter in high school, and that kept her from enjoying that particular luxury.

Carrying her cup of coffee to the table, Lora sat down and selected an apple fritter from the pink pastry box. "Well, maybe I'm in a good mood because you let me off early last night."

"Yeah, to go out and get yourself laid." Sydney turned from the counter, a mug of steaming coffee in hand and a sly grin curving her lips. "Dare I hope?"

Lora picked off a crispy edge of her fritter and popped it into her mouth. "Sorry to disappoint you, my dear friend, but my virtue is still intact." However, Lora had to wonder if the vividly erotic dream she'd had last night qualified as getting laid. It was as close to getting laid as she'd gotten in the past two years.

She'd been deep asleep, but the image of Joel's hands and mouth pleasuring her in such steamy, breathtaking detail had seemed so real. Intensely so. She'd felt the heat and strength of his big body stroking in and out of hers, and each hard, fierce thrust had sent her spiraling into the sweetest kind of ecstasy.

She'd woken up panting and moaning as her body clenched deep inside and the last ripples of an orgasm coursed through her. She'd been shocked, and realized that she'd had the female equivalent of a wet dream, proof that her body truly was sexually deprived.

Her face warmed at the memory, and she ducked her head to hide the flush on her cheeks before Sydney noticed and called her on it.

Sydney plopped herself down across the table from Lora and picked out a maple glazed doughnut, which was her favorite kind. "So, tell me all about your *platonic* date with the hunk."

"It really wasn't a date." Lora shrugged, and took a sip of her coffee.

"What do you mean it wasn't a date?" her friend replied in that affectionately sarcastic way of hers. "You went out with him, didn't you?"

"I had a cup of coffee with him. It wasn't any big deal." Or so Lora tried to convince herself, as well as Sydney.

Sydney made a grunting sound to the contrary. "Did he kiss you?" she asked hopefully.

She recalled all the playful banter and innuendo about Joel's motorcycle at the end of the evening, could still feel the way he'd strummed his fingers down to the base of her throat and how his touch had ignited such a powerful sexual awareness between them. At that moment, she'd wanted to kiss him—the kind of slow, deep kiss that was infused with a heady rush of sensation. She could have sworn by the heat and desire in his eyes that he was thinking the same thing.

She was certain a kiss would have been so good between them . . . until he'd stepped away, dispelling any notion she might have had about making out with Joel Wilde. Which was probably for the best, she thought with a sigh.

In addition to the fact that he had "bad boy" written all

over him, she really wasn't in the market for any kind of relationship right now. She just didn't have the time. Between her day job at the hotel, her evenings at The Electric Blue, and saving every spare dollar she earned so she could open up her own spa within the next year, Joel and his sexy smile and built-like-a-god body were a distraction she couldn't afford.

"Helloooo," Sydney singsonged as she waved a hand in front of Lora's face to get her attention again. "Considering how long you're taking to answer my question, I'm guessing you're *wishing* he had kissed you."

"Score one for you," Lora admitted, and finished off her apple fritter. "But it didn't happen."

"Damn." Sydney shook her head and licked the sticky remnants of maple cream from her fingers. "Why didn't you just plant one on him? Or better yet, just tear his clothes off and have your way with him out in the back alley? Trust me, judging by the way he was watching you in the bar last night, he wouldn't have refused."

Lora laughed at her friend's outrageous suggestion. "Maybe because I'm not that kind of girl?"

Sydney rolled her eyes. "Tell me something I don't already know."

"Well, here's something you don't already know," Lora said, and folded her arms on the table. "Would you believe that Joel knows Zach? They were in the service together. The same unit, actually."

"No kidding?" Sydney asked, surprised. "Talk about a small world."

Lora told Sydney about her conversation with Joel, about Zach and how long it had been since Lora had been in contact with him. She really needed to call her brother again, just to let him know she was thinking about him and missed him. Her brother had become a wanderer since leaving the Marines, a man who just couldn't settle down in any one place, and she just wanted to know that he was okay.

Sydney cast a quick look at the clock on the wall, then turned to yell down the hall toward the bedrooms, "Twenty more minutes before we need to hit the road for school, Cass! You need to eat breakfast, so hurry it up already!"

"Okay, okay, I'm coming!" Cass hollered back, her voice vibrating with teenage impatience.

Hiding a grin at Cass's bit of attitude, Lora stood up, retrieved the coffeepot, and refilled her mug, then Sydney's, figuring her friend could use another boost of caffeine. "Hey, have you decided on a costume for the Halloween bash you're having at The Electric Blue?" The bar was hosting its second annual Halloween party, and Sydney had made it mandatory that everyone dress up—from the employees, to the customers, and even the bouncers. No one entered the place without wearing a costume.

"I'm thinking of being a lady pirate. *Arrr*," she said in a deep, swaggering tone, then grinned. "What about you?"

Lora set the coffeepot back on the burner and returned to the table. "I'm not sure yet. Any good suggestions?"

"Well, there's always a nun habit and gown to go with your celibate life these days," Sydney teased, and batted her lashes at Lora. "Or how about Little Bo Peep? She's pretty innocent, too."

Lora shot her friend an indulgent glance. "Ha ha, very funny. I'm sorry I asked. I'll figure out something on my own."

Sydney finished off her maple doughnut and grew silent, subdued even, and Lora wondered what had brought on the change. Her friend was normally so outgoing and bubbly, and even used her vivacious and sometimes sarcastic personality to keep other people from getting too close emotionally. It was a defense mechanism for Sydney, and one that had served her well over the years, but Lora was the one person with whom she let down her guard. The one and only person she trusted to let see the vulnerable, insecure woman beneath all that seductive, and brash, bravado.

"You're awfully quiet all of a sudden, Syd," Lora said softly, knowing her friend needed to talk about something. "What's on your mind?"

Inhaling a deep breath, Sydney lifted her gaze to Lora's, giving her a glimpse of maternal worry and deep-seated fears. "Cassie asked me if she could go to a Halloween party at a friend's that Saturday night."

Lora certainly didn't see anything wrong with a young girl enjoying a party with friends, but Sydney obviously did. "And?"

Sydney traced her finger along the rim of her cup. "I told her I had to think about it, but that didn't go over well at all, as you can imagine."

"Why?" Lora asked curiously.

An incredulous burst of laughter escaped Sydney. "Because she's a moody, temperamental fifteen-year-old?"

Realizing that Sydney had misunderstood her question, Lora shook her head. "No, I mean, why do you need to think about letting her go to the party?"

"*Because* she's fifteen," Sydney said meaningfully. "And she already has a centerfold body to match mine and every guy from the age of ten to eighty can only think of one thing when they look at her." Sydney put her head in her hands and groaned. "Why couldn't she have been skinny and flat-chested?"

Lora would have laughed at Sydney's motherly complaint, but knew her friend wasn't joking. Sydney was thinking of her own troubling and unstable childhood, and how her deep yearning for love and security had led to her getting pregnant with Cassie at the tender young age of fourteen. Her very mature and voluptuous body, along with a boy's promise of forever, had prompted Sydney to ultimately give her heart and body to him. But she'd learned the hard way that he'd only wanted one thing from her, and in the end, when she'd needed him the most, he'd betrayed her in the worst possible way.

And now, Sydney's biggest fear was that some young guy would take advantage of her own daughter in the same way.

As Sydney's best friend, Lora was also the voice of reason in their relationship when it came to Cass, especially since she'd had her share of raising a teenager— her own brother. She didn't hesitate to set Sydney straight now, to give her the words she needed to hear.

"I know it's hard to watch her grow up, Syd," Lora said gently. "But it's going to happen. You've loved her and you've done a great job raising her. Don't hold those reins too tight, or you might find her doing just the opposite of what you want."

"I know, I know," Sydney agreed with a sigh, and dragged her fingers through her drying curls. "I just want her to make smart choices."

"Then give her the chance, and a bit of space." The advice was logical, but not to Sydney, who'd spent years being an overly protective mother. "We've all made mistakes, and she'll make her share. But you need to have a bit of faith in Cass, and she needs to know you trust her. Let her go to the party and have a bit of fun, Syd."

Her friend didn't look convinced, or swayed. "Well, I'll see what her math teacher has to say today before I say yes or no to the Halloween party."

Lora arched a brow mockingly. "You have to ask her math teacher's permission for her to go to the party?"

"No, smart-ass." Sydney stood and carried her mug to the sink and dumped the last of her coffee. "I got a call from him requesting a parent-teacher conference. Remember Daniel Barnett, Cassie's math teacher from last year?"

Lora nodded. Oh, yeah, she definitely recalled the good-looking high school math teacher very well. She'd attended Cassie's Open House Night with Sydney last year, and that's when Lora had also noticed the subtle attraction between the two. But Daniel Barnett, with his clean-cut appearance and genuine nice guy personality, was the kind of man Sydney avoided as a rule—she preferred bad boys, rebels, and guys who were out for a good time, and nothing more. She didn't do long-term commitment or emotional entanglements, and never, ever allowed her heart to get involved in any relationship. According to Sydney, she had her daughter, The Electric Blue, and Lora as a best friend, and there was nothing else she needed in her life.

"Anyway," Sydney continued as she rinsed out her cup and put it into the dishwasher, then dried her hand on a terry towel. "He's teaching Algebra Two this year, so Cassie has him again. He wants to talk to me about how she's doing in class, which is surprising, since she's always done very well in math. She even got an A in Algebra One last year."

Lora joined Sydney at the counter and grinned. "Maybe Daniel Barnett is just looking for a good excuse to see you again."

"Ummm, he's pretty straitlaced, Lora. Kinda like you are." Sydney flicked the collar of Lora's practical work smock and wrinkled her nose playfully. "Besides, he's not the type of guy to call me in for a parent-teacher conference just to flirt with me. Something's definitely up with Cassie."

Worry filled Sydney's gaze, but before Lora could address her friend's concerns, the object of their discussion walked into the kitchen, her normally curly auburn hair now straightened into the latest shoulder-length style most teenage girls were wearing these days. The silky strands framed her face in wispy layers and brought out the golden flecks in her hazel eyes.

Growing up, Cassie had always been a no-frills kind of girl, more of a rough-and-tumble tomboy. But in the past few weeks Lora had begun to notice that Cassie was starting to pay more attention to her appearance, and taking more time with her hair and makeup, and picking out the clothes she wore to school. She still favored jeans over skirts or dresses, though, and today she had on a pair of dark denim jeans, a pale pink T-shirt, and a matching denim jacket.

Truly, Cassie did nothing to flaunt her body, but there was no way for her to hide her mature curves, either. And that was one of Sydney's biggest concerns, since her daughter was around hormonal teenage boys all day long.

"'Morning, Aunt Lora," Cassie said as she slung the straps of her backpack over one shoulder. "I'm ready to go, Mom."

As Cassie passed her mother on the way to the front door, Sydney grabbed one of the straps on her daughter's backpack, effectively bringing her to a stop. "You need to eat something before I take you to school."

Cassie rolled her eyes and exhaled dramatically as she trudged back toward the refrigerator. "Fine. I'll drink a bottle of orange juice on the way."

Knowing that wouldn't be enough to appease Sydney, Lora grabbed a napkin and picked out a buttermilk bar from the pastry box for Cassie. "And take a doughnut with you, sweetie, so you don't have to listen to your mother lecture you about the importance of breakfast all the way to school."

Behind Cassie's back, Sydney stuck her tongue out at Lora, silently telling her what she thought about Lora taking her daughter's side in things. Lora barely held back the humorous laugh threatening to surface.

"Thanks, Aunt Lora." Cassie took the doughnut, gave Lora a bright, grateful smile, and headed out of the kitchen before Sydney could stop her again. "I'll be waiting in the car, Mom!"

"You are such a troublemaker," Sydney said to Lora once the apartment door slammed shut behind Cassie. "You know that, don't you?"

"Yeah, I do, but someone has to keep things balanced around here and between you two." Sydney was way too strict and protective of her daughter, though her friend didn't see things that way.

"She never wants to leave for school early." Frowning, Sydney picked up her purse and car keys. "Something's up."

"Oh, for God's sake, Syd," Lora said, her tone reflecting her exasperation. "Quit being so suspicious. She probably wants to spend some time with her friends before the first period bell rings." Grabbing her own pocketbook, she followed her friend to the front door.

"Or spend time with a boy," Sydney added, and didn't sound happy about the possibility.

"Which is a perfectly normal thing for a fifteen-year-old girl to do." Even as she tried to reassure Sydney, Lora knew that her friend's experiences at the age of fifteen had been vastly different from her own—which was a huge part of why Sydney was struggling with her daughter's transition from little girl to young woman now. "You need to face the fact that she's not your little Tinker Bell anymore."

Sydney smiled at the nickname she'd given Cassie

shortly after she'd been born. "Does she really have to grow up so fast, and so soon?"

Lora hooked her arm through Sydney's as they walked down the corridor together. "Yeah, she really does."

"That's what I'm most afraid of," Sydney said, and sighed.

FINISHED with her third client of the morning, Lora headed to the receptionist's desk to check on her next appointment and what spa treatment she needed to prepare for. She'd already completed a facial, a seaweed body peel, and a mini–refresher massage. After reviewing the session log on the computer, it looked like she had a body polish scheduled in the next half hour.

She turned to head toward the treatment rooms to get one of them ready for her next client, but was stopped by the spa's receptionist as the younger girl returned to the front desk.

"I'm glad I caught you," Brittany said as she brought up a list of the spa's daily appointments on the computer. "There's been a change in your schedule this morning."

"According to the log, I have a client coming in for a body polish at eleven."

"Not any longer." The receptionist cleared Lora's next two appointments and rescheduled them with other technicians. "You now have a hot stone massage waiting for you in treatment room five. He just came out of the steam room, so he's all set up, draped, and ready to go." Brittany glanced back up at Lora and grinned. "He must be someone important, considering Ashley St. Claire called up here herself to schedule him an appointment specifically with you today."

That was a bit of a shock. Ashley St. Claire was the

hotel owner's daughter, and while she indulged in a spa treatment every once in a while, she'd never pulled strings to make special arrangements for a guest, as she had today. And Lora was equally surprised that it was *her* services that Ashley had requested for the client.

But, important or not, the man was just another client to Lora, and she gave every customer the best treatment possible. "What's his name?" she asked Brittany, so she could at least address him in a professional manner.

"John Smith."

A nice, nondescript name, she thought, finding the whole scenario a bit strange. "Is he a guest at the hotel?"

"Not according to our records. I already checked. So, he must be a personal friend of the St. Claires'." Grinning, Brittany leaned closer and lowered her voice so other nearby guests couldn't overhear her. "By the way, I'm thinking you're going to want to give him lots of special attention."

Lora caught Brittany's not-so-subtle wink and smiled. "Oh, really?"

"Mmmm. A few of us saw him when he first arrived, and let me tell you, the other technicians were *begging* me to give him to one of them. He is super-fine and hotter than most of the preppy executives that come up here." The receptionist fanned herself with her hand for effect. "We want details when your appointment with him is over."

"Details?" Lora asked, not sure what kind of inside information they were all after.

The younger woman nodded enthusiastically. "Yeah, we all want to know if his body is as rock hard as it looks. *Everywhere.*"

Lora couldn't help but be amused, and was curious as all heck to see this John Smith for herself. "Sorry, but I never gossip about my clients. Or their attributes," she added with a grin.

"Yeah, I know," Brittany said on a disappointed sigh. "But I thought it was at least worth a shot to ask."

The spa's phone rang, forcing the receptionist back to work. She answered the call with a courteous greeting, and after a brief moment began describing what a Spa Signature Sampler entailed to the caller on the other end of the line.

Not wanting to keep her client waiting any longer than necessary, Lora made her way to his room. She quietly slipped inside, grateful to find the room already set up for her. A few aromatherapy candles had been lit, and the pleasant, woodsy-floral fragrance of rosewood filled the air. Soft music played in the background, adding to the soothing, relaxing atmosphere. But it was the gorgeous, well-built specimen of a man lying facedown on the massage table that made everything feminine within her sit up and take notice.

She'd seen a whole lot of nude male bodies during her years of being a massage therapist, and for the most part it was easy to remain indifferent and unaffected, but like Brittany had indicated, this man was unlike the normal executives and businessmen that frequented the hotel's spa.

This man was big and broad and well-defined in all the right places. Unable to resist, she took a moment to appreciate and enjoy the sculpted contours of his naked, muscular body. Starting at his bare feet, her gaze traveled over well-defined calves and up his long, strong legs. From mid-thigh to the base of his spine, he was covered with a towel, but there was no mistaking that he had an ass that was just as rock hard as the rest of him. The slope of his lean, sun-bronzed back led to wide shoulders and sinewy arms that spoke of the kind of power and strength no one would dare mess with.

He was facing the opposite direction, and she took in his thick, roguish, long and shaggy hair. Those textured, unruly strands, coupled with that amazing body, stirred an undeniable awareness and familiarity inside her. She walked around the table and confirmed her suspicions when she was met with vivid blue eyes and a positively sinful grin that gave her a thrilling rush of pleasure.

The tempting, fully naked body laying on her massage table was none other than Joel Wilde.

Four

LORA tipped her head, lifted an inquiring brow, and regarded Joel with an amused smile. "John Smith, I presume?"

He chuckled, the sound as intimate as the blue-eyed gaze traveling down the length of her body. "I wanted to surprise you."

"You definitely accomplished that."

His gaze slowly, gradually returned to her face, making her all too aware of how drab and sensible she looked compared to how he had seen her at her night job at The Electric Blue. Per the spa's rules for female employees, her hair was pulled back into a neat and tidy ponytail, and she had on a white smock, matching cotton pants, and rubber-soled shoes she wore more for comfort than style.

The outfit certainly wasn't something to inspire a man's lust, yet the spark of desire darkening Joel's gaze was as real as it got. And seductive as hell.

She turned away for a moment—to check the heat setting on the massage stones and make sure they were ready, as well as to compose herself and her response to him—before glancing back at Joel. "I don't know if I'm more surprised to see you here, or more surprised to find out that Ashley St. Claire made special arrangements to fit you in at the last minute."

"It's great to have connections," he said, and grinned shamelessly. "I never know when I'll need to pull in a favor, but it comes in handy at times like this."

"Times like this?" she asked as she picked up one of the warmed basalt stones and placed it on his upper left thigh.

"Yeah. Getting-to-know-you time. You're so busy that I figure I ought to take whatever time with you I can get."

She laughed, truly flattered that he'd call in a favor in order to pursue her. "You didn't have to go to this extreme." She added another stone to the middle of his hamstring, one to the back of his knee, and a smaller stone on the center of his calf.

"Yeah, I did." He let out a low, pleasurable groan as the heat of the stones penetrated the corded muscles along his leg. "I wanted to find out for myself just how good those hands of yours really are," he teased.

Despite the cheesy pick-up line, her pulse raced a bit faster. The conversation had definitely taken a turn toward the kind of sensual banter they'd indulged in the night before, and while she enjoyed flirting with Joel, she was at work and wanted to keep things on a purely professional level. If that was possible when she was about to touch, caress, and massage nearly every naked inch of the man.

She placed a new set of heated stones down the length of his right leg and turned the discussion back to something less tempting. "You seem to have connections all over town—last night at The Daily Grind, and now today, with Ashley St. Claire."

"Actually, Ashley St. Claire is really Ashley Wilde," he said in a low, relaxed tone of voice. "She's married to my older brother, Scott, but keeps the St. Claire last name for business purposes."

Lora had no idea, and was intrigued by that bit of information. "Are you serious?"

"Yep." He exhaled a seductive sigh as she set a pile of hot stones on his lower back to warm the muscles there. "So far, most of my connections are among my brothers' and cousins' spouses. That means lots of perks for me."

She heard the lilting humor in his voice and wondered just how large his family was. But instead of asking, she answered with a soft, soothing, "Ummm," and let the moment segue into a comfortable silence.

"Ummm?" He murmured back to her. "What's that supposed to mean?"

She smiled to herself and placed more of the therapeutic stones on his wide shoulders, around the nape of his neck, and down along the slope of his spine. "I'm trying to be quiet so you can relax and enjoy the experience."

"I'm enjoying it very much," he assured her in a sexy, rumbling voice that had the same effect as if he were stroking his fingers along her bare breasts and belly.

"Good. Now be quiet." She returned to his left leg, grateful that Joel's eyes were closed, because her nipples had tightened against her bra, and her body's reaction to him showed through her white work blouse. God, if the man's voice alone could elicit such a searing response, she could only imagine what a kiss, or a slow, deliberate caress of those big hands along her body, could do to her. Make her melt and unravel, she was sure.

"So, what if I want to talk and relax at the same time?" he asked, and groaned as she began massaging his calf and thigh with the warmed stones in firm, upward strokes. "Does that cost extra?"

His humor got the best of her, and she laughed. "No, but most clients would rather take in the music, along with the scent of the aromatherapy candle, and just de-stress." She moved around to his right leg, and gave it the same massage treatment with the stones.

"Well, I can do all that and talk, too," he assured her. "I'm multitalented that way."

Lora just bet he was. His tone was infused with pure male confidence, hinting at other, more provocative, talents he possessed, as well. "Pleasing the client is my job," she said, and before he could turn that innocent statement into something more suggestive, she added quickly, "What would you like to talk about?"

"You name it. I'm an open book."

And she had to admit that she was way too interested in, and fascinated with, Joel. Picking up two larger, newly warmed basalt stones, she glided them up the sides of his muscled back, all the way up to his neck, then repeated the process again.

"Okay, Mr. Open Book," she said, smiling, "tell me, just how big is your family, anyway? I'm curious about all those perks you get to take advantage of."

"In my family, there are four of us. I have two older brothers, Scott and Alex, and a sister, Mia." He groaned deep in his throat when she hit a particularly tense set of muscles along his neck, then added just the right amount of pressure to ease the taut group of muscles. "Mia is the only girl and the youngest in the family, including my three male cousins, Steve, Eric, and Adrian."

"So, there's seven of you in all," she mused, thinking that there must have been a helluva lot of male testosterone running rampant in the Wilde family, considering six of them had been boys. "Is everyone married or single?"

"The funny thing is, we all were single until a few years ago. And then one by one, my cousins got married and settled down, then my two brothers." His voice was as relaxed as his body, a lazy, deep-timbered sound that told her the massage was doing its job. "Just recently, my sister, Mia, got engaged to Cameron, who is my cousin Steve's business partner. He's a P.I."

Finished using the therapy stones, she removed them from his backside so she could begin the second part of Joel's treatment. "Ahh, one of the perks you were talking about earlier?"

"Definitely," he murmured. "Being a security agent, there are times when certain things need to be investigated or looked into, and Steve and Cameron are two of the best in the biz, with some great connections."

She poured massage oil into her palm and rubbed her hands together to warm the slick substance as she moved back down to the end of the table, to his feet. Wanting to know more about his sister, the lone female in his family, she kept the conversation going. "Where does your sister, Mia, work?"

"She used to work for the family tile business, as do both of my brothers, but she quit so she could concentrate on the stained glass designs she's been creating for some time now." His toes curled as she kneaded the balls of his feet and pushed her thumbs along the arch. "She's getting ready to open her own gallery here very soon."

She heard the pride in his voice and smiled as she went to work on his other foot, then began kneading the firm muscles in his calves with her palms and fingers.

"Good for her," she said, wishing she had the same kind of support from her own brother when it came to her life and dreams.

"We're all really happy for Mia. She's been through a lot, so it's really nice to see her settled down and satisfied with the direction her life is taking." There was no mistaking the affection and caring he felt toward his youngest sibling. "Now, with everyone pretty much married or heading toward the altar very soon, lots of babies are following. It's kind of cool watching the next generation of Wilde kids grow up."

The thought of Joel being an uncle to a bunch of adorable nieces and nephews, playing with them, warmed her deep inside. Yet, despite his siblings' and cousins' committed relationships and the families they were starting, he didn't seem at all bothered by the fact that he was still single and unattached.

She glided her hands along the back of his knee and up to his hard, muscular thigh. Using her thumbs, she rubbed the taut tendons along his hamstring, all the way up to his buttock, with firm, deep strokes. "So, I take it you're the token confirmed bachelor of the family?"

"Yeah, I guess you could say that," he said, and grunted when she dug deep into a knot of muscle to work out the tension. "I've pretty much resigned myself to being a bachelor. It suits me and my lifestyle, so I can't complain."

She switched to his other leg, telling herself that she ought to take his open and honest admission about his permanent single status at face value and proceed with caution. But the awareness between them was strong and sexual . . . and undeniable. And the temptation of physical pleasure beckoned to that part of her that had been without a man's touch and attention for so long.

A comfortable silence fell between them as she finished the lower portion of his body. As her hands slid beneath the towel to massage his toned buttocks, she realized that Joel's breathing had grown shallow and even, and his body lax and pliant. He was either in a deep state of contentment, or he'd fallen asleep.

Either way, she wasn't going to bother him with more conversation. She oiled up her hands again and went to work on his upper back. Placing both hands at the base of his spine, she slowly, gradually, made her way up all that hard, sleek flesh and contoured muscle, kneading out a variety of knots she encountered along the way and massaging the oil deep into tense muscles and his smooth skin.

The man had a body to die for. Amazingly well built, toned to perfection, and made for sex, sin, and all kinds of wicked delights. It had been forever, *if ever*, since she'd touched a body so incredibly strong and powerful, and because she had Joel in such a relaxed state, she did something she'd never, ever done before during a professional massage. Something forbidden and decadent and just for her. She closed her eyes and immersed herself in the sheer, sensual pleasure of stroking his warm, golden skin, and just let herself *feel* and enjoy.

She continued the massage, going purely by touch, skill, and years of practice. Her palms and fingers outlined the shape of his back and glided over hard planes and rippling muscle before she pressed her thumbs firmly along each one of his vertebrae, all the way up to his neck. She kneaded and massaged his broad shoulders, then went to work on each of his muscled arms.

With her eyes closed, her other senses came alive, adding to the desire unfurling within her. She could hear Joel's steady breathing and the soft background music, could feel the thickly corded tendons in each of his arms, despite how lax and pliant the rest of his body was. But most of all, every time she inhaled, she not only drew in the fragrance of rosewood, but also the arousing scent of a hot-blooded male.

Undeniably turned on, her own body responded to the onslaught of sensations. Her breasts grew tight, her stomach tumbled, and between her thighs she pulsed with a need she ached to fulfill. Not in a dream or in a fantasy, but for real, with this man sliding deep, deep inside of her . . .

She heard a moan and snapped her eyes back open, horrified by the possibility that the telltale sound had escaped *her* lips. But then she heard it again, the tone alternating between a low growl and a soft rumble of pleasure.

"God, that feels good," Joel murmured huskily. "You *do* have amazing, magical hands."

"Thank you." She felt herself blush, and wasn't sure if it was because of where her thoughts had strayed before he'd interrupted them, or from his compliment. "I'm ready for you to turn over."

He hesitated. "Ummm, so soon?"

"So soon?" She laughed lightly and moved down to the single towel draped over his butt, holding it in place so he could turn over without revealing any private parts. "I just spent forty minutes on your back side."

"I know, but . . . are you easily shocked?" he asked.

The odd question confused her. "No. Why?"

He lifted up on his forearms and twisted around to glance back at her. He wore an adorably sheepish grin on his face that made him look like a naughty little boy who was about to be caught doing something bad. "I *really* enjoyed that massage. A whole lot," he said meaningfully. "Especially having your hands all over me, and there was something incredibly sensual about your touch that, well, certain parts of my anatomy couldn't help but react to."

The warmth in her cheeks grew hotter as understanding sunk in. Obviously, the massage had aroused him as much as it had her. "Oh."

"Yeah. *Oh.*" His gaze flickered with laughter, along with something hotter, like lust. "I'm not a shy guy at all. The Marines pretty much stripped me of any modesty, but I just didn't want you to think I'm some kind of pervert. I swear I tried to keep my mind on other things during the massage, but considering how attracted I am to you, nature kind of took its own course."

At least she hadn't been the only one who'd allowed a few touches and caresses to get her all hot and bothered—a first for her, but then again she'd never been so attracted to a client before.

"I promise not to swoon or faint from embarrassment," she said with a grin. "But I do appreciate the warning. Now go ahead and turn over onto your back."

She pinned one end of the towel securely to the table with her hip, then discreetly lifted the other end a few inches so he could shift and move to his back. Once he was done and settled, she re-draped the towel and tucked the ends around his hips and thighs.

Oh, yeah, he was definitely, impressively aroused, and maintaining that professional exterior was going to take effort. Luckily, he closed his eyes and let her do her job. They both remained quiet during the hot stone massage, and she segued right into the actual hands-on massage. When she reached his left thigh, her hands slowed as she caught sight of a jagged line of puckered flesh—the only visible flaw on his otherwise perfect body.

Her fingers grazed over a long, thick scar, at least two inches in length, and beneath that light caress she felt the muscles in his leg tense. His reaction was enough to tell her that having her touch the healed wound made him uncomfortable.

"What happened?" she asked softly, curious to know how he'd hurt himself, and why the scar bothered him so much now.

"A large piece of shrapnel got lodged in my leg," he said gruffly, and didn't expand on the details of the incident.

She glided her thumb one last time over the disfigured skin before moving to his abdomen. "How?" she asked, and glanced up at his face. His eyes were still closed, but there was no mistaking the slight clench of his jaw before he replied.

"A roadside bomb in Iraq," he said, his tone brusque. "An IED, actually."

An *improvised explosive device*, she thought with a shudder, grateful that he hadn't ended up a casualty.

Her fingers stroked and kneaded over his solid stomach and across his impressive six-pack abs. "What was it like in the service and Iraq?" she asked, curious to know. "Was it really bad?"

His long, sooty lashes slowly lifted, revealing eyes that were carefully guarded. "Why do you want to know?"

She shrugged and glided her hands over his ribs to his chest and solid pecs, bringing her closer to his gorgeous face and his watchful expression. "No matter how many times I asked, Zach wouldn't tell me anything. He refused to talk about the war or his time in the service."

"There was a reason for that, Lora," he said quietly. "There wasn't a whole lot of good stuff to talk about."

And it was clear that Joel didn't want to discuss it, either. "I'm sorry."

"No, I'm sorry." He closed his eyes again and released a

heavy sigh. "I didn't mean to be rude, but our time in the service wasn't a pleasant experience. We saw and did things that no one should ever have to deal with, but we did what we needed to do. What was necessary. For our country, and to protect our own men that we fought side by side with for days on end."

Joel spoke matter-of-factly, but there was an underlying thread of emotion beneath his impassive attitude. Lora had no doubt that Joel and Zach had seen their share of death and heinous attacks, and she respected them both for risking their lives to save others. But at what cost to their own mental state? she wondered.

As much as that question plagued her mind, Lora let it go and finished up their session. She spent a good amount of time on his arms, shoulders, and neck, and felt him relax once again beneath her skilled hands. She worked out any last lingering stress and tension, and when she was finished, she lifted her palms from his body and stepped away from the table.

"You're all set," she said in a low, soothing tone as she recapped the bottle of oil and turned the heat off the stones. "I hope you enjoyed the hot stone massage."

"Ummm, I did." He moved to a sitting position, thankfully remembering to hold on to the towel covering all his manly assets. "Ashley said I'd feel like a new man afterward, and she wasn't kidding. That was beyond anything I could have imagined. Thank you."

"It was my pleasure." More than he would ever know. "Your clothes are behind that screen in the corner, and you can get dressed as soon as I leave the room." She started for the door.

"Wait," he said, stopping her before she reached the exit. "We're not finished yet."

She turned back around and tipped her head, which

caused her ponytail to brush across her shoulder. "Did you want another massage session?" She honestly didn't know if she could handle another hour or more of touching that body of his in a platonic manner.

"No. Not another massage, though the thought is very tempting." He winked at her, his blue eyes sparkling mischievously. "Actually, I want you to go out with me tonight."

A tiny thrill raced through her, until she remembered her hectic schedule that left little time for a social life. It was Friday, and that meant a late night shift at The Electric Blue. "I can't," she said, unable to disguise her disappointment and regret. "I'm working at the bar until closing."

"Tomorrow night, then?" he asked hopefully.

Normally, she worked a full day and night on Saturdays, but she'd managed to free up the entire day. Sydney had offered her the evening off, which Lora had taken, since it was rare that she had a weekend night off. As for the spa, one of the other massage therapists had asked Lora to switch her Sunday day off with the other woman's Saturday, and Lora had jumped at the chance to have an entire day and night to herself.

"Actually, Saturday is my only full day off this week." And she really did have errands to run and things she needed to catch up on that she'd been putting off for a good week, like laundry, grocery shopping, and paying bills.

"And what better way to spend the evening than with me?" He treated her to one of those devastating grins. Coupled with the fact that he was sitting only feet away from her, completely naked beneath that small towel and looking like a Greek god, she was hard pressed to resist.

She shifted in her rubber-soled shoes and bit her bottom lip, seriously considering his very persuasive offer. There were so many reasons why she ought to turn him down, but whatever was happening between her and Joel, she was oh-so-tempted to throw her normal caution to the wind, go for it, and enjoy whatever he was willing to give.

It had been so long since she'd done anything just for the sheer pleasure of it. And longer still since she'd had such a sizzling, captivating chemistry with a man, along with a connection that went beyond the physical. She liked the way he made her feel, so why not?

The best part was, she knew the score going in, and so did Joel. She wasn't looking for anything permanent, not with her erratic work schedule and visions of opening her own spa, and Joel had made it clear that he was a confirmed bachelor, and liked it that way. There would be no unrealistic expectations between them, just a few fun, enjoyable dates, and hopefully a whole lot of hot, satisfying kisses.

"Come on, Lora," he cajoled when she took too long to answer. "I'll even pick you up on my bike and take you for the ride of your life."

Oh, he was definitely pulling out all the stops to sway her, and there was no denying that he'd wanted her to think about that fast and fierce conversation they'd had the previous night, along with her being the first woman to ever ride his bike with him.

She was hooked. "Okay, I'll go out with you tomorrow night, but it's only because I really want a ride on your motorcycle."

He chuckled and watched as she crossed the room to one of the counters and pulled open a drawer to retrieve a pad of paper and a pen. "Hey, that works for me."

She jotted down her home and cell phone numbers, and her address, then turned back around to give him the piece of paper. Realizing he had nowhere to put the information—not unless she wanted to tuck it into his itty-bitty towel—she set the note back on the counter for him to get later, when he was dressed. "You can pick me up at six."

"Perfect." He grinned like a man who was very pleased with his powers of persuasion. "I'll be there."

She left the room with a smile on her face, thinking that Sydney would be very proud of her for saying yes to Joel.

Five

IT was nearly four o'clock in the afternoon when Sydney arrived at Cassie's high school for her conference with Cassie's math teacher. She'd left her daughter at home, mainly because she wanted to know what was going on with Cassie without any ready excuses or interruptions during her meeting with Daniel Barnett. She wanted direct and uncensored information so she could decide how to get Cassie back on track—pronto.

She entered through the school's main gates and followed the directions Cassie had given her to Building C. She passed through the quad area, and other than seeing a few teenagers and staff on campus, the place was fairly deserted, which made sense, since it was Friday and the start of the weekend for teachers and students.

Finding the two-story structure, she entered the quiet building and headed down the long corridor toward the math wing, the sound of her heeled boots echoing in the hallway. Her gaze took in the rows of metal lockers lining the corridor, the glass case filled to capacity with student awards, and the colorful posters taped to the walls announcing an upcoming dance.

A dull, disconcerting sensation settled in the pit of her stomach, and she tried to shake it off. It wasn't the first time she'd been to Cassie's high school and walked the halls, yet doing so never failed to bring back memories of her own teenage years and how very difficult and painful high school had been for her.

As a freshman, she'd not only had the stigma of being a foster kid who wore used and outdated clothes purchased at the Salvation Army, but being a fourteen-year-old pregnant teen living in a halfway house made her the target of gossip, ridicule, and scorn. No one cared to know the circumstances of her past, or her pregnancy—they only chose to believe that she was a tramp and a whore, and the kind of girl that would screw any guy interested in getting into her pants.

But what hurt more than the rude stares and whispers behind her back was the fact that the boy who'd taken her virginity and fathered her baby, *her own foster brother*, had only reinforced the notion that she was a slut who put out, and that made her the target of unwanted advances from other guys, as well. The only person who'd remained a true friend through those four torturous years had been Lora Marshall. Sydney knew she never would have made it to graduation without her best friend's love, support, and understanding.

High school had been nothing more than a means to an end for Sydney. Despite how hard it had been to raise a toddler during those years and still maintain a B average, she'd been driven to get her education and be more than her heroin-addicted mother had amounted to. She'd also been fiercely determined to give Cassie the kind of life and unconditional love that she, herself, had grown up without.

As for Tim Carson, the guy who'd fathered Cassie—a boy that Sydney had truly believed had loved her and who had said all the right words to get her to have sex with him—well, he'd denied any part in her pregnancy. And his mother and father, *Sydney's foster parents*, had immediately thought the worst and accused her of trying to trap their son by claiming the child was his. Then they'd promptly given her back to the state to deal with. Since no one wanted the responsibility or hassle of taking in a knocked-up teen, she'd been assigned to a state-run halfway house for unwed mothers.

Her memories of her teenage years weren't fond ones, but she'd learned a whole lot of hard, emotional lessons during high school, especially from Tim Carson. He'd been the first to teach her that guys took one look at her voluptuous body and curves and wanted only one thing: to fuck her. It had been a perpetual occurrence in her life when it came to men, but instead of allowing the situation to make her bitter, she'd learned to use her sensuality and seductive figure to her own advantage. To get what *she* wanted, too—whether it had to do with business or her own physical pleasure. Her decision had served her very well over the years, not only putting her firmly in control of any sexual situation, but also allowing her to keep emotions out of the equation.

She refused to let any man exploit her the way that Tim Carson had. When she went out with a guy, she knew exactly what she was getting into. To that end, she preferred to date men who were out for a good time and nothing more. She had a daughter to raise and a bar to keep successful in order to pay off her business loan, and she didn't want or need the distraction of entanglements or attachments getting in the way of her priorities. Which wasn't an issue since she never let a man get close enough to threaten her emotions.

Arriving at Daniel Barnett's classroom, she inhaled a deep breath to regain her composure and redirected her focus to why she was here today. Because of Cassie, and to discuss any potential problems that her daughter was having with math.

She opened the door, stepped inside, and found Daniel standing at the front of the room. His back was to her as he wrote the following Monday's class assignment on the chalkboard, and he gave her a quick glance over his shoulder, and added a polite, "I'll be with you in a minute," before finishing up his task.

As he jotted down page numbers and a note to the class that there would be a test at the end of the week, she casually strolled her way toward his desk. A moment later, he dropped the chalk into a tray and turned around to face her. Her mouth quirked as she took in Mr. Preppy's attire—with his navy chinos, long-sleeved button-up shirt, and matching tie, he was the epitome of a conservative, traditional type of guy. The kind she wouldn't normally give a second glance because he was so opposite of the rough-and-tumble bad boys that normally drew her eye.

Yet she had to admit that Daniel Barnett was very nice looking, in a clean cut, polished sort of way. There was no denying his wide shoulders and a lean body he obviously kept in shape. His thick, dark blond hair was cut short and neat, and his features were nicely chiseled. His eyes were a warm shade of brown that reminded her of the fine whiskey she served at the bar, or rich caramel, depending on how the light reflected off his irises, and he had a mouth that was decidedly sensual and prompted her thoughts to stray down a very naughty path she had no business traveling with this particular man.

"Hi, Sydney," he said, and extended his hand toward her as a friendly smile curved the lips she'd just fantasized about. "Thanks for coming in. I appreciate it."

"Of course." She shook his hand, all too aware of the heat of his large palm against hers, and how long and strong his fingers felt wrapped around her hand. In contrast to his undeniable masculinity, she almost felt *delicate* . . . when she was anything but.

She pushed the ridiculous notion from her mind and kept her thoughts strictly on business. "Nothing is more important than my daughter and her education, Mr. Barnett." And she was determined to make sure that Cassie had every advantage, and the grades to get accepted to a reputable university. Sydney might have scratched, clawed, stripped, and slept her way to being able to open her own business because she'd lacked any type of college degree, but her daughter would hopefully never, ever have to stoop to that kind of level. Not if Sydney could help it.

"Call me Daniel, please." He rounded his desk and pushed aside papers and textbooks on it in search of something. "I have to say, if all my parents had your same positive attitude and showed more interest in their kids' academic achievements, my job would be so much easier and far more enjoyable."

She shook her head, a smile playing at the corners of her mouth. "I can't even imagine how difficult it must be to teach a classroom of hormonal, moody, and temperamental teenagers." Considering she could barely handle Cassie's mood swings, the thought made her shudder.

He glanced up at her and chuckled, a warm, deep sound that did funny things to her insides. "It's definitely a challenge. If I didn't love math so much, I would have quit my first year, which was pure hell, and followed in my brother's and father's footsteps and joined the family medical practice. Except I'm not that great when it comes to blood and guts, and stitches and shots make me queasy." He pressed a hand to his stomach and grimaced.

This time, *she* laughed, because it wasn't often that a man admitted to such a weakness. "Well, if you do ever quit, you can always come to work for me as a bartender at The Electric Blue."

He lifted an inquiring brow, bringing her attention to the amusement glimmering in the depths of his eyes. "Don't the workers dance on the counters and tabletops there?"

"Yeah, they do." She bit the inside of her cheek, unable to imagine a reserved guy like Daniel shaking it for the crowd. She was guessing he came from a blue-blooded type of family who preferred the exclusivity of a posh, upscale country club over a loud, rowdy bar. "It's part of the job description. You've got to be willing to be a little uninhibited."

"Ahhh, it's a tempting offer, but I'm much more comfortable holding a calculator and textbook than juggling bottles of beer and liquor, not to mention the whole dancing thing," he said, and picked up a file folder he found beneath a pile of papers. "I'm an analytical, problemsolving kind of guy, and the whole bump-and-grind scenario just isn't my thing. At least not in public, anyway." Grinning, he winked at her, then started for a small table and chairs set up in the corner of the room.

She stared after him for a moment before following, uncertain whether she was more shocked at his sense of humor, or the fact that he'd just openly flirted with her.

She sat down in the chair across from him and put her

purse on the table, recalling Lora's comment about the possibility of Daniel being interested in her. Okay, so maybe he *was* attracted to her, especially if she took into account the way his gaze had briefly dropped to her full breasts, clearly outlined in her snug blue sweater, before he averted his eyes to the papers in the file he'd brought with him.

His reaction and quick glance at her chest certainly didn't surprise her. She was used to the blatant stares, the bold and unabashed ogling. With men, it always came down to her physical appearance, and the fact that she had a body built for down-and-dirty sex. And Daniel, being a man, was no different, except for the fact that he was more subtle about checking out her curves than most.

Too bad for him, he truly wasn't her type at all, because she was certain he'd be a fun, temporary romp to end her own dry spell. However, he'd revealed just enough about himself in the past ten minutes since her arrival for her to know that their lifestyles were as different as night and day. A nice, conservative teacher and a wild, anything-goes bar owner just didn't mix, in her opinion.

"About Cassie," he said, getting back to the reason why she was there. "I wanted to show you her work over the past month and a half of school, from the first week in September to this week's review test." He laid out a series of papers for her to look at and compare. "Here, as you can see, she started out the school year with a good grasp of what she was learning. But in the past three and a half weeks, her test scores have dropped substantially. From high As to mid Cs."

As Sydney took in her daughter's decreasing grades, she felt her stomach drop. The decline was startling, and disconcerting, especially since Cassie had always done very well in her math classes.

Daniel's gaze met hers, a troubled frown creasing his brows. "What's odd is that Cassie's homework is perfect, and she rarely has anything more than one or two problems wrong. So, to see her doing so poorly on the review tests, which are taken directly off of the homework I give them, really concerns me."

"It concerns me, too," she said on a rush of breath.

He gave her an understanding nod. "Another thing I noticed is that she's changed answers on her tests and ended up getting the problem wrong, when it was correct to begin with." He pointed out a few of those instances on the papers in front of her. "Something isn't quite right, but I can't put my finger on it. I know Cassie's grades and what she's capable of doing from last year, and this just isn't a normal pattern for her."

"Maybe she's confused about how to do the problem," she said, and wondered if she sounded like she was grasping at straws for an answer. Because if Cassie was able to ace her homework, it didn't make sense that her test scores would be so low.

"Could be," he replied, not discounting her theory. Leaning back in his chair, he tipped his head and regarded her thoughtfully. "You're a single parent, right?"

She stiffened, her defenses instantly rising. Shit. She hated, *hated*, this line of questioning—and Daniel certainly wasn't the first person to scrutinize her ability as a single parent. "Yes." She couldn't keep the irritable bite from her tone.

He didn't seem to notice her annoyance. "And Cassie's father?"

Her teeth clenched before she replied. "He isn't a part

of her life." Tim Carson never had been, and never would be a father figure to her daughter. Especially considering he'd never acknowledged his child's existence, which was more than fine with Sydney.

"Okay," Daniel said, much too calmly, and with too much consideration, for Sydney's liking.

She could only imagine that he was judging her, just as so many before him had, and her irritation spiked. She leaned forward in her chair and braced her forearms on the tabletop, her entire demeanor taking on an aggressive, I'm-not-about-to-take-your-shit stance. "Look, I don't know what kind of information you're digging for, but what do any of Cassie's problems with math have to do with me being a single parent?"

Judging by the barely perceptible smile tugging at the corner of his mouth, it appeared the man actually had the audacity to find her indignation humorous. It was also obvious that he wasn't at all threatened by her confrontational attitude.

"Sydney, I didn't mean to imply anything by the question, and I'm sorry if I offended you in any way," he said, his voice genuinely sincere. "I'm just trying to get a better feel for Cassie's home life. Is something going on with her that might be distracting her from school and testing? Anything in her normal routine that has changed lately?"

Choosing to believe that Daniel was truly interested in her daughter's welfare and hadn't meant to insult her, she gave his question serious thought. Sydney knew all the good friends that Cassie hung out with, along with their parents, and though the girls had normal teenage issues that they occasionally dealt with, everything was fine for the time being. She regularly checked her daughter's e-mails and text messages to make sure Cassie wasn't doing something she wasn't supposed to, and she stayed on top of her extracurricular activities and her whereabouts. So, other than a regular fifteen-year-old attitude that came with frequent mood swings, there wasn't anything abnormal or troubling about her daughter's behavior.

Sydney shook her head. "I honestly can't think of anything that has changed or is out of the ordinary for Cass."

"Then it's possible that this is just a bump in the road, so to speak, and we'll just have to get things back on track again."

"What do you recommend I do?" she asked, unwilling to walk out of his classroom without some kind of proactive plan in place for her daughter. "I can get her a private tutor, if you think that's necessary."

"No, not yet I don't." He picked up the papers and slipped them back into Cassie's file. "At this point, I wanted to make sure you were aware of the problem. So, before I recommend your hiring a tutor, I'd first like to try and work through this with Cassie myself."

"Okay." She was fine with that. Despite running her own business, anything beyond basic math was out of her realm of comprehension, and that included algebra. She wouldn't be much help to Cassie at all.

"I tutor my own students on Tuesday and Thursday afternoons," he went on, meeting her gaze from across the table. "I'd like to have Cassie come in on those days so I can work with her one-on-one, which most of my students don't get during class time because we only have an hour to review the day's work. By working directly with her, I can get a solid idea of how she's doing and make a better evaluation of the situation. I can find out if she's truly struggling in the class, or if something else is going on that needs to be addressed."

Of course, Sydney's mind conjured up all kinds of worst-case scenarios. Like drugs. Depression. Hooking up with a horny boy who said all the right things to flatter a girl, but only wanted one thing from her: sex.

Panic made Sydney's heart race. She'd like to think that as Cassie's mother she would be aware of, or at least notice, such extreme activities, but she was far from being that stupid or naive.

"What else would be going on?" she asked.

"Hopefully, nothing too serious or dramatic." He must have seen the stricken look on her face, because his own expression softened with understanding. "Look, I know Cassie well enough to know she's a good kid. But, she's a teenager, and she's at the age where there's a lot of peer pressure and outside distractions that can interfere with schoolwork. Unfortunately, I see it happen all the time."

Sydney's stomach clenched. "Well, I'll definitely be having a talk with Cassie when I get home today and see if I can find out what's going on."

"That would be good," he said, encouraging her with an easy smile. "But don't push too hard for answers, or go searching for trouble where there is none. It could be as simple as her needing extra help in math."

That said, he stood and walked back to a tall filing cabinet, where he put away Cassie's academic folder. While she accepted his input, she'd like to think she could handle her own child, without any extra advice from him. After all, she knew Cassie and her personality best.

Figuring their parent-teacher conference was over, she stood, too, and stopped in front of his desk before leaving. "I appreciate you staying on top of Cassie."

He turned back around. "It's not a problem. It's my job to make sure each student does their absolute best in my class." He came around to where she was still standing, and tipped his head, regarding her curiously. "By the way . . . can I ask you a personal question? It's something I've wondered since the first time I met you last year."

"Uh, sure," she said with a carefree shrug, though after his inquiry about Cassie's father, she couldn't help but feel cautious about what was currently on his mind.

His warm gaze traveled over her face, taking in her features, then lingered on her lips a few extra seconds before he raised his brown eyes back to hers. "How old are you?"

Another question she absolutely hated. Especially when she knew it related to being Cassie's mother. "Why does it matter?"

He shook his head and laughed. "Are you always so defensive about everything?"

"Are you always so nosy about people's personal life?" she shot right back.

"No, not normally," he said with a sexy grin that told her that he was purely interested in just *her* personal life, which completely unnerved her. "Most of my kids' parents are in their midthirties to forties. You, on the other hand, look young enough to be Cassie's sister, not her mother."

The man had a way of throwing her off balance, with his direct questions, the too-charming way he had of dealing with her brash replies and personality, and the undeniable interest in his gaze that struck a spark of restless excitement deep inside her belly.

Jee-sus. She was starting to lust after a buttoned-up, conservative teacher. Un-freakin'-believable.

"I'm twenty-nine," she said, not at all surprised at the disbelief she saw pass across his expression when he made the quick mental calculations that told him how young she'd been when Cassie had been born.

She was certain her announcement had just put a huge damper on his interest, just as she'd intended. She'd come across a few nice guys like Daniel Barnett over the years, and her past indiscretion resulting in a child born out of wedlock when she was only fourteen never failed to make them back off, and fast. At least when it came to anything more than a brief affair. Which proved that when it came to polished, educated men, she was the type of woman they slept with, but didn't take home to meet Mom and Dad.

"I guess I was right, wasn't I?" he said, a good dose of humor chasing away his initial shock. "You *are* young enough to be Cassie's sister."

She rolled her eyes at his flattery. "You should have been a politician instead of a teacher."

"That definitely would have made my parents happier," he said meaningfully, but his grin never wavered.

His comment again told her too much about his family and his way of life. She adjusted the strap of her purse over her shoulder and decided it was time for her to leave. "I should be going."

"I'm done here, too." He rounded his desk, tossed some papers into a leather briefcase, and snapped it shut. "I'll walk out with you."

Her point had been to get far away from this man who provoked way too many unexplained feelings within her. However, saying "I'd rather you didn't" was too rude, so she waited for him to join her at the back of the class, and together they headed out of the building, a surprisingly comfortable silence settling between them.

Walking side by side as they passed through the campus to the parking lot, she was acutely aware of just how tall he was, how masculine. The cool, crisp afternoon breeze ruffling through her long, unbound auburn curls also tousled

Daniel's short honey-blond hair, giving him a mussed, un-kempt look she found much too appealing.

There were only a few cars left in the lot, and she started toward her ten-year-old Honda Accord. The vehicle was old and used, but it was completely paid for and ran like a dream, and that's all she cared about. When Daniel continued to follow her, she cast him a sidelong glance filled with amusement. Undoubtedly, he'd been raised a gentleman, and that included walking a woman to her vehicle. "I think I can make it to my car on my own from here."

"Actually, my car is right over there," he said, and pointed to a vehicle that was parked just beyond hers—a sporty Volvo convertible coupe that most people wouldn't be able to afford on a teacher's salary. "And, there's something I wanted to ask you."

Coming to a stop on the driver's side of her car, she dug her keys from her purse, then met his gaze and allowed a derisive smile to curve her lips. "Another personal question?" She unlocked the door and opened it, just in case she needed a quick escape from him and what was beginning to feel like a relentless interrogation.

He thought for a moment, then replied. "Yeah, I guess it would be."

After tossing her purse into the passenger seat, she folded her arms across her chest and braced herself for another curious inquiry about her life, her past, or some other quest for private answers. "What would you like to know?"

His gaze drifted briefly to the cleavage she'd unintentionally created, then came back to her face. "Would you like to go out sometime?"

His question caught her completely off guard. That was the last thing she'd expected him to ask, and she wasn't even sure she'd heard him right. After all, checking out her breasts and flirting with her were one thing, but it just didn't make sense that someone so conservative would want to interact socially with *her*. "Excuse me?"

He casually braced a hand on the top of her car, subtly caging her in between the vehicle door and his body. "I asked you if you would you like to go out on a date."

Okay, so she had heard him correctly, and somehow she found the fortitude to laugh off his absurd question. "You're kidding, right?"

"No, I'm not joking." In fact, he appeared downright serious.

She shook her head, causing her hair to swirl wildly over her shoulders. "I don't think so."

His gaze remained persistent. "Why not?"

Wanting to let him down easy, she came up with the most logical excuse without stating the obvious—that their worlds just didn't mesh. "Well, for one thing, I'm sure my daughter wouldn't appreciate my dating her math teacher."

"Actually, it's not Cassie's choice to make."

He was right. But here was the best reason of all why going out with Daniel Barnett just wasn't a good idea: "You're so not my type."

He shifted on his feet, the movement bringing him closer somehow. Certainly within touching distance. "Now how would you know that?" he asked in a soft, sexy drawl that was equivalent to a sensual caress along her spine.

She ignored the tingling sensation making her nipples tighten and pucker. "A woman just knows these things."

"What if you're wrong?" he countered, all charm and temptation rolled into an irresistible package she was certain many woman found hard to ignore.

Herself included, it seemed.

"I'm not wrong," she insisted, then inhaled a deep breath. But instead of the cool, fresh air she'd expected to fill her senses, she drew in the scent of *him*. A heady combination of heat and sandalwood, and something else that made her stomach clench with shameless desire for a man who never should have affected her so physically.

"Look," she tried, this time more firmly, "I'm flattered you asked, but it just wouldn't work between us."

Amusement tipped up the corner of his mouth. "It's just a date, Sydney. I'm not asking you to marry me."

The wry note to his voice and the mirth dancing in his gaze prompted an indulgent smile from her. "That's a good thing, because then I'd have to turn you down twice."

He paused for a long moment, and just when Sydney thought she'd finally convinced him she wasn't interested, he managed to throw her another curveball. Reaching out, he caught a long strand of her hair and slowly, gently wound it around his long index finger, ensnaring her in more ways than one. The gesture struck her as oddly tender, if not a little possessive, especially when his fingers grazed the side of her neck. She shivered and damned her lack of willpower and that gnawing need making itself known deep inside her soul.

"Are you always so tough with men?" he asked, his tone low and caring.

She tried to pull back, but he still had her hair between his fingers. "No, not all men." With some of them she played easy to get, usually to satisfy her own purposes. But her reasons for being tough with Daniel had more to do with him being a genuinely nice guy—and her being a very bad girl.

"Then why me, Sydney?"

God, even the way he said her name, so soft and reverent, made her want to hear it on his lips in the throes of passion. And that thought was enough to force her to take drastic actions with him.

"Why you?" Deliberately, she stepped closer to him and ran her finger down the front of his dress tie while giving him an upswept glance infused with a whole lot of unabashed confidence and reckless aggression. The kind that considerate, conservative guys found too bold and brazen for their tastes. "Because I eat stuffed shirts like you for breakfast."

He raised a brow, then burst out laughing. Once he got all those deep, good-natured chuckles out of his system, he regarded her with a lopsided grin. "I don't know what amuses me more, the fact that you think I'm a stuffed shirt, or that you'd eat me for breakfast." His eyes darkened with something wicked and playful. "I have to admit that would definitely be a first for me, but I'm willing to let you try your best."

Did nothing dissuade this man? She dropped her arms to her sides and sighed. "Daniel . . . you're a really nice guy, and—"

"Ahhh," he interrupted, the word laced with a wealth of understanding. "Too nice for *you*?"

Now he was getting it. Finally. "Trust me. I'm doing you a huge favor by telling you no."

"I'm a big boy, Syd," he replied confidently. "I think I can handle a night out with you."

She stared into his compelling caramel-colored eyes and realized that Daniel was no different from any other guy and it was all about getting laid. It had to be, because there just was no other explanation for his determination, despite her rejection.

Well, two could play that game. It had been months since *she'd* gotten laid, and there was something about Daniel Barnett that made her wonder what he was like in bed. There was a definite attraction between them, so it wasn't as though she were settling, or even taking advantage of him.

What the hell, she decided. He thought he knew what he was getting into, that he could handle *her*. It would be interesting to see if that was true.

"Fine," she said, giving in for the sake of enjoying a night of mutual pleasure with him. "I'll go out with you, but it will have to be next weekend so I can get someone at the bar to cover one of my late night shifts."

"That works for me." The grin that appeared was pure male satisfaction. "Next weekend it is."

Having gotten what he wanted, he slipped on a pair of sunglasses and walked away toward his sporty Volvo, his stride self-assured and cocky even. She watched him go, appreciating the width of his shoulders and his firm backside before she slid into her car. She closed the door and started the engine, unable to remember the last time, if ever, that a man had been able to wrap her around his finger, as Daniel just had.

The feeling was disturbing . . . and very exciting.

Six

IT wasn't often that Lora bought new clothes for herself, but she hadn't been able to resist buying a new top for her first real date with Joel. Besides, the shirt had been on sale for half price, so it had been much easier to justify the purchase, because she'd gotten such a great deal.

The long-sleeved, plum-colored, thermal ribbed top was perfect to ward off the chill of the late October weather, and the low, rounded neckline and row of small silver snaps securing the front would no doubt stir Joel's imagination, and hopefully a good amount of lust. She'd paired the top with her favorite low-rise jeans, which did great things for her butt, and a comfortable pair of heeled boots, since they'd be taking Joel's motorcycle. The overall look was simple, but sexy and alluring at the same time—which was exactly the result she'd wanted to achieve.

After a girl-to-girl talk with Sydney earlier that afternoon and a much-needed boost of confidence from her friend, Lora had decided that tonight she was going to indulge wholeheartedly in the mutual attraction simmering between her and Joel, and follow wherever it might lead. She wanted to discover just how hot and intense all that sexual chemistry was, and just how far it would take them.

She fluffed her unbound hair with her fingers one last time, then exited the bathroom into her bedroom. Cassie was still where Lora had left her five minutes before— lying on her stomach on the queen-sized bed, thumbing through one of the month-old fashion magazines Lora had brought home for the teen from the hotel spa. Every month when the new magazine subscriptions arrived for the reception area, Lora collected the expired periodicals for Cass before they were thrown away.

The young girl had dropped by half an hour earlier because she wanted to hang out before heading back to her place for the night, but Lora suspected there was something else distracting Cassie. Since arriving, she'd been quiet and subdued, and Lora was fairly certain that the talk Cassie had with her mother the previous night about her math grades was weighing heavily on her mind. As a result of Sydney's meeting with Daniel Barnett, she'd restricted Cass's weekend and weeknight activities until her grades improved, and while Lora thought her friend's limitations were a bit extreme, Sydney had been adamant about her decision.

"So, what do you think, Cass?" Lora asked in an attempt to draw the young girl out of her funky mood. "Does this outfit look okay for a casual date?"

"How would I know?" Cassie replied sullenly, without glancing up from her glossy fashion magazine. "I've never been on a date before."

"But you will," Lora assured her. "Someday."

When she didn't get a response, Lora sat down on the bed next to Cass and gently smoothed a hand over her soft, auburn curls. She'd always been able to talk to Cassie and reason with her in a way that Sydney couldn't grasp. Sydney was the strict one, the disciplinarian, and Lora was the softer, gentler voice of understanding. It was a good balance for Cassie, and she at least trusted Lora enough to open up to her, rather than keeping everything buried inside where it could build into the kind of resentment that drove a kid to do drugs or to hang out with the wrong crowd in an attempt to rebel against a parent's rigid rules.

Flipping the last page in the magazine, Cassie tossed it aside with a sigh and finally looked up at Lora, her expression filled with teen angst and frustration. "Do you really think my mother will let a boy get close enough to ask me out?"

The sarcastic tone of Cassie's voice had Lora biting the inside of her cheek to keep from laughing. Cassie didn't need her amusement, but rather her support and assurance, and Lora did her best to provide it. "Cass, hon, you're only fifteen. You're young and have plenty of time to date boys."

An indelicate snort escaped the younger girl, and she flopped dramatically onto her back and stared up at the ceiling fan above the bed. The position accentuated Cassie's figure, especially the round firmness of her breasts that most grown women would kill to possess. And those very adult curves were a big reason why Sydney felt the need to shelter her teenage daughter.

"Most of the girls in my classes already have boyfriends. I'm probably the only one who's never been kissed." She slung her arm over her eyes as if the thought traumatized her. "God, if my mother had her way, I'd die a virgin!"

A truer statement had never been spoken, but Lora wasn't about to add to Cassie's anguish by admitting that out loud. "Losing your virginity isn't all that it's cracked up to be, you know."

Cassie lowered her arm, her pretty hazel eyes brimming with a young girl's hopes and wishes. "I'm not looking to lose my virginity," she said adamantly. Then her voice turned soft and forlorn. "I just want to be able to say *yes* if a guy asks me out on a date. Is that so much to ask?"

No, it wasn't a whole lot to ask for at all, but unfortunately Lora wasn't the one who made those kinds of decisions in Cassie's life. All she could do was talk to Sydney and fight the good fight on Cassie's behalf. Maybe she could suggest a group date with friends, which would be far safer and not nearly as intimate as a single date.

As Lora mulled over that idea, a thought occurred to her. "Does this conversation about dating have anything to do with the Halloween party you want to go to?"

Cassie averted her gaze and shrugged. "Maybe."

Lora took her answer as a yes, but didn't push the issue for now. When Cassie was ready, Lora had no doubt she'd bring up the subject. Or, the boy she was interested in would garner up the nerve to ask her to the party, which would then send Cassie to Lora with pleas for help to convince her mother to let her go out on the date.

"Aunt Lora . . ." Cassie's curious tone drew her attention back to the young girl. "How do you know if a guy likes you?"

The question made Lora smile, as well as think about the initial attraction between her and Joel. The man's smoldering looks, shameless interest, and direct approach had been some of the first clues that he was interested in her. Then came the kind of arousing sexual tension that sparked between them whenever they were

near one another. Heated glances. Unspoken desires. A
subtle caress that made her entire body crave a more ex-
plicit touch.

Yeah, those were definitely some of the signs that a
guy was into you. However, considering adult attraction
was far more blatant and sexual than teenage infatuation,
Lora did her best to try and remember back to when she
was fifteen years old and in high school. She recalled her
first crush and used those memories as a guide for Cassie.

"Well, it usually starts out with a glance your way
when he thinks you're not looking," she said, watching as
Cassie listened intently to her descriptions. "Eventually,
he'll meet your gaze, and maybe even give you a smile. If
he's confident that you like him, too, he might approach
you, and talk and flirt with you. When that happens,
you'll probably feel a tickle of excitement in your belly,
and your heart will beat a bit faster."

A telltale blush swept across Cassie's peaches and
cream complexion, but the teen didn't give Lora long to
wonder about its source before she asked, "Is that how
you feel about the guy you're going out with tonight?"

Lora nodded. "Yeah. Those kinds of feelings don't
change as you get older." They just grew more intense.
More tempting and deliciously seductive.

The doorbell rang, interrupting her talk with Cassie
and jarring Lora into the realization that it was a few minutes after six. She jumped up and hurried over to her
dresser. "Ohmygod! He's here and I'm not ready yet."
She'd gotten so caught up in Cassie and their conversation
that she hadn't been watching the time. "I still need to put
on my watch and earrings and get my coat and purse—"

"That's okay," Cassie said as she quickly scrambled
off the bed. "I'll let him in for you."

She was out the bedroom door before Lora could stop

her, and it was obvious that Cassie wanted to meet her date. So Lora let her answer the door while she quickly put on her jewelry and stuffed her cell phone, driver's license, and lip gloss into her small purse. She heard Joel's deep, sexy voice, but couldn't make out what he'd said. A moment later, Cassie popped back into her room with a big grin on her face.

"Wow, Aunt Lora," she said in a giddy whisper, her pretty features alight with girlish delight. "He's so *hot*!"

Lora laughed as she grabbed a warm jacket from her closet—a dark brown faux-suede coat that was lined with fleece. "I can't believe you're checking out my date."

"I wasn't—" Cassie began, then cut herself off before the denial could escape. Then, an adorably sheepish look replaced her indignation. "Okay, I'll admit I was curious to see what he looked like."

"Well, I'm glad you approve."

Cassie grabbed the magazine off the bed and gave Lora a quick kiss on her cheek. "I do. I've got to get going. Thanks for, you know, talking," she said a bit awkwardly before adding, "Oh, and have fun tonight."

"I'll do my best," Lora said with a smile, though she planned to have more than just *fun* with the hot, sexy guy waiting for her in the living room. "Tell Joel I'll be right out."

"Okay." The young girl started out of the bedroom, but stopped and turned back around before reaching the door, her magazine hugged to her chest. "By the way, I didn't answer your earlier question, but I wanted to tell you that you look great, Aunt Lora. He's a very lucky guy to be going out with you," she said, then was gone.

Out in the other room, she heard Cassie tell Joel goodbye, then the front door closing as she left.

After one last check in the mirror, Lora gathered up her

purse and jacket and went to greet Joel. She found him standing in the middle of the living room, wearing his classic black jeans, boots, and a T-shirt beneath a black leather jacket that was unzipped. His roguishly long hair was a rumpled mess around his head, which accentuated his disarming blue eyes and added to those too-appealing bad boy looks of his.

But instead of gracing her with one of those irresistible, breath-catching smiles that turned her inside out with wanting, his hands were braced on his hips and a deep frown creased his brows instead.

"Hey there," she said, unable to guess at what might have set him off. "Is everything okay?"

"Hi," he said gruffly, then hooked a thumb toward the front door, where Cassie had just exited. "Who was that?"

Good God, had Cassie said or done something to annoy Joel? "That was Sydney's daughter, Cassie. Since we live in the same apartment building, she's here quite often."

If possible, his displeasure increased. "Does she always open the door without asking who's on the other side?"

Lora stared at Joel, surprised at his question. "I knew it was you."

He cocked his head to the side and regarded her with a good measure of male arrogance. "What if it *weren't* me?"

"Who else would it have been?" she countered as she set her purse on the couch so she could slip into her jacket. "You said you'd pick me up at six, and it was a few minutes past six when you knocked on the door."

Still, he didn't let up. "Do you know how many defenseless women get attacked by opening their door to a stranger?"

"Ummm, no." She would have thought that he was yanking her chain if he didn't look so serious about the subject matter. "But judging by how upset you are, I'm guessing it's a pretty high percentage?"

"Higher than you might think." He dropped his hands back to his sides, but his entire body remained tense. "Just do me a favor. Always ask who it is before opening your door, and don't open it for anyone you don't know or aren't expecting."

She did her best to keep her amused grin from reaching her lips. "Okay."

As Lora straightened the collar of her jacket, she realized the source of his annoyance. The man obviously possessed a protective instinct when it came to women, whether due to having a sister or his time in the military, she wasn't certain. But she'd been on her own for a very long time, and as much as she appreciated his concern, she didn't need someone being her guardian.

As if he sensed her willful thoughts, he narrowed his gaze and added, "Promise?"

She refrained, just barely, from rolling her eyes at his insistence and gave him the reassurance that would hopefully put an end to the conversation. "Sure, I promise."

"Good." He released a breath and finally relaxed.

He looked relieved, but now Lora was slightly miffed by the fact that his interrogation, and that frown of his, had put a damper on the start of their evening together, instead of them leaving her place on a high of excitement and anticipation of the night's events. "Now that you've gotten that off your chest, do you think we might be able to start this date of ours over?"

He blinked at her in confusion. "What do you mean?"

When it came to romancing a woman, he was obviously a typical, obtuse man who didn't realize the importance of setting the tone for a date. Well, she'd just have to *show* him what she meant.

Closing the distance between them, she placed a hand on his chest, tilted her head, and brushed her mouth against his in a slow, sweet caress. His lips were soft and warm and slightly damp, and she caught the faintest hint of peppermint on his breath.

After a moment, she pulled back. The chaste kiss wasn't nearly enough to satisfy her desire for him, but it was sufficient to trigger a deeper longing and start their date off with a slow buzz of sexual tension. She figured the evening was still young, and the rest of the night still held a whole lot of promise.

She slowly smoothed her hand down his chest, relishing the heat of his skin radiating through his cotton T-shirt, and the way those well-defined muscles of his flexed beneath her fingertips.

Lifting her lashes, she met Joel's gaze and smiled up at him. "Hi," she said huskily.

"Hi, yourself," he murmured, an odd mixture of surprise and uncertainty in his eyes. "What was that kiss for?"

She shrugged. "I thought I'd get our first kiss out of the way. Now it's done, and you don't have to worry about making the first move, because I just did." Her meaning couldn't have been more clear, or inviting.

An amused smile tipped up the corners of his mouth. "I wasn't worried about making the first move, but I wouldn't want something like that to distract you all evening."

"Yeah, me, either." She grinned and picked up her purse. "It was just something I had to do."

"I completely understand. Are you ready to go?"

She nodded. "As ready as I'll ever be."

They left her apartment, and once they were outside the building, they took the walkway toward the parking lot.

"Did you bring your motorcycle?" she asked hopefully.

"Yep. It's right over there." As they turned a corner, he pointed toward the sleek, black bike parked in one of the stalls.

Exhilaration filled her at the thought of riding on such a powerful machine, with the cool, crisp evening air on her face, her arms around Joel, and her thighs tight against his hips. "Remember, I like it fast and fierce," she teased.

"Trust me, sweetheart, that's something a guy's not likely to forget," he said in a low, seductive drawl as he unhooked one of the shiny black helmets from the bike and handed it to her.

"I just want to make sure you're up for the challenge," she said playfully, and slipped the helmet on her head, then buckled the strap beneath her chin. "Wouldn't want you to get performance anxiety, or anything like that."

He arched a brow her way at the double entendre she'd just issued. "You are a *very* naughty girl."

She laughed and had to admit, she *was* feeling decidedly naughty.

"Here, put these on, too." He retrieved a set of gloves from a small compartment at the back of the motorcycle and handed them to her. "It can get cold on the ride."

Grateful that he'd thought ahead, she pulled on the insulated gloves, while he did the same with a black pair that molded to his long fingers and strong hands.

"This, too," he said, and wrapped a dark, plaid scarf around her neck, then tucked the ends into her jacket.

"Thanks." The soft material was warm, and when she inhaled she caught the arousing scent of Joel's aftershave. "So, where are we going tonight?"

He took her purse and put it into the compartment, then snapped the lid shut. "I thought I'd show you my regular hangout."

"You mean your regular hangout when you're not at The Electric Blue?"

"Yep. It's far more casual and you aren't required to dance on the tabletops." Grinning, he straddled the seat of the Ducati with ease, his long legs enabling him to keep his feet flat on the ground to keep the bike steady. He started the engine, then glanced back at her. "Hop on."

She settled herself behind him, her chest to his back, and braced her boots against the back footrests. He grabbed her hands, pulled her arms around his waist, and pushed her gloved fingers beneath his zipped-up jacket so that her hands were clasped firmly in his lap.

"Hang on tight," he said.

Those were the last words Joel spoke as he navigated the bike onto the street, then proceeded to accelerate and took her on the fast, exhilarating ride that he'd promised.

"JUDGING by those come-and-get-me looks Lora keeps throwing your way, I take it she finally fell for the Wilde Man charm, huh?"

Joel glanced at Ben—a good friend and one of Elite's partners—who was sitting with him at a table at Nick's Sports Bar. His two other partners had joined them for the evening, as well. At the moment Jon was flirting with a petite blond woman across the room, and Kevin had whisked Lora off to play a game of pool with him.

Joel shrugged evasively, refusing to let Ben's observation turn into a more personal discussion about his relationship with Lora. "Yeah, I guess you could say that. It makes keeping an eye on her a whole lot easier if she believes we're dating."

Ben leaned his arms on the table and grinned. "And considering the way you're watching her, like you wouldn't mind mixing a bit of pleasure with business, I'm assuming she's gotten under your skin, too."

Annoyed at Ben's persistence, along with his too-accurate presumption of the situation between him and Lora, Joel clenched his jaw. "I'm watching her because it's my job." His tone was clipped with impatience.

Ben held up both of his hands as if to back off. "Okay, if you say so."

Figuring that was the end of their conversation, Joel finished off the last of his beer and turned his gaze to the gaming area of the bar, where Kevin and Lora were playing their second game of pool—this time with a twenty-dollar wager on the table.

Kevin had made the mistake of assuming that Lora didn't know the specifics of the sport, but the sparkle in her eyes was a dead giveaway that she was playing along with Kevin's assumption. Currently, Lora was bent low over the pool table as she lined up a shot, giving Joel and every other guy in the place a mouthwatering view of her rounded breasts pressing tight against her top. Joel's lips pursed and he narrowed his gaze as Kevin moved beside Lora and leaned way too close for Joel's liking as he oh-so-helpfully gave her advice on attempting a combination. She made the shot, not because of Kevin's guidance, but because of her own skill.

"You know, you really don't need to glare at Kevin," Ben said in amusement. "He's just teaching Lora a few shots. He's no threat at all to whatever is going on between the two of you."

Joel had had enough of Ben's ribbing and transferred that dark scowl to his friend. "Shut the fuck up, will you?"

Ben laughed heartily, not the least bit offended by Joel's brusque and rude comment, which was a dead giveaway of just how on edge Joel was over Lora. Instead, Ben picked up a potato skin from the appetizer platter they'd all munched on earlier and took a big bite.

Thankful that Ben's mouth was full, which meant Joel had a few minutes of peace, he redirected his attention to something more productive than the unaccustomed jealousy making itself known. Instead, he gave the filled-to-capacity establishment a quick look around to make sure that there wasn't anyone in the bar that looked suspicious or out of place. This was his turf, a place he was familiar with when it came to the patrons and layout of the bar, and that made him feel far more comfortable and in control than he did at The Electric Blue. And, here he had three other guys keeping an eye on Lora, too.

Joel's gaze slid past Ben, who smirked at him knowingly but didn't say a thing. Joel felt himself bristle all over again. He hated that Ben was able to peg his attraction to Lora when he was trying so damn hard to keep his desire for the woman under wraps.

This entire pretense with Lora was a double-edged sword as far as his libido was concerned, and it had gotten a whole lot sharper and more dangerous with that kiss she'd planted on him in her apartment. Despite how sweet and platonic it had been, he hadn't missed the underlying hunger in the way her lips had pressed against his, and the overwhelming temptation that beckoned him to take the kiss to a hotter, deeper connection. The kind that included open mouths, mating tongues, and wandering hands over warm, smooth flesh.

So far, he'd managed to maintain his physical distance with Lora and hadn't so much as encroached on the hands-off policy he'd sworn himself to when he'd agreed to this favor for Zach. Not only was protecting Lora a job for him, there were other issues that made any kind of affair between them impossible. Without her even knowing it, their relationship was a complex one, based more on deceit than honesty, and he wasn't about to add to his guilt by succumbing to his own lust and the undeniable need to lose himself in her soft, lush body. No matter how much he might wish otherwise.

Lora deserved more than a few nights of sex with him that weren't even grounded in complete honesty. He'd deliberately entrenched himself into her life because he'd promised to keep her safe from the thugs who were after her brother, and carnal pleasure was all he had to offer any woman, because he just didn't do long-term commitments.

Unlike his brothers and cousins, who were all enjoying marital bliss, Joel had come to the conclusion that he wasn't the home and hearth type. After the death of his mother, with Scott and Alex taking over the family responsibilities and making their main focus raising their baby sister, Mia, Joel felt as though he'd gotten lost in the shuffle. He didn't have an important role in the family, as his older brothers did, which had given him the feeling of not quite fitting in.

As a young boy, it had been easier to keep his emotions bottled up inside and just do his own thing, and that rebellious streak had led to a thirst for risk and adventure and the kind of adrenaline rush that kept him on a natural high. He'd become the black sheep of the family, the one who wasn't cut out to be a part of his father's construction business like Scott and Alex. The one who'd always kept women at a distance because he'd rather be on an exciting assignment than tied down.

That's why he'd joined the military, because his only obligation had been to Uncle Sam. And now, with Elite Security Specialists, he was able to take on jobs that satisfied his restless need for something different, yet were temporary and didn't demand anything more than he had to give.

Those were the facts, his lifestyle and his reality.

The story was rock solid, but it didn't diminish the fact that Lora Marshall tested his honorable intentions in so many ways, with her seductive overtures, flirtatious touches, and bewitching, come-hither eyes, which she'd been using to her advantage all evening long. The woman was determined to drive him to the brink of sexual frustration, and while he'd managed thus far to maintain control of his own aching need to get horizontal with her, he had to admit that his restraint was stretched nearly to the limit.

"What are you doing back here so soon?" Ben asked as Jon returned to the table sooner than any of them would have expected. "Did you strike out with the blonde?"

Jon shook his head as he sat down. "She was definitely a sure thing, but when she started talking about how her biological clock was ticking, then started looking at me as a potential sperm donor, I was so outta there." He shuddered for effect. "The last thing I need to do is hook up with a woman who has me in mind to father her baby. Jeez, an uncomplicated fling is hard to find these days."

Ben chuckled. "Maybe we've just become more discriminating," he suggested philosophically, then sent Joel a sly glance. "Not all of us are lucky enough to find a smart, sexy woman like Lora."

Joel's fingers tightened around the neck of his empty beer bottle, making him wish it was Ben's neck instead. He chose not to reply, knowing that the guys were just giving him shit, as they always did.

"Watch out, guys, this one's a hustler," Kevin said, hooking a thumb over his shoulder toward Lora as they rejoined the table after their game.

"I did *not* scam you," Lora insisted with a sassy grin as she took the empty seat next to Joel, and Kevin settled into the chair next to her. "It's not my fault you underestimated my skills just because I'm a woman."

"That is so *not* true," Kevin denied emphatically, but Joel knew that's exactly what had happened. Kevin had made it way too easy for Lora to dupe him.

"If you didn't think that Lora could play, then why were you teaching her all the different shots?" Ben asked, taking great delight in giving Kevin a hard time.

Joel was just damn grateful that Ben was no longer focused on harassing him.

Kevin slanted Lora a chastising glance. "She didn't bother to tell me that she knew how to play pool."

"That's because you made your own assumptions without giving me a chance to tell you otherwise," she informed him with a very sweet smile. "Besides, I was having too much fun watching your mouth drop open in shock when I cleared the table on that last game."

"Yeah, and now I'm twenty bucks poorer," he grumbled good-naturedly. "You're a pool shark."

"It was like taking candy from a baby," she teased as laughter danced in her green eyes.

Joel couldn't take his gaze off of Lora, especially not when she unconsciously shook her hair back and away from her face in a move that was as feminine as it was sensual. Her cheeks were flushed pink, her expression vibrant as she reveled in her recent victory over Kevin. The graceful curve of her neck and the upper swells of her breasts, and in between, were damp with perspiration from the warmth in the bar. All that glowing, dewy skin made Joel think about how she'd look after a night of hot, illicit sex. With him, of course.

He shifted in his seat as his body reacted to that little

fantasy, and swallowed back a groan at the torturous, it's-never-gonna-happen thought.

"You know, I'm going to have to demand a rematch," Kevin said in an attempt to preserve his manhood.

Lora braced her elbow on the table, rested her chin in her hand, and batted her lashes at Kevin. "I don't know if that's a good idea. I really hate to see grown men cry."

Both Jon and Ben burst out laughing, and even Joel couldn't help but chuckle at Lora's quick wit and amusing banter. Their humor at Kevin's expense earned them all a dark look from their friend, but it was all in good fun.

"By the way, the next round of drinks is on me, boys," Lora said as she slapped the twenty-dollar bill on the table, then signaled for the nearby cocktail waitress to come by after she was done with her other customers. "Or rather, drinks are on *Kevin*, since this is his money."

Kevin dragged his hand through his hair. "Man, I'm not going to be able to live this down, am I?"

"Not anytime soon, I'm guessing," Lora said with a grin.

"Well, the least you can do is tell me how you learned to play so well."

She shrugged. "I've worked in a lot of bars over the years as a cocktail waitress. It was decent part-time work while I was going to college, and some of the places had pool tables. So on occasion I'd stay after work and play with the guys."

Joel continued to listen to Lora, as well as watch how easily she managed to capture not only Kevin's attention, but Jon's and Ben's, as well. She was so genuine, so easy to like, and definitely a guy's kind of girl. The type who was comfortable in any situation, and effortlessly fit in and meshed well with his friends. And she was the exact opposite of the high-maintenance women he normally hooked up with . . . then promptly dumped when they began to cling, make demands, and make him feel way too stifled.

Lora was far from the clingy, demanding type. And that made his job of watching over her a helluva lot easier.

"What can I get you all to drink?" the waitress asked as she came up to their table a few minutes later.

Ben, Jon, and Kevin ordered fresh beers, and Lora stuck with her drink of the night, an iced water with a lemon twist, keeping with her claim that she didn't drink liquor. Joel passed on a refill, since it was getting late and they'd be leaving soon.

"I need to go to the restroom," Lora said after the waitress was gone, then stood up and glanced at Joel with a too-tempting smile. "How about a dance when I get back?"

Hell, no, he thought firmly. He'd seen the way she danced at The Electric Blue, and he knew for certain he'd never be able to handle Lora brushing her body sinuously along his, tantalizing him with a shimmying sway of her hips, an intimate press of her soft, yielding breasts against his chest.

His pulse thudded through his veins as he looked into her inviting gaze. There was no way he'd survive such a close, erotic encounter without showing her, and the rest of the patrons in the bar, just how much this woman affected his libido. One dance, and he'd be walking around for the rest of the night with his cock raised at full mast.

Yet . . . how could he tell her no? "Uh, sure," he finally said.

She flashed him a smile that told him she definitely had seduction on her mind. "Great," she said, then headed off in the direction of the women's restroom, which Joel luckily had a perfect view of so he could watch her the entire way.

Chuckling, Ben gave Joel an amicable pat on the back. "Oh, yeah, you are so in over your head with this one."

This time, Joel didn't bother denying Ben's claim. It was no use, because he could feel himself falling under her spell, with no cure in sight.

Seven

"HAS there been any more word from Zach?" Jon asked, once Lora was out of earshot. It was the first time the four of them had been alone all evening and could talk business.

Joel shook his head, watching as Lora pushed the door open to the women's restroom and slipped inside. "He hasn't contacted me since his initial phone call. There haven't been any threats against Lora, either."

"Yet," Kevin added grimly.

"There won't be a *yet*," Joel stated adamantly. "She's covered twenty-four/seven, by either myself or one of you. That doesn't give someone a whole lot of opportunity to get to her."

Even as he said the words, Lora was leaving the restroom and making her way back to table to get him for the dance he'd promised her—while a guy in his midthirties was walking directly toward Lora. The man could have been headed to the john, but the way he remained purposefully in Lora's path, instead of veering to the left to let her pass him, made the approach far more personal.

Joel stiffened as every primal instinct within him surged to life and he automatically went into military combat mode. His sudden, intense reaction caused his three friends to turn in their seats to see what had captured Joel's attention. As soon as the guy stopped in front of Lora, which forced her to come to an unexpected halt, Joel knew some kind of trouble was about to erupt. The big question was, was this one of the thugs who was out to terrorize Lora on Zach's creditors' behalf, or was he a harmless guy looking to hook up with a woman for the evening?

Either way, Lora wouldn't be involved.

"*Fuck,*" Joel muttered beneath his breath, and abruptly stood up, ready to tackle the problem.

At the same exact moment, three other chairs scraped against the hardwood floor as Ben, Jon, and Kevin joined him in his stance, instantly prepared to provide additional reinforcement. Their unwavering fidelity reminded him of their time in the military and the way they'd always banded together whenever a threat was imminent.

Joel appreciated his friends' support, but he didn't want to make a scene if it could be helped, and the daunting sight of four big, strapping guys striding across the establishment would attract way too much attention.

"I'll take care of this," he said, 100 percent certain that he could handle the smarmy guy on his own.

"We've got your back if you need it," Ben told him, even though it went without saying.

With a nod, Joel made his way through the crowded bar, his gaze never leaving Lora or the blond-haired guy who was invading way too much of her personal space. His temper spiked when he saw her shake her head at something the other man said, then try to step around the guy only to have him grab her arm to stop her.

Ten more seconds and he reached Lora's side, every one of his five senses sharp and alert, along with a strong protective impulse that went above and beyond the call of duty. This unfamiliar feeling was far more possessive, and it set off warning signals he pushed aside in order to deal with the issue at hand.

He pinned the other man with a dark, menacing look. "I suggest you let go of her and back off, unless you'd rather I remove your hand for you."

The man had the good sense to drop her arm, but was stupid enough to challenge Joel. "Who the hell are you? Her bodyguard?" he sneered, his breath reeking of whiskey, which explained his show of bravado.

"Actually, I'm your worst fucking nightmare," Joel said with deadly calm. "The lady is with me."

The man looked him up and down, his gaze brimming with alcohol-induced insolence. "Yeah? Why don't we let *her* decide who she's with? She might not like the Neanderthal type." He shifted his gaze to Lora and attempted a cocky grin designed to charm her. "Come on, sugar, let's get out of this joint and go somewhere quiet and private where we can get to know each other better."

Lora opened her mouth to speak, but Joel squeezed her arm to shut her up.

Confident that Lora was interested in him, the guy took a step toward her. Blood simmering with annoyance, Joel instantly stopped him with a flattened palm to his puny chest. He ruled this particular man out as a suspect, and saw he was a too-aggressive womanizer who thought way too much of his power of persuasion when it came to the opposite sex.

Still, Joel wasn't about to let any guy near Lora—a direct threat or otherwise. "Do *not* touch her again. If you do, I'm going to have to kick your ass."

The other man let out a bold, you-don't-scare-me laugh. "Yeah, you and what army?"

Joel could easily take the guy single-handedly. All it would take was two seconds and he would have the man's arm jammed up the middle of his back and his face pressed against the nearest wall, but Joel truly didn't want to engage in any kind of physical altercation if it could be helped.

So he opted for a more intimidating tactic. "Me, and that army right over there." He pointed to his three friends, who were still standing across the room as they watched the scene play out. Their arms were folded over their chests and the ominous expressions they wore would make any man think twice about doing something stupid.

This guy was no exception. Finally realizing just how outnumbered he was, he cast a disgruntled look toward Joel. "She's not worth the trouble." He turned around and went back to the bar to order a drink and nurse his bruised ego.

Once Joel was certain he'd diffused the situation, he glanced back at Lora. He wasn't sure what to expect from her, but it damn sure wasn't the amusement glimmering in her eyes or the way she was biting her bottom lip to contain her laughter. She didn't display an ounce of fear or trepidation over the man's overzealous confrontation, and Joel wanted to shake her for being so trusting. So naive. Just like she'd been earlier in the evening by not checking who'd been at her door.

She had no idea what she was up against. Or just how vulnerable and defenseless she was right now. That any guy who approached her could be someone who wanted her *dead*.

That thought, mingled with the realization of just how personal this job, and Lora, had become to him, increased the gut-twisting turmoil within him. His entire body was strung so tight he felt as though he was going to snap.

He made a split-second decision based on his surly mood. "Let's get the hell out of here."

Before she could suggest otherwise, or remind him that he owed her a dance, he grabbed her hand and led her back to their table to collect her purse and jacket, then escorted her out of the joint. As if sensing his need for space, she didn't say a word when he handed her a helmet to put on, nor did she ask where they were going as he revved up the motorcycle and told her to get on behind him.

Once he was on the interstate, he increased the speed of the bike, which also gave him the surge of adrenaline he was looking for. His motorcycle had always provided a therapeutic release for him when he was feeling irritable or restless, a way for him to relax and take the edge off of any aggression or tension that might be riding him hard.

Then again, hot, mindless sex had always been a great stress reliever for him, too, and with the provocative feel of Lora straddling the bike behind him, that's exactly where his mind and body had wandered. And it didn't help matters that her gloved hands were splayed on his thighs instead of clutched around his waist. Between the heat and throbbing vibration of the bike between his legs, the grip of her thighs against his hips as they leaned into a curve in the road, and the occasional brush of her fingers against the fly of his jeans, he was hard enough to pound nails.

She was teasing him again. Making him achingly aware of her willingness to indulge in the kind of carnal pleasures that would put an end to his sexual frustration. To that end, she was slowly, seductively driving him out of his ever-loving mind.

Needing a breath of cool night air to douse the arousal humming through his veins, he turned his bike off the main road and onto a narrow pathway. The trail led to a secluded area along Lake Shore Drive that he'd discovered a few years ago but hadn't visited in a while. The clusters of large trees gave the place a modicum of privacy and seclusion, and had always provided a peaceful, solitary escape for him. Especially during the first few months after he'd returned from Iraq, when the nightmarish memories of that last mission in Baghdad seemed to drag him down.

He wasn't sure why he'd brought Lora here now, considering he'd never shared this spot with anyone else, but it was the first place he'd thought of heading to after leaving the bar.

He brought the motorcycle to a stop, cut the engine, and parked the bike up on its kickstand. Lora slid off the back of the seat, pulled her helmet off, and shook her hair out so it fell in soft waves around her shoulders. Pale, silvery moonlight shimmered and gleamed off of those long, lustrous strands, making him wonder if its heavy weight felt as soft and rich as it looked.

She took off her gloves and jacket and set them on the seat behind Joel, but left on the scarf he'd given her earlier to wear. After giving the place a quick look around, she flashed him a dazzling smile that accentuated the mischievous light in her eyes.

"Mmmm. This is a nice, quiet, make-out spot," she said with all kinds of insinuation lacing her tone. "Do you come here often?"

"It's been a while." He took off his own helmet and hooked it over the end of the handle bar, then pulled off his gloves. "And just so you know, I've never brought anyone here to make out."

"Maybe we'll have to do something to change that," she said, her low, husky voice wrapping around him like a sensual promise she intended to keep.

Or maybe not, he thought to himself as he got off the bike, then unzipped his leather jacket, welcoming the rush of cool night air against his T-shirt and the heated skin beneath.

She walked to the edge of the trail, which overlooked Lake Michigan and the sandy beach stretching out below them. He came up beside her, and a few quiet moments passed as they admired the gorgeous evening view of the harbor lights off to the right.

"You know," Lora said, finally breaking the companionable silence between them, "I have to say, between you and your guys, that was quite an impressive front back at the bar."

Grateful for a conversation that wasn't laced with sexual undertones, he chuckled as he recalled how fierce and formidable Jon, Ben, and Kevin had looked as they backed him up. From the moment they'd been assigned to the same unit, it had always been that way with them, a strong, united front all the way. In good times and in bad.

A smile pulled at the corner of his mouth as he stared at her lovely face. "What can I say? Old habits die hard. For all of us."

She tipped her head to the side. "Once a marine, always a marine?" she guessed.

He nodded. "In a lot of ways, yes."

She was standing so close, the urge to reach out and caress his fingers along her soft cheek, down the side of her neck, and across the full swells of her breasts pushing against her top nearly overwhelmed him. Instead, he slid the tips of his fingers into the front pockets of his jeans, which forced him to keep his hands to himself.

"Well, all that fuss over me at Nick's wasn't necessary," she told him, her voice vibrating with feminine confidence. "I could have handled that guy on my own."

He raised a brow at her claim, though he couldn't help but approve of, and be attracted to, that fiery independence of hers. Couldn't help but imagine how all that bold self-assurance would be a huge turn-on in the bedroom. "You think so?"

"I *know* so. I deal with jerks like that all the time at The Electric Blue." The impudent smile on her lips made Joel grin, too. Then her lashes fell to half-mast as she stepped toward him, placed a hand on his chest, and slowly, brazenly stroked her palm down to his abdomen, leaving a trail of burning desire in its wake. "On the other hand, it was kind of nice having a big, strong man like you staking his claim."

He curled his hands into tight fists, even as his dick throbbed to life when he considered just how close her fingers were to his fly. "Is that what I did?" he asked, his voice rough with arousal. "Stake a claim?"

"Yeah." Her sweet, tempting mouth held a delectable curve of humor and sensuality. "And just for the record, it *was* a tad barbarianlike."

"Can't say I'm sorry."

"Me, either," she admitted, and shifted closer so that her mouth was only inches away from his and invited his kiss. Her hand, still splayed low on his belly, seared his skin through his T-shirt. "I've never had any guy come to my defense the way you did," she said softly.

"Not even your ex-fiancé?"

Her eyes widened in startled surprise at his abrupt comment. She dropped her hand and took a step back, giving him breathing room that no longer contained her warm, enticing female scent, which was wreaking havoc with certain parts of his anatomy.

Her brows creased in confusion and curiosity as she stared at him. "How do you even know I had a fiancé?"

It was an easy enough question for him to answer. "You wrote to Zach while he was in the service, and we talked about our siblings and what was going on back home. He happened to mention your engagement, though I don't know the specifics of your breakup." And right now seemed like a great time to discuss something that would cool his ardor. "What happened?"

She shrugged, as if her broken engagement no longer mattered to her heart or her emotions, and Joel hoped that was true. "Soon after I accepted Brent's proposal, I moved into his place with him. I figured since we were getting married anyway it made sense that we cut costs and live together, instead of paying for two apartments."

She looked away, providing Joel with a silhouette of her profile and the way she absently stroked her tongue across her soft bottom lip before speaking again. "A few months after that, Brent started acting strange. He'd pick fights with me over ridiculous things, like me taking up too much room in his closet, or if I cooked something he didn't like, and even the way I folded his clothes. I honestly thought it was because he was having a hard time adjusting to living with someone when he'd always lived on his own and that we'd eventually find some kind of balance."

"Except you obviously didn't," Joel said.

"No, we didn't." She glanced back at him. A faint smile touched her lips and her hands tugged on the ends of the scarf wrapped around her neck. "Things just got worse. Brent grew distant and started spending more time at work, and he'd even take off for a weekend, claiming it was for the ad agency he worked for."

Joel knew exactly where all those classic signs were heading, but he didn't say anything, just listened to her tell the story her own way.

"The stupid arguments we had, and Brent's behavior, reminded me exactly of the way my own parents' marriage started disintegrating, then eventually fell apart. I was only twelve at the time, but I remember it all so vividly. Having lived through my father's infidelity and what it did to my mother, I emotionally prepared myself for what I knew was coming. And it did."

She wrapped her arms around her stomach and exhaled a deep breath. "Six months after I agreed to marry Brent, he finally broke down and admitted that he'd been seeing someone else on the side for the past three months. And if that wasn't enough of a blow, he also told me that she was pregnant and he planned to marry her."

"Jesus, Lora." He scrubbed a hand along the late-evening stubble on his jaw, hating that some prick had treated her so badly. "I'm so sorry."

Her chin lifted, showing him that gutsy, defiant spirit that never failed to impress him. "You know what? I'm okay now. Better than okay," she added as a light breeze ruffled through her silky, unbound hair. "At the time I was devastated, but I wasn't about to be defeated. And I wasn't about to repeat my mother's mistakes by wallowing in regrets and wishing for something that wasn't meant to be."

He didn't know many women, if any, that could survive such a painful breakup and be stronger for the experience, instead of angry and bitter. Only someone as stubborn and determined as Lora could push forward with such a positive outlook and attitude, he thought with an internal smile.

"What about you, Joel?" she asked, turning the tables on him with a not-so-coy grin. "How many hearts have you broken over the years?"

"None," he replied easily, and honestly.

She gave him a dubious look that was tempered by the playful gleam in her eyes. "Oh, come on, Romeo. I find that hard to believe."

Now that she was standing far enough away, he pulled his hands from his pockets and folded his arms over his chest. "Let me rephrase that. I've never *intentionally* broken anyone's heart," he said, not wanting her to think that he was the type of guy to string a woman along with false expectations. "The women I've dated know right up front what I'm willing to give to a relationship."

Tipping her head to the side, she eyed him curiously. "And what's that?"

He shrugged and gave her the truth. "A good time, in and out of the sack."

"But no emotional ties," she murmured, more to herself than to him. "You like to play it safe."

It both amazed and annoyed him how effortlessly she'd nailed his MO, when he was normally very guarded when it came to the opposite sex. It was an unsettling feeling knowing that Lora could get into his psyche so easily, and it made him realize how important it was that she understood his own personal rules when it came to women and relationships.

"I'm straight up with women about what to expect because I don't want anyone to get hurt when I'm ready to walk away." And he always did. Either he grew restless and bored with the affair, stifled by constraints, or some woman would get it into her head that she was the one who could domesticate him. All three situations were clear signs that it was time for him to move on.

"What made you so jaded?" she asked, her gentle, caring voice reaching out to him like a physical caress.

He ignored the sensation, as well as the all-too-knowing tenderness that softened her features and seemed to see past all those internal barriers he'd erected long ago. "I'm not jaded," he said, but knew that denial was a lie. He'd learned at a very young age that it was so much simpler, and less painful, not to open himself up to any kind of emotional involvement, and it was a lesson that had served him well ever since.

"There isn't any room in my life for commitments and promises," he went on, before she could dig any deeper into the depths of his subconscious. "And it has more to do with my lifestyle and my job than anything else."

In the starlit shadows, he watched as a slow, sultry smile claimed her lips, and his gut clenched with heat and desire, mingling with the frustration twisting through him.

"I know this sounds clichéd, but maybe you just haven't met the right woman yet," she said.

He laughed, but the sound held no humor. In fact, considering the topic of conversation, and his own uncontrollable lust for this woman, he was beginning to feel downright cantankerous. "And you think you're her?"

His dark, argumentative tone didn't seem to faze her. "Who knows? Only time will tell." She followed up that flirtatious reply with a seductive wink.

"Don't set yourself up for heartache, sweetheart," he warned, narrowing his gaze at her. "I can't give you what you need."

She raised a dark brown brow, highlighting the *amusement* in her gaze that seemed to taunt him. "How do you know what I need?"

His jaw tightened in growing aggravation, and he jammed his hands onto his hips, wondering how in the hell this one woman could push all his hot buttons. She had him tied up in knots on so many levels. Emotionally. Physically. Sexually. All because he wanted her soft and naked beneath him, in a variety of ways. God, why couldn't she be the kind of woman he could just fuck, get out of his system, and forget?

But he instinctively knew there would be no forgetting Lora Marshall, and not just because she was Zach's sister.

He answered her question, using the direct, no-nonsense, male approach so there'd be no misunderstanding what he meant. "You want and need all that emotional hearts-and-flowers kind of crap that all women eventually want. I'm not that kind of guy, Lora. I never have been and I never will be."

She stepped toward him and opened her mouth to speak, but he cut her off before she could say a word. Or touch him again. If she did either, she'd send him right over the edge with no hope of turning back.

"I like living alone," he went on, impatience roughening his voice. "I like my life uncomplicated, and I like being able to come and go as I please. I don't do love, Lora, and don't think that you'll be the one to change me. Many have tried, and all have failed."

Her mouth curved ever so slightly, as if she wasn't thoroughly convinced. "Wow, that's quite a speech."

"It's the truth."

"Okay. Your position has been duly noted." She held up both of her hands, clearly backing off, just as he wanted. Unfortunately, the movement caused her full breasts to lift and bounce, drawing his attention to the front of her snug top and the clear outline of her chilled nipples straining against the fabric.

Heat shot straight to his groin, thick with the aching, pulsing need that constantly smoldered just below the surface when it came to her. Inhaling a steadying breath, he raised his gaze back to her face, ignoring the fact that she'd noticed him staring at her breasts—and didn't seem to mind at all.

Shit. "I think it's time I took you back home," he said gruffly.

Before he said to hell with the moral quandaries surrounding their relationship and succumbed to the awareness enticing him to do all the things he fantasized about doing to her in the dark of the night, he forced himself to turn around and head back to his motorcycle.

But despite his admirable discipline at the moment, Joel feared it was just a matter of time before this particular woman shattered his quickly dwindling willpower.

At least he'd adverted giving in to any temptation for tonight.

THE man was a bundle of contradictions, Lora thought as she watched Joel stalk toward his bike. Pure walking sex with a body made for sin, yet so unconscious of his masculine appeal. Fiercely protective of her, as he'd been earlier in the bar, yet dangerously possessive in a way she found shamelessly exciting.

Then there was the dark hunger in his eyes that clearly stated he wanted her—yet every time she tried to get close enough to indulge in her own desires, he immediately put physical distance between them to keep things platonic. And now, with his lecture about women and relationships, he'd just erected all sorts of emotional walls, too.

What the heck had that been all about, she wondered, feeling confused and baffled by his odd behavior. She didn't understand his resistance when there was so much sexual tension between them just waiting to be explored and exploited to its fullest potential for pleasure. Especially when *he'd* asked *her* out on a date—yet had spent most of the evening avoiding any one-one-one contact with her.

It was as though he was fighting himself and what he truly wanted. She didn't know why, but considering he'd made it clear during their discussion that he only wanted one thing from a woman, she figured they were pretty much on the same page. She had her own reasons for not getting tangled up in a committed relationship right now, but what was wrong with the two of them enjoying a bit of sexy fun?

As he slid onto his bike and reached for his gloves, Lora decided it was time to go after what *she* wanted. Time to really shake Joel up and let him know she'd more than welcome some one-on-one attention. Obviously, the seductive, flirtatious cues she'd been tossing his way all night long hadn't done the trick, so she needed to ratchet up her efforts.

He glanced her way, frowning when he found her still standing where he'd left her. "Let's go."

It was a brusque order, tinged with impatience to match his restless need to get out of this secluded area with her. She started toward him, adding a slow, purposeful sway to her hips as she walked—like a woman on a sensual mission who wouldn't be dissuaded. Not this time, at least.

"I'm not ready to go back home." The anticipation of executing her plan infused her voice with a low, husky quality.

His gaze, so dark and intense, narrowed at her, as if he was trying to figure out exactly what she was up to. "It's late."

"It's Saturday, and the night is still young." Before he realized her intent, she slid her hip onto the leather seat in front of him, between his spread thighs. Then she plucked the gloves from his grasp before he could put them on, and tossed them aside.

Lifting her hand, she caressed her palm along the taut line of his strong, firm jaw, trying to ease the tension vibrating off his entire body. "Besides, I don't have a curfew. Do you?"

He didn't touch her as Lora ached for him to. In fact, he went to great pains to make certain he kept his hands to himself, even though she was practically draped across his lap, his for the taking.

"Lora—"

She silenced his oncoming protest with her fingers against his mouth. His lips were so warm and pliant and tempting, and all she could think about was tasting him and making that precious control of his shatter. Feeling the barely leashed aggression beneath his reserve, along with the solid length of his shaft pressing against her hip, she knew she was close to doing just that.

Lora's greatest wish was to be ravished by this man, except he didn't seem willing to oblige, and that meant she'd have to do the persuading, and the seducing. "I've been dying to kiss you," she whispered as she eased her right leg over the bike so that she was facing Joel, her legs draped atop his muscled thighs in a position that was oh-so-intimate. "*Really* kiss you. Slow, and long, and deep."

Sinking her fingers into the soft, richly textured hair at the nape of his neck, she lowered her mouth to steal one of those kisses, but right before her lips made contact with his, he jerked his head back.

She sighed. His reaction was disappointing, of course, but Lora wasn't completely surprised, considering he'd been thwarting her attempts to get close to him all night long. But she wasn't discouraged, and she didn't take his rejection personally, not when he was staring at her with eyes that were dark and tormented with wanting, and the struggle within him was nearly palpable. The big question was, why was he still denying her, and himself?

Since her bold and assertive advance hadn't worked, she opted to handle the situation by taking a more humorous approach that would undoubtedly get some kind of reaction out of him.

She tipped her head to the side and schooled her features into a mask of seriousness. "Are you gay?" she asked, even though the fierce erection straining against the fly of his jeans made his sexual orientation a nonissue. Still, the transformation in Joel—from controlled and collected to severe shock—was too comical, and she had to bite her lower lip to keep from laughing out loud.

"*Jesus!* Of course I'm not gay!" Joel stared at her in horror, his expression appalled. "What in the hell would make you ask that?" he demanded.

Clearly, he wasn't amused by her question, but she was enjoying herself, and his response, immensely. Enough so that she decided to keep up the pretense a bit longer. "Well, you've been avoiding any kind of physical contact between the two of us, and you don't seem very interested in kissing me." She sighed, trying to sound and look dejected. "Do I just not do it for you?"

He exhaled a long, harsh breath and curled his hands into tight fists at his sides, still not allowing himself to touch her. "I've got a goddamn raging hard-on that states otherwise."

"Yeah, you do," she agreed as she stroked her palms up his jean-clad thighs until her fingers grazed that very impressive bulge. "So, since we've established that I do turn you on, what's the problem?"

"I'm *trying* to be chivalrous," he said through clenched teeth.

"Who asked you to be?" Certainly not her! God, she was doing everything in her power to entice him, all to no avail. "Not only does chivalry not suit that risk-taking personality of yours, but you strike me as the type of guy who has no qualms about taking what a woman offers, no questions asked. So why are you fighting what we both want so badly?"

Pale moonlight washed across his gorgeous features and gleamed off his black-as-midnight hair, making him appear every inch the rebel. But it was the candid, caring look in his eyes that captured her attention the most and made her realize just how serious this moment was to him.

"Because I don't think I can stop at just one kiss," he told her.

His words were so real and honest, they made her heart skip a beat to think he found her that irresistible. "I guess that's a risk *I'll* just have to take."

Smiling, she leaned toward him and nipped gently at his bottom lip, teasing him with the promise of something hotter, deeper, sweeter. "Kiss me, Joel," she breathed against the corner of his mouth while she brazenly tugged his shirt out of the waistband of his jeans so she could slip her hands beneath the warm, soft cotton material. "Touch me," she urged as she splayed her palms on his rock-hard stomach and glided them upward, aching to feel his hands on her, too. "Take me, *please.*"

A low, untamed growl ripped from his chest, and that stubborn, unyielding control of his finally, *finally*, gave way to all the pent-up desire and hunger he'd been struggling against all evening long. His hands, which had been so idle before, now came up and tangled in her hair, and in the next moment he crushed his mouth to hers. Her lips parted on a gasp of surprise, and he took advantage and slid his tongue inside, reckless and demanding, sweeping every one of her senses into overload.

His response was absolutely, positively heavenly.

She'd managed to unleash his lust, and now all that alpha male aggression was spilling over into the hottest, most erotic kiss she'd ever had the pleasure of receiving. Returning the kiss with equal abandon, she wrapped her arms around his waist beneath his T-shirt and jacket, trying to get as close to him as she could.

Judging by the restless shift of his body against hers, he seemed to want the same thing. She felt the impatient tug of the scarf from around her neck as he unraveled the strip of knitted material and let it drop to the ground, revealing her neck to the chilly evening air. She shivered, then moaned in pure delight when he buried his face against her throat and warmed her skin with his breath and the hot, damp press of his lips nuzzling just beneath her jaw.

Closing her eyes, she let her head fall back to give his mouth better access, while one of his hands skimmed down her back to the base of her spine and the other gave a gentle tug to the snaps securing the front of her top. One, two, three, four . . . they popped open, exposing her bra and the full upper swells of flesh nearly overflowing the lace-edged cups. He lifted his head, watching as he pushed the stretchy fabric down and released one of her breasts, then the other, to his dark, avid gaze. Her nipples hardened instantly, and he saw that, too.

An involuntary sound escaped her lips, a whimper of need that Joel recognized and understood. He covered both of her bare breasts with his hands, the slight roughness of his palms abrading the sensitive tips as he gently kneaded the soft mounds of flesh. Then the lazy friction of his thumbs joined in on the action, stroking and swirling around her areolas, rasping across her nipples—gentle at first, then harder, firmer, creating a firestorm of sensation that spiraled straight down to the pit of her stomach, and lower.

She groaned, in surrender, in anticipation of feeling his mouth on her. The wanting made her weak. The waiting made her impatient. Sliding her hands into his hair, she pulled his head down and arched her back, silently begging him to take her into his mouth—and ready to strangle him if he refused.

Obviously done denying her, or himself, he licked at her stiff nipples, a wet, velvet swipe of his tongue over each tender peak. A slow, lazy lap designed to torment and tease. A soft, heated stroke that made her tremble and moan. The gentle scrape of his teeth was both sweet bliss and exquisite pain. When he finally sucked her deep into his mouth, the pleasure was so immense, her entire body shuddered and she cried out.

Her wanton response tore a groan out of him, too, and his mouth came back to hers in a desperate, needy kiss that made her mind spin. The deep, assertive stroke of his tongue echoed the decadent, erotic rhythm of hot sex. He circled his strong arms around her and pulled her close, but when that didn't seem like enough—for either of them— he skimmed his flattened palms all the way down her back to her hips. She was still straddling his thighs, but that didn't stop him from tucking his hands beneath her bottom and hauling her up onto his lap, then gently tipping her backward, until she was laying on the metal gas tank with her legs all but wrapped around his waist.

Her top gaped open, and pale moonlight painted her naked flesh and lush curves with an opalescent hue. She'd never felt more beautiful, or more desirable, than she did at that moment with Joel staring down at her, worshipping her with his reverent gaze. Soon, though, the chill of the evening washed over her, causing her to shiver.

Keeping the bike stable with his feet braced on the ground, Joel bent over her, pressing his muscled body intimately, insistently into hers with his thick erection fitting naturally in the crux of her thighs. Threading her fingers through his silky hair once again, she welcomed another deep, drugging kiss, and sighed against his lips as his hands caressed her breasts and warmed them in his palms. His mouth eventually followed, trailing a searing path from her neck to her tight, puckered nipples. With the wet heat of his tongue, he lavished each one with a generous amount of attention before kissing and nuzzling his way down to her soft belly. When he reached the low waistband of her jeans, instead of unsnapping her pants and continuing the journey, which she would have more than welcomed, he instead stopped and laid his head on her stomach.

She was panting, and he was breathing just as hard. Hot, damp puffs of air caressed her belly, and the stubble on his jaw chafed her skin. She waited, knowing exactly what he was going to say, even before he said it.

"We have to stop." His voice was rough and strained, and it was enough to tell Lora that it was taking Joel tremendous effort to bring things to a halt.

Aroused beyond belief, she squeezed her eyes closed, trying to ignore the way her body was clamoring for release. She could have told him that they didn't have to stop, that she was on the Pill and protected, if that was his concern. But for as much as she wanted Joel—and for as badly as she ached to know how he'd feel inside of her—she didn't want their first time together to be like this, out in the middle of nowhere on his bike. She wanted a warm, soft bed and lots of time to enjoy everything about making love with Joel Wilde.

"Okay," she said softly.

He lifted his head, clearly surprised that she hadn't argued. "I really am going to take you home now." He straightened and helped her to sit up, too.

She immediately missed his warmth, the heat and strength of his body pressing into hers. Humored by his insistent, back-in-charge tone, she readjusted her bra while he watched. "Okay."

Pulling the sides of her top together, he snapped them closed in a very efficient manner, as if he wanted her covered as quickly as possible. "And we are *not* going to finish what we just started here tonight when we get back to your place."

She almost laughed at his ridiculous order, but managed to hold it back. "Okay."

He frowned at her easy acceptance after she'd spent most of the night trying to seduce him. "When did you become so agreeable?"

"Since I got what I wanted."

He raised a dark brow, and much to her relief she caught a glimpse of amusement softening the depths of his bluer-than-blue eyes. "Oh, yeah? And what was that?"

This time, she didn't bother stopping the grin from appearing on her lips. "A hot kiss, and knowing there's a whole lot more where that came from."

And for tonight, that kiss, and Joel's uninhibited reaction, was enough for her.

Eight

"HAVE you gotten lucky with you-know-who yet?"

Lora grinned at Sydney from across the bar as her friend started in on the drink order Lora had just given her. Since Lora had worked a full eight-hour shift at the spa earlier that Sunday, and had arrived at The Electric Blue only half an hour earlier, she hadn't had a chance to talk to Sydney about her date with Joel the night before. At the moment, the bar was only mildly busy, but it was still early and the real crowd usually didn't pour in until after eight, so Lora indulged her friend with a few juicy tidbits.

"Not yet," Lora replied as she placed a stack of fresh cocktail napkins on her tray. "But it was damn close." She might not have gone all the way with Joel, but their hot make-out session had been enough to keep her satisfied for now. She figured it was just a matter of time before they made that natural progression to mutual pleasurable sex.

Thinking of Joel, she cast a glance over her shoulder to where he'd settled himself at a small table located in a darkened corner of the bar. He'd shown up without any of his buddies, and she wasn't sure what to make of him spending his evenings at The Electric Blue just to watch her work when he no doubt had better things to do with his time. But she secretly found his nightly appearance romantic and charming, not that she'd ever tell Joel that.

From across the room, their gazes met, and a corner of his mouth kicked up in a slow, sexy smile that warmed her from the inside out. She replied with a flirtatious grin of her own, then returned her attention back to her drink order. Since their encounter the previous night, he seemed less uptight and more relaxed, and she hoped he remained that way.

Sydney set an Amaretto sour on the bar, a sly smile on her lips. "Judging by that flush on your face, your 'damn close' must have been very satisfying."

Lora laughed and didn't bother being modest with her best friend. "Oh, it was," she admitted, but kept the more intimate details of just how amazing Joel's hands and mouth were to herself. "And look at you with your new admirer sitting at the other end of the bar." Lora subtly nodded her head in that direction, where Daniel Barnett had taken up residence on a barstool and was nursing a Jack and coke while watching Sydney mix drinks.

Sydney poured triple sec and vodka into two shot glasses and topped the kamikazes off with a splash of lime juice. "He was here last night, too."

So, it appeared that Sydney had a suitor, and he seemed like a genuinely nice guy, too. "It's very sweet," she said, as she placed both shots on her tray.

"Well, if Daniel is expecting sweet in return, he's going to be very disappointed." A naughty light glimmered in

Sydney's eyes, a sure sign that she had something mischievous on her mind. "Our date isn't until next week, but if he insists on being here every night until then, I'm going to give him something to look forward to. I think I'll be doing some dirty dancing on the bar tonight." She winked at Lora.

Her friend's shameless suggestion was enough to tell Lora that Daniel was in for a whole lotta trouble where Sydney was concerned. The kind that was going to leave him hot and bothered by the end of the evening. "You are *so* bad."

Sydney shrugged indifferently as she uncapped a Corona and added the bottle of beer to Lora's order. "He might as well know right up front what he's getting into with me. Then again, guys don't ask me out for my sparkling, witty conversation, now do they?"

No, Sydney believed that they dated her expecting something else entirely, and talking wasn't a requirement. Lora knew that her friend was jaded for good reason, but she hated that Sydney judged all men the same. And especially Cassie's math teacher, who, in Lora's estimation, held so much potential—if Sydney didn't scare him off before their first real date.

"Maybe Daniel isn't like every other guy you've gone out with," Lora suggested as she topped the Corona off with a wedge of lime.

Sydney let out an indelicate snort and reached for a bottle of Grey Goose vodka. "He has a penis, Lora," she said wryly. "Trust me, getting laid is a priority. Lucky for him, I'm not one to play hard to get. It's been a long dry spell, and I'm more than willing to accommodate him."

"Okay. Fine," Lora conceded, not wanting to end up in an argument with Sydney about how she never gave the opposite sex a fair chance. It was a discussion they'd had

many times before and the end result was always the
same: emotional barriers went up, and nothing changed.

Lora picked up her drink-laden tray and balanced it in
one hand, unable to stop herself from issuing one last parting remark. "I just wish you'd give yourself more credit,
Syd. Maybe if *you* expected more than just sex from men,
then they'd treat you with the same respect in return."

"Thanks for the advice, Dr. Marshall," Sydney replied
with a hint of sarcasm in her tone. Then she leveled a
look at Lora as she cleared dirty drink glasses off of the
bar. "Now go and deliver your order before I write you up
for insubordination."

"Yeah, yeah," Lora drawled, not at all bothered by her
friend's intimidation tactics. The throwaway threat was
Sydney's playful way of saying "discussion over," and
Lora knew better than to say anything more.

She went back to work and spent the next few hours
taking orders and delivering drinks to the increasing deluge of customers flowing into The Electric Blue. When
she had a few spare moments, she'd cruise by Joel's table
and flirt with him, until she was just too busy with drink
orders and bar dancing to pay him anything more than a
quick passing visit.

Before long, the place was absolutely packed with
their normal patrons, and plenty of new ones, too. Over
the next few hours, the crush of people in the bar got
thicker, the music amplified to a throbbing beat, and the
crowd grew loud and boisterous from too much liquor
and a whole lot of fun. It was all Lora could do to squeeze
her way from one end of the establishment to the other.

Just as Lora had taken a huge drink order for a table of
six, Sydney rang the cowbell behind the bar, generating a
frenzy of cheers, whistling, and overall excitement for
the entertainment about to begin. Strobe lights pulsed and

flashed overhead, the music changed to a raucous song with a sexy beat, and employees abandoned their posts to give the customers what they'd come to expect at The Electric Blue.

Lora groaned. Exhaustion was settling in after working two shifts in one day, and she just didn't have the energy to put on another performance for the crowd. She decided to skip this round, and instead of letting orders pile up while Sydney, her backup bartender, and all the other waiters and waitresses strutted their stuff on the bar and stage, she'd mix her own drinks and at least *she'd* stay ahead of the crowd's demands. She was certain she wouldn't be missed, since the other staff were riling up the throng of customers just fine.

Lora navigated her way through the crush of bodies, and grinned when she caught sight of Sydney up on the main bar, dancing right in front of where Daniel was sitting. True to her word, Sydney was executing some of her best dirty dancing moves—gyrating her hips to the beat of the music, hands brazenly tracing her alluring curves, fingers stroking across the bare, flat expanse of her belly exposed by her tight, cropped T-shirt. As if that weren't enough to make a guy hard, she grabbed the brass pole at the end of the bar and spun around it, all long legs, voluptuous breasts, and smooth, provocative moves she'd perfected during her days as a stripper.

Dozens of guys crammed against the bar, whistling, cheering, and overall encouraging Sydney as she slid up and down the pole, but Lora knew that her tempting, teasing performance, and the hot promise in her eyes, was all for Daniel. But unlike the frat boys making fools of themselves, Daniel played it cool, refusing to outwardly react to Sydney's attempt at seducing him. Instead, he sat casually on the barstool, watching her with an appreciative male smile as she ran her hands through her long, wavy hair and swayed her hips in time to the music.

Lora had to give Daniel credit for maintaining his composure so well when every other guy in the place was clamoring to get her attention with the hopes of getting their own private performance. The fact that Daniel wasn't responding to Sydney's sexual overtures made Lora hopeful that he'd be the one guy who could get past Sydney's bold and brash personality to the softer, sweeter woman beneath all that bravado.

Once she finally stepped behind the bar, the disarray of liquor bottles, dirty glasses in the sink, and nearly overflowing garbage made Lora realize that she'd be far more helpful if she washed up the glasses and restored some order for Sydney and her backup bartender before they returned to fill drink orders again. In fact, she figured she could at least take the two bags of trash out to the Dumpster and be back before the song was done, which would give them more room to move around behind the bar.

Setting her tray down, Lora grabbed both bags of trash and made her way down the hallway that led to the men's and women's restrooms and the employee exit that connected to a back alley and the Dumpster they used. Like she'd done a dozen times before, she pushed the door open and twisted the bolt lock so that the metal bar kept the door from closing and locking behind her.

Cold, damp wind assaulted her as she stepped out under the small four-by-four awning protecting her from the rain that had begun to fall sometime during the past few hours. Unfortunately, the Dumpster was across the alley, and she cursed beneath her breath as she ducked her head against the rain and sprinted toward the garbage bin.

Of course, Mother Nature chose that moment to open

up a thundercloud and let it pour. Lora lifted the metal lid and quickly tossed the bags of trash inside, just as she heard the employee exit door open, then shut securely behind her with a solid click.

Panicked, she whirled around to find two big men pulling ski masks over their faces as they strode purposefully toward her from the door she'd just walked out of. She stood there, frozen to the spot, a foreboding chill racing up her spine that had nothing to do with the fact that she was nearly soaked to the skin by the ice-cold rain and wind.

Before she had the chance to react to the imminent threat, and before she could draw the breath to scream for help, one of the men grabbed her, spinning her around, and clamped a strong hand over her mouth. He pulled her head back so it butted against his shoulder and he could hold her immobile. She caught the flash of something long and shiny right before she felt the sharp prick of a blade against her neck.

Oh God, oh God, oh God. Her heart slammed painfully against her chest and her legs went weak at the realization that nobody was going to come to her rescue. Not when no one knew where she'd gone. Eyes wide with terror, and fearing the absolute worst, an involuntary whimper escaped her throat.

The other masked man stepped in front of her, lifted an open cell phone, and snapped a few pictures of her in the midst of being attacked. The flash went off, and Lora blinked furiously to clear her vision and keep her wits about her.

"Got it," the accomplice said in a low, gruff voice, then snapped the phone shut.

The guy behind her pressed his mouth near her ear. "Maybe seeing these photos will remind your brother that we're serious about getting our money back. *Dead* serious. And next time, we'll stick around and let you provide a down payment." The hand at her neck slid down and gave her breast a hard, brutal squeeze, leaving no question in her mind exactly how they'd exact whatever payment they were after.

"Come on, let's get the hell out of here before someone comes looking for her," the other man said urgently.

"You scream, and it will be the last sound you make." The hand covering her mouth fell away, then the man behind her shoved hard between her shoulder blades. Lora tripped forward, lost her balance, and fell onto her hands and knees on the ground. Gritty asphalt scraped across her palms, and the torrent of rain pelted her back and soaked through her hair to her scalp. She remained in that position, waiting for the sound of running footsteps to fade away into the distance. Then, and only then, did she push to her feet.

A sob caught in her throat and tears stung her eyes as she stumbled back toward the employee exit and the promise of safety. She pulled on the handle, and let loose another hoarse sob when the slab of metal didn't so much as budge.

She could hear the loud music blasting from inside the bar, could feel it vibrating against the outer walls of the building, and knew the noise would drown out the sound of her knocking. She thought about going around to the front, but she was too terrified of running into the two men again.

So she pounded desperately on the door anyway, praying that someone, anyone, would hear her attempts and let her back inside.

ONE minute Joel was watching Lora work behind the bar, grateful that she wasn't up on the stage dancing for the customers like the rest of the employees, and in the next minute two big guys directly in front of where he was sitting jumped up from their seats and started yelling at one another in a heated, drunken argument. Joel automatically stood, too, just as the pushing and shoving match between the duo escalated into a fistfight.

And that's when all hell broke loose. Acquaintances of the two fighters surged forward to defend their friends and ended up a part of the hostile exchange and physical assault. Boozed-up patrons encouraged the brawl by rooting for their favorite team. Chairs crashed to the ground and a table tipped over, spilling drinks and bottles of beer across the floor. The obnoxious noise and the shuffle of bodies finally caught the attention of one of the dancers from atop a counter, and she quickly signaled to the bouncers that there was trouble that needed their attention.

Knowing it might take a few minutes for the two brawny security guys to work their way to the back of the bar, Joel stepped in to help pull the two apart before someone really got hurt. He'd seen his share of bar fights over the years, and it was just a matter of separating the two most aggressive opponents in order to get everyone else to back off.

With the assistance of another sober patron willing to step into the fray, they managed to secure the fighters' arms behind their backs so neither one could throw any more punches. As soon as that was accomplished, the rest of the crowd settled down. By the time the bouncers finally arrived, the fight was under a semblance of control, and it was just a matter of escorting the disruptive group out of The Electric Blue.

Once the ruckus had come to an end, business went back to normal and Joel sat down at his table, his gaze automatically searching the place for Lora. She was no longer behind the bar, and as far as he could see, she wasn't in the main area, either. Figuring she probably went to get something from the storeroom, or needed to visit the restroom, Joel waited for her to reappear. Long minutes passed, and he drummed his fingers restlessly on the table as he grew increasingly impatient for her to return. Finally, unable to sit tight any longer, he got up and headed across the room to the bar, where Sydney was back to making drinks.

He sidled up to the counter next to Monique, who was waiting for one of the bartenders to fill her drink order. "Have either of you seen Lora in the past ten minutes?" he asked, loud enough to be heard over the blaring music.

Sydney shook her head as she reached for a bottle of liquor and poured a generous shot. "I haven't seen her since that fight broke out."

"Me, either," Monique said as she added a pineapple wedge and cherry to a fruity-looking drink. "I'm sure she's out in that crowd somewhere, probably clearing tables or taking drink orders."

"Yeah, you're probably right." Joel didn't bother telling Sydney and Monique that he'd already scoured the main area from one end to the other for Lora, all to no avail. Considering nobody knew his real purpose for being there on a nightly basis, he didn't want to appear too anxious or worried.

But as the seconds ticked by with no sign of Lora, her absence definitely started to concern him. Leaving the bar, he casually headed down the hallway leading to the back of the establishment. The door to the office was closed and locked, but he rapped his knuckles on the solid wood, anyway, just in case she was inside. There was no answer, so he did the same thing at the storeroom. Again, nothing.

There was only one place left to look, and Joel was

desperate enough to infringe on someone's privacy in order to locate Lora and give him the peace of mind he was searching for. He pushed open the door to the women's restroom and glanced inside. The three females standing at the bathroom mirror immediately stopped their chatting and primping and looked at him with wide, shocked eyes.

Then the woman in the middle, with big blond hair and even bigger breasts, gave him a sultry once-over. "Hi, sugar," she drawled as a come-hither smile curved her glossy lips. "Looking for someone?"

The interested look in her kohl-lined eyes told him that she'd gladly be that person, but he did nothing to encourage her hopes. Instead, he cast a quick glance toward the stalls and experienced a jolt of frustration when he found them all wide open and unoccupied.

"Yeah," Joel replied calmly, even as his tension and unease seemed to coil into a tight, strangling knot within him. "But she's not here. Thanks, anyway."

Where in the hell was she?

The question ate at him as he let the restroom door shut. He turned to head back to the bar to give it another search just as he heard a loud pounding at the employee exit door at the end of the corridor. Jesus, had Lora accidentally locked herself out of the bar? Frowning, he started in that direction, and as the banging grew more frantic, he tried to ignore the apprehension spreading through him.

He pushed the door open and found Lora standing on the other side, a torrent of rain deluging the ground beyond the small, protective awning she was standing beneath. Still, she was absolutely soaked to the skin—from her hair all the way down to her work shoes. Her wide eyes were filled with gut-wrenching horror, and her expression reflected a stark fear that sliced straight to his soul.

Joel immediately reached out to her, and as soon as she realized it was him she collapsed into the safety of his embrace, buried her face against his neck, and broke down crying—deep, convulsing sobs that wracked her entire body. He wrapped his arms securely around her, and feeling the vivid terror emanating from her, he instinctively knew that this wasn't a simple case of her getting locked out.

Something bad had happened, and he hadn't been there to protect her. His remorse was overwhelming, but he forced his own emotions aside to focus on Lora and making sure she hadn't been hurt in any way.

She was clinging to him like he was her lifeline, and he gently grasped her shoulders and pulled her away so he could see her face, which was now streaked with tears and smudged with mascara. "Jesus, Lora," he said, his tone gruff with his own painful recriminations. "Are you okay?"

She stared up at him, a fresh surge of tears welling up in her green eyes. "Oh, God, Joel," she choked out as her hands gripped the front of his T-shirt. "There were two guys . . . and they had a knife and . . . *oh, God*!" She squeezed her eyes shut, as if the memory of what had happened was too horrible for her to go on.

They had a knife. The words slammed through his mind like a brutal sledgehammer. His own panic increased, and he gave her shoulders a small shake to get her attention again. "And *what*, Lora?" he demanded. "What did they do to you?"

"They held the knife to my throat . . . and threatened me." She sucked in a gulp of air and buried her face in her hands, shuddering at the memory.

Rage flowed through Joel's veins, and he wanted to kill the men who'd dared to lay a hand on Lora—no thanks to him! He tipped her chin up with his finger and glanced at her neck, and felt physically ill when he saw the long red scrape marring her smooth, creamy flesh. His rage boiled over into a white-hot violence, and it took everything in him not to slam his fist against the metal door in fury and frustration.

"Lora?" Trisha, one of the bar's waitresses, who'd been heading toward the women's restroom, now rushed down the hall toward them. "You're soaking wet. What happened?"

"She got locked out in the alley in the rain," Joel replied before Lora had the chance to launch into another round of hysterics. "I need to get her into the office where it's warm and dry. Who has a key?"

"Sydney does. I'll go get her for you," Trisha said, and hustled off to find the boss.

Knowing how unsteady Lora's legs were, Joel draped one of her arms over his shoulder and slid his other arm around her waist, holding her upright as he guided her back down the hallway. By the time they made it to the office, Sydney was already there with the door wide open.

Sydney followed them inside, her brows creased in worry. As soon as Joel eased Lora into one of the chairs in front of the metal desk, Sydney rushed to her side.

Once Sydney was assured that Lora was okay, she let loose. "What in the world were you doing in the back alley?"

It was a question that Joel was eager to hear the answer to as well. There was a whole lot more to this story, and he needed to hear it all.

Lora began to shiver from being wet. She crossed her arms over her chest and rubbed her bare, damp arms with her hands. "I was taking out the trash."

"What!?" Sydney jammed her hands on her hips,

clearly not happy with Lora's reply. "That's the guys' job, not yours! You know that! And for good reason, obviously," she added, waving a hand at Lora's condition.

Lora had the good grace to wince at her boss's chastising. "The trash was piling up, and I've taken it out to the Dumpster many times before. It only takes a couple of seconds to toss the garbage bags out, and I was just trying to help, since we're so busy."

Sydney shook her head, causing her cascade of red curls to bounce wildly around her face. "Well, you do it again and you're fired." The warning was issued in a caring, loving tone.

As Lora's tremors increased, Joel grabbed the sweater hanging on a coatrack behind the desk and draped it over Lora's shoulders. She glanced up at him gratefully as she pulled the edges of the sweater closer together to keep warm.

Christ, she looked so scared and vulnerable, and he wasn't used to seeing her that way. Another jolt of guilt punched him hard in the gut, but he couldn't dwell on his part in her attack right now. Later there would be plenty of time for recriminations. At the moment, his concern was solely for Lora's safety and mental state.

Finding a spare chair, Joel dragged it over to Lora and sat down in front of her, spreading his legs wide apart so he could get as close to her as possible. Whether she was ready or not, the interrogation was about to begin.

He placed his hands on her jean-clad knees, certain she must be extremely uncomfortable with the cold, wet fabric plastered to her skin. "Lora, what, exactly, happened out there?"

She pushed her wet hair away from her face with a shaky hand and took a few seconds to gather her thoughts. "When . . ." Her voice cracked, and she swallowed hard to clear her throat before trying again. "When I went out back, two men followed and made sure the door locked behind them so I couldn't get back in. I didn't get a chance to see what they looked like because they pulled ski masks over their faces."

Joel waited patiently for Lora to continue, while Sydney started pacing anxiously beside Lora's chair.

Lora's fingers fluttered up to her throat and touched the angry red welt one of the thugs had put there. "One of the men grabbed me from behind and put a hand over my mouth and a knife up to my neck, while the other snapped pictures of him doing it."

Sydney came to an abrupt halt and gasped aloud. "Jesus, Lora. They could have killed you!"

"I know," she whispered, the anguish in her gaze vivid and real.

Joel gently took both of her hands in his and rubbed his thumbs over her knuckles, trying to warm her chilled fingers. It was then that he felt the fresh scrapes on her palms and realized that the thugs must have shoved her to the ground at some point. "Did they say anything to you at all?"

She nodded jerkily. "The one standing behind me said something about the pictures reminding my brother that they were serious about getting their money back. *Dead* serious."

She'd just confirmed that her attack hadn't been random, but rather a deliberate setup to send a message and warning to Zach. Joel swore beneath his breath, drawing on every ounce of control he possessed so that he didn't come unglued right then and there. "Anything else?"

This time she closed her eyes and began rocking back and forth, a sure sign that those bastards had instilled a whole lot of fear in her, just as they'd intended. "They said that the next time they'll stick around and let me provide a down payment, and I don't think they were talking about money."

"There won't be a next time," Sydney said angrily, and reached for the phone on the desk. "I'm calling the police."

"No!" Lora slapped her hand over Sydney's so she couldn't lift the receiver. "Please, don't," she begged.

Sydney frowned at her. "For crying out loud, Lora. You were assaulted by two men, and it could have been much worse than them issuing a few threats."

"I'm okay," Lora said, but Joel knew that she was anything but fine. She was shaken, confused, and still terrified out of her wits. "There's not much I can tell the police anyway. They were wearing ski masks, so I can't even give them a description."

"We should at least file a report," Sydney insisted, though she'd taken her hand off of the phone.

"No, Syd," Lora implored. "Please, *no*."

Desperation tinged Lora's voice and Joel was fairly certain he knew the reason why. She was scared, yes, but also concerned about her brother. Involving the police could jeopardize not only her safety, but Zach's, too, and Lora obviously wasn't going to take that risk. Lora's loyalty to her brother was unwavering, and under the current circumstances, Joel knew Zach didn't deserve one bit of it.

Sydney crossed her arms over her ample chest. "Fine," she said curtly, even as she gave in to Lora's pleas. "But I'm not happy about it." Then she turned to Joel. "Maybe *you* can talk some sense into her."

Joel nodded. "I'll try." For as much as he agreed with Sydney about filing a report, there truly wasn't much the police could do without a physical description of some sort. Therefore, Joel wasn't inclined to force the issue when Lora was still so panicked.

Lora glanced at Joel, looking so achingly fragile and defenseless that he wanted to pull her into the security of his arms and never let go. "Just get me out of here," she said as her teeth began to chatter. *"Please."*

Whisking her away from the scene of the crime was the one thing he could do for her, but he wouldn't be driving her back to her apartment. No, from now on, he wasn't letting her out of his sight if it could be helped.

One look at Sydney, and he could easily read her thoughts. She was chewing on her bottom lip, her concern for her best friend etched plainly on her face. "Don't worry, Syd. I'll take care of Lora," he promised. "I'm going to take her to my place for the night so she won't be alone."

A small, grateful smile touched Sydney's lips. "Good idea. Thank you."

He stood up and unclipped his cell phone from the waistband of his jeans. "I just need to make a quick phone call before we go."

"Sure." She waved to the corner of the office to give him some privacy, then sat down next to Lora to talk to and fuss over her like a mother hen.

Joel pressed one of his speed dials, and before the first ring ended Ben picked up the line. After giving Ben a quick rundown of what had happened, Joel informed him that he'd be taking Lora to his place, which meant no one needed to play watchdog at her apartment for the night.

Snapping his phone shut, he turned back around. "Okay, I'm ready to go."

Lora stood up, and Sydney gave her a hug, then pulled back and smiled at her friend. "I love you, Lora, and I'm so glad they didn't hurt you."

Lora managed a shaky smile of her own, and her eyes welled with moisture, telling Joel that she was still very emotionally unstable. "I love you, too," she rasped.

A quick knock sounded at the door before Trisha stepped inside. "Here's your jacket, Joel," she said, handing him the black leather coat. "I didn't want to leave it at your table."

"Thanks." Gently pulling the sweater off of Lora's shoulders, he handed the garment to Sydney, then helped Lora slip into his much warmer, dryer jacket.

Tucking her under his arm, he ushered her through the bar and out the front door. It was still raining heavily, and because of the cold, damp weather, he hadn't brought his motorcycle, but instead had driven his black SUV. He sprinted with her to the vehicle through the downpour, got her situated in the passenger seat, then settled himself behind the wheel. He headed out of the parking lot, keeping an eye on his rearview mirror to make sure they weren't being followed by anyone.

The drive to his place started out quietly, with only the spatter of raindrops on the windshield and the scrape of the wipers punctuating the silence. He glanced over at Lora and found her clutching his jacket around her while staring out the window. Even though he'd turned on the heater, she was still shivering, and now that her initial rush of adrenaline had receded, his biggest concern was that she might go into shock.

"Hey, you doing okay over there?" he asked in an attempt to keep her alert and conscious.

She slowly turned her head to glance at him, and even in the dimness of the cab he could see the vacant, faraway look in her gaze. "I keep thinking about what that man said to me about my brother, but I don't understand what they want from me."

Joel's fingers tightened on the steering wheel as he returned his attention to the road. He knew exactly what those thugs wanted from Lora, and in a clearer state of mind, he was sure she'd figure out what they intended, as well. But at the moment he was so fucking torn about what to do or say to her. After what she'd just gone through, she deserved to know the truth—the *whole* truth, but right now she wasn't in the frame of mind to hear, or even comprehend, her part in Zach's scheme.

But come morning, when she was more cognizant, he decided he was going to tell her everything—how her brother had involved her in his addiction, and even his own role in protecting her.

Ultimately, she needed to understand just how dangerous the situation had become.

Nine

JOEL was saved from having to answer Lora's painful question as he pulled up to his house. He hit the garage door remote, and once the panels had lifted open he parked the SUV, he cut the engine, then got out and rounded the vehicle to the passenger side. He opened the door for Lora, but she didn't move—except for the tremors still running just below the surface of her skin. The bluish tint to her lips worried him, and if he didn't get her warmed up, and quick, they'd be making a trip to the emergency room.

He gently helped her out of the car and into the house, her movements sluggish and unsteady. She stumbled a few times and looked around, clearly disoriented and confused.

"Where are we?" she mumbled.

"We're at my place." With a firm hold around her waist, he led her back to his bedroom, then into the adjoining bathroom.

Immediately, he turned on the shower to warm up the

water as quickly as possible, then flipped the switch for the overhead heating lamp, doing whatever he could to increase the temperature in the bathroom. He slid the leather jacket off her shoulders and down her arms, his fingers brushing along her chilled skin as he pulled the garment off. Her bare flesh was pebbled with goose bumps, and it was difficult not to notice the stiff points of her nipples pushing against her thin, wet T-shirt.

"You need to get undressed and into the shower," he told her, meeting her gaze. "You're freezing cold."

She gave a jerky nod of her head, and he turned and exited the bathroom to give her privacy to strip naked and step into the shower. Less than a minute later he heard a soft whimper and didn't hesitate to glance back inside. Still fully clothed, her cold, fumbling fingers couldn't unfasten the snap on her jeans. She was shivering all over again, and when she glanced up at him, her glassy eyes were filled with tears.

"I . . . can't," she said as her teeth began to chatter.

Obviously, giving her privacy wasn't going to be an option. There was no question in Joel's mind what he had to do, and he stepped back inside the bathroom to help. Pushing her hands aside, he tackled her top first, quickly and efficiently skimming the damp, clinging T-shirt up over her head and off, doing his best to work around her sluggish, awkward movements. Leaving her bra on for the moment, and for his own sanity, he turned his attention to her jeans. Once they were unzipped, he pushed them over her hips to her thighs. She swayed on her feet, and he made her sit on the closed toilet seat so he could kneel in front of her and remove her boots and socks, then drag the saturated denim down her endlessly long legs as the bathroom filled with warm, soothing steam from the shower and overhead lamps.

Standing again, he pulled her back up, too, unclasped her bra, and let it fall to the floor. Her silky panties followed right after, and one glance at her completely naked had his dick swelling with typical male lust. Up until that point, he'd managed to remain detached and focused on undressing Lora as fast as possible, and even though his brain recognized the situation as dire, his body obviously had a mind of its own.

Ignoring the tightening ache in his groin, he guided Lora into the shower and positioned her beneath the heavy spray of water. She moaned and crossed her arms over her stomach as the heated water hit her cold skin and sluiced its way down her trembling body.

Knowing he couldn't leave her alone, he kicked off his shoes and removed his own T-shirt and jeans. Keeping his black boxer briefs on for a number of reasons, he joined Lora in the glass enclosure, then shut the door to keep in the rising steam. Wrapping his arms securely around her back, he pulled her as close as two bodies could get, to generate a more natural, instinctive kind of heat.

She was rigid and unyielding at first due to how cold she was, but as the water and heat lamps bathed her in warmth and gradually chased away her chill, fear, and shock, she grew soft and pliant in his embrace. Water cascaded over her shoulders and between their bodies as he caressed his hands down her back, then up again in slow, soothing strokes. Before long, she released a soft, shuddering sigh and relaxed completely against him, trusting him to keep her safe and protected.

From now on, he swore, he would.

Her calm, slack response was exactly what he'd been trying to achieve, yet he'd failed to take into consideration the intimacy of the situation once the urgency of raising her temperature was no longer an issue. Now she was burrowed close with her head on his shoulder and her lips mere inches away from his neck. Then there was the soft cushion of her breasts pressing against his bare chest, and the exquisite feel of her silky smooth belly and supple thighs aligning so perfectly with his own.

Despite his best efforts to remain unaffected, arousal thrummed heavily through his veins. His cock pulsed with need, and he was grateful that he'd worn his boxer briefs, which was the only thing keeping his raging hard-on confined and under a semblance of control.

Needing some kind of distraction, he swept his hands up the provocative curve of her spine and beneath the fall of her hair. The heavy strands were wet, and the nape of her neck was the one place that was still cold to the touch. Tangling his fingers around those tresses, he gently tipped her head back so that the spray soaked her hair and warmed her scalp. With a low, appreciative moan, she closed her eyes and lifted her chin even more, so that the water cascaded over her face, down her slender throat, and across the generous rise of her breasts.

She looked so incredibly sensual, like a water nymph with her sleek, wet skin and the ribbons of steam swirling all around her. His gaze took in her slightly parted lips, then slid down the arch of her throat—and came to a stop on the red slash on her neck. One of the thugs had exerted enough pressure to leave a mark, but not enough to badly break the skin, *thank God*.

Still, he couldn't stem the surge of anger that gripped him anew—directed at the men who'd terrorized her, at Zach for involving Lora, but mostly at himself for allowing something so horrendous to happen when he'd sworn to keep her safe and protected.

The attack never should have happened on his watch, and knowing she could have been hurt much worse, he nearly choked on a fresh wave of anguish and remorse. Without thinking, he lifted his hand and gently stroked his fingers along the slight abrasion on her neck. Her skin was so soft, so delicate and fragile, and he couldn't help but feel solely responsible for putting her through such trauma.

"I'm sorry, Lora," he rasped, his voice sounding like rough sandpaper. "So, so sorry."

She brought her head back down, and her water-spiked lashes lifted, revealing beautiful green eyes that were far more lucid than they'd been ten minutes ago. Her face was flushed with warmth, and she met his gaze with a small smile that was so incredibly sweet and guileless.

"I'm okay," she said, misunderstanding his apology for concern, and he couldn't bring himself to explain the truth just yet.

As they stood beneath the pelting spray, a slow, seductive awareness gradually took hold. He could feel the subtle change from relaxed to aroused in Lora in how she shifted against him and the way her flattened palms slid around his waist and up the slope of his spine. He watched as she licked droplets of water from her bottom lip, and felt himself respond to the desire darkening her eyes. His cock throbbed and ached, the material of his boxer briefs too tight and confining against his stiff shaft.

"Joel . . ." she whispered, the one word filled with a wealth of emotion that struck a chord deep within him, too. Eyes closing, she leaned forward and pressed her lips to his.

Her mouth was soft and yielding, a heavenly temptation he couldn't resist, so he didn't even try. Her lips parted, and he accepted the invitation to deepen the connection, to slide his tongue inside and curl around hers, dragging her into a hunger so dark and hot he burned with the intensity of it.

He kissed her with a fierce urgency born of knowing that she was truly okay and unharmed. Kissed her with an abundance of relief and gratitude and something else far more profound that echoed in the farthest recesses of his soul—an emotional, intimate bond that rocked the foundation of the solitary man he'd always been.

Driven by pure sensation, encouraged by the uninhibited way her fingers dug into the muscles bisecting his back and the arch of her hips against his, Joel backed her up against the shower stall, pressed the length of his body along Lora's lush curves, and ravished her mouth with an overwhelming amount of passion and heat. His craving for her blazed through him like an out of control wildfire—a reckless, insatiable need he could no longer deny.

More. He needed more of Lora. Needed to touch and taste and savor every nuance that was uniquely hers.

With only that thought in mind, he tore his mouth from hers and trailed his lips along her jaw, licked his way down to the base of her throat where her pulse beat strong and steady. She moaned softly and sifted her hands through his wet hair, twisted the too-long strands around her fingers and guided his mouth lower, to the firm swells of her breasts. He followed willingly, giving her what she wanted and what he so desperately needed.

He drew a taut nipple into his mouth, flicked the rigid tip with his tongue, and sucked her deep and hard. With his hand he squeezed and kneaded her other breast, traced lazy circles around her areola with his thumb before lightly pinching and rolling the firm, aroused nipple between his fingers. She gave a helpless, impatient whimper, the restless sound urging him to venture toward more forbidden territory.

With his large hands, he traced the dip of her waist and

the flare of her hips, then dragged his thumbs over her belly before sliding his hands around to the base of her spine and down her perfect ass to the backs of her thighs. The feel of her smooth, sleek skin against his palms was a luxury he'd denied himself for too long, and he memorized every sensual curve of her body, along with the sweet, uninhibited sighs that accompanied his bold exploration.

If he thought touching her was pure bliss, then allowing his mouth to follow in the same direction as his hands and tasting her warm, wet skin was like experiencing a slice of heaven. He licked and gently bit his way down to her stomach, and dipped and swirled his tongue in her navel. Another erotic moan echoed in the shower stall, and the slender fingers still wrapped in his hair tugged him lower still.

Instinctively, he dropped to his knees in front of her, his heart racing a mile a minute as a heady surge of desire tore through him. Knowing what she wanted, what she *needed*, he took one of her hands and wrapped her fingers around the small metal bar built into the shower to help her keep herself steady and balanced, then draped one of her legs over his shoulder to give him better access to her.

The water poured down on both of them, and curls of steam immersed them in a sultry warmth as he leaned forward and laved the inside of her thighs, slowly, leisurely, until he reached the very heart of her femininity. Her sex was soft and swollen, and he parted the plump folds of flesh with a slick caress of his tongue that had her arching her hips against his mouth, seeking and silently begging for release.

He closed his eyes and groaned, doubling his efforts to give her exactly that. He drew her clit into his mouth, used his tongue to stroke and caress and increase her pleasure. Her fingers knotted tighter in his hair and a soft mewling sound escaped her lips. In response, his balls drew up hard and his cock jutted painfully toward his belly, aching with the need to be buried to the hilt inside her, to feel her convulse around him as she came.

Knowing that wasn't going to happen, he entered her with his tongue instead. Deeply. Relentlessly. With heat and possessive intent.

She inhaled sharply, jolted against him in shock, then gave herself over to his erotic assault. Before long, he felt her thighs quiver, felt her legs buckle as her orgasm crested, heard her lusty moan as she tumbled headlong into that powerful rush of sensation rippling through her. He kept her from completely collapsing with a strong hand pressed to her stomach, and when he was certain he'd given her every last bit of pleasure he could, he stood back up and braced his hands on the wall on either side of her head, not trusting himself to touch her when he was harder than granite and there wasn't much left of his self-control.

He lifted his head and looked into her face, expecting to see a languid, sated expression. Instead, her eyes were bright with a desire that didn't bode well for his good intentions. Neither was the way she slid her hands around to his backside and slipped her fingers beneath the elastic band of his boxer briefs. She grasped his buttocks and pulled his hips to hers, so that his confined erection nestled right at the crux of her thighs. Right where she was hot and slick and ready for him.

She leaned into his chest and pressed her lips against the side of his neck. "Joel," she whispered as she twined one leg around his, aligning them even more intimately. "I want you inside of me."

There was so much longing in her voice, the kind that

could easily chip away at his resolve if he let it. He curled his hands into tight fists against the wall. "Lora—"

Whatever he'd been about to say went up in smoke as her fingers followed the waistband of his briefs back to the front, then dipped inside and wrapped around his erection. She stroked once, twice, and glided her thumb over the swollen head of his dick. His heart hammered in his chest and the muscles in his stomach clenched as he resisted the urge to thrust into her snug grasp.

"Please," she said huskily, her gaze soft and imploring. "I need to feel pleasure, not the terror and fear of tonight. I need *you.*"

A terror and fear he'd been responsible for, and it was that thought that made him want to do whatever possible to chase away those awful memories for her. Except . . . "I don't have any condoms," he rasped. He hadn't needed any lately, and he hadn't dared to buy any when Lora had presented such a temptation. It was the one thing, the last thing, that was keeping him from fulfilling her wish.

"I'm on the Pill." The knowledge snapped the last thin thread of his control, as did her next words. "Please don't tell me no. Not tonight."

He groaned as her tenacious grip on his shaft and the sluice of warm water created a slick, suctioning sensation that made him crazy-wild to come. With her. In her. Done resisting what he wanted so badly, he gave up the fight. Pushing all ten fingers into her wet hair, he crushed his mouth to hers.

There was nothing slow and sweet about the way he kissed her. Greedy and ravenous, he tilted her head for a better fit and let loose all the pent-up hunger, need, and lust clawing at him. Now he took without hesitation or re-serve, then took some more, and she was right there with him, giving him her mouth, her tongue, and soon, her soft, willing body. A sense of urgency and impatience built between them, hotter and more vital than anything he'd ever experienced. It made his head spin and his erection throb and pulse.

He could have easily taken her right there, in the shower, pushed up against the tiled wall with her thighs riding his hips, but he wanted her beneath him. Wanted leverage to get as deep inside her as he could get.

With that in mind, he blindly reached out to shut off the shower and started to pull back, but she mewled in protest and clung to him. Undoubtedly she believed he was going to end things, and he sought to reassure her.

"Don't worry, sweetheart," he murmured against her lips. "I'm not done with you yet." He was beginning to wonder if he ever would be.

He silenced the answer to that question with another aggressive, soul-searing kiss and maneuvered them both out of the glass enclosure. The bed was much too far away, and he pushed her down to the thick, plush rug laid out on the floor. After quickly shucking his soaked boxer briefs, he joined her.

Nudging her legs wide apart, he settled between her sleek thighs and slid up and over her wet body. She splayed her palms on his chest, glided them up to his shoulders and around his neck as she arched against him and hooked her calves against the back of his thighs, urging him to complete the act. He drove into her in a seemingly endless stroke, and growled deep in his throat as she took every hard, solid inch of him. Until he didn't know where he ended and she began.

The pleasure of being inside Lora was so intense, so surreal, that he shuddered and tried to absorb the moment, how agonizingly perfect, how incredibly right, she felt beneath him. Hot, slick, tight. Bracing his forearms by her shoulders, he framed her face in his hands, grazed her plump bottom lip with his thumb, and watched as her gaze darkened with need.

Then she closed her eyes, whispered his name, and rolled her hips sinuously against his, beckoning him to finish what he'd started.

He wanted this to last. Wanted to linger and savor and watch her as she came again. His cock, however, refused to take the slow, leisurely route, and because his overly aroused body demanded he do so, he withdrew and surged back into her, again and again, long, hard strokes that increased in power and strength and depth.

She met him thrust for thrust, moving in perfect rhythm with him as he pumped into her. She slid her hands down the slope of his back, her fingers digging into muscle and flesh as she tried to drag him closer, deeper, with every fluid stroke. She bit his shoulder and writhed against him in wild, reckless abandon.

Their mating was raw and primitive, a culmination of every desire they'd suppressed, every seductive tease between them, every erotic fantasy he'd had of possessing her just like this. It didn't take long for the heat coiling low in his belly to spiral down to his groin. As if in sync with his body's impending release, her lashes fluttered back open, and she met his gaze, whimpering helplessly as she started to convulse around him.

Her orgasm triggered his own, and he followed her right over the edge with a rough, guttural groan. His climax was scorching hot, an unbridled surrender of body and soul that left him shaken and stretched across her limp, sated form, his face pressed against her damp neck as he struggled to come back to his senses.

And when he did, it was with the realization that if this one night was all he had of her, it would be enough. It would have to be.

LORA walked out of the bathroom after drying her hair and into Joel's bedroom, just as he entered from the hallway with a mug in one hand and a spoon in the other. His gaze took in the long-sleeved, thigh-length flannel shirt he'd given her to wear, sans underwear, and lingered on her bare legs just long enough to remind her of how wantonly she'd wrapped those same legs around him in the throes of passion less than an hour ago. The erotic memory made her skin flush all over again.

As for him, he'd pulled on a pair of baggy black sweatpants, leaving his well-built chest and muscled arms naked for her appreciative gaze, though she had no problem remembering how equally impressive he was below the waist. He'd taken a quick shower after making love to her, and while she'd opted to dry her hair, he'd combed the damp strands of his hair away from his face with his fingers, leaving it an appealing, tousled mess. He looked hotter and more gorgeous than ever, this incredible man who'd taken such good care of her since the attack and made her feel so safe and secure.

"I made you some chicken noodle soup to help keep you warm." He lifted the steaming mug he was holding as he approached her. "Why don't you get into bed and beneath the covers."

She smiled, amused by this take-charge side to Joel, along with the small, concerned frown marring his brows. After their hot shower and now that he'd switched the heater on in the house, she was plenty warm, but she did as he suggested. After pushing the pillows up against the headboard, she sat down on the bed and pulled the comforter and blanket all the way up to her lap.

"I've got your clothes running through the wash so they'll be clean and dry by morning," he said, and handed her the mug and spoon.

She grabbed the cup by the handle and dipped the spoon inside, stirring the heated liquid. "You've been busy while I was drying my hair. Who would have thought you had a domestic side?"

He braced his hands on his hips and shrugged. "I just thought you'd like to be able to wear your own clothes home tomorrow."

"Oh, I don't know," she said, giving him a playful grin. "Your flannel shirt is pretty darn comfortable."

Normally, a light flirtatious comment like that would have earned her one of his sexy smiles, and maybe an equally teasing reply. Not tonight. He looked much too serious, and she wondered if it was all worry on her behalf, or was he having regrets about what had just happened between them? She certainly harbored none, not when she'd been the one to beg him to make love to her.

"I should have asked you long before now, but how are your hands?" he asked, smoothly changing the subject.

"A little sore." She looked at her left palm, which had a few scrapes and scratches from the asphalt, then showed the red marks to Joel. "I might have to keep myself off the books at the spa for a few days when it comes to client massages, but I'll be okay."

"Good." He nodded and started around the bed to the other side. "Eat your soup before it gets cold."

She brought the mug closer so she didn't spill, lifted the spoon to her mouth, and inhaled the familiar scent, which was accompanied by a rich broth, noodles, and little pieces of chicken. "Ummm." She swallowed the warmth, feeling it slide all the way down to her stomach. "This tastes really good. Thank you."

He settled himself on the mattress next to her, sitting upright against his pillows. "I wish it was something better than canned, condensed soup, but it's all I had."

"I don't mind." She took another bite, realizing that she was actually very hungry. "I grew up eating cheap canned soup, so it's sort of one of those comfort foods for me, if you know what I mean."

"Your mom never made homemade chicken soup?" he asked, surprise in his tone.

"Actually, she did. She was a great cook and I loved the fresh, homemade chicken soup that she'd make when either myself or Zach got sick," she said, remembering those happier days when her mother had reveled in her position as Bill Marshall's wife and her role as mother to two children. "But that was before my father told my mother he was having an affair and wanted a divorce, then packed his bags and walked out the door. My mother was never the same after that, and Zach and I learned pretty quickly how to fend for ourselves."

He regarded her curiously. "Never the same how?"

She finished taking a drink of the broth and stared at him in bewilderment. "Zach never told you about what happened with our mother?"

"Just bits and pieces." He clasped his hands over his bare stomach, drawing her gaze to that taut, lean belly of his and the sprinkling of hair that whorled around his navel and made an enticing trail south. "He mentioned that your parents divorced when he was young, and that both of them have since died, but he never shared details. Whatever happened between your parents wasn't something he liked to talk about."

Neither did she, because it stirred up a lot of hurt and

pain. Even now, she felt old, buried resentment rise to the surface. "What my father did was rough on Zach." And accounted for a lot of her brother's rebellion and reckless behavior when he was a teenager, and even now as an adult.

"I'm sure it was rough on you, too," he said softly.

The dark, smoky blue hue of his eyes searched hers, silently offering the kind of comfort and compassion that made her feel connected to Joel, in a way that she'd never experienced with any other man. Startled by that notion, she glanced away from his mesmerizing gaze, scraped out the last bit of noodles and chicken from the mug, and told herself not to read too much into his interest, and his too-knowing comment.

"It was rough on all of us," she told him. Their father's reckless, egotistical choices had not only devastated their mother and destroyed their family as a whole, but it had also shattered her and Zach's illusion of love and security, as well. "As for me, after my father walked out, someone had to make sure that our lives continued as normally as possible, especially mine and Zach's, and that became my responsibility."

He frowned at her. "Where was your mother during all this?"

"Oh, she was there physically, but the day my father left she checked out mentally and emotionally."

Finished with her soup, she set her empty mug on the nightstand beside the bed, then turned back toward Joel. She wasn't sure how they'd gotten so immersed in her past, gone from canned soup to her turbulent childhood, but she didn't mind sharing that private part of herself with Joel. And that realization said a lot, considering she didn't like thinking about, or talking about, what had happened so many years ago.

"My mother had centered her married life around pleasing my father, and him doing everything for her in terms of financial support. She honestly didn't know how to cope without him." Facing Joel, she crossed her legs and settled the covers up around her waist. "After the divorce, she became withdrawn and depressed. She slept most of the day away, and when she was up, she was barely functional, despite the medication her doctor prescribed for her. Things got even worse after my father was killed in a car crash, along with his then-girlfriend. I think my mother always harbored the hope that he'd come back to her."

"So you pretty much became a parent to both your mother and Zach," he guessed, his deep voice rich with understanding.

She nodded. "Like I said, someone had to keep what was left of our family together, and I did what I could. Zach didn't cope well with my father's abandonment or the divorce, and he was a moody, temperamental teenager. Then, the summer after I graduated from high school, I came home from work one day to find that my mother had deliberately overdosed on a combination of painkillers and other barbiturates." Her throat clogged with emotion and the sadness that always accompanied thoughts of how her mother had died.

Joel reached out, took her hand, and gave it a gentle, comforting squeeze. "I'm sorry, Lora. I know how hard it is to lose a parent. My mother passed away when I was just a kid, and it changes everything."

"Yeah, it does," she said, wondering what had changed for him and his family after his mother's death. The shadows lurking in his gaze told her that he'd been deeply affected by the loss of his mother in a way that still remained a part of him.

Pushing her own curiosity aside for the moment, she continued with her story. "I was eighteen at the time, and Zach was sixteen, so I filed for guardianship so we wouldn't be separated and I could raise him for the next two years. And let me tell you, he didn't make things easy on me. He ran with the wrong crowd and thought alcohol, drugs, and courting various kinds of trouble were the way to deal with his pain and anger over what happened with my mother and father."

She shook her head and gave Joel a small half smile. "Somehow, someway, I managed to keep him out of juvenile hall, and when he turned eighteen and joined the Marines, I couldn't have been happier. I really hoped that this would be his chance to make a good, stable life for himself."

She exhaled a deep breath and absently picked at a piece of lint on the dark brown comforter. "But I've had to bail him out of a few situations over the past few years due to his gambling habit and alcohol abuse, and now with tonight's incident, it seems that Zach hasn't changed at all. And even though I'm angry that he's gotten himself into trouble again, and I'm somehow involved, I really do miss him and I hope he's okay."

"That's understandable." Joel's long, warm fingers stroked across her jaw and brushed away stray strands of her hair, his gentle touch stirring feelings deep inside of her. "He's your brother and your only family, and you love him, despite his faults."

"Yeah, I do." She sighed, and eyed Joel's solid chest, thinking how wonderful it would be to curl up against him and forget about everything for a little while longer. At least until tomorrow morning, when reality would no doubt intrude on this idyllic time with him. "I'm really worried about Zach and I wish he'd get in touch with me so I can help him get out of whatever mess he's in."

"If you've bailed him out before, maybe it's time that he learns to handle the situation himself," Joel said gruffly.

She couldn't argue with that, yet . . . "If those guys had no qualms about putting a knife to my throat and threatening me with further harm, I can't imagine what they'll do to Zach."

Lora shuddered at the horrible thoughts passing through her mind, of Zach alone and susceptible to those evil men wanting whatever money her brother owed them. She was suddenly very thankful that she was here with Joel, instead of by herself at her apartment. "I want you to know that I'm so grateful that you were there for me at The Electric Blue tonight."

"It's not as though I was able to stop the attack." His jaw clenched in a flare of anger, and his eyes flashed with the same spark of fury. "It never should have happened to you, Lora."

She studied him for a moment, from the tension radiating off his body to the self-reproach in his gaze. He made it seem as though he was responsible somehow, and that was an absolutely ridiculous notion. "There's no way you could have anticipated something like that. Nobody could have. But you did find me out in the back alley, and who knows how long I could have been out there if you hadn't heard me pounding on the door. And you've taken great care of me ever since."

She moved closer, wanting him to know how much his attention and concern meant to her. "I can't remember the last time someone took care of *me* the way you have. It seems like I've always been the one taking care of everyone else, so to have you take charge of the situation like that, and me, was so reassuring. I needed you, and you were there for me, and I'm so glad that I'm here with you now and I don't have to be alone after what happened tonight with those men."

His sensual lips tightened. "Sydney wouldn't have left you alone."

"You're right," she conceded, though she wasn't sure why he was arguing the point. "I'm a pretty independent woman, but there's something about you that makes me feel safe and protected."

"Lora . . ." His gravelly voice trailed off, and he looked torn about something. "About those men who attacked you—"

Reaching out a hand before he could finish his sentence, she placed her fingers against his warm lips, stopping his flow of words. "I don't want to talk about what happened, or think about it," she said, and moved closer to him. "At least not right now."

No, at the moment she had other things on her mind, and they included taking advantage of Joel's magnificent body. She wanted him again, ached to lose herself in his sensual kisses, the knowing stroke of his hands, and the heat of his mouth tempting her beyond thought or reason. And judging by the dark desire sparking to life in his gaze, he craved the same things.

Emboldened by that knowledge, she closed the distance between them. Sliding her fingers into the waistband of his sweatpants, she tugged them down and off, then pushed his knees apart and knelt between his spread legs. He was already hard and thick, his erection curving up from his body as if begging for her touch.

That she could arouse him so quickly was a heady notion that made her want to please him all the more. Earlier, he'd given her exactly what she'd needed, generously, intimately, and unselfishly. This time, she wanted to be the one to seduce him, just as indulgently.

Flattening her hands on his strong thighs, she slid her palms upward. Her fingers traced the long scar on his left leg that he refused to talk about, then moved higher, until her thumbs brushed across the heavy sacks beneath his shaft, until the fingers of one hand were wrapped snugly around the base of his heated flesh.

She glanced up the length of his torso, watched the rapid rise and fall of his chest, and finally met his gaze. His eyes were dark and intense and hypnotic, and when she stroked him all the way to the tip of his cock then glided her thumb over the swollen head, she felt him shudder and jolt against her erotic caress.

Smiling, she lowered her head and teased him with slow, languid licks and wet swirls of her tongue. Tempted him with the promise of a deeper, moister heat. His fingers slid into her hair and cupped the back of her head, gently urging her to take more of him, all of him. Parting her lips, she drew his cock into her warm, wet mouth, as far as she could, loving the taste of him. She gradually withdrew, adding just enough suction and friction to rip a helpless groan from his throat.

Her own arousal pitched higher, and because she wanted him inside her when he came, she moved up and over him, until she was kneeling above his hips, poised less than an inch away from his jutting erection. His hands settled on her thighs as she began unfastening the buttons on the shirt she wore. She made him suffer through her slow, seductive strip tease, made him watch as the flannel material parted and she caressed her bared breasts with her hands and grazed her rigid nipples with her thumbs.

Feeling shamelessly uninhibited, and encouraged by the lust and need chiseling his features, Lora skimmed her palms down her ribs, over her belly, and let her fingers dip between her legs. She was already slick and wet, her flesh incredibly sensitive to the touch, and she couldn't hold back the moan that escaped her lips.

Joel's fingers dug into her thighs, and his breathing grew ragged. She knew she was pushing his restraint, and making him lose complete control became her ultimate goal. She inched downward, until just the swollen head of his erection glided along the weeping folds of her sex, and shivered at the delicious, erotic sensation of him sliding rhythmically against her cleft. Letting her lashes fall to half-mast, she bit her bottom lip and rocked sinuously against that smooth, hard column of flesh once, twice, three times . . . and felt the beginnings of an orgasm start to unravel deep inside her.

She heard Joel swear as his control finally shattered, a dark, ripe curse that was raw, primal, and wholly sexual. Grabbing her hips firmly in his hands, he jerked her body down onto his engorged cock at the same time he thrust upward, impaling her to the hilt in one long, hard, driving stroke. She gasped in shock, and her head spun at the sudden, unexpected invasion, but he didn't give her time to think. Didn't give her time to react or adjust before he was bucking into her, grinding against her, repeatedly, impatiently, relentlessly.

She might have been on top and in the dominant position, but the man beneath her was far more powerful, far more demanding, and there was nothing she could do but match him stroke for stroke and ride out the sensual storm.

His hands tugged at the shirt she wore, shoving it down her arms and off so that she was as naked as he was. His splayed palms slid around to her back, moved firmly up the slope of her spine. Long, warm, insistent fingers curled around the nape of her neck, and he pulled her down toward him to fuse their mouths together, even as their lower bodies continued to mate and strain for release.

The kiss was deep. Hot. Bold and aggressive and ultimately possessive—a ravenous clash of lips and tongues that imitated the unbridled way he moved against her, inside of her. Then his hands were gripping her bottom, dragging her closer, increasing the heated friction between their bodies. Intense pleasure saturated her senses, and she clenched around his shaft as the beginnings of a climax rippled through her.

She groaned raggedly against his mouth, and unable to hold back, she let her orgasm wash over her. The release was strong and overwhelming, tearing a soft cry from her lips as she rode out the exquisite sensation.

Even as she was still convulsing from the aftermath and trying to catch her breath, Joel's body tightened beneath hers and he came, shuddering hard against her.

Ten

JOEL had always been a light sleeper, made more so by military training and the living conditions he'd endured during his time in Iraq. He'd learned to always be alert, anticipate danger, and react to the slightest sounds, even while sleeping. *Especially* while sleeping. Because that's when you were most vulnerable to the enemy.

So, before the first vibrating sound against his night-stand ended, Joel jolted awake, had his cell phone in hand, and was checking the caller ID. He saw PRIVATE CALLER flash across the display, which automatically ruled out his partners at ESS, and cursed softly beneath his breath even as his stomach twisted with dread. It was never a good thing when someone got a call at three in the morning, and Joel instinctively knew that this one was going to be a hellish wake-up call.

He managed to move off the bed quickly and without disturbing Lora, who was sound asleep on the other side of the mattress, then grabbed his sweatpants from the floor and headed down the hall to the living room. The unit in his hand buzzed again, and he flipped open the cell phone and tucked it between his ear and shoulder as he pulled on his pants.

"Hello?" he said, keeping his voice low.

"Jesus Fucking Christ, Joel!" came the loud, pissed-off voice he'd been anticipating since Lora's attack. "What the hell is going on with my sister? I just got a few snapshots of her sent to my cell phone and she's got a goddamn knife pressed against her neck. *Is she okay?*"

Beneath the justified fury in Zach's tone, there was a trace of panic Joel couldn't ignore. "She's okay," he reassured Zach. "She's here with me at my place."

"What the hell happened?" Zach demanded heatedly. "How did these guys get her alone when you were supposed to watch over her twenty-four/seven?"

Joel pressed his thumb and forefinger against the bridge of his nose and squeezed his eyes shut. The question prompted a fresh surge of guilt to rise to the surface, now compounded by the fact that he'd slept with Lora. Twice. He was beginning to think he was in way over his head when it came to Lora, and he wasn't quite sure what to do about that realization.

Still, he'd been responsible for her safety, and he'd failed to keep her out of harm's way, and that was something he couldn't deny to his friend. "They caught her when she went outside to throw away some trash at The Electric Blue."

"Jesus, Joel. They could have really hurt her, or worse, and I have no doubt that the next time they'll do more than just threaten her," he bit out furiously. "I trusted you to protect Lora, and if that's too much to ask, then let me know and I'll find someone else who can do the job."

Despite his own remorse, Joel felt his anger toward Zach spike. "You're the one who got her in this fucking mess in the first place, Zach," he said as he paced restlessly across the living room floor. "How about you take some responsibility for that, huh?"

"I'm doing what I can to get the money," Zach replied, backing down a fraction.

But Joel was fired up, and he wasn't about to let his friend off so easy. "If you would have been honest and up front with your sister about what you did, this *never* would have happened. She would have known to be careful and to watch her back. It's not easy to protect someone when they have no idea that their life is in danger."

Zach had no response, and Joel had no problem filling up the silence. "When is this going to be over, Zach?" he asked in a low, harsh tone. "How long are you going to string these guys out for the money you owe them?"

"Luck hasn't exactly been on my side lately," Zach said cynically. "I need a few more weeks."

Joel jammed his fingers through his hair in frustration, because he knew what kind of "luck" his friend was referring to. The kind of big break that compulsive gamblers prayed for as they tossed borrowed money into a poker pot. "This is bullshit, Zach. You're throwing good money after bad. When are you going to wake up and face the truth that you have a gambling problem?"

"The only problem I seem to have is finding someone to keep my sister safe," Zach replied in an attempt to deflect the focus off of him and his personal issues.

"Fuck you, Zach," Joel hissed into the phone, feeling unduly provoked.

"Yeah, well, I already *am* fucked," Zach said, unable to disguise the thread of fear in his voice. "But that doesn't mean my sister has to be. Can I trust you to keep her safe from here on out, or is that too much to expect?"

Joel hadn't forgotten the fact that he owed Zach his own life, that all his friend had asked in exchange was this one small favor. "I won't let her out of my sight again," he promised, and meant it. "But this situation is bigger and more dangerous than you want to admit. Call your sister and tell her the truth, man. She deserves to hear it from you."

"I . . . can't. I just can't. She'll never forgive me for what I've done, and I don't want her to ever find out about what I did with that damn insurance policy." Zach's voice cracked with shame and desperation. "Now that you know how serious these guys are, *please* do whatever it takes to keep her safe."

"Zach—" The line disconnected before Joel could say anything more. *"Goddammit,"* he growled beneath his breath as he snapped his cell phone shut. Irritation over the whole situation flowed hot and fast through his veins, and it was all he could do not to crush the phone in his hand to ease some of his frustration. Instead, he hung his head and released a slow, taut breath.

"Tell me the truth about what?"

The sound of Lora's soft voice drifting from behind where he stood in the living room, along with the realization that she'd woken up and had overheard a good part of his conversation with Zach, had Joel's stomach dropping out.

Shit.

Reluctantly, he turned around and found her standing a few feet away, wearing his flannel shirt once again and looking all warm and soft and sleep-tousled. In that moment, all he wanted to do was take her back to his bedroom, strip off their clothes, and make love to her again. To lose himself, mind and body and soul, in her giving body, in her sweet, drugging kisses, and forget about Zach and his lies, and Joel's own deceit.

But that wasn't going to happen. In fact, it wouldn't happen again, *couldn't* happen again, because Joel was forced to admit that Lora had become more than just a job or temporary assignment to him. More than just a client he could watch over dispassionately and without any kind of involvement other than whatever the job entailed.

No, somewhere along the way the entire situation had gotten emotionally complicated, and so fucking personal. And as a result he'd lost his edge and his ability to remain focused. Lost those instincts that kept his senses sharp and honed and enabled him to keep his client out of danger. It was obvious to him that his desire for Lora had become too damned distracting, to the point that he'd grown lax. Too comfortable. So caught up in the awareness and sexual tension between them that he'd let his guard drop long enough for Zach's thugs to get their hands on her.

Knowing that the next time could be deadly, he couldn't afford to make that kind of mistake again. Which meant he had to distance himself from his attraction to Lora, and keep his lust in check. Had to keep his head in the game and make her safety a priority, and he couldn't do that if he was constantly thinking about getting Lora naked again.

"You were talking to Zach, and he is obviously keeping something from me that you know about," Lora said, bringing his thoughts back to the discussion at hand. "What's going on, Joel?"

He watched as she approached him, her gaze searching his for answers in the still dim, shadowed room. He'd prefer that she heard the full story from her brother, but Zach hadn't given Joel that option, and he was done lying, done pretending to be someone he wasn't, and done covering Zach's ass.

He switched on a nearby lamp, set his cell phone on the coffee table, and released a deep sigh before facing her again. "Zach's in trouble, Lora. *Big* trouble. And it involves you."

She crossed her arms over her chest, drawing his gaze to the full swells of her breasts peeking from the low V where she'd buttoned his shirt. "I think I've figured out that part already," she said wryly. "Why and how does Zach's situation involve me?"

There was no easy way to couch the ugly, disturbing truth, so he didn't even try. "Because Zach used the life insurance policy on you as collateral for a loan so he could gamble some more and get himself out of debt," he said bluntly. "Except now he's in deeper shit than before and his 'friends' are demanding payment, or they'll go straight to the source to get it themselves."

Lora's eyes widened in disbelief and her hand fluttered to her throat, her fingers pressing against the red mark still visible on her neck. "And that's me. Dead."

"Yeah, that's usually how those insurance policies work," he said grimly.

"Oh, God," she breathed. Stunned, she sat down on the sofa, then her gaze cut to his. "And all this time, you knew."

It wasn't a question, but a statement of fact. "Yeah, I knew. Zach called me a few weeks ago and told me everything. He knew those guys were going to come after you eventually, and he asked me to watch over you until he could get the money together to pay back the loan."

She swallowed hard. "How much does he owe them?"

"Over fifty grand," he said, and watched her complexion pale even more.

She was quiet for a long moment, and Joel gave her the time to process everything he'd just told her. He'd always known that she was a strong, capable woman, but her relatively low-key reaction to learning that her brother pretty much sold her life to enable his gambling habit proved it. Most people would have been frantic, hysterical, and emotionally distraught, yet here Lora sat, trying to sort out the facts. He couldn't help but admire her for that internal fortitude and her ability to remain calm in the face of such devastating news. However, he also suspected that this was the calm before the storm, that soon her composed demeanor would shift to a very justified anger.

"So," she said, a small, pained smile on her lips. "Our meeting at The Electric Blue wasn't some kind of coincidence, was it?"

He shook his head. "No, it was planned."

"Oh, wow." Lora exhaled a deep breath, feeling as though her world as she knew it had tilted on its axis. And in a big way, it had, considering nothing had been as it seemed.

But knowing the truth now explained so much. Like Joel's single-minded pursuit in order to stay close to her. His resisting the attraction between them because it went against that code of honor of his when their meeting had been based on a pretense. But there were other questions, important ones, that still remained unanswered.

She glanced back at Joel, who stood just a few feet away, his arms crossed over his wide chest and his expression as guarded as his attitude. Last night he'd been her rock, her anchor in a very stormy, turbulent sea of shock and confusion. Now, he looked like what she knew him to be . . . her protector, a man who'd promised her brother that he'd watch over her. And he was back to taking that job very seriously.

"Why didn't you tell me about Zach's debt and my part in it?" she asked.

A muscle in his cheek ticked, and he scrubbed a hand over the dark stubble on his jaw before answering. "Because I promised Zach that I wouldn't tell you the truth."

Judging by the reserved look in his eyes, she suspected there was more to that simple reply than he was letting on. "Why not?" she asked curiously. "Wouldn't it have just been easier if I knew what I was up against?"

"Hell, yeah," he said with a dry little laugh. "If you knew, last night with those thugs *never* would have happened. I'm sure of it."

"So why keep everything a secret?" she persisted.

He hesitated, his reluctance to reveal that part of his agreement with Zach nearly tangible. Then, he obviously decided that honesty at this point was the best option. No more lies between them. "There's two reasons, actually. First, Zach didn't want you to know what he'd done, because he was afraid this would be the final straw for you when it comes to him, considering this isn't the first time he's gotten himself into this kind of situation."

"As upset as I am about Zach's gambling addiction and what he did with my insurance policy, he's my brother and I love him. Nothing will ever change that, but it's so clear that he needs professional help."

"Yeah, he does," Joel agreed gruffly.

"And the second reason?" she asked, wanting to hear it all.

"I owed Zach for saving my life in Iraq." His eyes grew dark and shadowed, and uncompromising. "If that meant promising him I wouldn't tell you that your life was in danger while protecting you, it was a small favor to agree to, considering what he did for me."

Lora stared at Joel in shock. Her brother had saved his life? Good Lord, what had he endured in the military? What had Zach gone through, as well? A huge lump formed in her throat, and she spoke around it. "What happened?"

"Look, this conversation isn't about me," he said, pushing aside her too-personal question to redirect the discussion back to business. "It's about you and keeping you safe until Zach gets his shit together."

Lora knew it was a very real possibility that her brother wouldn't be able to come up with the fifty grand, or more, that he owed. Which meant not only her life was in danger, but Zach's as well. And that thought was enough to make her feel physically sick.

Knowing she had to do whatever she could for Zach, she stood up and approached Joel with her idea. "I have over twenty-five thousand sitting in a savings account that I've accumulated over the years. I've been putting it away so I could use it to open my own spa one day, but if that money means helping Zach get out of the trouble he's in, then I'm willing to use it for that."

Joel's brows rose incredulously. "Just a few hours ago you told me that you've bailed him out of similar situations before. And now you want to do it again?"

"He's in trouble, Joel, and he's my brother," she said, a little angry that he'd question her solution.

"You don't get it, do you?" He jammed his hands onto his hips and moved closer, so that he was in her face and being brutally honest and straight with her. "You're *enabling* him, Lora. Making it okay for him to go and do it again. He's got a huge problem, an addiction. Just a few minutes ago you said that he needs professional help, yet here you are, ready to bail him out again!"

She felt tears of frustration burn the backs of her eyes. Frustration and fear for Zach's life, she knew. "He can't get professional help if he's dead!"

The tension riding across Joel's broad shoulders eased, and his voice softened, too. But not his words. "Those people are still going to want the rest of the money, Lora."

"I'll take out a loan," she said, desperate for some kind of solution.

Joel shook his head sadly. "I'm not going to let you do that. You have to understand that Zach's behavior has become a vicious cycle, Lora. Unless you make him accountable for his actions somehow, instead of making it easy on him every single time he finds himself in a bind, then this gambling addiction of his will never end."

As much as it pained her, she knew deep down inside that Joel was right. It was hard to accept that truth, even more difficult to let her brother find his way out of this mess alone. "There has to be *something* I can do."

As if understanding her dilemma, he closed the distance between them and rubbed his hands down her flannel-covered arms, his caress as gentle and caring as the look in his eyes. "Right now the best thing you can do for yourself, and for Zach, is to keep yourself out of harm's way. That said, I don't think it's a good idea for you to return to work, at the spa or the bar, until this is over."

For her, that wasn't an option. "I don't intend to cower or hide, or keep myself cooped up for who knows how long." She lifted her jaw stubbornly, refusing to back down on the issue. "I have a life, and I have a job that means a lot to me, and there's no reason for me to take a leave of absence. Now that I know what's going on, I'm not going to do anything stupid like I did last night. Besides, didn't you promise Zach you'd protect me?"

He narrowed his gaze at her, and his arms dropped back down to his sides. "Yeah, I did, but I'm not Superman, Lora. It's difficult enough being responsible for someone *without* them making themselves a direct target." He paced away from her, then spun back around. "You saw what those men were capable of, and while I don't plan to let you out of my sight again, there are things that I can't anticipate, or that are out of my control, that can happen."

"I'm not a coward, Joel," she said, and meant it. "Sure, those men scared the hell out of me, but I've never run or hidden from anything in my entire life, and I'm not about to start now. If they want me bad enough, they'll find a way to get me, whether it's on the street with you, or in my apartment. I'm not changing every aspect of my life just because I'm afraid."

He studied her for a long moment, then, obviously realizing that there was nothing he could do or say to change her mind, he exhaled a long, harsh breath. "Fine."

She relaxed, grateful that that particular fight was over. "Thank you. Now that we've settled that argument, I'm going back to bed to try to get some sleep." As if. But she felt so drained and exhausted, emotionally and mentally, and crawling back under the warm covers held immense appeal.

"Lora, wait," he said when she started to leave the living room. "There's something else we need to talk about."

She faced him again, and immediately knew by the reserved look in his gaze, coupled with the gruff, direct tone of his voice, that their conversation was about to take a more personal, intimate turn. She steeled herself for what he was about to say.

He didn't disappoint her. "About last night—"

"Don't." She cut off his apology before it could leave his lips. "Don't you *dare* say you're sorry for what happened between us last night."

Even though she now understood why he'd resisted her overtures for so long, there wasn't anything about being with Joel that she regretted. He might have been sent to protect her, but the feelings between them were real.

"We're both adults, and I knew exactly what I was doing when I asked you to make love to me," she went on before he could interrupt her. "And we've already had the discussion about your position on sex, relationships, and how you don't like messy emotional attachments, so we don't need to go that route again. I get it, Joel, and I'm not going to start making demands or become some kind of clingy female, so don't worry about it." Unfortunately, the dull ache in her chest contradicted those words, made a mockery of what she knew to be true.

She was falling in love with Joel Wilde, a man who liked things uncomplicated and commitment free, and truly believed he wasn't capable of giving a woman what she craved beyond physical pleasure. Yet last night he'd been everything she'd ever needed in her life, everything she'd yearned for as a woman, and so much more. The desire between them had been mutual and real, soul stirring, and deeply, irrevocably emotional.

And he obviously didn't have a clue. He was a typical, stupid, stubborn man when it came to admitting anything that had to do with his feelings or emotions. And she wasn't one to push or cling to false expectations. She'd learned with her last relationship that you couldn't force someone to love you back.

"I wasn't going to apologize," he said with a frown, clearly not happy about her tossing his own lecture right back at him. "But it won't happen again."

She knew exactly what "it" referred to, and though his abrupt about-face didn't surprise her, his steely resolve made her all too curious. "Because?"

"Because my attraction to you is too damned distracting, and it gets in the way of my job of protecting you," he admitted roughly, and dragged his long fingers through his tousled hair. "I need a clear, focused head, and thinking about having sex with you isn't conducive to maintaining a sharp and alert presence. That's what got you into trouble with those men last night. My mind wasn't one hundred percent on the job, as it should have been, and I'm not about to make that same mistake again."

She held back the smile threatening to curve the corners of her mouth. At least he'd admitted to their attraction, even if he was now trying to do the honorable thing by establishing a more professional relationship between them in order for him to keep her safe from harm. That he had to physically and mentally remove himself from the temptation of sleeping with her again said a whole lot about Joel and his true feelings—that sex with her hadn't been easy, casual, or forgettable like every other affair he'd ever had. Because if last night had been all about pure gratuitous sex, he'd be taking advantage of the no-strings-attached fling instead of scrambling to put distance between them, as he was attempting to do right this second.

She could tell him that by not sleeping with her he'd be twice as distracted, but decided to let him figure that out on his own.

For now, she'd let him have his way, and she'd respect those professional boundaries of his. For now, she'd let him believe that their involvement had been a one-night deal, a result of heated passion and the need for her to replace bad memories with more pleasant sensations.

And maybe, if she was lucky, when this situation was over he'd realize that there was more between them than just incredible lust, sizzling desire, and one night of sex.

Eleven

"SINCE you've never been to Santori's, I can personally guarantee you're in for a real treat."

Walking side by side through Little Italy toward the restaurant Daniel spoke of, Sydney smiled at her date, still unable to get over the fact that she was going out with a *teacher*. Cassie's math teacher to be exact. A man who wasn't nearly as uptight and stuffy as she'd originally pegged him to be. He might not possess those bad-boy tendencies she was normally attracted to, but he was definitely hotter and sexier than she'd originally given him credit for.

Gone were the slacks, dress shirt, and tie he wore to work, replaced by casual, form-fitting blue jeans and a neatly pressed oxford shirt. The tan leather jacket added to his striking good looks and overall appealing package. One she was more and more tempted to unwrap and enjoy.

She planned to. Later. After an evening of being wined and dined by him. "I'm definitely looking forward to dinner. I was so busy with inventory at The Electric Blue this afternoon that I missed lunch, so I'm absolutely starved." Having taken off a Saturday evening, which she very rarely did, she wanted to make sure she left the bar well stocked and the place fully staffed.

"Ahhh, a woman with a healthy appetite for food." The tone of his voice was warm and appreciative, with just a hint of flirtatious innuendo. "How refreshing. Women like you who actually *eat* on a date are becoming a rare breed, you know."

She laughed lightly. "Trust me, I'm not a salad-with-dressing-on-the-side kind of girl." She pushed her hands into the pockets of her coat and shivered against the cold October evening breeze. "I love carbs. You couldn't have made me any happier than by feeding me authentic Italian food."

He grinned and his brown eyes sparkled mischievously, as if he'd just discovered the secret to capturing her heart and soul. "I'll be sure to remember that."

She had no doubt that he would. The man had proven to be far more direct and determined with her than she ever would have anticipated. Much to Sydney's surprise, and a bit of personal, private delight, he'd spent a few nights this past week at The Electric Blue, nursing a drink while she worked behind the bar. She'd given Daniel a good dose of her bold, daring behavior and equally brazen attitude, more than enough to scare him off, and yet here he was, still taking her out to dinner.

Which just confirmed that he was interested in the same thing that every guy wanted from her once they got a good look at her centerfold figure. Hot, fast, raucous sex. Daniel was just going about his quest in a more considerate and polite manner than all the rest, but the end result would be the same.

She'd already decided that it was going to be his lucky night, and hers, too. Hell, she was as primed and ready as a woman could get, and it had been way too long since she'd been with a guy. She'd spent the past week tempting and teasing Daniel with plenty of naughty innuendo and dirty dances on the bar's countertop, deliberately building that delicious sexual tension that eventually led to a night of hot, satisfying, physical pleasure. Oh, yeah . . . she was definitely looking forward to getting down and dirty with Daniel tonight.

A group of young kids was heading toward them, and Daniel settled a large hand at the small of her back to guide them away from the teenagers and keep her near so they didn't get separated on the sidewalk. She was wearing a black winter trench coat, yet his touch, the alluring press of his palm, seemed to sear right though the heavy material and elicited a surge of awareness within her.

Her hip bumped against his, and he could have easily taken advantage of the opportunity to slide his arm around her waist and pull her closer to his side in a show of male possession, or to *accidently* graze the full underside of her breast while he was at it. She'd come to expect those not-so-subtle tactics from most guys, but Daniel's hand remained in place at the base of her spine. Protectively. Respectfully. In a way that unnerved her more than if he'd copped a feel.

Go figure.

As soon as they reached Santori's, Daniel opened the door for her to enter before him—another gentlemanly gesture she wasn't used to. With a murmured "thanks" she stepped into the establishment, grateful for the rush of warmth that replaced the early evening chill outside. She inhaled the rich, redolent scents of authentic Italian food, and her stomach growled hungrily in response.

A woman in her midsixties made her way through the crowded lobby of customers, her bright gaze focused on Daniel. She was wearing a pretty, flowery dress accessorized with a cute I LOVE PASTA pin with a fork and spoon twirling strands of spaghetti and a dangling meatball. As soon as she reached him, her lovely face lit up with genuine fondness.

"Well, look who decided to stop in for a visit!" The woman's lightly accented voice held distinct tones of pleasure and a slight reprimand. "It's been too long."

"I know. I know." Daniel ducked his head sheepishly, looking far too charming and appealing for Sydney's peace of mind. "I had a craving for some deep dish pizza, and we all know this is the best place in the city for that."

"You got that right." The woman gently patted his cheek before taking his face in both her hands to scrutinize him closer, as a mother would a young boy. "Just look at you. You keep getting more and more handsome each time I see you." Then she finally dropped her hands back down to her sides and shifted her gaze to Sydney, her curiosity evident in the slight arch of her brow. "Who's your friend, Daniel?"

"This is Sydney," he said, that clever hand of his finding its way back to her spine to urge her forward. "Sydney, this is Rosa Santori."

"It's very nice to meet you." Sydney extended her hand courteously toward Rosa.

"No, the pleasure is all mine," the other woman insisted as she took Sydney's hand and gave it a warm, welcoming squeeze that was far more affectionate and personal than a handshake. "I can't remember Daniel ever bringing a woman friend here before. He must be trying to impress you."

Sydney laughed. Oh, this woman was sly. And incredibly sweet. "He's well on his way to doing just that."

Daniel glanced around at the crowd of people waiting to be seated for dinner. "I didn't even think about it being a Saturday night and the restaurant being so busy." He checked the time on his watch then sent Rosa a hopeful look. "Do you have a table open, by chance? We have a movie to catch in about an hour."

The man obviously wasn't opposed to using his acquaintance with Rosa to pull a few strings and eliminate the long wait for a seat, which led Sydney to believe that maybe he did have a bit of a rebellious streak in him after all. That possibility made him all the more sexy and irresistible to her.

"For you, I have the best seat in the house available," Rosa said, happy to accommodate him. "Come this way."

She crooked her finger at the two of them, grabbed a few menus from the hostess stand, then led the way to a quiet, secluded table at the back of the restaurant, which was decorated in traditional, old-world pizzeria style. Here, the lighting was low, with a flickering candle in a Chianti bottle adding to the relaxing and cozy atmosphere.

Once they were seated in the booth across from one another Rosa handed each of them a menu and gave them the specials for the day. "Now you two enjoy your dinner, and I'll send Tony over with a bottle of wine, on the house."

She left, and moments later a good-looking man came up to their table, a bottle of Chianti in one hand and two wineglasses in the other. He greeted Daniel with a firm handshake and some friendly ribbing that made it obvious that they'd known each other for a long time. Then another round of introductions ensued for her, and she learned that this man named Tony was one of Rosa's sons.

Wine was poured, and when their waitress arrived to take their order, Sydney went with Daniel's recommendation to try the deep dish pizza, which was his personal favorite. With that out of the way, he shrugged out of his jacket, and she untied the sash around her waist and did the same with her coat.

When he'd arrived at her apartment to pick her up, she'd been dressed and ready to go—including wearing her coat. Now, as she peeled off that outer layer and watched his eyes take on a dark, appreciative gleam, she was pleased to see that her outfit had the desired effect on him. Especially her long-sleeved, lace-up, corset-type top, which she'd chosen with pure and deliberate seduction in mind. The dark burgundy fabric molded to her curves, and the low scoop neckline emphasized her best, and most lusted after assets—her breasts.

Satisfied that her blatant display of cleavage didn't escape his notice, she settled back against her seat and reached for her glass of wine. "I take it that the Santoris are friends of the family?"

His gaze met hers and he smiled. "Yeah. I've known Mr. and Mrs. Santori since I was a kid. My brother and sister and I went to school with the Santoris. And my mother and Rosa were always involved in the PTA, booster clubs, and that sort of thing, so our families spent time together."

It sounded as though Daniel had a close-knit family and had grown up in a normal, well-adjusted household. She envied that sort of childhood simplicity, things that most people took for granted. "So, you've lived here all your life?"

"Yep. Born and raised right here in Chicago." Daniel took a long drink of his wine, his deep brown eyes studying her for a moment over the rim of his glass. "What about you? Where did you grow up?"

She shrugged, and kept things vague. "I'm from various parts of Illinois."

He tipped his head curiously as he stroked his fingers along the stem of his wineglass. "I take it your family didn't stay in one place for long?"

How could she forget that this man had a penchant for asking personal questions, despite her reluctance to answer them? He'd done the same thing after their parent-teacher conference regarding Cassie's math grades, coaxing information out of her about her past that she normally kept to herself—and here he was, doing it again.

She wanted to tell him that getting to know her on a deeper, more intimate level wasn't a prerequisite for getting laid—she'd agreed to a date, so sex was a given. Wanted to tell him that she preferred a no-strings-attached affair, the kind that didn't require sharing secrets or trading personal information beyond their sexual preferences. A casual, friends-with-benefits type of arrangement, because anything beyond that with a man, any man, just wasn't going to happen.

The physical connection and attraction between them was one thing, but she wasn't about to let him in emotionally, and she couldn't think of a better way to ensure he backed off than by being completely honest and up front about her past. All of it. Including the sordid details that a nice, blue-blooded guy like Daniel wouldn't want in a future mate. And she was fairly certain that by the time their first date was over and he knew just how scandalous a past she'd had, he wouldn't be chomping at the bit for a second go.

That worked for her.

"I never had a family, to speak of," she said, giving him the reply he was waiting for. "Just a string of foster homes from the age of twelve, until I got pregnant with

Cassie when I was fourteen. I spent the four years after that in a halfway house for unwed mothers, going to school, working part time, and raising Cassie."

If she'd shocked him with her blunt response, he had the good manners not to show it. In fact, the interest in his gaze increased, and he didn't hesitate to act on it. "That had to be tough," he said, gentle understanding in his tone. "Are your parents deceased?"

Sydney's stomach twisted relentlessly. More ugly truths to reveal. If her answer to that question didn't turn him off completely, then she didn't know what would. "My mother died of a heroin overdose in a back alley somewhere, and I have no idea who my father is. I don't think my mother even knew, considering she prostituted herself in order to afford her next fix."

Daniel watched as Sydney's chin lifted defensively and her eyes flashed fire—the kind that warned him that he'd just trudged onto very sensitive territory and he needed to take a huge step back before he got burned.

Despite his father's opinion to the contrary, Daniel had always considered himself a smart man, and intelligent enough to know when he'd backed someone into a corner—and that's what he'd unintentionally done to Sydney. He'd hit on a raw and painful topic, and she was lashing out, trying to protect her emotions with a fearless and defiant attitude.

He could easily understand how that approach would keep other, lesser men at a distance, but Daniel hadn't come this far with Sydney to let her shut him out now. After years of dealing with problematic kids being shuffled through the public school system, he easily recognized her behavior as purely a protective instinct. She was no different than some of those students—rough and tough on the outside because life had dealt them a crappy hand, yet vulnerable deep down inside, where it mattered the most.

Now he knew just how difficult part of Sydney's life had been, and as much as she wanted him to back off and keep things impersonal between them, he wasn't going to. He wanted to know everything about her. Every little detail. Everything that had shaped her into the fiercely independent woman she was today.

As she finished off her glass of wine, he took in her fiery auburn hair and those sensual green eyes that guarded deeper, painful secrets. She'd intrigued him from the very first time he'd met her, a year ago. At first glance, he'd seen what every other guy saw when they looked at her—a body made for pure pleasure and sin, and one she flaunted to her advantage. She was so unlike the sweet, traditional women his mother was constantly foisting on him. This woman had energy and spirit, and was feisty enough to hold her own in any situation.

Undoubtedly, she was a man's walking fantasy, but it was the way she cared about her daughter that showed him another side to her personality. A softer, tender side that he suspected she didn't show to the outside world very often. Judging by her past, she had good reason to be cautious, even suspicious of other people's motives, and he hoped that in time she'd come to realize that his interest in her was honest and real.

Their waitress came by to deliver their order, which helped to relieve the tension that had settled over the table. Daniel served them each a thick slice of the deep dish pizza and refilled their wineglasses, then watched as Sydney ate her dinner with a gusto few women would have the nerve to display on a first date.

After a few bites, he decided to switch to a lighter, mutual subject between them. One they both could relate to.

Her daughter. "So, how does Cassie feel about the two of us dating?" he asked.

Just as he planned, the mention of Cassie immediately grabbed Sydney's attention and her gaze met his with amusement, all traces of their previous exchange gone. "She took the news about as well as any typical teenager would. She wasn't thrilled about us going out, but she does like you, so you do have that going in your favor."

"That's good to know," he said, and grinned. "By the way, I spent some time with Cassie this week during the afternoon tutoring sessions."

"And?" she asked anxiously. "How's she doing?"

"For the most part, it appears that she's comprehending the daily lessons, but there still seem to be a few areas that she's struggling with." Despite working directly with Cassie, he'd yet to figure out the source of her inability to grasp certain aspects of their lesson, yet understand the more complicated equations he'd given her. There was an inconsistency there that didn't make sense to him. "I had a lot of students show up this week for after-school tutoring, so I wasn't able to spend as much one-on-one time with her as I would have liked to, but she did do better on her review test this past Friday."

Finished with her first slice of pizza, Sydney reached for a second and set it on her plate, matching his own appetite without a hint of self-consciousness. "That's good, right?"

"Yes. Very good. Overall, it's positive progress." He grinned at her, trying to allay her concerns. "I told you not to worry."

She rolled her eyes as she took a drink of her Chianti. "Easier said than done. Being a parent breeds all sorts of paranoia and concern." Then she smiled at him, her gaze now soft and mellow from the wine and amicable conversation. "Besides, weren't you the one who mentioned all the things that could be a part of the reason her grades are falling behind, like peer pressure and other distractions?"

Now knowing what Sydney had endured as a teenager, her overprotective demeanor toward Cassie made perfect sense. "She's a good, smart girl and sometimes it's a matter of getting kids back on track before they fall too far behind. However, I'd still like for her to come in twice a week for after-school tutoring, at least until I know for certain she's back to working at grade level. I'll keep working with her when I can, and I also encourage the students to pair up, which helps to hone their problem-solving skills, as well."

She nodded in agreement. "Okay, I completely trust your judgment on this."

And trusting him, a man, said a lot from this wary, cautious woman. He decided he'd take whatever he could get at that point. "So, are you going to let Cassie go to that Halloween party next weekend?"

She blinked at him in surprise. "How do you know about that?"

Done with his dinner, he wiped his fingers on his napkin and set it on his empty plate. "I heard Cassie talking to a friend before class started, and she said something about wanting to go to the Halloween party, but she wasn't sure if she'd be able to." Actually, Cassie had told her friend that her mother was being difficult, but Daniel didn't think *that* information was necessary.

She sighed, as if the decision was a tough one for her to make. "I haven't decided yet. I told her I'd consider letting her go if her math grades improved." She finished off her last bite of pizza and licked her fingers clean.

As Sydney's tongue swirled around each digit and she sucked the tomato sauce off the tips, Daniel felt his groin tighten with heat and desire. She had an incredibly sensual mouth, and it was so easy to imagine her using it on him in the same exact way. Her gaze caught his from across the table, and a small smile curved the corners of her mouth when she realized where his thoughts had wandered.

He shifted in his seat and forced his mind back to their discussion about Cassie. "Her grades *have* improved."

She pushed her plate aside and crossed her arms on the table in front of her in a way that accentuated those full, voluptuous breasts of hers that were straining against her lace-up top. "They could be better though, right?"

"Yes, but taking something away, or denying Cassie the opportunity to go to a party and have some fun, isn't going to help her grades."

She laughed dryly. "God, you sound just like Lora."

He casually swirled the last of the wine in his glass and took the direct approach. One that scraped off surface layers and tapped into more emotional issues. "What are you really afraid of, Sydney?"

She stiffened noticeably. "I'm not afraid of anything. I'm trying to be a good parent, one who makes sure that her daughter doesn't end up making bad choices or getting herself into trouble that can be avoided. Letting her go to a party at this age, *any* party, I'm taking the chance of her being exposed to drugs and alcohol and sex."

"Fair enough. But that's going to happen eventually, and a part of growing up is learning to make the right choices, even if that means making a few mistakes along the way. But she can't become her own person if you don't give her the chance, and sheltering her from the big bad world isn't going to keep her your little girl forever."

Just as he'd braced himself for a bristling argument from Sydney, their waitress came by to clear their dirty dishes from the table and ask if they wanted dessert, defusing the potentially explosive moment between them.

They both declined, their waitress delivered their check, and Daniel paid for the meal, determined to make the next segment of their date far less serious and much more fun.

THE Will Ferrell comedy Daniel took her to see had been hilariously funny. Sydney couldn't remember the last time she'd laughed so much during a movie, or been so aware of a man sitting beside her in a darkened theater. Especially at the same time. Most of her dates, if she could even call them that, consisted of going to a rowdy bar or a loud and crowded club with a guy. There'd be a few drinks and a few dances and a whole lot of expectation at the end of the night that resulted in mutual satisfaction. It was always the same . . . until tonight.

As she sat in the passenger seat of Daniel's sporty Volvo as he drove back to her place, Sydney couldn't help but wonder how *their* evening would end.

Despite the intense conversation they'd had about Cassie over dinner, the rest of their time together had been surprisingly relaxing and enjoyable. After the movie, he'd taken her to a nearby Starbucks for a coffee, and they'd sat at a table and talked—this time about inconsequential things. She learned that he loved to cook, that he collected old James Bond novels, and that he was a self-proclaimed computer geek. She was unexpectedly touched by the affection in his tone and expression when he talked about his two nephews and how he enjoyed taking them to the batting cages on the weekends and coached their little league teams during the season since his brother didn't have the time. He was a dedicated uncle, and it was clear that he connected with kids of all ages.

He shared bits and pieces about his parents and siblings and how he was treated as the odd man out for choosing a less-than-illustrious career as a high school math teacher. It was enough for Sydney to realize that she'd never, ever, fit in with his family, and she was grateful that she'd never have to make the effort.

But mostly, he made her smile and laugh and feel younger and more carefree than she had in a long time. Made her forget, for a little while, just how different their lives were while he made her the sole focus of his attention. There was nothing awkward or uncomfortable about being with Daniel. No pretenses, either. What you saw was exactly what you got—a man who was smart, amusing, honest, and caring to a fault.

As they left the coffee shop and were walking back to his car, their hands swung together in one of those accidental ways, and before she could pull her arm back, he laced his fingers through hers, securing her hand in his large, warm male grasp. Her stomach did one of those funny little flips, a silly, girlish reaction that was as thrilling as it was unnerving.

He was almost perfect. Almost too good to be true. Definitely the kind of guy a woman could fall hard and fast for given the chance.

But not her.

She reminded herself that he was just a temporary diversion, a pleasurable fling she had every intention of following through on tonight. To give them what they both wanted, and go their separate ways.

Now, as he walked her up to her apartment, hand in hand once again, she decided it was time to put her plan for seduction and sex into motion.

When they reached her door, she turned around and faced him. Giving him one of those inviting, come-hither smiles that made most men weak with lust, she brazenly slipped her hand inside his jacket, flattened her palm on his chest, and stroked her way down to the flat, hard contours of his abdomen. She could feel the heat of his body through his shirt, watched as his eyes darkened with desire, and experienced that powerful surge of excitement that came from being the one in control, the one to make a man, *this man*, want her.

Her own body thrummed in response.

"Would you like to come in?" she asked huskily, and there was no misinterpreting the sultry invitation in her voice.

He stared at her, dark-eyed and oh-so-tempting, with a sexy, bone-melting smile on his lips. "No, not tonight."

She dropped her arm back to her side and blinked at him, certain he was joking with her, or maybe was playing hard to get. That was the only thing that made any sense, because what normal, healthy, red-blooded man turned down a sure thing?

"Are you sure?" she asked, then wondered if he was worried that they might get interrupted. She cleared up that possibility real fast: "Cassie is staying the night at a friend's."

Undeterred, he shook his head in true gentleman fashion. "I'm sure."

A flicker of annoyance got the best of her and she exhaled a frustrated breath. "Daniel, you don't have to work so hard for it, you know." She was his for the taking. More than once, if he'd like.

Amusement—at her expense, no less—danced in his gaze. "I have no idea what you're talking about."

Oh, he most certainly did. And because he was being deliberately difficult and obtuse, she was about to abandon subtlety and take the blunt approach, which was more to her liking anyways. "Then let's just get it out in the open so there's no mistaking what I'm talking about." She licked her lips provocatively. "I want to have sex with you." Hot, hard, mindless sex. The kind that had nothing to do with talking, and everything to do with sweaty bodies, tangled sheets, and if she was really lucky, an orgasm or two.

He considered her proposition for a moment, not at all shocked by her candidness. "You know, I'm really flattered, but I don't have sex on the first date."

She opened her mouth, then closed it again, disbelief rendering her speechless—and that certainly didn't happen often. He was flat out turning her down. Was this guy for real?

He casually slid his fingers into the front pockets of his jeans, his smile never wavering. "What I would like, though, is to go out with you again. You name the day and time. Whatever works for you, since I'm open."

Oh. My. God. In that moment, Sydney realized that he was going to make *her* work for it. String her along. Build the tension and desire between them. Make her hot and bothered to the point that *she* was the one begging.

She'd never allowed a man that kind of control over her, and she wasn't about to start now, either. But she wasn't ready to say good-bye to Daniel just yet, not without finishing what he'd started. He'd just issued her a challenge, a seductive game between them, and one she had every intention of winning. They *would* have sex, and when they did, it would be on her terms, as it always was.

"Fine," she said, and mentally reviewed her upcoming week at The Electric Blue for the slowest evening to take off. "How about Tuesday night?"

"That's great." With their next date settled, he stepped

closer, leaned in, and slowly lowered his mouth to hers for a kiss.

His lips were warm and sensual as they slid across hers in an enticing, heated caress. Surprisingly soft and damp . . . yet wholly, deliciously male. She wanted a hot and aggressive exploration, mouths fused, tongues mating, and bodies straining for more intimate contact and friction.

Figuring that this was as close as she was going to get to any satisfaction tonight, she attempted to make their kiss a good one, but Daniel wasn't cooperating with her efforts. Every time she shifted closer or pressed for a deeper connection, he'd pull back ever so slightly, teasing her with the promise of something more lasting and erotic . . . in his own sweet time.

He nibbled softly, gently, on her bottom lip, and an impatient noise escaped her throat. The man was destined to drive her absolutely crazy with need, and there wasn't a damned thing she could do about it except let him saturate every one of her five senses with his slow, leisurely kiss.

By the time he was done and finally lifted his mouth from hers, Sydney's entire body was thoroughly aroused, from the sensitive tips of her breasts to the insides of her thighs, and everywhere in between. And he hadn't even used his hands, since they were still tucked into his jean pockets.

Judging by Daniel's triumphant and too-smug grin, he was well aware of his affect on her.

"Good night, Sydney," he said huskily.

Knowing there was nothing she could do to persuade this man who possessed such ironclad willpower to stay, she dug her apartment keys from her purse and unlocked her door. "Yeah, well, thanks for what's certain to be a long and restless night for me," she said wryly.

He chuckled humorously. "Me, too."

One quick glance downward at the erection clearly outlined against the fly of his jeans told her that he'd been just as affected. A part of her admired that impressive restraint of his, but she knew it wouldn't last for long.

She'd make sure of it.

Twelve

"WOULD you stop fidgeting already?"

Joel grunted in response and shifted in his seat once more, wishing like hell that *one*, Lora would stop fussing over him, and *two*, she wasn't standing in between his wide-spread legs, her full breasts right at his eye level. The pink bra top she wore, encrusted with faux jewels, lifted those full mounds like an offering, and his mouth watered just thinking about how all that creamy skin tasted, and how her nipples could pucker so sweetly against his tongue.

He swallowed back a groan and tried not to move again as she cuffed the sleeves on his stark white T-shirt, which seemed so glaring in comparison to the black shirts he preferred. He hadn't so much as touched her since the night she'd gotten attacked, but his awareness of her couldn't have been more keen, and the reality of that made him cantankerous and easily provoked.

Just like with every other woman he'd slept with over

the years, he would have thought that after making love to Lora and slaking that lust and need that had been riding him hard since the moment he'd met her, that maintaining his distance and keeping his focus on protecting her would be a cinch. No such luck, because this woman had the opposite effect on him. Now that he'd had her warm and soft and willing beneath him, now that he'd experienced how she came alive when he was deep inside her, he craved her even more.

And now, it didn't help matters, or his unruly libido, that she was currently scantily clad in a genie costume for The Electric Blue's Halloween bash, and all he could think about was asking this particular genie to grant a few of his most erotic wishes.

He exhaled a rough, serrated breath as she began applying gel to his hair, to slick back the long strands and make him look more like one of those greasers from the 1950s. "Is all this *really* necessary?" he asked grumpily, enjoying way too much the feel of her fingers running against his scalp.

"Yes, it's *really* necessary," she mimicked him, laughter in her tone. "If you don't dress up for the Halloween bash, you won't be allowed inside the bar. No exceptions. Not even for you, so stop being such a grouch about it."

"I'd prefer that we not go at all," he replied gruffly.

"Sorry, but that's not an option, either." Finally, she moved away to wash her hands in the kitchen sink, giving him some much-needed breathing room. "Besides, tonight is going to be a great night for tips, and right now money is a priority."

Despite their discussion about her enabling Zach, Joel knew Lora was driven to save as much cash as she could to hand over to her brother to help pay off his debt. Except

Zach had made himself very elusive and unreachable lately. He wasn't answering the daily messages that Lora left on his cell phone asking him to call her, and while that didn't bode well for the entire situation, Lora refused to believe that anything bad had happened to Zach.

Joel wanted to believe that, too.

So far, there hadn't been any other attempts against Lora, but that didn't mean those men weren't out there lurking, watching, and waiting for the perfect chance to strike again. But between Lora being more cautious and aware of her surroundings and Joel making sure she was protected at all times, there hadn't been any opportunity for those thugs to get her alone to assault her, or worse.

Unfortunately, Joel had to let Lora out of his sight when she was at the spa, because he couldn't follow her from appointment to appointment and stand in the corner of the room while she gave a client a massage or facial. Because Lora had been adamant about working at the hotel spa, he'd called his sister-in-law, Ashley St. Claire, to request another huge favor. Since Joel was unable to be by Lora's side during those daytime hours, he'd asked Ashley to make sure that Lora was only scheduled guests of the hotel, preferably women, and no one from off the street. That, at least, reduced the possibility of one of those men getting to her through the spa.

After drying her hands on a paper towel, Lora turned back around and headed toward where Joel was still seated on a kitchen chair, his gaze drawn to the enticing sway of her hips and the veils of fabric fluttering all around her half-naked body. The genie outfit exposed all of her soft stomach, and the waistband of the pants, if you could even call them that, rode way below her navel. Other than the bikini-type shorts she was wearing, the rest of the bottoms were sheer and slit down the sides to her ankles. The flowing, gossamerlike material swirled around her bare legs when she walked and made him think of an Arabian harem girl. And that thought made his mind spin off into more provocative scenarios that included her as his private love slave.

His groin tightened and he gritted his teeth. "You have way too much skin showing."

The corners of her pink, glossy lips twitched with an amused smile. "It's just a Halloween costume, Joel."

One he wanted to rip right off her body so he could have his wicked way with her. Right here. Right now. And if he was having those kinds of depraved thoughts, there was no doubt that other guys at the bar would be contemplating the same thing. The very idea sent a possessive streak surging through him.

"I'm sure there will be more scantily clad women at the bar than me." She picked up his black leather jacket, which he'd draped over the back of a chair earlier. "I'm not going to change or cover up, so deal with it."

Stubborn, independent woman! "Fine," he bit out irritably.

Satisfied that she'd won the argument, she snapped open his leather jacket and held it out for him. "Now stand up so we can complete your costume."

He did as she ordered and let her slide his jacket up his arms to his shoulders. She fussed with the collar, smoothed a hand down his plain white shirt and made sure it was tucked nice and neat into his blue jeans. With his hair slicked back and looking like a throwback to the '50s, Joel couldn't help but feel ridiculous, and was eternally grateful that his friends weren't going to be at The Electric Blue to see what a fool he looked like.

Just as he'd had enough of Lora touching him, which was starting to arouse him all over again, there was a knock

on the front door, then it opened and from the other room
a young girl's voice called out.

"Aunt Lora, it's me, Cassie," she announced.

"Come on in, sweetie," Lora replied. "We're in the
kitchen."

Right after Lora's attack, Joel had made it very clear
to everyone close to Lora that her front door would remain locked twenty-four/seven, and that Sydney and
Cassie were to use their keys to get in. And also to make
sure they made their presence known right away so Joel
didn't end up scaring the crap out of them thinking
they were an intruder. So far, his rules had been very effective.

Cassie walked into the kitchen, looking literally like
an angel. She wore a pretty, white, ankle-length dress
with long flowing sleeves that gave her the appearance of
an ethereal heavenly creature. Gold cording crisscrossed
at her slender waist, and the iridescent wings attached to
her shoulders fluttered as she walked. Completing the en-
semble was a golden halo set atop the auburn hair she'd
left in loose curls instead of straightening as she normally did. With her green eyes lined in a soft shade of
kohl, and her lips a shiny peach hue, she easily looked
eighteen years old, instead of the young fifteen that she
actually was.

Lora had told him about the dynamics between Sydney and her daughter, and since he'd spent the past week
at Lora's apartment and Cassie visited her "aunt" on a
regular basis, he'd gotten to know the teen fairly well. Tonight they were dropping Cassie off at her party on the
way to The Electric Blue, since Sydney had gone to the
bar earlier that afternoon to make sure everything was
stocked, set up, and ready for the huge crowd she was anticipating for the Halloween bash.

Cassie grinned as she gave Joel's quick, homemade costume a once-over. "Hey, Joel, you look *tight*."

Joel raised a brow. "Tight?" He had no idea if that was good or bad.

"Don't worry, it's a compliment," Lora assured him. "It's teen-speak for *cool*."

"Ahhh." He adjusted the black leather jacket across his shoulders, then zipped it halfway up, still feeling silly despite Cassie's enthusiastic endorsement. "Well, in that case, thank you."

"What do you think of my outfit?" Cassie asked, and did a cute little pirouette in front of them that made the skirt of her dress billow out around her legs. Her angel wings shimmered beneath the kitchen lights, as did her halo.

"Definitely tight," Joel said, testing out the new word he'd just learned.

Cassie laughed, her eyes bright and happy, and Joel knew why. According to what Lora had told him, attending this Halloween party with her high school friends was a big deal for Cassie, and Lora suspected that a certain boy was the reason for the young girl's excitement and exuberance. As of yet, though, Cassie hadn't confirmed Lora's hunch.

"I think you look absolutely gorgeous," Lora said, a bit of melancholy in her tone as she straightened one of Cassie's wings. "You really are growing up way too fast."

Cassie rolled her eyes, then checked out Lora's genie attire. "I wish my mom would let me wear a costume like yours," she said enviously.

"Don't push your luck, honey," Lora said on a drawl. "I think your mother let you choose that angel costume you're wearing for a reason, and as it is, I'm sure you're going to have the boys clamoring for your attention."

Cassie actually blushed, and Joel quietly agreed with

Lora's assessment. Cassie was a very beautiful girl, with a pretty face and peaches-and-cream complexion, and a body much too mature for a fifteen-year-old to handle. Undoubtedly, most of the teenage boys at her school weren't able to walk past her without their gazes dropping to her chest. If Cassie were his daughter, he'd keep her dressed in a potato sack until she turned twenty-one, so it was easy to understand Sydney's concerns regarding Cassie.

"I'm glad your mother came to her senses and decided to let you go to the Halloween party," Lora said as she brushed a stray curl back from Cassie's cheek.

"Me, too."

Lora gently grasped the young girl's shoulders in her hands and met Cassie's gaze, her expression both loving and stern. "Giving you permission to go to this party wasn't an easy thing for your mom to do, so don't do anything to make her regret her decision, okay?"

Lora's meaning was very clear, and Cassie nodded her haloed head in understanding. "I won't. I promise."

"Good." With that light lecture out of the way, Lora grinned. "We have a few more minutes before we have to leave. I have some pretty sparkle powder that we can dust on your cheeks and your collarbones, and add a little to your makeup, if you'd like."

"I'd love that," Cassie said eagerly.

The two girls headed off to Lora's bedroom to do some last-minute primping, and Joel went into the living room and sat on the couch to wait for the duo. The cell phone clipped to the waistband of his jeans vibrated, and he checked the caller ID before answering the unit.

"Hey, Mia," he said, greeting his younger sister.

"So, you *are* alive," came her sassy reply.

Joel grinned. "What's that supposed to mean?"

"Well, it's been a few weeks since I've heard from

you, so I thought I'd take the direct approach with your cell phone to make sure you're okay."

"I'm fine," he said, not certain what his sister was getting at. He'd gone long periods of time without talking to her, so her comment confused him. "Were you *supposed* to hear from me?"

"I left you a message on your machine at home, and I sent you an invitation in the mail for my gallery opening next weekend. You're the only one in the family that hasn't RSVP'd yet."

He winced, because he'd known that big day was coming up, and how much it meant to Mia. In the midst of everything with Zach and Lora, he'd honestly forgotten about the opening of her stained glass art gallery.

"Sorry 'bout that," he said apologetically. Since Lora preferred to stay at her apartment where all her things were, Joel hadn't been home in the past week to check his piled-up mail or go through messages. Obviously, he needed to make time for that this weekend. "I'm not sure if I'm going to be able to make it."

"Why not?"

His sister's disappointment traveled through the phone line, and Joel hated that he was responsible for Mia's crestfallen tone. Out of all his siblings, he related the most to Mia, and was closest to her. They'd both been adversely affected by their mother's death, in ways that had bonded them and made each of them understand the other's wild, adventurous behavior over the years.

Luckily, his sister had found a man to settle down with. A man who accepted Mia, flaws, smart mouth, and all. She seemed so happy and content with Cameron Sinclair, secure in herself as a woman and an artist, yet Joel being at the gallery opening meant more to Mia than he'd realized.

Torn, he scrubbed a hand along his jaw. "I'm on assignment right now."

"Are you out of state?" she asked.

"No. I'm in Chicago, but I'm standing in as a bodyguard for a friend's sister, and I have no idea what the situation will be like by next weekend." He'd like to hope that Zach's predicament would be settled somehow by then, but Joel wasn't holding his breath for any quick and easy resolution.

"Why can't you bring her with?" Mia suggested. "Squeeze in a bit of fun around business if you can. It would mean so much to me to have you there."

It was difficult for Joel to resist those words. Even more difficult to say no to his sister. "Okay. I'll see what I can do."

"Thank you," she said, and he heard the relief and pleased tone of her voice.

"So, how are *you* doing?" he asked, wanting to make sure that everything was going well for her.

"I'm busy with the gallery opening, but overall, I'm good."

He smiled. "Does Cameron still want to marry you?"

She laughed at his teasing question. "Of course," she said confidently. "The guy knows a good thing when he's got it."

Joel chuckled, though he knew the feeling was mutual, that Mia realized how lucky she was to have found a man like Cameron. He loved seeing his sister so happy and mellow. So content with her life. Just like the rest of his siblings and cousins. Being the only single one left in the family, Joel was beginning to feel like the odd man out.

After a few more minutes of conversation, he said good-bye and promised once again to do his best to be at the gallery opening. Just as he snapped his cell phone shut and stood up from the couch, Lora and Cassie exited the bedroom—with Cassie more sparkly than before.

"Okay, we're ready to go," Lora announced, her sexy genie costume wreaking havoc with his best intentions all over again.

He led the way to the front door and prepared himself for another long night at the bar—made more so because now, with that peekaboo outfit she was wearing, he had to worry about fending off all those unruly frat boys who drank too much, then decided the waitresses were fair play.

And he absolutely *hated* when other men touched Lora.

LORA made her way through the growing crowd of customers entering The Electric Blue and stopped at a table to take a drink order. Though it was still early, the atmosphere was already loud and festive, with the strobe lights flashing above, black and orange streamers fluttering overhead, and the Halloween song "Monster Mash" blaring through the speakers. A fog machine pumped out plumes of gray mist that rolled across the dance floor and added a graveyard feel to the bar, while rubber bats and big, fat spiders swung from the ceiling.

Everyone was dressed in some kind of costume, from the basic witch, devil, and Playboy bunny, to a fireman, jailbird, and even Elvis. There was a guy dressed as the tooth fairy, and another as Batman with Catwoman as his sidekick. Then there were the typical scary outfits, such as a zombie, Hannibal Lecter, and other gruesome masks that were straight out of a horror movie.

Currently, Lora was stopped at a table with a vampire, Cleopatra, and a mermaid. "Can I get you guys something to drink?" she asked over the noise and music.

A sumo wrestler bumped into her as she was jotting

down the table's order, his big, cushy stomach causing him
to bounce from her to another customer, who laughed at
the man's wacky choice of costume. The vampire ordered
a Bloody Mary, the mermaid asked for a Blue Hawaiian,
and Cleopatra requested a Screaming Orgasm.

After collecting a few more drink requests, Lora
headed back to the bar, set her tray on the counter, and
placed her order with Sydney. Her friend looked like a
sexy wench in her very provocative pirate costume, and
the roguish outfit suited her personality perfectly.

"I've been meaning to ask if you noticed anything unusual when you dropped Cassie off at the Halloween
party." Sydney asked oh-so-casually as she started mixing Lora's drinks.

Lora unloaded the dirty glasses she'd cleared off a
table and glanced back at Sydney, who was way too anxious and worried about her daughter's fun night out. "Unusual how?"

Sydney frowned at her, clearly annoyed that Lora was
making her spell things out. "You know . . . did any certain boy rush up to greet her when she arrived?" she
asked as she grabbed two bottles of beer, uncapped them,
then set them on the bar top for Lora. "Were the parents
there at the house like Cassie said they would be? Did
you see any evidence of any alcohol one of the kids might
have snuck in?"

Lora shook her head and laughed, truly amazed at how
a fifteen-year-old could shake her best friend's normally
cool, calm, and collected composure and make her a bas-
ket case.

"What's so funny?" Sydney demanded, much too defensively.

Lora added fresh napkins to her tray. "You are."

"Yeah, well, I'm glad you're so amused," Sydney

retorted in a mocking tone as she poured the liquor for a Screaming Orgasm. "I'm just trying to be a responsible parent."

More like overbearing and too protective, Lora thought, but kept that observation to herself. "There was no particular boy ogling her," she finally said to put her friend out of her misery. "And yes, I met the parents, who seemed to be good, decent people. And if any of the kids brought alcohol, they didn't leave it out for the adults to find."

Sydney made a face at her, the jaunty set of her pirate hat on her head making her look all the more comical. "Gee, thanks, I feel sooo much better now."

"It's a Halloween party for high school kids, Sydney. There's no predicting what's going to happen. All I know is that you did the right thing by letting Cassie go, and trusting her. I haven't seen her that excited about something in a long time."

"Yeah, yeah, I know," she admitted reluctantly, and dropped a celery stalk into the Bloody Mary she'd just made. "But I don't have to like it."

That was fair enough, Lora supposed.

As Sydney started in on a blended drink, Lora added a wedge of lime to the rim of the tomato-based cocktail and glanced across to the other end of the bar, where Joel now sat on a nightly basis, rather than at a table out in the middle of the crush of people. He'd told her that he felt more in control, and more at an advantage, being seated up at the bar, where he could see everything going on around him. And, quite honestly, she felt safer, too.

He'd taken the seat next to Daniel, and over the past week the two had become friends as Joel alternately watched over her and carried on a conversation with Sydney's new guy. And despite Joel's numerous complaints and protests about dressing up for the Halloween bash,

Lora had to admit that Joel looked gorgeous and incredibly sexy in his simple '50s costume, like her own personal James Dean.

Then there was Daniel's outfit as a swashbuckling pirate, complete with a parrot perched on his shoulder, which made him and Sydney a perfect pair.

"Don't you and Daniel look cute," Lora said when Sydney finally turned off the blender. "Did you plan on matching costumes?"

"Of course not," she said with a shake of her head as she poured the frozen, frothy piña colada mixture into a tall glass. "Daniel asked what I was dressing up as, and picked his outfit to match mine." She cast a quick glance over her shoulder at the man in question, a slow smile kicking up the corners of her lips. "I do have to say, he looks damn good with an eye patch."

Lora garnished the fruity drink with a slice of pineapple and a paper umbrella. "Ummm. I take it you're having wild and wicked fantasies of being ravished by a pirate?"

"Don't I wish." Sydney's tone was wry, and borderline annoyed. "I swear, I've never been so frustrated and sexually on edge in my entire life. I've been on *three* dates with Daniel, and I've made it very clear that I'm game for sex, yet we've barely made it to second base. He's driving me crazy."

Lora laughed, because it was so much fun to see her best friend so tied up in knots over a man, instead of the other way around. "Yet you keep going back for more, don't you?" That she hadn't dumped Daniel spoke volumes about just how much Sydney liked the man.

"Hey, at this point I'm counting on a huge payoff when we finally do the deed." She cleared off the empty glasses and put them into the sink behind the counter.

Lora couldn't help but wonder what kind of payoff *Daniel* was hoping for. Having gotten to know the guy a bit over the past few weeks, she was guessing that Daniel wanted the real deal with Sydney, and was willing to wait until she came around to his way of thinking—to accept that their relationship wasn't just about quick, temporary sex, but something deeper and more lasting.

"You know what I think?" Lora asked as the "Monster Mash" song segued into a beat-heavy number that had people heading toward the dance floor.

"No, but I'm sure you're going to enlighten me."

"I think Daniel Barnett is a good influence on you and your wild ways." Before Sydney could come up with some kind of smart-ass comeback, Lora picked up her full tray and headed back toward the sitting area to deliver her orders.

Over the next few hours, The Electric Blue swelled to capacity. The Halloween bash was a huge success, with a long line of costumed patrons waiting outside for customers to leave so they could enter and join the party. After a few drinks, the people inside lost inhibitions and grew rowdy and raucous, which made it difficult for Lora and the other bar waitresses to take and deliver orders, not to mention trying to squeeze their way from one end of the establishment to the other.

It was also strange to Lora to see everyone dressed in a costume, and while most of the outfits were fun, outrageous, and even eccentric, it was the customers who wore masks over their faces that bothered her the most. The gorilla, funky chicken, and Darth Vader all made her feel uncomfortable, and then there were the more gruesome disguises like Chucky, Freddy Krueger, and Jason from Friday the 13th that completely unnerved her and made her think of those two men who'd attacked her—both of whom had been wearing ski masks.

She tried not to think of that awful night as she cleared tables and attempted to keep up with the demanding crowd. But as a jester with a painted face bumped into her, then a werewolf with a hairy mask trapped her between himself and a guy dressed as a skeleton, she started to panic and wonder if those men were here tonight wearing masks, just waiting for the chance to get her alone again.

She was jostled from person to person, and each masked costume seemed to mock her. Too many people were touching her—a hand grazed her bare back, then another slid down her arm, and she shuddered, trying desperately to keep her growing anxiety at bay. Someone pulled on one of the veils attached to her costume and the opening of her genie pants caught on something, nearly yanking her off her feet. Her tray slipped from her fingers and clattered to the floor, but she couldn't bend down to pick it up since she'd been pushed out to the middle of the dance floor, with an evil clown bumping and grinding against her, his depraved, leering grin sending chills down her spine.

Everything closed in on her and she suddenly couldn't breathe. With the thick fog curling around her and the strobe lights flashing, she felt as though the room was shrinking in size, and she had no way to escape. As she was shoved against a man wearing a Bart Simpson mask, and he caught her by the arms in a firm grip, adrenaline and terror spiraled through her.

It was all too much, and more than she could handle mentally. She'd been so strong since her attack, so determined to live her life as normally as possible and not let trepidation and fear rule her every thought or every move she made. But now, tonight, it all came to a head and she could no longer hold back all those emotions and feelings she'd bottled up tight inside of her.

Her heart pounded hard and fast in her chest, and she struggled out of Bart Simpson's grasp. Struggled to find a way out of the crush of people pushing and shoving and suffocating her with their bodies and masked faces. She started to sweat and gulped for air, but oxygen seemed in short supply, and she couldn't seem to inhale a sufficient amount into her lungs. Her head spun, her vision blurred, and a dry, frightened sob nearly strangled her.

As she was frantically pushing her way toward the bar, and Joel, she felt an arm snake around her waist and haul her against a hard, solid chest. Then she was being dragged away. She opened her mouth to scream for help, but no sound emerged.

Oh, God, she thought. Not again. Please, not again.

She grew lightheaded and dizzy, her entire body tingling in cold, stark terror as she kicked and clawed and did everything she could to escape this man's steel embrace. It was no use. The more she fought, the more the person behind her tried to subdue her efforts—and he was much bigger, and more powerful, than she was.

"Goddammit, Lora," a familiar male voice growled into her ear. "It's Joel. Stop fighting me so I can get you out of here!"

Her relief was so profound that her entire body went weak, and she let Joel pull her out of the thick mass of party revelers and into Sydney's office, where her best friend was waiting for the two of them to arrive. The whole scene had an odd sense of déjà vu to Lora, reminding her too much of the night she'd gotten attacked, and how Joel had come to her rescue then, as well.

Once they were safely inside the room, Sydney let her

worry spill forth. "Jesus, Lora!" she said, her own voice shaking. "Are you okay?"

Lora couldn't answer. Couldn't talk. The pressure in her chest was still so painful, her throat raw and just as tight as she struggled to take big gulps of air and breathe normally.

"She'll be fine," Joel finally answered calmly, though Lora heard the concern in his voice, too.

The next thing Lora knew, Joel was pushing her onto a chair. Once she was seated, he cupped the back of her neck in his large hand and guided her head down between her legs. Then he crouched in front of her so he remained close by.

"Breathe slow and easy through your nose, sweetheart," he instructed in a low and gentle tone of voice. "Close your eyes, try to relax, and concentrate on taking deep, even breaths."

His voice was so soothing in the midst of her scare. Knowing she was well and truly safe, Lora did as he ordered, inhaling slowly, despite the rapid beating of her heart.

"What's wrong with her?" Sydney asked, pacing beside Lora's chair.

"She's hyperventilating." Joel's fingers stroked the back of Lora's neck, comforting her with his warm touch, his presence. "She'll be okay in a few minutes."

True to Joel's word, Lora's pulse gradually returned to a normal pace. When she finally felt as though her anxiety had subsided and she could breathe without feeling as though she was going to pass out, she lifted her head and stared into Joel's dark blue eyes. His jaw was clenched tight, his gaze narrowed as he searched her face for any other signs of trauma.

"Are you okay?" he asked, tipping her chin up with his fingers to get a better look at her.

Still unable to speak, she moistened her dry lips with her tongue and nodded. Minutes ago she'd been sweating and hot. Now, her skin felt cool. She shivered and wrapped her arms around her bare stomach, suddenly wishing her costume was more substantial than the bra top and sheer material it was made out of.

Joel straightened back to his full height, shrugged out of his leather jacket, and draped it over her shoulders, instantly enveloping her in his warmth and male scent. "Did anything happen out there?" he asked her. "Did anyone try and hurt you?"

His voice was neutral in tone, but the tension radiating from his body and the steel glint in his eyes told her that he'd charge right back into the bar in search of anyone who'd dared to harm her.

She shook her head. "No . . ." Her voice cracked and she swallowed to ease her parched throat so she could explain. "It was just me. I felt suffocated and closed in with all those masked people crowding around me. I kept thinking that any one of them could be those guys who attacked me, and I completely freaked out." Even now, the thought of going back out into the bar, and being surrounded by so many people, made her stomach twist into knots all over again.

"Well, you certainly scared the crap out of me," Sydney cut in, and fisted her hands on her hips, swathed in a striped pirate sash. Then she pointed a finger at Lora. "You are *so* done here at the bar. You're not working here until this thing with your brother is over, do you hear me? Because if something happened to you again while you were here working, I'd never forgive myself." Her stern voice softened toward the end, her caring and concern tangible.

Lora didn't have the energy to argue, so she managed

a half smile and attempted to lighten the moment. "Are you firing me?"

"I will if I have to." Sydney was completely serious, and Lora knew her friend would have no qualms about following through on the threat. "Whatever it takes to make you start thinking about yourself, and your safety, for a change. I have to get back to tending the bar before things get totally out of control, but as of right now, you're on a forced vacation, which has been long overdue, anyway. This place is off-limits for you. Got it?"

Sydney's curt attitude left no room for negotiation over the issue, which was what made her such a good boss and businesswoman, Lora knew. "Yes, ma'am," she murmured.

Clearly surprised by Lora's too-easy assent, Sydney stared at her for a long moment. When Lora said nothing more, her friend spun around and left the office, closing the door behind her.

"She's right, Lora," Joel said once Sydney was gone and they were alone, backing her friend's decision 100 percent. "I don't like you working here at the bar, either. Now you know why. It makes you too much of a target, whether you like it or not. And it makes my job of protecting you difficult as hell."

She burrowed deeper into the warmth of his jacket. "You did just fine tonight," she said gratefully.

His lips flattened into a grim line. "Yeah, well, getting to you through that thick mob of people wasn't an easy task."

At the time, Lora had felt as though she'd been trying to wade her way through quicksand, so she could only imagine how hard it had been for Joel to reach her so quickly. Which brought up a curious question. "How did you know that I wasn't okay?"

"Because it's my job to know." It was that simple and straightforward for him. "I've done nothing but watch you the past few weeks, and I've pretty much learned and memorized every one of your facial expressions and what they mean. Trust me, it was easy to recognize the fear in your eyes, and when I realized that something was wrong, I couldn't get to you fast enough."

Suddenly, she saw the entire situation from Joel's perspective, and just how difficult she'd made things for him by insisting she keep working at the bar. Was it really fair to put him through that tension, and to expect him to be responsible for her safety when she was the one putting herself in the direct line of danger?

The answer came easily. *No.* She'd been so stubborn and adamant about not letting Zach's predicament affect her life, but the truth was, it *did* affect her life, on many levels. And until Zach was out of trouble, she needed to be careful, and far more cautious.

But how long would it take for this nightmare to end? Another week? Another month? Longer? The thought made her stomach roil, and brought on a healthy dose of resentment and anger.

She was so tired of constantly looking over her shoulder, waiting and wondering when the next attack would happen. That slight bit of fear was always in the back of her mind, and she hated when it played tricks on her psyche, as it had tonight.

"I want this to be done and over with," she said, frustration getting the best of her. "The more time that passes without knowing where Zach is or what's going on, the more anxious I'm getting." Tonight proved it.

"You and me both." Joel leaned against the office desk behind him and crossed his arms over his chest. "But until we know something, or we hear from Zach, laying low until this is over is the best thing to do."

And Lora knew that the waiting, and the not knowing, was going to be the hardest part of all.

LATER that same night, Joel waited until Lora was asleep to make some phone calls and put an idea into action. After tonight's incident at the bar, and witnessing Lora's distress over Zach, he'd decided that something had to give.

And that something was Zach.

It was time for him to stop being so self-centered and be the kind of man the Marine Corps had trained him to be. A man who was honest and loyal and unafraid to face the consequences of his actions. A man willing to step forward, admit mistakes, and make amends. Considering what Zach had put Lora through, he owed it to his sister to make that attempt.

But even as Joel set up the clandestine meeting and contacted his partners at ESS for a conference call to line up a way out for Zach if he had the guts to take it, he wondered if Zach was capable of that kind of redemption. Or was Zach so far gone that he'd completely and irrevocably turn his back on the one person who loved him unconditionally, despite the fact that he'd sold her soul to a loan shark?

In a few days, Joel would find out exactly what kind of man Zach was. And so would Lora.

Once he'd finalized his plans and secured his partners' approval, Joel called Zach's cell phone, which went straight to voice mail. No big surprise there. Joel left him a detailed message, and had no problem playing on the other man's conscience, or using guilt to get the results he wanted. At this point, Joel was willing to do whatever it took to make this reunion happen and offer Zach the chance to get the help he needed for his addictions.

The big question was, would Zach show up? Or would he take the coward's way out?

Only time would tell.

Thirteen

THE man could cook, and that was a huge point in Daniel Barnett's favor.

Meeting his gaze from across the dining room table at his house, Sydney leaned back in her chair and placed a hand over her full stomach. She couldn't believe how much she'd eaten, but the pecan-crusted chicken he'd made, along with buttered green beans and roasted herb potatoes, had tasted so good she hadn't been able to resist a second helping. The man kept impressing her at every turn, with his culinary talents, his dedication to his job as a math teacher, and the seemingly effortless way he resisted her sexual advances.

Yeah, especially that, damn him.

Even last night, after she'd closed down the bar following the Halloween bash and the rest of her employees had gone home once the place had been cleaned up, she'd hoped to have a little fun with Daniel and their pirate costumes. Except he hadn't cooperated. Oh, she'd managed to get some hot and heavy kissing out of him, more than enough to get her juices flowing, but that had been it, despite her protests for more.

So when he'd invited her over to his place for dinner the next night, she saw it as the perfect opportunity to fire things up between them, in a way he wouldn't be able to refuse.

Seduction and satisfaction were the goals for the evening.

"I take it you liked dinner," Daniel said, his tone pleased. "Either that, or you were being very polite with that second helping."

She laughed, enjoying his humor. Heck, she enjoyed most everything about this man. More than she ever would have anticipated. "Trust me, I don't waste good calories on second helpings unless it's truly worth it. Dinner was delicious. In fact, if I didn't see you prepare and cook the meal yourself, I would have thought you had it catered in," she teased.

"Not a chance." His caramel-hued eyes were warm and mellow with his own brand of playful flirtation. "I told you I love to cook."

She reached out and strummed her fingers along the stem of her wineglass. "Yeah, well, when a guy says that, it usually means boxed potatoes, canned green beans, and chicken on the barbeque, not this gourmet meal you put together."

He winked at her. "Stick with me, sweetheart. I have all kinds of tricks and talents up my sleeve."

Oh, she was hoping so.

The term of endearment he'd used, along with the husky tone of his voice, sent a pleasant warmth seeping through her that had nothing to do with the expensive wine he'd served with dinner, and everything to do with *him*. "So, what's for dessert?"

"Something chocolate and absolutely decadent."

"Mmmm." She let the sexy sound roll up from her throat in a tantalizing purr. "I like the sound of that."

He laughed deeply. "Does everything have a sexual connotation to you?"

"Only when I'm being sexually deprived," she retorted sassily.

"Awww, poor baby," he crooned, though his eyes held a devilish glint that told her he wasn't at all sorry for his part in her sexual frustration.

Releasing a breathy sigh that snagged his attention from across the table, she lifted her hand to her throat, then slowly skimmed her fingers along the opening of her blouse, and was immensely gratified when his gaze followed the trail. Her nipples puckered from her own caress, and he noticed that, too.

She wet her bottom lip with her tongue, a long, slow swipe that would hopefully add to his own arousal and discomfort. Or, at the very least, make him think of all the wicked ways she could use her mouth and tongue on him. She was more than willing, given the chance.

His eyes grew dark with desire, and she smiled. "You know, there is more than one way to put me out of my misery." Hot, hard sex was her preference, but hell, at this point she was willing to settle for some heavy petting and a few orgasms.

"What, and spoil all this fun between us?" he drawled. He thought for a moment, then shook his dark blond head. "Nahhh. I'm having way too good a time just the way things are."

He stood to clear the dining table, and she joined him,

deciding that the man was the female equivalent of a cock-tease. Amazing. She was used to dealing with aggressive men who couldn't keep their hands off her—until they got what they wanted. And here she was offering it up to Daniel, and he'd just politely turned her down. Again.

She placed her utensils on her plate, and when she reached for his dishes across the table, he stopped her.

"I'll do this," he insisted, taking the plate from her grasp. "Why don't you go ahead and make yourself comfortable in the living room while I clean up the kitchen real quick. I'll be there in five minutes, max."

"Okay."

She headed into the adjoining room, and instead of sitting down on one of the brown suede couches to wait for Daniel, she strolled over to the wall unit and casually scanned the items on the shelves. There were hardbound books, most of which were spy novels, along with the James Bond novels he'd told her he collected. There was a nice stereo unit and a stack of CDs ranging from jazz and country to rock, but what drew her attention the most was the array of framed photographs he had on display.

She smiled at the picture of Daniel with two little boys dressed in baseball uniforms—his nephews, she guessed. And it was obvious by Daniel's affectionate grin and the way he was ruffling one of the boys' hair just how much he adored them. Another photograph showed him with another man his age, who possessed similar looks but appeared very serious in nature, and a beautiful woman caught laughing at something just as the snapshot had been taken. Siblings, she assumed, and moved on to another picture of an older couple who were clearly his parents.

His father was handsome, with distinguished features and the appearance of a well-established doctor. In the photo, his mother was wearing a designer summer outfit, and the left hand resting on her husband's chest sported a huge rock of a diamond and an equally impressive diamond tennis bracelet. They were standing next to a new Jaguar, with a two-story estate home in the background, confirming what she'd known all along—that despite the modest salary he no doubt made as a high school math teacher, Daniel Barnett came from a wealthy, upscale, and classy family.

And Sydney was as far from classy as a woman could get. Considering her checkered past and the things she'd done to get to where she was today, there was no way that she'd ever fit in Daniel's world beyond a brief fling. And he had to know that, too.

It was time to be assertive, to heat things up, get the deed done, and move on before she got any more involved with Daniel than she already was.

With that plan in mind, she scanned the stack of CDs and chose The Fray and slipped it into the disc player. Seconds later a rhythmic beat filled the room, along with the lead singer's smooth, rich vocals. Closing her eyes, she inhaled a deep, relaxing breath and let the seductive cadence invade her mind, her body, and her senses.

"Nice choice of music," Daniel said from behind her.

Blinking her eyes back open, she turned around and gave him a slow, sultry smile. "I'm glad you approve."

He sat down on the couch and met her gaze from across the room. "You never did say how everything went with Cassie and the Halloween party she went to last night."

It figured that the man wanted to talk. He probably assumed they'd spend the next hour or so just chit-chatting, as they had on all their dates thus far. But not tonight. She'd allow him this one last question, and then it was show time.

"She was in bed asleep when I got home from work,"

she said, and started a slow dance by herself, with her hips swaying oh-so-subtly, and her gauzy skirt swirling enticingly around her legs as she gradually strutted her way closer to him. Her fingers toyed with the top button on her blouse, which effectively drew his gaze to her chest. "This morning she told me she had a good time and everything seemed fine, so I'm going to have to trust that it was."

He shifted on the couch and forced his gaze back up to hers. "See, letting her go to the party wasn't so bad now, was it?"

"No," she admitted, and unfastened the first button on her blouse, then another, as he watched. Truth be told, she was starting to relax with Cassie, just a little. Her daughter had given her no reason to worry or suspect that anything had happened outside of normal teenager fun, and she was trying to take Daniel's advice and not go searching for trouble unless there was a good reason to.

Another button slipped open, giving Daniel a quick, seductive peek at the pink and white lace push-up bra she'd bought a few days ago, specifically for an occasion like this. The cups were lined, and while the bra showcased the full mounds of her breasts to their best advantage, it also left enough covered to stir his imagination.

His gaze darkened as she neared, his irises like rich, burnished gold. "Sydney . . . what are you doing?" His tone was an interesting combination of curiosity and desire.

"I'm taking things between us to the next level." With a practiced roll of her shoulders, her blouse slid down her arms and off. She let it fall to the floor, then brushed her fingers across the bare skin of her abdomen until they reached the elastic waistband of her skirt.

"It's called a *relationship*," he said huskily.

She smiled and inched the skirt over the swell of her hips, teasing him from only a short distance away. "It's called an *affair*," she corrected him, because it was important to her that he not read more into this connection between them than there was. A relationship implied that there was a commitment and emotional ties involved, and that kind of intimacy wasn't something she was willing to give to any man.

Sex, however, was all about mutual pleasure, and that was her goal tonight. "Ever had a personal, private lap dance?" she asked.

He shook his head, still looking way too calm and casual, when most guys at this point would be panting for more. "Can't say I have, but I suppose there's a first time for everything."

She laughed, liking the idea that she was going to be Daniel's first. With a slight shimmy of her hips, her skirt fluttered to the plush carpet around her feet, leaving her scantily clad in the bra and a pair of matching lace bikini panties designed to make a man drop to his knees and beg. Then there were the high heels she was wearing, which did great things for her legs as she picked up the beat of the music once again.

His breathing, she noticed, had deepened, and he didn't look so casual and relaxed anymore. She held back a triumphant smile and lifted her hands to her hair, striking a very provocative pose. "You know, when I was a stripper, private lap dances were where I'd make all my big money."

Daniel did his absolute best not to outwardly react to that comment, because he knew that's exactly what Sydney was angling for. To shock him. To force him to see and think of her as nothing more than a physical object, as other men did. And admitting to what she perceived as a scandalous past was the equivalent of her putting up barriers around her emotions, and in her mind made this *thing* between them all about the physical.

Physically, yeah, he was aching and hard just watching her dance in front of him like temptation and sin, wearing nothing more than a skimpy bra, barely there underwear, and fuck-me high-heeled shoes.

"I didn't know you were a stripper," he managed evenly, though he honestly didn't care about her past. It was the present, and the possibility of a future with this woman who intrigued him at every turn, that mattered to him.

"Yep, and a damn good one at that." To prove her point, she turned her back on him, and with her legs straight and slightly parted, she bent over and stroked her ankle and calf, giving him an up-close and personal view of her smooth, perfect ass. The position was uninhibitedly sexual, as was the coquettish way she glanced over her shoulder at him. "I had clients come in nightly and ask specifically for me."

He barely had enough blood left in his brain to think coherently. At least with his *bigger* head. He swallowed thickly and did his best to remain impassive about this brazen display of hers, when he knew she was doing everything in her feminine power to get a reaction out of him. "You were that good, huh?"

From her upside-down position, her gaze narrowed ever-so-slightly, then a sly smile curved her lips and she straightened, facing him again. She sauntered purposefully toward him, all long supple limbs, lush undulating curves, and a soft sexy tumble of auburn waves bouncing gently around her shoulders.

Her tongue darted out to moisten her lips, and she touched her fingers to the upper swell of one breast, then traced the inviting curve of flesh to the deep V of her cleavage. "I think I ought to show you just how good I was," she said, a challenge in her low, naughty tone.

Okay, maybe he'd pushed her too far, goaded her just

a little too much, but there was no backing down now. Her giving him a lap dance was going to test every bit of his control, possibly shatter his restraint when it came to her, but he had a feeling that's exactly what she was striving for. Which made him all the more determined to make sure this scenario didn't escalate into a physical encounter, not when she still wanted to believe that he was in this purely for sex.

Give it your best shot, sweetheart. "Please, do," he murmured, daring her right back.

She nudged his legs apart and moved in between, just as the song playing ended and another began. This one had a slower beat, and Sydney's body eased right into the rhythm, hips circling, thighs shifting, as her hands touched and caressed all that smooth, bare skin. Eyes closed, her head fell back on a sigh, and her torso undulated, slowly, sinuously—just inches away from his face. So close he could smell her soft, feminine scent, could see the tight points of her nipples straining against the fabric of her bra.

The urge to reach out and stroke her, everywhere, was strong, and he closed his hands into tight fists at his sides. Undoubtedly, this woman was every man's erotic fantasy, and that was part of the problem—he didn't want to be just another man in a long line of them, and he refused to fit into the same low class as all the other jerks in her life. He wanted more than Sydney's body, more than one night of hot sex, and convincing her of that, and his honest intentions, meant suffering through this sexual game of hers.

With an amazingly lithe move, she turned around in the V of his legs. Bracing her hands on his knees, she lowered herself toward his lap, slowly, leisurely sliding her bottom along his thighs and barely grazing the thick, aching erection pressing insistently against the fly of his pants.

His heart pumped hard and fast in his chest, and it was all he could do to hold in a deep groan as she added to the torture, grinding down gently against his crotch and adopting a forward and backward motion with her hips that increased the burning need surging through his veins. Just when he thought he wasn't going to last, she laid back against him in a full body slide. Her head came to rest on his shoulder, which gave him an unobstructed view of her gorgeous breasts, the slope of her belly, her slightly spread legs.

She took advantage of that fact, arousing herself, and him, with her hands. Her fingers dipped into her bra and cupped her breasts, while her thumbs played with the rigid tips. She moaned, wriggled against him, and glided her flattened palms over her stomach . . . then lower, between her thighs.

Lust and desire inflamed him, threatening to unravel not only his control, but all his good intentions, too. Knowing that watching her pleasure herself was going to be his undoing, which she no doubt was hoping for, he glanced away and started going through complicated math problems in his head . . . anything to keep his cool, which wasn't an easy feat when he had a near-naked woman rubbing up against him.

The music continued, and she rolled over gracefully so that she was sitting on his thighs facing him, with her knees straddling his hips. Placing her hands on his shoulders, she scooted closer until his constrained cock was nestled right up against the damp panel of her panties.

And still, he didn't so much as touch her.

He looked up into her face, which was flushed a warm shade of pink that continued down her throat and spread out toward her breasts. Her lashes were at half-mast, but he could still see the soft, sultry green of her eyes, glittering with heat and hunger. Her lips were parted, her breathing as ragged as his own. Oh, yeah, she was thoroughly aroused, and the sudden determination that flashed in her gaze didn't bode well for him at all.

Neither did the wicked smile curling her lips as she smoothed her hands down over his chest. He was wearing a shirt, but her palms burned him straight through the thin material to his skin. Her slender fingers found his taut nipples, and she scraped over them with her thumbnails, eliciting a deep groan from him that seemed to give her a tremendous amount of satisfaction. Lower those sweet hands of hers traveled, until they reached the waistband of his trousers.

Before she could unfasten the first snap, he grabbed her wrists and pulled her hands away. No words were spoken as they stared at one another in a silent battle of wills, but then again, none were needed. He was so damned close to surrendering, and she knew it, too. Sex was her goal, and there was no doubt in his mind, or hers, that if she released his shaft and touched him, stroked him, he'd be unable to resist her.

With her hands still firmly in his grasp and held out to the side—he wasn't about to let her go—she used other feminine wiles to get what she was after. She rolled her hips into him, subtly, skillfully, simulating the erotic grind and thrust of sex, and no amount of algebra equations could stop his body from responding. His own need kicked up a notch, pushing him closer to the point of no return.

She dropped her head back, arched into him, and moaned. Her breasts were inches away from his mouth, so tempting, and it took every ounce of willpower he possessed not to lean forward and taste her with his tongue . . . to push her down onto the couch and give her exactly what she was begging for.

Another rhythmic stroke against him and she gasped
out loud. Again, and she shivered and started to come with
a soft, unraveling moan, and he knew he was done for, too.
Hell, he might as well have been deep inside her for the
way she was gripping his hips with her thighs and pressing hard and deep against his cock. His own release grew
and intensified, until he couldn't hold back any longer.
With a rough groan, he climaxed right along with her.

After one last final shudder, she collapsed against him,
her face buried into the curve of his neck and her warm,
damp breath caressing his skin. He let go of her wrists and
fully expected her to move off his lap and gloat at the fact
that she'd managed to get a reaction out of him after all.

Instead, she cuddled into his chest, surprising the hell
out of him with that unguarded gesture. But he took advantage of the moment and gently caressed his hands
along her back, relishing just how soft this woman was,
inside and out. That despite how rough and tough she
tried to act, she did have a tender, vulnerable side. He
smiled as he skimmed his fingers down her spine, and
just when he thought that maybe, just maybe, he'd made
some headway with Sydney, he felt a distinct change in
her body language, as if she'd realized just how much
she'd revealed by her relaxation.

Slowly, she pushed away from him, going from being
sated and content and enjoying an intimate embrace to all
sass and bravado.

Still sitting astride his thighs, she glanced down at his
lap, then met his gaze with a satisfied, cocky grin. "Well,
that settles that."

He arched a brow and played along, because it was
clear she wasn't ready for a deep, emotional conversation
about the two of them. "What settles what?"

She ran a playful finger down the middle of his chest.

"I was beginning to think you were impotent, but that's clearly not the case."

Unable to help himself, he laughed. "Everything functions quite well, as you can see."

"Then why are you making this so difficult? We could be having hot sex right now." A slight edge of frustration vibrated in her voice, then was replaced with sarcasm. "Oh, wait, don't tell me you're one of those guys who won't have sex until they're married?"

"Hell, no." She was trying to push all his buttons, possibly angling for an argument to make sure she distanced herself from him, but he wasn't going to let her take the easy way out. "But I'm not into casual sex, either, Sydney."

And that, too, seemed to piss her off—probably because she understood the underlying connotation to his comment. That sex, for him, was an intimate and personal connection. And for her, it was all about the physical.

Her lips pursed in annoyance. "Okay, whatever," she said, dismissing the entire incident with a wave of her hand. Then she moved off his lap and started picking her clothes up off the floor. "I think it's time I went home."

Knowing that they'd just reached a stalemate, he didn't try and convince her to stay. He could only hope that in time she'd come to realize that he wasn't like all the other men had she dated. That he wanted more than just her body or a quick lay.

He wanted *all* of her, and he'd accept nothing less.

LORA had no idea where Joel was taking her, and quite frankly, she didn't care. He'd told her they were heading out of the city for a few days, so she could rest, relax, and regroup. She appreciated the gesture more than he could know. After falling apart at The Electric Blue during the Halloween bash, she was forced to admit that she was more on edge about Zach, and the situation he'd gotten her into, than she'd realized.

On the long drive, they made a stop for lunch at a roadside café, then again at a market to pick up groceries, which made Lora all the more curious to find out where they were going. But with each mile that passed between Chicago and their destination, she felt the tension that had been crowding in her chest ease. She decided that if Joel was making the effort to take her out of the city and away from the stress in her life, then she was going to enjoy the time away with him.

She cast a glance at the man sitting beside her in the car, his gaze pointed straight ahead as he drove. Now if only she could get Joel to lighten up, they could have a great time together. But so far, he was still in "bodyguard" mode—way too serious and all business.

A while later, they passed a sign that read KANKAKEE RIVER STATE PARK, and Joel turned off the highway and began following a paved road that eventually gave way to a dirt path. All around them, they were surrounded by large overhanging trees, lush foliage, and craggy rocks. She caught sight of a large creek with flowing crystalline water just as they rounded a bend and Joel brought the vehicle to a stop in front of a cabin that was located, quite literally, out in the middle of nowhere. There was nothing around them but nature for miles, which made the place a perfect hideaway retreat.

"Whose place is this?" she asked curiously. She'd been expecting a hotel somewhere, possibly a small town off the beaten path, but not a secluded cabin. "Does it belong to one of your connections?" she teased.

"You could say that." He cut the engine, withdrew the keys from the ignition, and briefly met her gaze. "The cabin belongs to my aunt and uncle." He opened the door and headed around to the back of the SUV to unload their stuff.

She followed from the other side. It was early afternoon, and while the sun was shining overhead, the air was crisp and cool, making it an absolutely gorgeous day. "It was nice of them to let you use it."

Lifting the rear door, he reached in and handed her a few of the grocery bags filled with food and other necessities, then grabbed the small duffel bags they'd packed. "They'd never tell their favorite nephew no."

She laughed in amusement. "Don't you have two brothers?"

A hint of humor lurked in his bright blue gaze as they walked side by side toward the front steps leading to the cabin's porch. "Yeah, but *I'm* their favorite."

"Well, you can certainly be charming when you put your mind to it."

Though, admittedly, it had been way too long since she'd seen that playful side to Joel's personality, and she missed his sexy smiles and flirtatious comments, along with the comfortable, amicable companionship they'd shared. Then there was the undeniable awareness still simmering between them that he was doing his absolute best to avoid and resist.

He unlocked the front door and held it open for her to enter before him. She walked inside, admiring the small but cozy interior of the cabin. From the living room, she could see two individual bedrooms, a bathroom, and a compact dining area that adjoined the kitchen.

With her arms loaded with groceries, she headed toward the kitchen while Joel dropped their duffel bags off in separate bedrooms, making it very clear that this was a *working* vacation for him, and he wasn't about to allow any distractions—meaning her and their attraction—to change that.

She sighed as she shelved the canned goods they'd bought, then put away the items that needed to remain cold in the small refrigerator, which had been left on. There were already frozen meals in the freezer for them to use, and plenty of other dry foods stored in tightly covered containers.

Hearing Joel's footsteps behind her, she turned around and found him standing in the doorway, looking as gorgeous as ever dressed in all black. She tried not to think about that amazing body of his beneath those tight, dark clothes, and instead focused on what they could have for their next meal.

She grabbed a canned item, glanced at the label, and decided to keep things simple and easy. "How does navy bean soup and grilled cheese sandwiches sound for dinner?"

"Great." He absently pushed his fingers through his too-long hair and rubbed at the back of his neck with his hand, looking much too tense and on edge. "If you wouldn't mind putting away the rest of the groceries, then opening up the place to let it air out, I'm going outside to get some things done. I also need to chop some fresh wood for the fireplace. A storm is supposed to be moving in by this evening, so I want to be prepared."

Considering the nice weather she'd just encountered, she had to wonder if he was using an approaching storm as an excuse to keep his distance from her. "Sure. No problem."

Once he was gone and she heard the screen door shut behind him, Lora finished putting the rest of the groceries away, then opened the windows in the cabin to let fresh air in, as he'd requested. Before long, she heard the steady *thump, thump, thump* of Joel splitting logs outside, and found herself drawn to one of the windows overlooking the side yard where he was working.

He was wearing a T-shirt, but she could still see the play of corded muscles in his shoulders, back, and arms as he swung the axe downward, then lifted it once again to repeat the motion. Too easily, she recalled how all that firm skin felt beneath her hands, along with the heat and strength inherent in every inch of his body as he moved over her, inside her.

She felt the familiar stir of longing when it came to this man, the tug and pull of desire deep inside of her. A cool breeze blew outside, ruffling his long, inky hair around his head and at the back of his neck. Those thick strands, she knew, were silky soft as they sifted through her fingers, and it had been much too long since she'd enjoyed that luxury. Much too long since Joel had allowed her to get close enough to touch him in any way that might be construed as too intimate.

Sighing, she leaned against the window frame and continued watching Joel as he worked. Since the night of the first attack and his claim that their attraction was too much of a distraction when it came to keeping her safe, she'd been waiting patiently for him to come around, to realize that what they shared was more than a one-night stand. To admit that he was far more distracted, not to mention grumpy, denying what was so obviously between them.

But it was more than just sex that she wanted from Joel, and that was a huge revelation for her. When she'd first met him, she'd been so adamant about not allowing herself to get involved with any man—especially after enduring such a tumultuous and emotionally devastating relationship with Brent. Work and making a life for herself had been her main focus, along with her future goal of opening her own spa one day soon.

But she'd never expected to meet a man like Joel. He was everything that Brent hadn't been. Joel Wilde was the real deal, a man with honor and integrity. And unlike her own father, then Brent, and even her brother, Zach, Joel was a man she could depend on, trust, and give her whole heart to, if he'd let her. And despite his own warning that he didn't have any room in his life for commitments and promises, and that he didn't do love, she believed differently.

Maybe it was time to make him realize that for himself.

She watched him turn and toss a split log onto a growing pile. Just when he would have picked up another slab of wood and continued chopping, he caught sight of her standing at the window, staring at him. Their gazes met, and even with the distance separating them she could see the wanting and carnal hunger in his expression.

Her heart raced with that same blatant need. She didn't move or look away, refusing to be the one to put an end to that intimate moment between them. Not surprisingly, he was the first to break the visual contact.

She decided that she was done waiting for Joel to come around. She'd agreed to let him do his job without distractions while they were in the city, but they were a world away from Chicago and the threat lingering there like a black cloud. Out here, with just the two of them at a secluded, isolated cabin, there was no need for Joel's protection. No need to look over her shoulder for danger, or rely on him to keep her safe.

Now, they were just two people who were very attracted to one another, and as far as she was concerned, all bets were off.

Fourteen

IT didn't take Joel long to realize his monumental mistake in bringing Lora to the remote, secluded cabin. When he'd originally come up with the idea of setting up a meeting between Lora and Zach, his only thought was to make sure it happened somewhere far outside the city limits, at a place that was difficult to find or trace without specific directions, and his aunt and uncle's cabin provided the kind of isolation he'd been looking for.

He'd deliberately withheld the real reason why he'd brought Lora there. She believed it was for the sole purpose of taking a minivacation and being able to rest and relax without worrying about being attacked again. But the truth was, he didn't want Lora to be disappointed if her brother didn't show up, and considering Zach's track record thus far, Joel knew that was a huge possibility.

Tomorrow would tell.

In the meantime, Joel hadn't accounted for the fact that he'd be spending a whole lot of time alone with Lora.

Or that she'd view this time away together as an opportunity to rekindle their affair and put the *heat* back into their relationship. He should have known better, though. Despite the fact that he'd kept his hands, and other body parts, to himself since the night of her attack, the sexual tension between them had only increased to the point that one simple touch from her had the ability to short-circuit his brain and make him forget everything except the aching need to be deep inside her again.

Shit.

Annoyed at himself, and the entire situation, he slammed the axe down hard, splintering the last log into two clean pieces. He wished he had a truckload of wood left to chop to keep him busy well into the night, but no such luck. This was it. His current diversion was done, and sooner or later he was going to have to face Lora again.

After carrying a night's worth of wood into the cabin and stacking the rest in the corner of the porch to keep it dry, he came up with an idea to stave off the inevitable. Since they still had a few good hours of daylight left, he figured they might as well take advantage of the outdoors, and the decent weather while it lasted.

He found Lora inside, reclining comfortably on the sofa and reading a book that someone had left behind at the cabin. When she heard him walk into the living room, she glanced up from the novel and gave him a too-knowing smile.

"Are you all done outside?" she asked, much too innocently.

"Yeah." She was so on to him, and he felt the beginnings of an answering grin tug at the corners of his mouth. "I was thinking of going for a walk along one of those trails before it gets too dark. Care to join me?"

She snapped the book shut, sat up, and started putting

her sneakers back on. "I would love to go on a walk with you, as long as you're willing to protect me from any snakes or wild creatures we might happen to run into. I so am *not* a Girl Scout."

He nodded. "I think I can manage that."

"Oh, and it would be really nice if you'd just relax around me, instead of being so serious and formal all the time. Especially out here." Standing, she approached him, her eyes turning a soft shade of green as she searched his expression. "And just so you know, I *really* miss the old Joel. You know, that fun, irresistible guy who took me to a coffee shop for our first date and used to flirt and tease. I know he's in there somewhere, and it would be nice if you could try and coax him back out, maybe just a little bit?"

He exhaled a deep breath and scrubbed a hand along the slight stubble on his jaw, forcing himself to relax and just enjoy being with her. He could at least manage that. "Okay. I'll do my best."

"Great." A sweet, enthusiastic grin lit up her entire face. "Can we take one of the trails along the creek?"

"Sure."

They left the cabin and headed toward a dirt path located near the flowing stream. All around them were a profusion of wildflowers, large trees, and foliage giving way to beautiful autumn colors. A cool, light breeze blew, and in the distance Joel could see clouds moving in, but there was still enough daylight left for them to kill a good hour or two outdoors.

As they strolled along the winding trail, he pointed out the poison oak fringing the edge of the trail so she didn't come into contact with the toxic plant. And luckily for Lora, the only wildlife they happened upon were a few twittering birds nestled in the tree branches overhead, and a raccoon ambling his way across their path. The furry animal stopped to look at them with beady eyes as they approached, then hustled off into the brush, which made Lora laugh.

A good half an hour passed, filled with easy, companionable conversation before they reached an open clearing with rugged rock formations and a clear view of the creek. They headed in that direction, and came to a stop at the edge of the stream, where the water was shallow and slow moving.

Ever since Joel had spoken with Mia on the phone, he'd been meaning to bring up the gallery opening event with Lora and figured this was as good a time as any. "I've been wanting to ask you something," he said casually.

She glanced at him and tipped her head curiously. "Sure. What's up?"

He couldn't help but notice that her skin was flushed as a result of their hike, and her hair was tousled around her face from the breeze—reminding him too much of the sensual, disheveled way she looked after sex. He swallowed hard, looked away, and rerouted his thoughts back to the more mundane.

"My sister, Mia, is having a gallery opening this coming weekend and I'd like to know if you'd come with me." He squatted down, picked up a small, smooth rock, and ran his thumb over the flat surface. "I don't know if this situation with Zach will be over by then, so I wanted to be sure you wouldn't mind going."

"I'd love to go with you." She lowered herself down to his level and dipped the tips of her fingers into the clear, cold water. "She does the stained glass designs, right?"

"Yep. Except her designs have a bit of a twist to them."

He wanted to make sure Lora knew that right up front, so she wouldn't be shocked when she realized how risqué some of Mia's designs actually were. "She creates these beautiful designs that seem ordinary at first glance, but when you look a little deeper, the design actually transforms into something else entirely."

"Such as?"

He pitched the small rock in his hand out into the creek and watched as it skipped three times along the surface before sinking. "Well, she made this gorgeous stained glass pattern of a peacock, and the colors were absolutely striking. But the longer you look at the original design, the more your eyes start focusing in on another image within the picture, of a couple in an intimate or erotic embrace."

She grinned in amazement. "How clever."

He agreed, and was incredibly proud of his sister and her accomplishments. "The concept is very remarkable, and she did well enough selling her pieces on consignment that she was able to open up her own gallery."

"I'm definitely intrigued, and I can't wait to see her designs." Cupping her hand, she brought a drink of the creek's fresh, clean water up to her lips to quench her thirst. After a few long sips, she glanced at him, her gaze turning inquisitive. "You and your sister . . . you're close, aren't you?"

He picked up another stone and weighed it in the palm of his hand. "What makes you say that?"

She stood back up, dried her damp palms down the front of her jeans, and shrugged. "It's the way you talk about her. There's a certain affection in your voice when you mention her name. It's enough to make me think you two have a special brother-sister kind of relationship."

And one she apparently envied, he thought, hearing

the wistful emotion in her soft voice. "I think out of all my siblings, Mia and I relate to each other the best. We have similar personalities, so we understand one another pretty well."

"You're so lucky to have that connection with her." Smiling, she brushed back the strands of hair tickling her cheek from the breeze. "You mentioned that your mother passed away when you were a kid. What happened?"

He tossed the stone out onto the water with a snap of his wrist, giving it just the right spin for it to bounce five times before dropping to the bottom of the stream. His first instinct was to brush off her too-personal question, or attempt to change the topic of conversation, but something stopped him from doing either.

He couldn't remember ever talking to anyone about that part of his life—when his mother had died and the aftermath of that loss. Not with his family, and never with any of the women who'd tried to get him to open up about that part of his past, and that usually happened when they felt the end to their affair was near. He knew it was their way of trying to establish an emotional bond between them, yet it always had the opposite effect and made him feel stifled, and that only made it that much easier for him to break up with them.

But he knew that wasn't Lora's intent at all. She'd suffered similarly with the death of her parents, and he knew her well enough now to realize her question was based more on that mutual experience than any attempt to manipulate his emotions. Her interest was as real and genuine as she was, and that made it easy for him to tell her what she wanted to know. For the first time he wanted to open up to someone, and that was because it was *her*.

"My mother died in a car accident when she was visiting

her sister in Florida," he said, and straightened to his full height. "It was a strange thing, actually, because one day she was leaving to go on a short vacation, and then we never saw her again. It was almost like she just never came back."

"I'm so sorry. That couldn't have been easy," she said softly. "But at least you had the love and support of the rest of your family to get you through that rough time in your life."

Which she'd never had. No, this amazing woman had taken on most of the burden of her parents' deaths, and then had gone on to raise her brother on her own. Alone. Without any help from anyone.

"Like with you, everything changed dramatically after my mother passed away," he said, thinking back to that difficult time. "My father was devastated, of course, and my sister, who was only five at the time, had a hard time adjusting to the fact that her mother was never coming back. My two older brothers, Scott and Alex, did their best to handle a lot of the family responsibilities, and their main focus was Mia, and making sure she was taken care of while my father was at work."

"And what about you, Joel?"

He wasn't certain what she was getting at, and he didn't want to assume anything. "What about me?"

"It sounds like everybody in your family was busy taking care of everyone and everything else." Her comment was insightful and incredibly intuitive. "Where did that leave you?"

"As the odd man out?" he said automatically, and even though his voice was tinged with a teasing quality, too late he realized just how much he'd revealed.

Her gaze met and held his, delving past those tough, guarded layers of his. "Yeah, I think it did," she said gently, and without an ounce of humor to indicate she was joking, too.

He inhaled a deep breath until he felt his lungs burn. How in the hell did this woman see past the surface and understand him so well?

"And, I also think that's a good part of the reason why you try and keep everyone around you at an emotional distance," she said, adding to her psychoanalysis. "You felt disconnected from the family, didn't you? Like you didn't have a purpose like your dad and older brothers did."

She wasn't even close enough to physically touch him, yet he felt as though she'd reached deep down into his soul and released years' worth of personal anguish. With anyone else, he would have told them they were overthinking things, but he found that he couldn't deny the truth, not with Lora.

"Yeah, I guess I did feel that way." He stared across the creek at nothing in particular, then shifted his gaze to the dark gray clouds heading their way. "So, while my brothers were busy being responsible and dependable and trying to take care of Mia, who became quite rebellious after my mother's death, I did my own thing. Eventually both Scott and Alex went to work for my father's tile company, and when I graduated from high school and realized that there wasn't a place for me in the family business, I decided to join the Marines."

"They told you that they didn't need or want you in the business?" she asked incredulously.

"Well, no, not exactly." He didn't care for the harsh way her question sounded and tried to explain. "But everything was running just fine without me, even after my father remarried and retired from the company."

"So, you just *assumed* they didn't need you," she said, more a statement than a question.

He frowned. "I didn't belong there, Lora."

Even as he said the words, there was something about her comment that made him wonder if maybe, in his youth, he'd judged the situation too hastily, based on emotion rather than logic or reason. That maybe he'd come to his own conclusions without giving his father or brothers the opportunity to make him a part of the business. Or worse, they'd thought he wasn't interested, which now, looking back from an adult perspective, would have been understandable considering he'd always distanced himself from that part of the family.

It was a disconcerting notion, yet he'd never regretted his choice to join the Marines. He'd loved the sense of adventure the military had to offer, and even the risks and rush of adrenaline that came with the missions he'd been sent on. He knew he never would have been happy sitting at a desk pushing paperwork. For him, the tile business would have been too mundane, and he would have eventually felt too stifled.

It was difficult to admit that his lifestyle had been one of his own making, and not a result of anything his brothers and father had, or hadn't, done. That he'd cut himself off on many levels and especially with relationships, because it was so much easier than putting himself out there emotionally.

The sound of thunder rumbled in the distance, a distinct warning of the impending storm approaching them. Lora shivered at the sudden drop in temperature and rubbed her hands along her arms. "We should probably head back to the cabin before we get stuck in the rain."

He'd been so caught up in their conversation that he'd

forgotten about the storm moving in. But it was definitely on its way, and judging by the dark, bloated clouds drifting overhead, it was going to be one helluva downpour. "I think you're right."

They were at least half an hour away from the cabin, and despite their brisk walk along the open trail, the rain quickly caught up to them. Large, fat drops fell, sporadically at first, then gradually increasing into a heavy deluge that soaked right through their hair and clothes.

With a low curse, Joel grabbed Lora's hand and picked up the pace to a light jog, searching for some kind of shelter until the worst of the rain passed. Behind him, Lora laughed at their comical situation, and he found himself chuckling, too—and had to admit the playful moment felt incredibly good.

Finding a large tree with long, thick branches and dense leaves, he pulled her in that direction, until they were finally beneath the large overhead canopy that protected them from the worst of the storm. She was still laughing as she gathered her hair over her shoulder and wrung out the dripping wet strands.

Her white blouse was thoroughly saturated—and now completely transparent, enabling him to see her bra and the tight, rosy-hued nipples straining against her top. The wet fabric clung to her luscious breasts and outlined her curves like a second skin, and all he could think about was how soft and lush the rest of her body was beneath those clothes.

Amusement shimmered in her gaze, and a drop of water dripped from her cute little nose. "Wow, what's with me getting caught out in the rain?"

At least this time there was no threat to her life. But still, Joel felt bad for getting them in this predicament and for not paying more attention to the changing weather.

"I'm sorry. We should have headed back sooner." And now, with the rain falling hard and steady around them, they'd be much safer waiting beneath the shelter of the tree for the worst of the storm to pass.

"I don't mind." She grinned at him, her lips wet from the rain. So pink and sweet and kissable. "If I'm going to be stuck out in a downpour, I can't think of anyone else I'd rather be stranded with."

As much as the situation lent itself to seduction, that wasn't what her comment was all about. No, she meant it in a way that implied that she truly appreciated being with him, no matter the cause or the reason.

God, she was unique, and so far removed from the usual high-maintenance women he dated who'd be pissed as all hell that the rain not only ruined their hair and clothes, but that they were stuck out in the wilderness indefinitely. But Lora didn't seem to mind at all. In fact, she appeared to be enjoying herself and the spontaneous change of plans.

Standing next to him, she shivered, obviously chilled. Gooseflesh rose on her skin, and she crossed her arms over her chest. "I should have worn a jacket."

Another roll of thunder shook the gray skies, and a brisk gust added to the cold, wet conditions. Feeling responsible for their situation, and knowing the best way for them to keep warm was sharing body heat, he grabbed Lora's arm and gently pulled her to him.

"Come here, so I can keep you warm," he murmured, even as she came willingly into his embrace.

Knowing they had a while to wait before the storm eased up enough for them to head back to the cabin, he moved back a few feet until he was resting against the thick tree trunk. Spreading his legs, he pulled her closer, so that his thighs bracketed hers and protected her from the wind. She snuggled into him, her hips aligned much too intimately to his, and her full breasts and tight nipples pressed against his chest in a way that had his lower body instinctively growing hard. Her head rested on his shoulder, and her face was nestled into his neck. Her nose was chilled from the elements, but her lips, when they touched his skin, were warm and soft—her breath equally so.

Arousal shot through his system like a drug he'd been craving for too long. He closed his eyes and inhaled a deep, steady breath that did absolutely nothing to curb the insistent ache in his groin.

She kissed his neck and somehow, when he hadn't been paying attention, had managed to pull his shirt from the waistband of his jeans and slip her hands beneath the damp material. Flattening her palms on his abdomen, she slowly stroked them up toward his chest, then back down again.

"How can your body be so warm when it's so cold out?" she asked as her lips nuzzled just below his jawline.

"I've always been warm-blooded," he said gruffly, and swallowed back a low groan when her thumbs grazed his taut nipples. "The cold weather doesn't bother me much."

She shifted closer, if that were even possible, and he felt her mouth curve into a smile as it traveled up to the shell of his ear. "Well, you definitely feel good to me, and I'm thinking there are plenty of other ways to generate some heat. Lots of rubbing and friction is always good for that. And kissing and making out, too."

This time he did groan, because the images that slipped into his mind were just too damn erotic to ignore. She was tempting him, driving him beyond crazy with lust and desire. And he had no doubt that was exactly her intent.

"We're out here, all alone, and there's absolutely nothing you need to protect me from while we're at the cabin," she whispered in his ear as she skimmed her hands around his waist and up the slope of his spine. "There's no reason why we should deny what we both want."

He wanted to argue the point, tell her that there was more at stake than him keeping her safe from Zach's thugs. There were already too many emotions swirling between them, bonding them in ways he'd never felt with any other woman, and that in itself was reason enough for him to keep his distance. Making love with Lora again just wasn't a smart idea, because the biggest threat of all was the possibility of breaking her heart when this job ended and he walked away.

And him walking away *would* happen. It always did.

Besides, realistically, there was no place for Lora in his life, a life that consisted of a hectic schedule and workload with Elite, and spontaneous assignments that were sometimes dangerous and other times grueling. She deserved a stable relationship with a man she could depend on on a regular, daily basis—not someone who'd never endured a long-term commitment with a woman and didn't know if he was even capable of doing so.

But Lora didn't give him the chance to say any of what he was thinking. Her mouth found his and she kissed him softly, nibbled on his lower lip, then teased the seam with her tongue, seeking an invitation to explore deeper territory. He'd spent *days* ignoring this sizzling attraction between them in order to stay focused on protecting her, and it had been fairly easy to do since she'd been on her best behavior, but how was he supposed to resist such a blatant sensual assault when she tasted so damn good, and felt even better in his arms?

A kiss . . . he could handle a kiss, he told himself, and it didn't have to lead to anything sexual. But what he wanted from her wasn't a sweet, playful kiss. No, if this was all he was going to allow himself to take from her, then he wanted something hotter, harder, and a whole lot more carnal and satisfying.

Bringing a hand up from where it had been secured around her waist, he sank his fingers into the damp strands at the nape of her neck, tipped her head to the side, and slanted his lips across hers in a demanding, open-mouth kiss. With a soft moan, she gave him exactly what he craved, responding like a woman equally starved for him. Their tongues mated eagerly, dueled aggressively and with a driving, passionate force that matched the storm raging inside them, and around them.

And just like every other time they'd touched or kissed, it wasn't nearly enough.

The tips of Lora's fingers stroked their way down his back, kneading skin and muscle with those talented hands of hers until she reached the waistband of his jeans. She strummed those same graceful fingers around to his bare abdomen, then slid them lower as she traced the stiff length of his erection confined beneath his button fly, making him swell and harden even more. Boldly, she cupped his cock in her palm and squeezed gently, but firmly enough to make him groan deep in his throat and forget everything but the hot need surging through him.

Then her mouth was gone, and before he had the chance to clear his head and realize what she meant to do, she was already down on her knees in front of him on the wet grass, her hands working to unbutton his jeans. Just as she hooked her fingers into the waistband of his pants and underwear and started to pull them down, he came to his senses and grasped her wrists, stopping her just inches from baring his aching shaft to her gaze, her touch, her incredibly sensual mouth.

"*Lora*," he rasped, the one word infused with a warning for her to stop.

She tipped her head back and looked up at him, her eyes dark with temptation and a little bit of sin. "I want to do this for you. *Please*. I'm not asking for anything in return."

He instinctively knew she wasn't referring to a reciprocal act of sex, but rather, she was making it very clear that she didn't expect any of those sentimental promises from him. She just wanted him, right now. Here. For the moment and while it lasted.

"Please, Joel. *Let me,*" she whispered huskily, another soft plea, and this time when she leaned forward and kissed his stomach, then nipped at his flesh with her teeth, he let himself surrender to the undeniable need she inspired in him.

He released her wrists, and with a slow, gradually tug at his jeans and boxer briefs, he was freed. Seconds later, she had him in her hand, her fingers wrapped tight around his thick length. She caressed his shaft slowly, leisurely, drawing out the process and teasing him unmercifully— because she could. She glided her thumb over the sensitive crown, followed that with a lazy lick of her tongue, and smiled oh-so-seductively when he shuddered from the exquisite pleasure.

Just when he thought he couldn't take any more of her sensual torment, she parted her lips and replaced the snug grip of her hand with the liquid heat of her mouth. Exchanged the stroke of her fingers for the silken swirl of her tongue and the suctioning pull of her lips dragging up and down his cock.

The white-hot sensation jolting through him was so intense, he could barely remember to breathe.

With a ragged groan, his head fell back against the trunk of the tree. Closing his eyes, he reached down and slid a hand into her hair, gently grabbing a fistful of the damp strands as she took him slow and deep, using her tongue in incredibly erotic ways that inflamed him even more. Over and over, she drove him to the brink, only to ease back just enough to keep him right on the edge of what promised to be an explosive orgasm. She lingered and played, as if there was no other place she'd rather be than right there with him. As if they had all the time in the world and she wanted to make this last.

Her mouth enveloped him once more, all the way to the base of his erection, then back up again, sucking him harder, faster, deeper, and finally giving him the release she'd been withholding.

The coil of desire wound tighter and tighter inside him, and before long there was no holding back the pulsing orgasm rising to the surface. He tried to issue a raspy warning, tried to pull free from her mouth, but instead of stopping, she merely moaned and slid his shaft all the way back inside, until he reached the back of her throat. He felt her swallow around the head of his cock, and the tight, squeezing sensation was his final undoing.

A haze of pure ecstasy fogged his mind, and he uttered a curse as he fell headlong into a blissful kind of oblivion and his entire body clenched in the hottest, most intense and all-consuming release he'd ever had. It trapped the breath in his chest, nearly stopped his racing heart, and left him completely spent and shaken.

While he struggled to recover—he was eternally grateful for the support of the tree behind him—Lora rose back to her feet to face him. With his gaze still a bit unfocused, he took her in. She looked beautiful, triumphant. Her cheeks were flushed an alluring shade of pink and her green eyes glittered mischievously.

He couldn't ever remember a climax that had left him so dizzy and weak. So thoroughly wasted, yet undeniably sated. He opened his mouth to speak, but all he could manage was a hoarse, "Jesus, Lora."

She laughed, way too pleased with herself. "I guess it was good for you?"

Grinning, he pulled up his pants and buttoned them up, his movements still unsteady. "Good is just too tame a word to describe that out of body experience. I was thinking more along the lines of phenomenal."

He glanced around them, beyond the shelter of the tree, and realized that while it was still raining, the initial torrent had passed. But that didn't mean they were in the clear, and they needed to take advantage of the slight lull while it lasted.

"We really need to get back to the cabin before the storm and winds kick up again, or else we could be out here for hours, and it's starting to get dark." They had about half an hour of any kind of daylight left, and it was getting gloomier by the minute. "I say we make a run for it."

"You're on." He hadn't meant it as a challenge, but she took it as one and upped the ante. "How about first one there gets the shower, and the other one has to make dinner?"

"Sure," he agreed, and pushed away from the tree. "Just so you know, I like my grilled cheese sandwiches nice and brown and crisp."

She laughed at him, and his presumptuousness. "I don't know why you're telling me this, since I'll be taking a long, hot shower while *you're* making dinner."

She took off down the trail, and he started after her, figuring he'd give Lora a bit of a lead before passing her up. Except he didn't take into account how sluggish his legs would be after that draining, and amazing, climax she'd given him, and that closing the distance between them would take too much effort and work when he was actually enjoying the view from behind.

As he followed after her and kept her in his sight, he came to the decision that he wanted this one last night with Lora, no matter how selfish it might be. Because tomorrow, when and if Zach showed up, everything was bound to change, and not necessarily for the better.

Fifteen

LORA walked out of the bathroom after a hot shower and into the living room, where Joel had built a fire in the hearth to help warm up the front rooms. With her hair towel-dried and wearing her favorite pair of pink cotton sweats and fuzzy socks, she headed into the kitchen, where Joel was pouring their steaming soup into bowls. She felt her stomach grumble hungrily, and realized that she was starved.

"That hot shower sure did feel good," she teased as she came up beside Joel at the counter. While he'd taken the time to change into dry clothes, his hair was still damp from getting caught out in the rain.

"I wouldn't know," he said, and cast her an envious look, one that lingered longer than necessary on her lips before lifting to her eyes. "I was busy slaving over the stove making your dinner."

She laughed and picked up the plates with their grilled cheese sandwiches to take to the small dining table.

"Now don't be a poor sport. We made a deal, and you lost. I can't help it if you're a slowpoke."

He carried over the bowls of soup, along with spoons, and set them down on the placemats. "Yeah, well, I didn't expect you to cheat."

"What?" Her tone rose incredulously, and she arched a brow his way as she sat down. "How do you figure that I *cheated*?"

He took the seat next to her. "You took complete advantage of a weakened man." His gaze took on a sexy glimmer, and the corners of his mouth twitched with a playful smile, leaving no doubt in her mind as to what, exactly, had worn him out.

Remembering her bold and shameless seduction, a warm blush swept over her cheeks. "You know, I'm finding it very hard to feel sorry for you."

"It was worth a shot," he said with a wink, and started in on his navy bean soup.

Taking a bite of her grilled cheese sandwich, she shook her head and pondered the change in Joel, from his earlier brooding attitude while chopping wood, back to the fun, flirtatious guy she'd originally met. He might have willingly surrendered to her lip service out in the middle of the storm, but she'd truly expected him to revert right back to being serious and all business once they returned to the cabin. She'd even anticipated the possibility of him expressing regrets for giving in to his desires, or launching into one of those "we shouldn't have" kind of speeches, and she was grateful that he hadn't done any of those things—because if he had, she would have had to just deck him.

It must have been the fact that they were a world away from civilization and the threat they'd left behind, she mused as they continued to eat their dinner in compan-

ionable silence. Or maybe the carefree, laid-back atmosphere out there lent itself to a more relaxed attitude and
mind-set. Whatever the reason, she was going to enjoy
Joel's fun, cheerful mood while it lasted.

Finished with their meal, Joel leaned back in his chair
and let out a contented sigh. "That was pretty darn good,
if I do say so myself."

She rolled her eyes and decided to humor him. "Yeah,
you're a regular Chef Boyardee."

He gave a low, lazy chuckle. "Yeah, that's about as
good as it gets when you're a bachelor."

They stood up, and when he started stacking their
plates and bowls to help clear the table, she brushed his
hands away. "You go take your shower," she said, and carried the dirty dishes to the sink. "Since you made dinner,
the least I can do is clean up the kitchen."

"You won't get an argument out of me." He put his
hands up and took a step back. "Cleaning up the mess is
the worst part."

He headed out of the kitchen, and she filled the sink
with hot, soapy water so she could hand wash the dishes,
along with the pot and frying pan Joel had used. She
wiped down the table and counters, and put away the left-
over butter and cheese into the refrigerator, then went
into the living room.

Joel must have thrown a few more logs on the grate,
because the fire was burning bigger and brighter than it
had been when she'd come out of the bathroom earlier.
She was grateful for the warmth, considering how windy,
cold, and wet it was outside.

While Joel took his shower, Lora searched the bedroom closets for extra blankets and brought them, and pillows, out to the living room. She spread out a soft, cushy
comforter in front of the fireplace, and added the pillows

and covers. Then she went to her duffel bag and retrieved a last-minute item she'd decided to bring along right before they'd left her apartment.

When Joel came out of the shower and saw the makeshift bed she'd created on the floor, he glanced at her curiously. "What's all this?"

He was wearing a pair of black sweatpants, and nothing else. His magnificent chest was bare, the golden glow from the fire giving his skin a smooth, tawny hue, and she couldn't wait to get her hands on him. "I have a surprise for you."

"Really?" He came around the couch to where she was sitting on the comforter, his interest definitely piqued. "What is it?"

"Well, I packed some of my massage oil . . . you know, just in case." Suddenly uncertain of how he'd react to the offer, and wanting to make sure he knew it came with no sexual strings attached, she added in a light, teasing tone, "I thought I'd give you a nice, relaxing massage, free of charge, of course. I wouldn't want to lose my touch as a masseuse while I'm not working." She reached for the bottle that she'd put on the coffee table, which contained a rich, orange-scented body oil.

"I doubt that would ever happen." He came down to his knees in front of her and plucked the bottle from her hand. "How about *I* give *you* a massage?"

The offer surprised her. "It's okay, I don't mind being the giver."

"Neither do I." His coaxing grin was difficult to resist. "Besides, when was the last time someone did something for you?"

She thought about that for a moment, and came up blank. "Honestly, I can't remember."

"That's because you're too busy taking care of everyone

around you, or worrying about them," he said so softly, so knowingly, she felt her throat tighten with emotion.

"I always have," she said with a nonchalant shrug. "That's just the way it's always been for me." Not necessarily by choice, but circumstances had dictated that she be responsible for so many things at such an early age, and those traits had spilled over into other areas of her life. Now it was just a part of who she was, and something that came naturally and without thought.

"But what about you, Lora?" He tipped his head, his gaze gentle, yet direct. "Who takes care of you?"

"Me." The reply was automatic, and truthful. "Don't worry, I've gotten used to it being that way."

He reached out and caressed his thumb along her jaw, and she turned her head ever so slightly into his warm, soothing touch. "Let me take care of you tonight," he said huskily. "Just relax and let me make you feel good, okay?"

The offer, coming from him, was inviting. So was the thought of having his large, strong hands massaging her tired and overworked body. For her, denying herself that kind of pleasure when she knew her time with Joel was so limited just wasn't an option. "Okay."

Since she hadn't put on a bra after her shower, she turned and pulled off her top, then started to lay down on the covers so he could work on her back, but he gently grabbed her arm before she could stretch out on her stomach.

"Not yet," he said with a shake of his head, even as the beginning of a wicked smile curved his sensual lips. "You need to ditch your sweatpants and panties, too, since this is going to be a full body massage."

Heat shot straight to her belly, the anticipation of what he intended to do blending into an exquisite shiver. He was the one setting the tone for the evening, and she decided to follow his lead . . . and willingly go wherever he decided to take her.

She stripped off the rest of her clothes as he'd requested. The fire cascading over her naked body was nice and warm, but his gaze as it raked down the length of her was even hotter. Her breasts swelled beneath his stare, her nipples tightened to the point of near pain, and a liquid kind of heat settled between her thighs.

"*Now* you can lie down," he said, his voice sounding like pure gravel.

She settled facedown on the comforter and bent her arms comfortably above her head. She heard him shifting and moving beside her, then he straddled her hips with his legs and rested his very bare butt on hers, startling her with that surprise. As he leaned over her and poured some of the oil down the line of her back, she could feel the heavy heat of his sex against the crease of her buttocks, and her desire for him increased.

She closed her eyes, inhaled a deep breath, and let it out real slow, trying her best to ignore the erotic thoughts drifting through her mind. Another long, slow breath as she forced herself to relax and enjoy this rare experience, which wasn't an easy feat when she was at the mercy of the naked, aroused man gently pinning her down to the soft covers.

But then those incredible hands of his, slick with the fragrant oil, began massaging her tense shoulders, and the only thing she could think of was how good it felt having someone pamper her for a change. He kneaded the knots in her neck, which she hadn't even realized were there before now, and rubbed the flat of his palm along the tendons bisecting her spine, applying just the right amount of pressure to make her groan with the sheer pleasure of it. He used his thumbs to dig into taut muscles, and soothed those sore spots with the firm stroke of his fingers.

He worked the entire expanse of her back, from the nape of her neck all the way down to where he was sitting astride her hips, then back up. Over and over and over again, until her body went slack and she felt absolutely, positively boneless.

He moved off of her, and seconds later he started in on her legs, his oiled hands giving the same luxurious treatment to her calves and thighs. Rubbing, kneading, stroking tendons and muscles. His palms glided higher with each sensual caress, until his fingers brushed along the crease that lead to softer, hotter flesh.

She instinctively parted her legs so he could touch her intimately and appease the sweet ache he'd created, and he didn't hesitate to drag his fingers along her cleft, then push them deep, deep inside her body. She moaned and arched her hips, then gasped when he bent over her from behind and touched his mouth to the base of her spine where she was ultrasensitive. His hot breath fanned her skin, and the evening stubble on his jaw rasped across her lower back, right before he licked her there. The combination of sensations was so erotic and arousing she felt the answering pull all the way to the very core of her, causing her inner muscles to clench around his fingers.

He groaned, too, and did it again, a slow, lazy sweep of his tongue right where her vertebrae ended and the curve of her butt began, while his fingers pumped rhythmically inside her. She curled her hands into the covers and writhed restlessly beneath him as he drew out the decadent, breathtaking pleasure, until she was panting and straining and begging with the need to embrace the orgasm he was dangling just out of her reach.

Ignoring her soft pleas for release, he continued to build the tension within her to dizzying heights as he trailed hot, moist, nibbling kisses over her bottom, which only added to the frenzy of sensations. Just when she thought she couldn't take his teasing any longer, he finally, *blessedly*, sent her spiraling over the edge.

With a soft, breathy cry, she came in long, hard shudders that seemed to go on forever. The orgasm was so strong and intense, her body seemed to become one endless wave of euphoric bliss that left her physically spent. Between the massage and the orgasm, she felt as though she'd died and gone to heaven.

Sated and content, she could have drifted right off to sleep, but Joel gently rolled her over onto her back. Hooking his fingers behind her knees, he bent her legs, spread them apart, then knelt in between. She glanced up at him with an appreciative smile, and one look at his fierce expression, along with his tight jaw and those hot blue eyes of his, was enough to warn her that he wasn't nearly close to being done with her. Lower, between his thighs and beside that warrior's scar marring his leg, his erection jutted out, thick and hard, the tip seeping with slick moisture and need.

And that quickly, that easily, her desire for him returned like a bright internal flame.

He brought his hands down next to her hips and lowered his head to scatter more of those soft, tantalizing kisses along her belly, her ribs, to her swollen, aching breasts. She threaded her fingers through his silky hair and sighed as he laved a nipple with his tongue, then drew the tip deep into his mouth and sucked while one of his hands cupped her other breast and his fingers plucked at the stiff peak.

His lips continued their upward journey. His tongue slid across her collarbone, and he nibbled at her shoulder before nudging her chin up so he could nuzzle and kiss her neck. He lowered his hips to hers, and she felt the head of his shaft glide along her soft, dewy flesh, then prod the entrance to her body, just enough to tease, but not fully penetrate—though Lord knew she was wet and ready for him.

His chest brushed across her tender nipples as he settled more fully over her, his arms now braced next to her shoulders. The feel of his naked body on hers was a warm, extravagant luxury she knew she'd never tire of.

His mouth reached her ear, and he was breathing hard and fast. "God, I want you," he said raggedly, as if she were something he'd never be able to have. Not in the way that mattered the most.

But she knew she already belonged to him—her body, her heart, and even the very depths of her soul. But he had to believe it for himself, and accept that he was worthy of her unconditional love. That was something she couldn't force upon him.

Tangling the strands of his hair in her fingers, she lifted his head, so he had no choice but to look down at her and see the sincerity in her eyes, and the emotion she knew was reflected in her expression. "Then take me, Joel," she whispered. "I'm all yours."

His eyes darkened as he oh-so-slowly pushed into her, his gaze turning hot and hungry as her body closed tightly around him and welcomed him home. He pulled out of her slightly, dragging the length of his cock against her still-sensitive flesh, as if he was trying to make the moment, and the pleasure, last. He groaned and shuddered, then thrust back in, harder and farther this time, causing her to gasp and arch beneath him.

And still, it wasn't enough. She wrapped her legs around the back of his thighs, urging him deeper. "I want more," she murmured huskily. "I want *all* of you." She wanted everything he had to give—physically and emotionally.

With a low, rumbling growl that reverberated in his chest, he sank back in, withdrew, and surged back again, his strokes lengthening, his pumping hips gaining momentum. Gone were any attempts to hold back. Instead, his thrusts grew urgent and demanding, and wholly primal. Friction, pressure, and heat fused together in a tangle of sensation, until her entire being focused on the connection of their bodies and the impatient, restless need swelling within her.

Framing her face in his hands, he seized her mouth with his, as if his next breath of air could only come from her. His kiss was deep and rapacious, and laced with a desperate kind of passion she could taste with every sweep of his tongue and feel in the aggressive way he possessed her body.

She slid her arms around him, flattened her hands on the firm, flexing muscles along his back, and held on for the tumultuous ride. Before long, he dragged his mouth from hers and stared down at her, his breathing shallow as his climax washed over him, through him. Eyes closed, he tossed his head back and arched against her hips, a helpless groan ripping from his throat as his flesh pulsed hot and hard inside of her and he shuddered from the sheer force of his orgasm.

When it was over, he collapsed on top of her, burying his face in the crook of her neck while his heart beat strong and steady against her breast. She closed her eyes and held him close, reveling in the quiet, tender moment while it lasted, and how perfect and right it felt being with Joel, in every way.

No other man, not even Brent, had ever made her feel this completeness, this kind of intimate connection, this stunning contentment. And when her time with Joel was over and they both went their separate ways, she instinctively knew that no man ever would again.

JOEL watched as another damp lock of black hair fell to the kitchen floor as Lora gave him a long overdue haircut. After he'd casually mentioned the need for a trim, she'd offered to do it for him. She'd found a pair of sharp-bladed shears in a kitchen drawer, told him to sit in one of the wooden chairs, and promptly went to work wetting his hair, then started cutting the length and bulk around his head.

A haircut definitely helped to pass the time. Joel had woken up extra early that morning, and had showered and changed and made coffee before Lora had roused herself from the makeshift bed on the floor a few hours later. He had no idea when or if Zach would show up, but according to the message Joel had left for him, today was the day he'd set up for the meeting between brother and sister.

It had been a waiting game all day long, made more frustrating as each hour passed without a sign of Zach. And now, considering it was past six in the evening, chances were that Lora's brother was going to be a no-show.

But despite Zach's lack of consideration when it came to his sister, it was clear to Joel that Lora had needed this time away. She was so much more relaxed than she'd been a few days ago, and for that reason alone Joel was glad he'd made the decision to take her out of the city, away from the stress of her everyday life and the threat still lurking out there somewhere.

Because it had been cold, windy, and rainy throughout the day, they'd stayed indoors, but Lora didn't seem to mind the seclusion. She'd finished reading the book she'd started yesterday, then took a nap, and when she woke up feeling rested and refreshed, she'd challenged him to a game of Scrabble she'd found in the hall closet.

He learned that Lora was very competitive and loved a good challenge. They laughed and teased one another over some of the ridiculous words they each spelled, and she argued passionately when she believed he'd made up a word just to use up his tiles and gain points. Usually, she was right.

It was so easy to be with Lora. So comfortable and enjoyable on so many levels. And even though the awareness had simmered between them all afternoon, she didn't pursue it, didn't try and seduce him again. It was as if she'd known that last night would be the final time that they would make love, and accepted, even respected, that knowledge.

Another thick strand dropped onto his thigh, and he grimaced, wondering if he was going to have any hair left by the time she was done. "I feel like I'm back in boot camp getting my first military cut."

Her fingers combed through the top of his hair, then snipped off another portion. "Your hair was this long when you joined the Marines?"

"Yeah, pretty much." She came around to stand in front of him, between his spread legs, to finish trimming the sides, and it was all he could do not to groan at the sight of her breasts beneath her long-sleeved thermal top, just inches away from his face. "It's just one of those things I don't hassle with until I absolutely have to."

"You were definitely overdue for a haircut," she said with a smile in her voice. "And I promise not to cut it too short so you don't feel like a jarhead again, but it already looks and feels much better."

He grinned at the use of the military term. "Did you learn that lingo from Zach?"

She ruffled her fingers through his hair and sent more snipped strands falling all around him before cutting the longer length off the back. "Yeah. Right after he joined the Marines, when he was calling me on a regular basis before he shipped off to Iraq, he'd always complain about the haircut the barbers gave him, and how he looked like a jarhead."

"Yeah, that's about right," Joel said with a chuckle. "It's far from a stylish haircut, but I have to tell you, when it's one hundred and twenty plus degrees in Iraq during the summer, the less hair you have on your head, the better."

She was quiet for a few moments as she continued to cut and trim, then finally she spoke. "Joel, there's something I've been wanting to ask you."

"Okay." Her comment made him both curious and wary, because he had no idea what was currently going through that mind of hers.

She came around to stand in front of him again and met his gaze, the scissors no longer active. "The night I was attacked behind the bar, after Zach called and you told me about what he'd done with the insurance policy and how he'd asked you to watch over me, you said something about owing Zach for saving your life in Iraq. What did you mean by that?"

He easily recalled that conversation, and he also remembered how he'd brushed off her question in favor of more important issues. Then there had been the time at the spa when she'd been giving him a massage and had asked about the scar on his leg, and he'd managed to evade the discussion there, too, and Zach's involvement in that harrowing mission.

"Why does it matter?" he asked gruffly.

"I guess I'm trying to understand my brother a little better," she said with a small shrug of her shoulder. Obviously done cutting his hair, she set the scissors on the table, then went to the sink to wash her hands. "I mean, if he's capable of saving someone's life, there has to be some good in him, right?"

Ah, hell. As much as he wanted to wring Zach's neck for what he'd done to his own sister, and how he was wasting his own life with booze and gambling, Joel could see that Lora was desperate to believe something positive about her brother. To know that, despite putting her life in jeopardy for his addictions, Zach wasn't as damaged and corrupt as he seemed.

As Joel stared into her soft green eyes, he decided that it was time to tell her about what had happened, to let her know just what kind of man her brother had been, and still had the potential to be. Joel firmly believed that with the right kind of help for his addictions, and with the support of his sister and friends, Zach had the ability to recover and be a man with integrity, honor, and a sense of right and wrong.

"He was a real good man, Lora," he said, his voice ringing with sincerity and truth. "And he was someone I was damn glad to have watching my back during our missions." Especially the one that nearly cost Joel his life.

"Tell me about it," she beckoned once again. She leaned against the counter behind her and crossed her arms over her chest. "Please?"

He exhaled a deep breath. Joel hated taking that particular trip down memory lane, but for Lora, he knew he'd do it.

With effort, he mentally put himself back into the situation and tried to make the story as succinct as possible.

"Our unit was on its way to conduct a search operation of a known terrorist ring in east Baghdad, when a young boy came running up to our Humvee, which is never a good sign. Three of us jumped off the vehicle, including Zach, to assess the situation and make sure the boy wasn't part of some suicide attack, and that's when one of the Humvees in our convoy was hit by a roadside bomb, followed by an immediate insurgent attack."

He combed his fingers through his now-short hair, which felt odd after months of dealing with the unruly, longer strands. "I was hit by a piece of shrapnel in my right thigh, and just as the guys in our unit started taking cover where they could, another blast went off nearby, which knocked me on my ass."

He watched as Lora pressed her fingers to her lips, her eyes wide with horror as she listened to his grim tale. "I ended up in the middle of the road, without any protection, and gunfire going off all around me from both sides," he went on as his hand absently rubbed at the scar on his thigh. "I tried to get up, but my right leg kept giving out on me, and just when I thought I was as good as dead, your brother ran back out into the open fire while the other guys covered him the best they could. He grabbed me beneath my arms and literally dragged me back behind one of the Humvees, where it was relatively safe."

"God, Joel," she said, her voice hoarse. "I had no idea."

Most American civilians never knew just how bad things could get in Iraq, that every day for someone in the military could be their last. Joel never took for granted just how lucky he'd been to get out of that attack alive.

"It could have been much worse," he said, eternally grateful that his injury hadn't been life threatening. "I could have died like a few of our men did that day, and I have Zach to thank for saving me."

There was no doubt in Joel's mind that if it hadn't been for Zach's bravery and spontaneous rescue, he would have ended up dead, too. But it was that tight band-of-brothers mentality that always had men risking their own lives to save others. Like one of their guys who'd thrown himself on top of a grenade during another mission in order to save the entire group. That had been just one of the many devastating acts of courage that Joel and Zach and his other comrades had witnessed.

"That's the kind of shit we dealt with, Lora, every single day," he continued. "And it takes men who are loyal and you trust implicitly to watch your back and do the unthinkable if necessary. And that's exactly the kind of marine and man that Zach was."

"Then what happened to him, Joel?" Lora's gaze was troubled and her voice trembled when she spoke. "What made that loyal, trustworthy man turn on his own sister?"

Her emotional turmoil was nearly tangible, and it twisted in Joel's gut like a knife. In no way did Joel absolve Zach of the mistakes he'd made over the past few years with his life and his sister's, but he tried to make Lora understand things from a military perspective.

"The war, and seeing the worst in humanity, and witnessing some of your good friends dying right in front of your eyes without any way of saving them, is enough to send anyone off the deep end." Leaning forward in his chair, he clasped his hands between his spread knees, his gaze holding hers as he recounted some of those situations. "There's a lot of pain involved in war, and not all of it is physical. There's guilt and remorse and regrets for things you should have done, or things you could have done differently. There's the anguish of watching innocent people die, and the guilt of not being able to save an

eighteen-year-old fresh out of boot camp who ends up getting killed in the line of fire."

Joel did his best not to dwell on the ugly, tragic aspects
of the war, but he knew that some people had a tougher
time blending back into civilian life than others. Like
Zach. Then there were the too-high statistics of depression and suicide that had afflicted some veterans of Iraq
once they returned home from the war.

"Everyone deals with that emotional upheaval in different ways," he said, and he highly suspected that Zach
had some form of combat post-traumatic stress disorder,
which would explain a lot of his choices and actions since
being discharged. "For Zach, maybe it's the gambling
and drinking that keeps him from remembering and dealing with what he'd endured. But those addictions are just
a temporary Band-Aid for the real underlying issues and
problems he needs to work through."

She nodded in understanding, then tipped her head, regarding him in a speculative way that made him uncomfortable. "What about you, Joel? How did you deal with
what you saw on a daily basis?"

He shrugged more casually than he felt inside. "Honestly, I try not to think about it, or the split-second
choices I had to make." Because if he did, he knew he'd
go insane and allow the mental distress of some of those
wrong choices to lead him down a destructive path, much
in the way that Zach had gone. "I keep myself busy with
work and don't dwell on the past." And he kept himself
emotionally detached, too. That part came easily. Since
his mother's death, other than Mia, he'd managed to distance himself from everyone else in his life.

Not wanting to dredge up any more of the past or his
time in the war, he stood up and brushed off the bigger

chunks of hair still on his shirt and jeans. "If you'll get me the broom and dustpan from that closet over there, I'll get this mess cleaned up."

Knowing by his change of subject that they were done talking about Zach and the war, she pushed away from the counter and went to retrieve the items he'd requested. "Why don't you go take a shower, and I'll do this."

Considering that the smaller hairs that had found their way down his shirt in the back were starting to make him itchy, he wasn't about to argue. "Thanks."

She stopped him before he could exit the kitchen. "Joel?"

He turned back around. "Yeah?"

"Thank you for telling me," she said softly, gratefully. "I really hope that it's not too late to get Zach the help he needs after this is over. I don't want him living like this anymore."

He felt the same way. "You and me both."

As Joel headed to the bathroom, he knew that someone had to save Zach from himself before the other man got himself killed. And that person would most likely be Joel.

Sixteen

A new storm raged outside the cabin, loud and windy and with enough furor to rattle the windows in the front rooms. The fire in the hearth had died down enough for Joel to feel confident that it was okay to retire for the night, as Lora had a few hours ago, yet he was still out in the living room, his mind, and his thoughts, working overtime.

He'd spent too much time mulling over what Lora had said about getting Zach the help he needed to overcome his problems, and Joel couldn't agree more with her. He, along with Ben, Kevin, and Jon, were ready and willing to give Zach the financial and emotional support he needed to dig himself out of his predicament, but accepting that help would require a huge dedication from Zach, personally and professionally.

But if Zach couldn't do something as simple as show up for a planned meeting, Joel had to wonder if he had it in him to make the commitment it would take to change his life for the better.

Knowing he needed to get some sleep so they could head back to the city in the morning, Joel got up from the couch and started toward the second empty bedroom down the hall. But instead of passing by the room that Lora was sleeping in, which would have been the smart thing to do, he came to a stop in the doorway and stared at her sleeping form on the bed.

She was curled up on her side, bundled beneath the covers. A flash of lightning from outside illuminated Lora's serene features, followed by a loud crash of thunder that shook the cabin and ultimately startled her awake. She came up on one elbow, her hair tumbling around her shoulders, and looked his way.

"Hey," she said, her voice soft and slightly raspy. "What are you still doing up?"

"I'm on my way to bed right now. I was just checking in on you." He forced himself to back away from the doorway before he gave into the temptation to crawl into bed beside her. "Good night."

"Wait," she called out before he could make his escape. Then she tossed back the covers, scooted over to make room for him, and patted the open spot next to her. "Why don't you sleep here with me? There's no sense in messing up two beds," she teased.

He chuckled, but there wasn't a hint of seduction in her voice. She wasn't looking for sex, and honestly, neither was he. He just wanted to be close to her, to take what he could while it lasted, no matter how selfish that might be.

More thunder clapped over the cabin, accompanied by a torrent of rain pounding on the roof, and Lora winced at the sound. "The storm is making me jumpy, and it sure would be nice not to sleep alone."

She didn't have to convince him any more than that, so accepting her invitation was incredibly easy to do. He moved into the room, and after stripping down to his boxer briefs, he slid into bed beside her. She turned to face the opposite way, and he cuddled up behind her, wrapped an arm around her waist, and aligned the front of his body to her backside.

His head rested next to hers on the pillow, and he breathed in the floral scent lingering in her hair. Interestingly enough, he discovered that she was wearing one of his T-shirts, and not her own pajamas. It appeared that she wanted to be equally close to him, in any way she could.

Smiling, he closed his eyes, and it didn't take him long to fall into a deep, exhausted sleep.

JOEL jolted awake, uncertain as to what, exactly, had disturbed him. Eyes open, he remained still, in the same position that he'd fallen asleep in, snuggled up behind Lora, and listened for any unusual sounds. Outside, the storm was still in full force, but it wasn't the distant rumble of thunder or the pattering of rain against the window that had roused him. It had been something else entirely.

Then he heard it again, the rattling of the front door-knob, this time followed by a *whoosh* of wind as the door opened, then closed behind someone.

The noise woke Lora with a start, and she looked over her shoulder at him. "What was that?" she whispered.

Joel had a feeling that their guest had finally arrived. Considering they were out in the middle of nowhere, and he'd only given one person the directions to the cabin, he'd deliberately left the front door unlocked, in the slim hope that Zach would eventually show up. Even though it was after two in the morning, it appeared that Lora's brother had finally found his way to the place.

Still, Joel wasn't ready to reunite brother and sister just yet, not until he confirmed that what he'd heard truly was Zach. "Just stay put," Joel murmured quietly. "I'm going to check it out."

He rolled out of bed onto his bare feet and stepped out of the bedroom into the adjoining living room just as the person switched on the lamp by the couch, illuminating none other than Zach Marshall. Joel came to a stop, and from across the room Zach stared at him, his chin lifting belligerently, as if anticipating some kind of confrontation or fight.

Joel's first thought was that his friend looked like shit. His dark brown hair was even longer than Joel's had been before his haircut, and the strands were dripping wet and tangled around his head, as if he hadn't bothered to run a comb through his hair in days. His eyes were dull, and what he could see of Zach's unshaven face was pale and gaunt.

Then there was the black-and-blue bruise ringing his swollen left eye and the fresh cut on his lower lip that added to his unkempt appearance. He was wearing a long, tan trenchlike coat that was old, worn, and dirty, and Joel noticed that his left hand and arm were plastered in a cast. He knew without asking that Zach's broken arm and his messed-up face were courtesy of the men who wanted their money from him. And those were just the injuries that he could see. There was no telling what else they'd done to Zach over the past few weeks.

As much as Joel hated seeing Zach in such a sorry

state, he wasn't about to pity the other man, or let him off easy. No, Zach had gotten himself into this predicament, and he needed to pull his head out of his ass before he completely flushed his life down the toilet.

"Nice of you to make it," Joel said dryly.

The corner of Zach's lip curled into a bitter smile. "Better late than never, huh, Wilde Man?"

Before Joel could reply to that snide remark, Lora came out of the bedroom behind him, obviously having heard the exchange and recognizing her brother's voice. She came to an abrupt stop next to Joel, her hand fluttering anxiously to her throat.

"Oh my God, Zach?" she asked, her voice trembling with shock. "Is that you?"

Zach's narrowed gaze traveled from Joel, to Lora, then back to Joel again in a heated and furious stare. Too late, Joel realized how the situation looked from Zach's perspective . . . with his sister walking out of the same bedroom Joel had, and her wearing one of his black T-shirts and her legs bare, while he was in nothing more than his boxer briefs.

The next time Zach looked at Lora, he managed a small smile meant solely for her. "Yeah, it's me." He spread his arms out in front of him. "In the flesh, big sister."

"Oh, Zach," she breathed, obviously still stunned to see him. After a moment, she rushed across the room to give her brother a hug.

Zach returned the embrace, though he still glared at Joel over Lora's shoulder. Joel crossed his arms over his chest and remained where he was, deciding to let brother and sister handle this reunion on their own and without any interference from him.

"It's been forever, and I've been so worried about you,

and . . ." Lora pulled back and glanced from his drenched hair and coat to her own damp T-shirt, and frowned. "You're all wet."

"Yeah, well, there just happens to be a rainstorm out there," he drawled, the beginnings of sarcasm lacing his tone.

"And your face . . ." She swallowed hard and reached up to touch his discolored cheek.

Zach flinched away before she could make contact. "I'm fine, Lora. Stop fussing over me."

"You're far from fine," she argued, a hint of anger creeping into her voice. "You've got a black eye, a split lip, and your arm is in a cast. And you've been drinking. I can smell the alcohol on your breath."

Zach's lips thinned, and his own temper flared. "If I'd known you were going to reprimand me like a little kid, I never would have shown up."

Now that her initial surprise had ebbed, Joel could see her mind working and trying to make sense of her brother's spontaneous arrival at a cabin miles away from civilization.

She shook her head in confusion and ran her fingers through her sleep-tousled hair, which only added to the appearance that she'd spent the night in Joel's bed having hot sex. "What *are* you doing here, Zach?"

"What, Joel didn't tell you?" he replied mockingly.

She turned around and tipped her head, looking to Joel for answers, just as Zach had no doubt intended. "Tell me what, Joel?"

Refusing to let Zach make him into the enemy, Joel moved forward into the living room, his gaze on Lora. "Tell you that I set up a meeting for you to see Zach," he said, and went on to explain his reasons for withholding that information before Zach could twist things around to suit his own purposes. "But I didn't say anything to you because I had no idea if Zach would show up, and considering he was supposed to be here, oh, a good sixteen hours ago, I'd given up hope of that happening."

Zach clearly didn't like taking responsibility for his actions and didn't hesitate to deflect the attention off of himself. "Well, it looks like it was more than enough time to nail my sister, now wasn't it, Wilde Man?"

Joel saw that confrontation coming from the moment Lora had walked out of the bedroom behind him, but *she* obviously hadn't anticipated such a derogatory remark. She gasped in shock and whirled around to face her brother again.

"Zach!" The one word rang with a firm warning for him to back off. "What the hell kind of comment was that?"

"Well, it's the truth, isn't it?" Zach said, and shifted his challenging gaze back to Joel. "I asked you to protect my sister, Joel, not fuck her."

The crude remark spurred Lora into action, and before Zach realized what she intended, she'd hauled off and slapped him across the face, hard enough to make his head snap to the side. "That's enough, Zach!"

Joel couldn't help but silently applaud her bold and gutsy move. She'd just made it more than clear that she wasn't about to take any crap from her brother, and if Zach had any smarts left, he'd watch what he had to say.

Zach worked his jaw and narrowed his gaze at Lora. "Wow, nice greeting, sis."

His obnoxious attitude pissed her off even more, and it seemed like all the pent-up fear and anger toward her brother that she'd been suppressing the past few weeks finally came bubbling to the surface.

"How dare you come here and make Joel the bad guy,

or make any kind of assumption about our relationship!" She punctuated her statement with a forceful finger jab to Zach's chest that made him wince. "It's none of your business what's going on between Joel and me. For that matter, I wouldn't be in this situation with Joel if it wasn't for you and your stupid, idiotic idea of using my insurance policy as collateral on a gambling loan. What were you thinking, Zach?"

The first faint signs of remorse flickered in his gaze. "I had no choice."

"That's a pile of bullshit!" she said, not letting sympathy for her brother get the best of her. Instead, she took a tough love approach that Joel admired. "Every time you put money down on a table in hopes of winning you make the wrong choice, Zach. The *right* choice is to walk away."

Zach's shoulders slumped in defeat, an oddity in a man who'd been trained to be strong and tenacious in any given situation. "You have no idea what it's like," he said quietly.

She exhaled a deep breath and dragged her fingers through her disheveled hair. "Look, you're here, and that's what matters," she said, her voice softening with concern. "Why don't you take a hot shower, and I'll make you something to eat, then we can talk."

Zach nodded. "Yeah, I'd like that."

Joel had been watching their exchange from the sidelines, and now addressed Zach. "Come on, I'll show you where the bathroom is and get you some dry clothes to change into."

He wasn't sure what to expect from Zach, but the other man suddenly appeared exhausted and weary, as if he just didn't have any more fight left in him. Most likely, he didn't. Zach was probably at the end of his rope and barely hanging on for his life, and his sister's.

Zach followed him down the hall to the second bed-room, where Joel first pulled on a pair of black jeans, then retrieved a shirt and a pair of pants for Zach, along with his toiletry bag, which contained shampoo, a razor, and shaving cream if Zach wanted to use any of it. After showing Zach where the bathroom was located, Joel joined Lora in the kitchen.

She was standing at the stove heating up one of the canned soups and buttering slices of bread to make Zach a few grilled cheese sandwiches. A fresh pot of coffee was percolating, and Joel knew they all could use a boost of caffeine considering how early in the morning it was.

As he came up beside her and leaned against the counter, he noticed that she, too, had put on a pair of jeans and traded in his black T-shirt for a sweatshirt. Mostly, he didn't care for how quiet she was and how she wouldn't look at him, and wondered if his decision to keep Zach's possible visit to himself was the reason.

If so, he owed her an apology, and he wasn't above giving it. "I'm sorry, Lora. I should have told you that I set up a meeting here with Zach."

She slanted him a quick glance before placing two slices of buttered bread on the hot skillet. "Yes, you should have, but I do understand why you didn't." She added cheese to the sandwiches and two more slices of bread, and this time when she looked at him, the pain in her gaze was unmistakable. "God, Joel, I've never seen Zach look like this. So dejected and hopelessly lost, and it scares me. What am I going to do?"

"Do you realize that to you it's always about what you can do for Zach, and not what Zach can do for himself? You can't take care of this, Lora. Zach has to do it on his own."

She shook her head, a tinge of desperation etching her features as she stirred the steaming soup. "I have money in my savings that would go a long way toward helping him out of this mess."

"And bail him out like you have every other time in his life?" he asked incredulously. "I'm sure a part of Zach is hoping that you'll offer him the money he needs to help pay off his debt, but I can guarantee that he'll take your money, go and pay off what he owes, and then he'll start gambling all over again." Frustration raised his tone a few decibels. "If you give him the money, he'll continue to think there're no consequences for his behavior. There will be no one forcing him to be accountable for his debt. It would be nothing more than free money for him."

"You're right, but it doesn't make it any easier not to do it," she said quietly, and flipped both of the sandwiches over to grill the other sides.

Her anxiety and despair grabbed at something deep inside him and tugged hard. Realizing he had the power to offer her some kind of comfort from that worry, he decided to let her know what he had planned for Zach. "There's something else I need to tell you."

"What, more secrets?" She turned off the burner beneath the soup and cast him a skeptical glance. "Should I be worried?"

Her comment made him realize just how much he'd withheld from her during the course of their relationship. Keeping things to himself was a part of his personality, a function of how he'd grown up and dealt with more emotional issues that had spilled into his life as a marine, then a security agent. But now it made him more aware that she was the one person who managed to drag these things out of him, that he trusted her with so much of himself, and that was a scary prospect for him.

He mentally filed that away to think about later. Right now, they had her brother's problem to deal with.

"No, there's nothing for you to worry about," he reassured her. "Not only did I ask Zach to meet us here for the two of you to see one another, but I also have a proposition for him that would enable him to pay off this debt and give him a chance at a solid future."

Her eyes grew wide, and though she didn't ask for specific details, the gratitude passing across her features spoke volumes. "You would do that for Zach?"

Without thinking, he reached out and caressed his thumb along her soft cheek, that simple touch affecting him more deeply than it should have. "And for *you*."

Moisture welled up in her eyes, and she swallowed hard. "Thank you," she whispered.

The urge to take her into his arms and comfort her was strong, but with Zach in the cabin and already tossing around derogatory remarks about the two of them, the last thing Joel wanted was to have her brother walk in on them in an embrace, no matter how innocent.

So, instead, he turned around and opened one of the overhead cupboards. "Would you like some coffee?"

She nodded and returned her attention to preparing Zach's meal. "Yes, please."

He retrieved three mugs and poured coffee into each one while Lora put the grilled cheese sandwiches on a plate and poured the soup into a bowl. By the time everything was on the table, Zach was done with his shower and joined them in the kitchen, looking much more human than he had when he'd arrived.

Zach had shaved the grisly stubble on his face, and he'd combed his now-clean hair away from his face. His eyes were still a bit bloodshot—from lack of sleep or too much alcohol, Joel wasn't certain—but overall his tidied-up appearance and change of clothes was a huge improvement.

They all took a seat at the table, and Zach immediately started in on his soup and sandwiches like a starved man, which he most likely was. Joel decided to wait and give the man some time to eat his meal before talking to Zach about his proposal.

Lora took a sip of her coffee, sweetened with cream and sugar, and was the first to speak. "Zach, what happened to your face? Those look like fresh cuts and bruises."

"They are," he admitted, already finished with one of the sandwiches. "This is what you get when you make a payment on an outstanding debt, so you can imagine what happens when you don't." He gave his sister a lopsided grin, obviously meant to make light of the situation.

Lora wasn't at all charmed by the smile. "You made a payment? How did you manage that?" She frowned at him in confusion, then realization struck before Zach could reply. "Don't tell me you're still gambling!"

Zach's demeanor immediately changed, his entire body stiffening defensively, which was an answer in itself.

Lora stared at her brother in shock, unable to believe the depths he'd sunk to, yet he was digging himself deeper and deeper into debt. "You have no money to gamble, Zach," she said, stating the obvious. "Or should I ask, whose life are you playing with now?" It was a low blow, she knew, but she wasn't about to sugarcoat the situation.

Animosity tightened the clench of Zach's jaw. "Look, I borrowed some money from a friend, okay?"

"A friend?" Her doubt rang clear in her voice. "How much interest does this friend charge?" she went on persistently. "No matter who it is, you're borrowing from Peter to pay Paul, not to mention that my life has been at a standstill since you handed over my insurance policy as collateral. What happens when you don't win a poker hand, Zach? When you lose all the money you just borrowed from someone else?"

Zach dropped his spoon into his empty bowl with a loud clatter, a muscle in his cheek twitching with suppressed fury. "I'm doing what I can to get myself out of this fucking mess."

"What you're doing is digging yourself deeper into debt, not to mention doing desperate things in order to keep yourself, and now *me*, alive," she replied heatedly. "Your life is spiraling out of control and it has to stop."

The hand Zach had on the table curled into a tight fist. "I'm handling it, okay?"

Lora glanced at Joel, who sat quietly across the table from her, watching the bitter argument between her and Zach. Up to this point she'd dominated the conversation, and judging by the understanding look in Joel's eyes, he knew that she'd needed to vent and had given her that opportunity. But now, she needed him to intervene with that proposition for Zach that he'd mentioned earlier.

Joel cleared his throat and sat forward in his seat, and Zach automatically looked his way. "I have an offer for you," Joel said calmly. "One that would pay off your debt, get those thugs off your back, and eliminate the threat hanging over your sister's head, too."

Zach's gaze narrowed with suspicion, but was quickly eclipsed by a curiosity that got the best of him. "Go ahead," he said gruffly. "I'm listening."

"I talked with Jon, Ben, and Kevin, and we're willing to pay off your outstanding debt with this Lanny Mendoza guy, and anyone else you owe, in order for you to start off with a fresh, clean slate." Joel paused for a second to let that sink in before adding, "But, the new loan from us and our company, ESS, comes with a few stipulations."

"Of course it does." Zach replied drolly, and crossed his arms over his chest. "Let's hear it."

"In exchange for us paying off your debt and getting your sister's life insurance policy off the block for collateral, you need to agree to rehab for your gambling and alcohol addictions. Once you've completed that program, the guys and I want to offer you a job at ESS, which will pay you enough to make a decent living as well as pay back what you owe us."

Lora's mind reeled at Joel's generous proposal, and she had to resist the urge to jump up and shout "yes!" to the offer *for* Zach. But, it wasn't hers to accept, and she glanced anxiously at her brother. While Lora was thrilled and knew what a golden opportunity this was for Zach to start a new life for himself, as well as get the help he desperately needed, her brother clearly didn't share her enthusiasm.

In fact, Zach looked downright furious. "What the hell is this, some kind of fucking setup?" he demanded, staring hard at Joel. "I come here to see my sister, and you accuse me of having a gambling and drinking problem and want to lock me up in some kind of psychiatric facility? Nice way to show your gratitude for me saving your life, Wilde Man."

Joel didn't so much as flinch. "This *is* my way of showing gratitude, you ass. Quid pro quo. You saved my life, I'm trying to save yours, and you damn well know it, so don't start looking for someone else to blame for your problems."

"Well, I don't have any problems to fix," Zach sneered. "This one thing got a little out of control, and you both are making a bigger deal out of it than it needs to be."

"Oh, really?" Joel leaned closer to Zach, his expression as ruthless and cutthroat as a man could get. "Look at your sister and tell *her* that, so when those thugs come looking for her again, she'll remember that you don't have a gambling addiction, and those men are going to kill her for no reason at all. How do you feel about *that*?"

Joel's deliberately brutal words had the desired affect on Zach, hitting him where he was most susceptible. Rage flared across her brother's features, and he stood up so fast his chair hit the back wall behind him. "Fuck you, Joel!"

"The truth hurts, doesn't it, Zach?" Joel's mouth flattened into a grim line.

"You don't know the first thing about my situation," Zach said through clenched teeth.

"I know enough, Zach." In a smooth, fluid motion, Joel stood, too, looking far stronger and more intimidating than Zach. "I know you're so far gone, and so desperate, that you really have no concept of what you're doing to your life, and your sister's. And if you go back to gambling and start losing and can't pay back your debt, those guys aren't going to kill you, Zach, because that doesn't do them any good at all. Instead, they're going to torture you, little by little, until you're barely hanging on and in so much pain you beg them to let you die, but they're not going to put you out of your misery. Then, they'll go and find your sister and kill her so *you* can collect on her insurance policy and pay them what you owe. And maybe, if you're really lucky, they'll finally leave you alone."

The picture that Joel painted with his harsh words was utterly morbid, and it chilled Lora to the bone. She understood what Joel was doing, that he was attempting to break Zach down and force him to face his demons. And, ultimately, to get him to admit that he did, indeed, have a problem and had dug himself into a hole so deep, there were only two ways out ... Lanny Mendoza's way, or Joel's way.

"This is fucking bullshit!" Despite Zach's brave tirade, he was trembling, and panic flashed in his eyes, along with a stark fear he couldn't conceal no matter how hard he tried.

Her brother's denial was so painful to watch that Lora felt her chest tighten to the point that it became difficult to breathe. She wanted to yell at him for being so stubborn and stupid and too proud to accept help, but Joel had everything under control and didn't need her falling apart on him, too.

"What it is, is your *reality*," Joel told Zach. "I'm offering you a clear-cut way out. You've already lost everything. You have absolutely nothing to lose by accepting my proposition, and so much to gain."

"Forget it." Zach backed away from the table, scrambling to put distance between himself and Joel and the truth threatening to strangle him. "I'm out of here." He spun around and strode out of the kitchen to the front room.

"Oh, God," Lora said on a sob, and started after her brother, ready to do or say whatever it took to make him see reason. She was terrified that if he walked out that door she'd never, ever see him again.

Joel caught her arm before she could chase after him. "Let him go, Lora," he said gently. "He has to *want* to change, or else we'll all be wasting our time."

The front door slammed shut behind Zach, and Lora felt her heart pound just as hard. Tears stung the backs of her eyes and her throat grew raw. "What is it going to take to make him want to change?"

Joel didn't bother to disguise his own pain over the situation. "Hitting rock bottom."

A harsh, humorless laugh escaped her, and she cringed

as she heard Zach's vehicle skid on the gravel drive as he left. "I thought he already had."

"Not quite." Joel pulled her into his arms, and she went willingly, needing his comfort and strength to get her through this agonizing experience. "I just hope he comes to his senses before it's too late."

So did Lora, because she knew that despite her brother's obstinance, she'd never be able to live with herself if anything bad happened to Zach.

AFTER Zach's abrupt departure, sleep was impossible. Lora tossed and turned in her bed and listened to the rain outside until six in the morning. She could hear Joel moving around in the living room, and she decided that there was nothing left for them to do at the cabin. It was time to get up and get dressed, pack their small bags, and head back to the city.

Within an hour, they were ready to go.

While Joel did one last check of the cabin and made sure that the fire in the hearth was completely extinguished, Lora stepped outside and came to an immediate stop when she saw a large figure huddled on the front porch. Instantly, she recognized the straggly, damp brown hair and dirty and stained coat covering the slumped form as Zach's.

"Oh, no," she breathed, her mind already thinking the absolute worst. She fell to her knees beside her brother and shook him, hard, and experienced a flood of relief when he lifted his head and opened his bloodshot eyes. "Zach, are you okay?"

"Yeah . . . just dandy." He tried to smile, but his expression was heartbreakingly bleak and desolate. He shifted on the cold wooden planks, and an empty pint of vodka rolled out from beneath his coat. He glanced from the bottle to Lora and murmured, "There's absolutely nothing left."

It was a bizarre statement, and she couldn't help but think that he was referring to more than just the empty bottle of booze that he'd undoubtedly consumed. She wondered if this is what Joel had meant when he'd said that Zach had to hit rock bottom, because her brother certainly appeared lost and bereft and she couldn't imagine him falling any further into his own personal hell.

Joel came out of the cabin and the screen door slammed shut behind him, the sound making Lora jump.

She glanced behind her, unsure what to do. "He came back," she said, praying that was a positive sign and a step toward Zach aiding in his own recovery.

Joel crouched down beside her so he could be on eye level with her brother. "What's going on, buddy?"

Zach met his gaze without the cocky, brash attitude he'd displayed toward Joel only hours before. "Is your offer still on the table?"

"That all depends on what changed your mind," Joel replied mildly.

Zach dragged both his hands down his face and released a rough exhale of breath, and it was clear to Lora that this wasn't easy for her brother. "I got as far as the main road when my car ran out of gas and I realized I didn't even have enough money to fill even a quarter of the tank." He shook his head pathetically. "So, I walked back here in the rain while drinking my last bottle of booze, and now I have nothing left. No money. No place to live. No job. And pretty soon, no life."

Emotion clogged Lora's throat, and she swallowed back the pressure so she could reassure her brother of the one thing that mattered the most. "You have *us*, Zach."

He looked at her, the pain and hopelessness in his gaze

more honest and real than anything he'd shown them so far. "I can't do this anymore, Lora," he said in a choked voice. "I'm just so damn tired of running and looking over my shoulder and not knowing if every day is going to be my last. I want out, and I want my life back," he whispered.

"Well, we can definitely help you with that," Joel said, and straightened to his full height once again. "It's not going to be a quick, easy process, but I do need a verbal commitment from you that you're willing to do whatever it takes to get the help you need for your addictions, and your life is yours again."

Zach nodded in understanding. "I'll do it." He pushed to his feet and stood.

"Good," Joel said, pleased with Zach's acquiescence. "Let's get you back inside the cabin. There's enough food here for at least another week, and I'm going to call and see which one of the guys can stay out here with you until we settle your debt and make sure your life, and Lora's, are no longer in danger."

At the mention of her name, Zach glanced at her. "I know I royally screwed things up, and I'm sorry, Lora," he said gruffly, putting aside his own pride to extend the apology she deserved. "I swear, I'll make this up to you."

She offered him a tremulous smile. "As of right now, you are." As grateful as Lora was for Zach's turnaround, she knew her brother had a long road ahead of him, most of which would be an uphill struggle before things smoothed out for him.

Zach turned back to Joel. "Thank you." He extended his hand to the other man. "Semper fi, Wilde Man."

The beginnings of a smile curved the corner of Joel's mouth. "Semper fi, Marshall," he replied, then shook the hand Zach offered, in friendship, camaraderie, and the kind of brotherhood that could have only been formed by their time in the military together.

Semper fi. Always faithful.

Lora could see and feel the integrity between the two men, and it made her believe that everything, in time, might just be okay for her brother.

Seventeen

DANIEL parked his Volvo in front of The Electric Blue and cut the engine. Other than Sydney's car, the lot was completely empty, which was strange to see since he'd only been there in the evenings, when the area was crammed with vehicles and there was usually a long line of customers waiting outside in hopes of getting into the bar for a guaranteed good time. Having his own intimate connections with the bar owner, he was always lucky enough to bypass that queue of people no matter when he arrived.

But his visit this afternoon had more to do with business than the kind of pleasure The Electric Blue had to offer. After watching Cassie over the past two weeks, throughout normal class time and again during after school tutoring, he'd finally figured out what was going on with the teen and the reason she was exhibiting inconsistent grades in her homework and math tests.

As soon as his students left his classroom after tutoring that afternoon, he'd called Sydney and told her that they needed to talk. Since she was trying to finish up payroll and inventory before her crew showed up in a few hours, he'd offered to stop by The Electric Blue on his way home.

He exited his car, hit the lock and alarm switch, and headed toward the establishment's front doors. Judging by Sydney's reaction over the phone, he knew she was anxious to discover why her daughter was having a difficult time in his class when Cassie had never had an issue with math before. Daniel had found the whole cause behind Cassie's apparent struggle in math amusing and typical of a teenager, but he'd learned enough about Sydney, and how overly protective she was of her daughter, to know that she was not going to take the news of Cassie's deception well at all.

He knocked hard on the establishment's main door, and less than a minute later Sydney was there, letting him inside, looking gorgeous and sexy, as always. Soft auburn curls spilled over her shoulders in a sultry disarray, and she was wearing a long-sleeved, low-cut cotton top that hugged her voluptuous curves, as did her skinny jeans. After a quick hello, she led him back to her office, where they could sit down and talk. She sat down behind her desk, and he took one of the chairs in front of her.

"So, what's up with Cass?" she asked, getting right to the point.

As Sydney stared at him impatiently, Daniel had the distinct and unsettling feeling that today's conversation was going to be a turning point for them, and not in a good way. That all the emotional headway he'd made with her over the past few weeks, all the dates and getting-to-know-you conversations they'd had, and the hot foreplay that he never let turn into the actual sex she wanted from him, was going to go up in smoke right before his very eyes.

He could tell by her rigid posture and the guarded look

in her gaze that she'd already erected those frustrating barriers between them. The ones that told him she was falling back into that self-preservation mode of hers that shut down her emotions and kept him at a distance. It was such a natural, ingrained response from her that he was pretty sure she didn't even realize she'd done it. But he read those signals loud and clear, and it didn't bode well for him at all.

"Earth to Daniel," she said, waving a hand in front of him to get his attention. "Are you still with me?"

"Sorry." He shook his head to wipe those other thoughts from his mind, and redirected his focus on the reason he was there. "You know I've been working with Cass over the past few weeks, and watching her during tutoring, and I'm pretty sure I've discovered what's up with her inconsistent homework and test scores."

She folded her hands on top of her desk, her fingers clasped tight. "Is everything okay?"

"Well, that depends on your definition of 'okay,'" he said lightly. Knowing they were about to tread upon a very serious topic, he choose his words, and explanation, carefully. "The good news is, Cassie is completely capable of doing the math homework I give out, and her test scores have improved."

"Thank God," she said, breathing a sigh of relief that also released the beginnings of a smile. "I've been trying to stay on top of her at home on a nightly basis, and I'm sure the after school tutoring is helping, too."

"Tutoring does have something to do with her improvement, but not in the way you think. The thing is, Cassie never needed the help in the first place."

Sydney's smile immediately faded, and confusion creased her auburn brows. "I'm not quite sure I'm following you on this."

Standing, he came around to where she was sitting, and propped himself on an edge of the desk that wasn't piled with paperwork. "Remember when I told you that I encourage students to pair up during after-school tutoring sessions to help one another while I'm working one on one with someone?"

She leaned back in her chair and nodded. "Yes."

"Well, I noticed that when I made the suggestion that the students choose a partner, Cassie was quick to pick hers." There was no easy way to tell Sydney what he knew, no way to sugarcoat the truth that would send this protective mother over the edge. So, he attempted to keep his tone and demeanor casual, in hopes that it would keep Sydney calm, too. "She chose a boy named Ryan, who I noticed also tends to flirt with her during regular class time."

Sydney's complexion paled, and her eyes grew wide with something akin to fear. "Oh, God, are you saying that Cassie deliberately dropped her test scores and grades to get into after-school tutoring in hopes of being with this boy?"

He slid his hands into the front pockets of his khaki trousers. "That's definitely how it looks, though I didn't want to call Cassie on her behavior until after I talked to you."

"Well you can be damn sure I'll set her straight as soon as I get home!" she said adamantly, then ran a shaking hand through her hair. "What the hell is she thinking, playing dumb and risking her grades for some boy?"

Daniel could tell that Sydney was on the verge of hysterics, and decided to share with her the *positive* aspects of the situation. "What's funny is that Cassie did most of the helping when she was paired up with Ryan, because she knew the problems, and as a result they both ended up with an A on a test I gave the class." He grinned.

"Hell, if she can tutor the boy and get his grades to improve, too, what's wrong with that?"

Her gaze narrowed at him. "What's wrong is that she has no business getting involved with this boy!"

"He's a nice, decent kid, Sydney," he said, trying to soften the situation and reassure her that Cassie hadn't gone after some hoodlum. "He's even a little shy. I've met his parents, and they're good people, too. The kind that care about their son and his education. Just like you do with Cassie."

"I don't give a shit if he's the Prince of England!" She abruptly stood up, her tone angry. "Jesus, was he the reason why she wanted to go to that Halloween party so badly?"

"I'm sure he was there," he said automatically, then wished he'd kept his mouth shut when Sydney grew even more furious.

She paced to the other side of the office, and he felt the distance she put between them like a cold chill. "God, now she's lying to me and sneaking around, too. What's next?" Her voice broke with anguish.

He sighed, trying to keep his own frustration in check. "I'm sure it's not as bad as it seems."

She spun back around and glared at him. "You did *not* just say that."

He truly didn't understand her extreme reaction to the situation. "It's normal teenage behavior, and I see it all the time at school. She's a fifteen-year-old girl who has a crush on a boy and wants to get his attention. In her mind, playing down her math skills so she could get into after-school tutoring was her subtle way of doing it." He moved off the desk and stood, facing her. "Trust me, kids do stupid things sometimes, and while I agree that Cassie never should have jeopardized her grades, I've seen kids do much, much worse." Cassie's actions were mild in comparison to the kind of peer pressure some girls caved into in order to impress boys.

Sydney's chin jutted out, and she crossed her arms over her chest defensively. "Yeah, well, I know what that 'much worse' is, and there is *no way* I'm going to let Cassie make the same mistakes that I did."

He had the feeling that they'd just crossed over into uncharted territory for him—that for as much as he knew about Sydney and her past, there was a whole lot more he didn't know that tied into her need to insulate her daughter from the real world. "What are you talking about, Syd?"

"I know exactly what teenage boys want from girls who show them the least bit of interest," she stated adamantly. "I already told you about my past, about my mother's heroin addiction and overdose and how I was sent to a foster home. Well, what I didn't tell you was that it was my own foster brother who took my virginity and got me pregnant with Cassie."

What came to mind was the worst kind of scenario he could imagine. "He raped you?"

She shook her head, causing her curls to tumble wildly around her face. "Oh, no, he didn't *have* to force me." Her tone was infused with bitterness and regrets. "I was fourteen years old, I already had the body of a centerfold, just like my own daughter does, and Tim Carson was two years older than I was. He said all the right things and led me to believe that he loved me, and because I was so young and naive and wanted more than anything to *be* loved, I gave in and had sex with him. Three months later I'm pregnant and Tim's denying that he's the father, and his parents chose to believe him. In fact, they accused me of trying to trap their son by claiming the child was his, then promptly called the state to come and pick me up."

The pain etched on Sydney's expression made Daniel's heart break. He'd known she'd had a rough past, but he had no idea just how bad it had been. Now he understood that tough attitude of hers, but he also knew it masked a more vulnerable, insecure side to Sydney, as well. Like the woman who craved love and acceptance, but had never received it. A woman who'd opted to be brash and bold in order to protect her emotions.

And most especially, a woman who based a relationship purely on sex, because she didn't believe herself worthy of love.

"After that, Tim told his buddies at school that I was nothing more than a whore who put out, which had most of the guys making lewd remarks and crude advances toward me, because being a slut and all, they were sure I'd have sex with them, too," she went on, and paced the small area across from where he stood. "They were pigs, all of them, and especially Tim, and I swore I'd never, ever, let any boy take advantage of my daughter that way."

"Not all guys are that way, Sydney," he said gently. *He* wasn't like that, but despite his numerous attempts to prove that to her, she didn't want to believe that, either.

She released a scoffing laugh. "Tim might have been the first one to take one look at my big breasts and curvy body and decide that he wanted to screw me, but it's been that way ever since. Guys only want one thing from me, and I've learned to deal with that in my own way, but my daughter is *not* going to be in that situation if I can help it!"

He moved across the small office, until he was close enough to feel the agitation radiating off of her. "So, what, you're going to put Cassie in a chastity belt until she's of age?"

She glared at him. "That is so not funny."

"You're right, and I'm sorry." He released a sigh and

gave it another shot. "I guess I see all this from a different perspective, along with my experience of being around hormonal sex-crazed teenagers all day long. The thing is, sooner or later, sex happens, Sydney. But to your credit, you've raised a really smart girl with a good head on her shoulders."

Sydney wasn't the least bit swayed by his point of view of the situation. "Yeah, well, that's not going to keep some boy from getting into her pants, now is it?"

"No, but neither is forbidding her from seeing or dating some boy, which will only force her to sneak behind your back to do it," he argued. "You just have to trust that when she's put into that kind of sexual situation, she's going to make the right decision and be smart about it." Reaching out, he caressed his fingers along her smooth cheek and softened his tone as he continued. "Besides, Cassie has one thing going in her favor that you didn't at her age. She has a loving and caring mother. There's no reason for her to go looking for those things, or to be swayed by a boy's declaration of love. Not if she doesn't want to be."

She jerked away from his touch, a hint of desperation shining through the fierce facade she was attempting to cling to. "You just don't get it, Daniel."

Ahhh, the evasive "you just don't get it" dictum, which, in Sydney's case, meant just the opposite. He was getting too close and too personal, and while she was doing her best to erect emotional walls between them, he was more than prepared to tear them all down. One by one, if need be.

"I get it more than you realize," he said, taking a more direct approach. "In fact, I get that this is more about you than it is about Cassie."

An impatient sound escaped her. "What the hell are you talking about?"

He shrugged. "It's about you and your past and how you've lived *your* life."

"How *I've* lived my life?" she repeated, brows raised incredulously. "Please, do tell me what you *think* you know."

If she wanted to play that kind of hardball, then he was game, and he didn't hesitate to step up to the plate. "I *think* that as a result of what happened with Tim and those other boys who thought you were easy, you decided to use sex to your own advantage, and as a way to keep any guy from getting too close. Sex is pleasurable and easy, and if you keep it all about the physical, it keeps you in control and there's no threat to your emotions. How am I doing so far, sweetheart?"

"Not very well," she lied. "You're *way* off base."

"Really?" he drawled lazily. "Then what have you been doing with me for the past few weeks? You've been trying to use sex to scratch whatever itch you think you might have, and you've been annoyed as hell that I haven't given in to your numerous attempts at seduction and screwed you, like every other guy that's come before me. That would have been ideal for you, wouldn't it have been?"

She jabbed him in the chest with a finger. "You are *so* full of shit."

He laughed, but the sound lacked any true humor. "Personally, I think I'm hitting way too close to the truth, and you don't like what you're hearing."

"Go to hell, Daniel." Her nostrils flared, as did her temper. "In fact, while we're at it, why don't we just put an end to this thing between us, right here and now."

That didn't surprise Daniel one bit. It was an easy way out, and she was taking it. "Just in case you didn't know, because you haven't had all that much experience with them, it's called a *relationship*, Syd."

She waved a hand between them and adopted an I-don't-give-a-damn attitude. "Yeah, whatever you want to call it, it's not going anywhere."

Oh, but it was, or else she wouldn't be scrambling to end things. "It's just not going where *you* want it to go. Isn't that what you mean?"

She glanced away and rubbed at her forehead with her fingers. He knew he was putting her through an emotional wringer, but it was necessary if they were going to have any chance at a future together, and he wanted that with her more than anything.

Finally, she looked back at him, her fortitude back in place. "The truth of the matter is that a relationship between us would never work. We're just too different, Daniel."

No way was he letting her off with such a simple, un-explained statement. "How so?" he persisted.

She clearly wasn't happy that he was pushing the issue, but to her credit she didn't brush off his question. "Look at you, and look at me. Compare your childhood to the one I just told you about. Compare my heroin addict mother and my father who was a nameless john, to your wealthy family who no doubt cares about those things," she said criti-cally. "Your parents would take one look at me, and once they found out I had a daughter at the age of fourteen out of wedlock, and that I own a bar where I dance on the countertops to entertain the customers and help sell more alcohol, they'd probably disown you for being involved with someone like me."

Disowning him would be a bit extreme, but unfortu-nately, he knew his parents had a tendency to judge peo-ple. "I don't give a shit what my parents think of you."

"Well, you should," she said, her gaze bright with con-viction. "They no doubt expect someone better for you.

Someone who is sweet and refined and loves going to Sunday brunch with the family and would be satisfied to be a stay at home mother and wife."

All the things she believed she wasn't. "My parents do expect a lot from me, but I've never bended to their expectations and I don't intend to now," he stated firmly. "If that were the case, I'd be a doctor, not a math teacher, and I would have married the sweet, refined debutante my mother set me up with when I was twenty. This is *my* life, not theirs, and I don't need their permission to date you, or anyone else."

She suddenly looked tired and weary, but she didn't back down from her own personal fight. "Let me set you straight, Daniel. I'm the kind of woman that men *fuck*, not the kind that they take home to meet their family *or* marry."

He met and held her dark gaze. "I disagree."

"Well, then it's time for you to pull your head out of the clouds and face the reality of who and what I am." Her expression hardened, grew cool and defiant and relentless in her quest to make him understand. "I was a stripper in a gentlemen's club for years, because the tips were outstanding and it helped me to survive and take care of Cassie. Men paid me damn good money for the illusion of sex, no big surprise there," she added wryly. "But do you know how I got the business loan to open up my own bar? The guy at the bank struck a deal with me. Sex in exchange for him pushing my loan application through. So, I slept with him to get what I wanted. Not exactly what a good girl would do, now is it?"

Knowing that she was baiting him, he didn't bother to answer the theoretical question.

"And like every other guy who's come before you, that's all this *thing* between us is about. Sex. Except you won't give me what I want."

A slight, mocking smile curved the corner of his mouth. "Yeah, imagine that."

Her annoyance spilled over into a deeper, darker resentment. "There's only one thing I want from you, Daniel, so don't make this affair into something more than it is. In fact, since you won't give me what I want, get the hell out of my bar and don't come back." She turned away and started back toward her desk.

Oh, she'd like that, and her pretense of indifference pissed him off more than anything else, because he knew that she felt something for him. That it was more than just a physical thing between them, and now she was quick to end their affair before those emotions had a chance to take root and grow. Well, he wasn't about to let her walk away without giving her something to think about.

He grabbed her arm before she passed him, and in the next moment he had her pressed up against the wall, his body pinning hers in place. Her lips parted to say something, most likely to tell him off with that smart mouth of hers, but he didn't give her the chance. He slanted his lips over hers and took full and complete possession of her mouth. His tongue sank deep, tasting, taking, ravaging—and being the bold and reckless woman that she was, Sydney kissed him back just as aggressively, and with an unmistakable edge of anger.

As their mouths and tongues dueled for supremacy, she pushed her hands between their bodies and skimmed her fingers down to the waistband of his pants. She started unbuckling his belt, and he grasped her wrists, pulled her hands away, and secured them at the sides of her head, refusing to let her take control of this situation, or make it all about sex.

No, this was about them connecting on a deeper, more

intimate level. This was about breaking down barriers and getting Sydney to open up and trust him with her heart and emotions.

A moan of frustration rose up in her throat, and he changed the tenor of the kiss. Easing up on the hard pressure of his mouth against hers, he kissed her slow and gentle, and used his lips to coax and seduce. Gradually, he felt the change in her, too. Her tense body relaxed and flowed against his, and the hands he'd pinned against the wall grew slack, as well. Her mouth softened beneath his, and he swirled his tongue around hers, tasting that soul-deep vulnerability of hers, along with the fear of letting someone close enough to hurt her.

By the time he lifted his head and stared into her glassy eyes, they were both breathing hard. But he still had a point to drive home, and this time he did it with harsh and direct words. "Giving you what you want—*fucking you*—would be so easy to do, Sydney," he said, his voice low and rough. "But I want to give you what you *need*."

Her bottom lip trembled ever so slightly. "You have no idea what I need," she whispered raggedly, still intent on denying any shred of feeling she had for him.

"That's where you're wrong. I do know what you need, because I need the same thing." Releasing her, he stepped back, and wasn't quite sure what to make of the flash of panic he saw in her eyes. But that was part of their problem . . . her inability to share those fears and insecurities with him.

But he had no qualms about putting himself out there for her, his heart and soul, wholly and completely. "It's okay to let someone love you, Sydney," he said gently, and felt his chest tighten when a telling moisture filled her eyes. "It's okay to let *me* love you, because I'm not going to hurt you, or disappoint you the way so many people in your past have. But I want more than a temporary sexual fix or a hot affair, and you deserve more than that, too."

She lifted her chin a fraction and said nothing. The woman was so damn stubborn, and deeply wounded, and she wasn't nearly as tough as she wanted everyone to believe.

"I'm going to go, just like you asked me to," he said, leaving any chance at a future together solely up to her. He managed a small smile. "If someday you decide you want to give the whole relationship thing a try, you know where to find me."

On impulse, he stepped back toward her and brushed his lips along her cheek in a soft kiss, and took a few self-ish seconds to breathe in her scent so he could memorize it for later. When he pulled back, he had to steel himself against the devastated look on her face, and it took every ounce of strength he possessed to turn around and walk out of her life.

Eighteen

"YOU'RE awfully quiet. Are you okay?"

Lora turned her gaze from the passenger window of Joel's SUV to the man sitting in the driver's seat as he navigated the way to his sister's gallery opening in downtown Chicago. Between watching the road and glancing at her, she caught glimpses of concern in his gaze and summoned a reassuring smile.

"Yeah, I'm good." As good as to be expected, she supposed, considering it was only a matter of time before the two of them went their separate ways.

It had been three days since they'd left Zach behind at the cabin with Kevin, and Joel's guys had begun the process of tracking down Lanny Mendoza to pay off her brother's debt. Once that was done, and her safety was no longer an issue, there was no reason for Joel to be by her side twenty-four/seven. He'd already made mention of a security case that was previously lined up for him, and he seemed anxious to get back to real work.

She knew the end was inevitable, yet there was that deep-seated hope she couldn't help but harbor that Joel would come around and give the two of them a chance. But he'd made his stand on relationships more than clear, and she was forced to accept that their affair had been as temporary as his presence in her life.

"Try not to feel too overwhelmed by my family, okay?" Joel's tone was light, as was the easygoing grin he cast her way. "According to Mia, just about everyone is going to be at the opening, so I'm sure you'll be whisked around for a dozen or more introductions. There's my brothers and their wives, and my cousins and their spouses, too."

"Actually, I'm looking forward to meeting everyone." And, she was interested in watching his family dynamics in action.

"The only ones you won't get to meet are the parents, and the little ones." He put on his blinker and made a right-hand turn down a side street. "Mia felt too uneasy about having toddlers in the gallery with all the glass designs, so the grandparents offered to stay at home and watch the rugrats."

She rested her head against the back of the seat and smiled at him. "That was nice of them."

"Are you kidding? They're loving having grandkids and want to be around them any chance they get." He pulled into a parking lot, which was already half filled, and found a spot near the entrance of the gallery. "Before long we're going to have an entire soccer team at family gatherings," he said, genuine affection in his tone.

She laughed, easily imagining Joel as an uncle, with little ones clamoring for his attention. Despite his rough and tough exterior, the man had a huge, caring heart. She'd seen it numerous times over the past few weeks, and it was just one of the many wonderful qualities he possessed that she'd fallen in love with.

Yeah, she was in love with Joel Wilde. Deeply. Irrevocably. In ways that defied anything she'd ever felt before, and she instinctively knew her heart would never be the same again.

Refusing to dwell on those thoughts tonight, she got out of the car with Joel and they headed toward the front of Wilde Designs. Joel's hand lightly touched that sensitive spot at the base of her spine that he'd kissed just days ago while doing other more erotic things to her body, and she shivered at the delicious memory.

"Are you cold?" he asked.

"Ummm, no." It was the first week in November, and there was a definite autumn nip in the air, but she'd worn a sweater top with a calf-length skirt and stylish boots, so she was plenty warm. It was other, more intimate things giving her the chills. "I'm okay."

He continued to escort her toward the gallery, the front of which was all framed in plate glass, enabling people who were window shopping to see directly into the shop and admire all the gorgeous stained glass designs glimmering beneath bright, strategically placed lights. Joel held the door open for her, and they stepped inside the shop, where a small crowd was already milling about and viewing all the dazzling works of art on display and for sale. The showroom buzzed with light chatter and bursts of delighted laughter, and an exuberant energy added to the lively atmosphere.

Since Joel didn't see any of his family right away, the two of them casually strolled from one partitioned room to the next to view the amazing artwork. There were butterflies and flowers and various animals all reproduced in colorful shards of glass, along with other abstract patterns, but Lora found herself drawn to one of the stained glass designs in particular—a stunning picture of a beautiful blond-haired fairy with iridescent wings who was sitting in a meadow of exotic flowers. The name of the piece was *Midsummer Dream*, and it was absolutely breathtaking.

Because Joel had explained to her that his sister's designs had a sensual twist to them, it didn't take her long to see the entwined couple meshed within the riot of wild-flowers.

"They're right here, aren't they?" she said in awe, and pointed to the subtle shades of glass that formed the couple's erotic embrace.

"Yes, they are," a female voice said from behind them, before Joel could reply.

Both she and Joel turned around at the same time. Lora smiled at the beautiful woman, with her thick, shoulder-length black hair, smoky silver eyes, and striking features. She was wearing a silk sapphire blue dress that was both elegant and sexy, and her face glowed with happiness.

The woman glanced from Lora to Joel, and she gave him a wide-eyed once-over. "Joel?" She asked incredulously. "Is that really you?"

He rolled his eyes at her dubious tone. "Cut the crap, Mia," he drawled good-naturedly, and pulled her into a heartfelt hug, which she returned just as warmly.

Mia was laughing when she pulled back. "You clean up real nice, Joel," she said, more sincere this time. "You were way overdue for a haircut, and it's always nice to see you in something other than *black*," she teased.

"You wound me." Joel spread his arms wide, showing off his black silk dress shirt, black slacks, and equally black loafers. "And here I dressed up just for you so I'd look presentable tonight."

"And you do," she insisted. "You look very handsome."

Lora had to agree. She'd only seen Joel in denim and cotton shirts, and now, with his new haircut, fashionable clothing, and smoldering masculine features, he looked as though he could have stepped right off the pages of a *GQ* magazine.

Mia turned her attention to Lora, her gaze bright with interest and speculation, before looking back at Joel. "And this must be Lora, the woman you told me about on the phone, right? The one that's a client of ESS?"

"Yes," he confirmed, obviously going with the client perception. "Lora, this is my pain-in-the-ass sister, Mia."

"Nice introduction," Mia said, and wrinkled her nose at her brother before grinning at Lora and extending her hand. "It's very nice to meet you."

Mia's handshake was friendly and welcoming. "Yes, it's a real pleasure," Lora said. "Joel has told me so much about you." Well, as much as she'd been able to drag out of him while they'd been at the cabin, anyway.

The other woman narrowed her gaze playfully at Joel. "All wonderful things, right?"

"Absolutely." His grin was full of charm, and his gaze was affectionate, making the bond between brother and sister evident to anyone who happened to see the two together.

"You've been trained well," she replied sassily. "Now, there's champagne and a dessert table, and soda if you prefer, so please enjoy whatever you'd like while you're browsing."

Joel frowned. "What, no beer?"

"Funny, but Cameron asked the same thing, as did Steve." She put her hands on her slender hips and shook her head in mock distaste. "Now come on, Joel. Does this look like a beer kind of joint to you?"

He chuckled in amusement. "Okay, I get your point." He glanced at Lora. "How about something to drink?"

"Sure. I'll take a glass of champagne."

"Me, too," Mia added with a persuasive smile.

"Two glasses of champagne, coming right up," Joel said, and headed over to the bar that had been sent up for the evening.

"Your designs are absolutely amazing," Lora said, once Joel was gone.

"Thank you." Mia beamed, basking in the compliment, and rightly so. "I have to admit, it's such a thrill to be able to open my own gallery. There was a time when I thought my designs would never see the light of day, let alone have people purchasing them."

"They're unique and gorgeous. All of them," Lora told her, then looked back at the one with the exotic fairy. "Though I do have to say that this piece is my favorite so far."

"I just finished that one a few days ago." Mia seemed to consider the jewel-toned design with a fresh perspective. "It was probably one of the most challenging designs I've ever done. Piecing together the shards of glass for the fairy's wings was a true nightmare."

Despite the complaint, Lora could tell that Mia loved what she did and was happy with the end results of this *Midsummer Dream*.

"You know, I can't help but think that you look so familiar to me," Mia said, studying Lora through inquisitive eyes. "Have we met before?"

"I don't think so." If they'd been introduced in the past, Lora would have remembered someone as vibrant as Mia. But she did get that do-I-know-you question every once in a while, due to where she worked. "Unless maybe you've been to The Electric Blue? I'm a waitress there."

Mia snapped her fingers. "That's it! That's exactly where I've seen you before, though I have to admit it's been a while since I've been there."

"Too busy working on your designs?" Lora guessed.

She flashed a nice-sized diamond solitaire encircling her left ring finger. "That, and The Electric Blue isn't quite the place an engaged woman should frequent." Her gray eyes took on a mischievous sparkle. "But I have to say that I did enjoy myself at that bar immensely when I was single."

"Ahhh, *there* she is." A tall, good-looking man with sandy blond hair and a charming grin approached the two of them, with Joel walking beside him. "No wonder I couldn't find you. You've been hiding out in this corner over here."

"I'm not hiding," Mia said, and took the glass of champagne that the man handed to her, while Lora thanked Joel for hers. "I'm just enjoying a conversation with Joel's . . . client." Mia slanted her brother a sly glance that said she didn't quite believe that their relationship was that simple. "Lora, this is my fiancé, Cameron. Cam, this is Lora."

Once the introductions were made, confusion creased Cameron's brows as he glanced back at Mia. "Did you say that she's a *client* of Joel's?"

Joel jumped in to explain the situation, but it was obvious that Mia had her doubts. Those expressive eyes of hers made it clear that she was wondering what the real scoop was when it came to her and Joel. Unfortunately, their relationship had truly reverted back to a platonic business arrangement and it didn't show any signs of changing back to something more intimate anytime soon.

Cameron gently touched Mia's arm. "I hate to be rude and steal you away, but there's someone I want you to meet."

Mia smiled at her fiancé. "Oh, okay." Then she transferred her gaze to Lora. "Don't be a stranger. Stop in at the gallery anytime. Oh, and I give a nice discount to family and friends."

"That's good to know. Thank you." Lora took a sip of her bubbly champagne, finding it incredibly nice of Mia to extend the discount to her, as well. "I'll be sure to bring my best friend by soon. She'll love your artwork."

"Wonderful." Mia waggled her fingers at them as she walked away with Cameron. "I'll see you two around."

"She's a little whirlwind, isn't she?" Joel said, chuckling and more relaxed than Lora had seen him in days. "Here one minute, gone the next."

"I really like her."

"The feeling is definitely mutual," he said, and smiled. "By the way, I saw my brothers and cousins when I went to get your champagne. Come on, and I'll introduce you to them."

His hand came to rest at the small of her back again as he guided her around the various partitions to the other side of the gallery, where it was more crowded. Guests were gathered in circles, talking and laughing, while others mingled from group to group to visit with everyone. Joel led her toward a fairly large cluster of people, and that's when she was introduced to his large family as a *client*—including his two brothers, Scott and Alex, his three male cousins, and all their spouses. The Wilde men were similar in looks, with their thick black hair and gorgeous blue eyes, and after a round of handshakes and friendly hellos, she felt quite overwhelmed.

She latched on to a familiar face standing next to her,

Ashley St. Claire, who was married to Joel's older brother Scott and managed the hotel where Lora worked. They chatted for a few minutes, then Ashley glanced at the other women in the group.

"Come on, ladies," Ashley announced, "let's let the men catch up while we indulge in a bit of retail therapy. We need to make sure we keep Mia in business for a long time to come."

At the mention of *retail therapy*, the men let out a collective groan, and the women just laughed.

"That sounds good to me," Alex's wife, Dana, said with a grin.

"Me, too," Chayse added, and made a big deal of batting her lashes coquettishly at her husband, Adrian, in an obvious attempt to soften him up. "Since we're supporting Mia, I take it I can buy whatever I want?"

All the men stared expectantly at Adrian, knowing that whatever his answer, it would set a precedent for their wives, too.

Adrian exhaled a deep breath and smiled down at Chayse. "You go right ahead and buy whatever your heart desires, sweetheart."

Another round of deep groans echoed from the other men, the mingled sounds echoing their disappointment in Adrian's response.

"Thanks, man," Alex said dryly, and slapped his cousin on the back. "You just gave all our wives carte blanche, you know that, right?"

Adrian shrugged unapologetically. "Hey, I like getting it on a regular basis, you know what I mean?"

The other guys caught on immediately and nodded in agreement, then made sure they issued the same bit of freedom to their significant others.

Liz and Jill joined them, too, both of whom were

expecting and appeared to be close to the same number of months along in their pregnancies.

Easy, friendly conversation ensued among all the women as they strolled around the showroom and looked at each individual design. By the time they were done a while later, Ashley had selected a few pieces of the stained glass artwork, one for herself and the others as gifts, and the other women had each purchased at least one design, too. When Lora didn't find anything she liked better than the fairy pattern, she decided to splurge and purchase the piece, but when she went back to buy the artwork, there was already a SOLD sticker on it.

Disappointed, but figuring it wasn't meant to be, Lora followed the women back to where the drinks and desserts were set up, which was close enough to see the men, but far enough away for the women to enjoy their own conversation. After perusing the desserts and everyone selecting a few items, they walked to a nearby lounge area, so that Jill and Liz could sit down in the two comfortable chairs and relax and rest their feet.

Jill gasped and pressed a hand to her belly, which looked to be the same size as Liz's. "This one sure is active," she said with an uncomfortable grimace.

Lora finished eating a delicious petit four and glanced at Jill, who was nibbling on a chocolate-covered strawberry. "Are the two of you due around the same time?" she asked.

Liz and Jill looked at one another and burst out laughing. Even Dana and Ashley chuckled, too, though Lora had no idea what was so funny.

"It's going to be a close call," Liz said with a sigh. "*Again.*"

Lora *still* didn't get the joke. "Again?"

"Yes, *again*," Jill said with a nod, then went on to

explain. "Believe it or not, our first babies were born on the same day."

Now, Lora understood and she grinned. "Ahhh, and you think that's going to happen this time, too?"

"Well, considering we found out that we were pregnant only one week apart from one another, it's a possibility."

"The guys are already taking bets on whose baby is going to be born first, just like they did last time," Liz said, and rolled her eyes at their husbands' antics. "Those men are so damn competitive, even when it comes to *this*."

While Liz and Jill talked about their most recent sonograms and what they thought the sexes of their babies were going to be, Lora casually glanced toward the Wilde men, and Joel in particular. Interestingly enough, she immediately noticed how he kept himself apart from everyone else in the group, mainly his brothers. His hands were pushed into his front pants pockets, and there was an air of reserve about him that she never would have equated with the Joel she'd come to know.

For a man who was so confident and take-charge in every other aspect of his life, when it came to his family he made himself blend into the background, when he was usually a guy who was bigger than life. And it wasn't as though they were excluding him from their conversation, but it was just so obvious to Lora, especially after her discussion with Joel at the cabin, that he felt as though he didn't fit in and didn't have that bond that his two brothers, Scott and Alex, did.

She supposed that over the many years since his mother's death, Joel's actions had just become routine and automatic, and everyone around him accepted his remote personality as all a part of his tough military image. But now, Lora knew his outward appearance of indifference went so much deeper. Knew that somewhere deep inside there was still a small part of that little boy he'd once been, the one who craved acceptance and a sense of belonging—despite the fact that he'd been the one to distance himself from his family.

But that's the man he'd become in order to cope with the loss of his mother at such a young age. He'd taken his feelings and shut them away, which had been so much easier than dealing with them.

But cutting off his emotions had affected him on other levels of his life, most obviously with relationships, and now especially with *them*. But she couldn't coerce him to change, or force him to love her—she'd learned that lesson with Brent and knew that it was all up to Joel to *want* to change. To allow himself to be loved in return.

Her own emotions tightened in her chest, and she finally tore her gaze from Joel and joined the conversation going on among the women.

From there, the evening went by quickly, and before long it was time to leave. She and Joel said their good-byes to everyone and headed back to her place. Just as they'd walked into her apartment, the cell phone clipped to the waistband of Joel's pants vibrated.

He flipped the unit open and pressed it to his ear. "Yeah?" Joel answered, and just by that informal greeting Lora knew it was one of the ESS guys. Instinctively knew, too, why they were calling.

She listened to the one-way conversation from Joel's end, feeling a jolt of anticipation that this situation was finally over, along with a sense of dread because of what it meant for her and Joel. The end, as well. There was nothing left for him to stay for.

A few minutes later, he snapped the phone shut and turned to face her. "It's done," he said quietly, his gaze not quite meeting hers. "All of it. Mendoza is paid off with interest, your insurance policy is off the table, and you and Zach are both in the free and clear."

After weeks of upheaval, the relief rushing through her was incredibly welcome. "What about Zach?"

"Kevin is taking him to a rehab center as we speak," he said, making way too much of a production of clipping his phone back in place—a stall tactic, she knew, so he didn't have to look at her and deal with the emotional fallout between them. "We already have him registered and the place is expecting him. Most likely, he'll be there for a few months."

"I don't care. Whatever it takes to get him over his addictions and back on track." When Joel still found reasons not to glance her way, she closed the distance between them and curled her fingers around his forearm, giving it a gentle, meaningfully squeeze. "Thank you, Joel, for everything," she said softly. "For taking care of me, and for saving Zach."

Finally he met her gaze. An easygoing smile curved his lips, belying the deeper, darker pain she detected in his eyes—a telltale sign that maybe, hopefully, walking away from her wasn't going to be so easy after all. "Taking care of you was easy," he said huskily. "As for Zach, I owed him. He saved my life, and now I'm going to save his ass. I'm sure he's going to go through more hell in that rehab center than I did when I got shot in my leg, but I'm hoping he'll thank me for it later."

"I'm sure he will." She let her hand drop back down to her side as an awkward silence settled between them. "So, this is it, then? We're done?" The last question deliberately held dual meaning, and considering how his jaw clenched ever-so-slightly, he'd caught her subtle double entendre.

He exhaled a ragged breath and reached for his duffel bag, which he'd left at the end of the sofa. "Yeah, we're done," he said, his tone low and rough, as if he'd just swallowed a handful of gravel. "Just let me pack up my things, and I'll finally be out of your way."

He'd never been in her way, and he knew it, too. Yet he was scrambling to get his things together and leave, instead of facing what was still between them. It was exactly what she'd expected, and his quick retreat shouldn't have hurt, but it did.

She sat down on the sofa as he went to retrieve his shaving kit from the bathroom. Already, she was dreading how alone and quiet it was going to be in her apartment once he was gone.

As she watched him pack his toiletries and finish stuffing the rest of his items into his bag, she realized that she didn't want him to leave without knowing how she felt about him. Mostly, she didn't want to live with regrets of what she should have said and done before he exited her life. She was going to lay her heart and soul bare. She'd tell him the truth, let him know that she'd fallen in love with him, and maybe, hopefully, he'd *allow* her to love him in all the ways he needed and deserved.

"I guess that's it." He zipped up his duffel bag and reluctantly glanced at her. "I'll be on an assignment for the next few weeks, but if you need me for anything at all, you have my cell number."

God, she needed him already. Before she lost her courage, she stood up from the couch and rubbed her damp hands down the sides of her skirt. "Joel, before you go, there's something I need to tell you."

He looked at her warily, then apparently sensing her nervousness, his gaze narrowed with a please-don't-go-there warning. The kind that men gave women when they sensed an emotional conversation on the horizon, and in this case he'd be right.

"Okay," he said, but his unwillingness to hear what she had to say was very obvious in the tense set of his jaw and the way his hands had curled into fists at his side.

But at least he stayed, and she was grateful for even that much from him.

"I know this isn't something you want to hear, but I'm going to say it anyway." She swallowed to ease the sudden dryness in her mouth. "I'm in love with you, Joel."

He looked away from her and swore beneath his breath, the sound filled with frustration and a hint of anger. His adverse response was as effective as rebuffing every bit of intimacy they'd shared, and felt the equivalent of being shot straight through the heart, leaving her breathless and aching.

She really shouldn't have been surprised by his reaction, because she'd known better than to expect a declaration of undying love in return. But she knew that Joel cared for her. Knew there was something real and honest between them that could grow into so much more if he'd let it. And therein lay their problem—his inability to open up and let her in to all those places that had been empty for so long, he didn't know anything else.

"Look, I don't expect anything in return," she said, knowing that was a big, fat lie. "You made your position on relationships and being committed very clear to me, and I'm not asking for any of that. I just wanted you to know how I felt."

"Lora . . . I can't." His tone was as tortured as the look in his dark blue eyes. "I just *can't* do it."

She walked toward him, closing the distance between them, and placed a hand on his cheek. "That's where you're wrong, Joel. You *could* do it. If you really wanted to." She skimmed her fingers along his jaw before letting them fall away. "You're just so used to being on the outside looking in, to being the odd man out, that you don't know anything else."

A frown creased his brows. "What are you talking about?" he asked gruffly.

"I saw it tonight at your sister's gallery, Joel. I saw how you were with your brothers, how you kept yourself apart from them because it's just an instinctive thing for you and something you've done since your mother's death. But it doesn't have to be that way. At least not with me."

He didn't say anything, but the pain in his eyes spoke more than words ever could. He *hated* being on the outside, but it was all he'd ever known.

"Sometimes you just have to put yourself out there emotionally and take a chance," she suggested, then shook her head at the irony of that statement. "I can't believe I'm saying that to someone who claims to be a risk-taker, a man who is strong and fearless and risks his life to protect others, and would willingly put himself in the direct line of danger if a situation warrants it. It seems the one and only aspect of your life that you *do* play it safe with is your heart and your relationships."

His eyes flashed with irritation. "With good reason."

She smiled, knowing better. Possibly knowing him better than he knew himself. "So you keep saying, but I've yet to find a reason that you can't work through, if you really wanted to."

He stared at her for a long, hard moment, then picked up his duffel bag, effectively putting an end to a conversation he didn't want to hear or face. "I need to go."

"I know," she said softly, and didn't say anything more as he turned around and headed toward the front door. He walked out without looking back, and she let him go, even though it was the hardest thing she'd ever had to do.

With a sigh that seemed to unravel her from the inside out, she sat back down on the couch, already feeling the quiet and solitude of her apartment closing in on her. Yeah, she had her life back, but it sure didn't amount to much without Joel in it.

Nineteen

SYDNEY stared at her reflection in the bathroom mirror, not sure that she even recognized the woman staring back at her anymore. Sure, she was very familiar with those green eyes—though currently red and puffy from a crying jag, and lined by dark circles due to her sleepless nights—and auburn curls, and even that voluptuous body that she saw on a daily basis and had been using to her advantage for years now, but she was referring to the person *inside* the body. And for the past few days since Daniel had walked out of her life, she'd spent a whole lot of time wondering how in the world she'd gotten to this point in her life . . . and, more shocking, she wasn't sure she liked who and what she'd become.

Oh, she knew that her past circumstances had molded her into someone driven, yet cautious when it came to relationships. Not to mention jaded and untrusting of men and their motives. Thanks to Tim Carson, it had become an instinctive part of her personality, as well as her way of protecting her heart and emotions and never allowing anyone to ever use her again for their own personal gain.

For years she'd been the one in control when it came to men and relationships. She called the shots. She took what she wanted and walked away when she'd had enough. For her and the guys she'd chosen to date, it had always been about having a good time and uncomplicated sex.

Until Daniel. He was the one man who'd ever wanted more than just sex from her, and it had scared the crap out of her. So did the emotions and feelings he'd stirred within her that were so foreign to her woman's heart. The wanting. The yearning. The need to let him be a part of her life beyond that physical attraction.

She drew in a shaky breath and swiped at the fresh batch of tears surging to the surface. She'd spent a whole lot of time thinking about everything Daniel had said to her, and now she tried to see herself from his perspective, beyond her looks, her ample curves, and all that superficial crap she'd hidden behind for much too long. And what she saw was a woman who wished she had someone to share her burdens with, beyond Lora. A woman who craved stability, the comfort of a man's embrace, and a shoulder to lean on during those rough times. But mostly what she saw was a woman who ached to be loved unconditionally.

Daniel had offered her all those things, and she'd pushed him away because she was too scared to believe someone like him, someone so honest and caring and a man who treated her with respect, could be for real. When he said he didn't care about her past, she'd desperately wanted to believe him. When he'd told her that it was okay to let him love her because he wasn't going to disappoint her like so many had in her past, instead of trusting him, she'd pushed him away out of fear.

And now, she was alone, and for the first time in her life, her heart *hurt*. And that brash and bold woman who used her body, and sex, to her advantage, no longer appealed to her.

It was a hard realization to face. Harder still to think about how her actions and feelings about men might have affected Cassie and her chance at a solid relationship with a man someday.

She'd spent years sheltering and protecting her daughter, because she never wanted Cassie to experience what she'd gone through. Yet, if her daughter judged Sydney by her actions and how she treated men and relationships, her less-than-exemplary behavior contradicted everything Sydney wanted to teach Cassie about relationships, and intimacy with the right person.

But in order to do that, Sydney needed to show her daughter that a monogamous relationship could work, that stability with one person was important. That a healthy, mature, and caring relationship could exist, if she made the right choices in her life. And it was time that Sydney changed her own ways and led by example.

With that decision made, she reached for a Kleenex, dabbed at her still-moist eyes, and blew her nose. She needed to go and talk to Daniel, and she prayed that she hadn't ruined any chance of a future together by shutting him out so completely.

"Mom? Are you okay?"

At the sound of Cassie's soft, worried voice, Sydney turned around and found her daughter standing just beyond her bathroom door. Quickly she summoned a smile, but there was nothing she could do for her puffy eyes and red nose from her crying jag. "I'm fine, honey."

"No, you're not," Cassie insisted with a concerned frown. "What's wrong, Mom?"

"Nothing, really." Sydney tossed the tissue into the trash and headed into her bedroom, with Cassie trailing behind. "Just a little PMS. You know how that is." She wasn't ready to talk about her relationship with Daniel with Cassie, not until she talked to Daniel himself to see where things stood between them.

Her daughter didn't look convinced, but she didn't push the issue, either. Instead, when Sydney started making her mussed-up bed, Cassie went the other side of the mattress to help smooth out the covers and pull up the comforter.

It was almost noon on Saturday, and as she glanced at Cassie, this time she noticed that her daughter had straightened her hair and had put on a light application of makeup, including lip gloss. She was wearing a pair of brown cords and a long-sleeved V-neck sweater, and while the outfit itself was casual, Sydney was used to seeing her daughter in jeans or sweats on the weekend. And more disturbing was the scent of the Love's Baby Soft perfume her daughter had put on.

"What's up with you?" Sydney asked lightly as she fluffed her pillow before folding the comforter over it. "You going somewhere today that I don't know about?"

Cassie shifted on her feet as Sydney rounded the bed to where her daughter was standing. She looked a little anxious, and the way she chewed on her bottom lip was a dead giveaway that *something* was going on with Cassie. It was one of those mannerisms that a mother picked up on early in her child's life that gave her the edge of being able to read her kid before they even learned to talk. In this case, that lip chewing thing was enough to tell Sydney that Cassie was feeling uncertain and nervous about something.

Finally, Cassie said, "I wanted to know if I could go to

the mall today with Becky, and maybe catch a movie, too."

Normally, a fun day out with her girlfriend wouldn't be a cause for concern. However, coming only days after Sydney's meeting with Daniel about her why her daughter had been deliberately sabotaging her math grade, Sydney couldn't help but wonder if an outing to the local mall was a ploy to meet a boy.

Sydney inhaled a deep breath and forced herself to remain calm. Since she'd been so upset and emotional after her conversation with Daniel, she hadn't talked to Cassie about her deception, but she knew it was time. Time to let her daughter know that she was aware of what was going on, and time to let her little Tinker Bell be the fifteen-year-old teenager she'd become—no matter how difficult that would be.

But first, she needed to know what she was dealing with, and what, exactly, her daughter was up to. "Is Ryan going to be there?" she asked.

Cassie's eyes widened into huge pools of panic at the unexpected question. "I . . . uh . . . how did you know about Ryan?"

It wasn't a yes or no answer, but overall Sydney was grateful that her daughter hadn't denied knowing Ryan, or worse, lied and said she had no idea what Sydney was talking about. And if she wanted to keep that trust and line of communication open with her daughter, then she knew it *had* to start here and now.

Sydney sat down on the bed, and patted the space beside her. "Come here and sit down, honey," she said gently, knowing that anger wouldn't resolve this situation. If anything, it would push her daughter away, and that was the last thing she wanted. "We need to talk."

Reluctantly, and with a worried look on her face, Cassie did as she asked.

"A few days ago, Daniel called me and said he needed to talk to me about your inconsistent homework and math tests," Sydney told her. "After watching you in class and at after-school tutoring and seeing how Ryan was flirting with you, he realized that you might be deliberately dropping your test scores and grades for the sole purpose of getting into after-school tutoring so you could be with Ryan. Is that true?"

Tears filled Cassie's eyes, along with a healthy dose of dread. "Yes," she said, her voice cracking.

Sydney closed her eyes, trying to process the truth, and trying, as well, to deal with this revelation on a rational level. When she looked at Cassie again, it was clear that her daughter expected her to come unglued over the situation. And oh, Sydney wanted to, in the worst way, but managed to tamp down the urge to yell at Cassie for doing something so stupid. She'd learned a lot from Lora over the years, and even more from Daniel.

So instead, she gently thumbed away a tear making its way down her soft cheek. "Cass, why would you do something like that?" Sydney wanted, *needed*, to understand, even though she suspected she already knew the reason—that Cassie's overbearing, way-too-protective mother had pushed her daughter to sneak around to be with a boy.

"Because I really like him, Mom, and I knew you'd never let me go out with him or see him after school," she said, confirming Sydney's greatest fears. "I'm so sorry."

There was a wealth of regret glimmering in Cassie's gaze, which reassured Sydney. Cassie wasn't a defiant child—never had been—and Sydney didn't want to give her any reason to start now. But there were a few more questions she needed to ask her daughter.

"Was he at the Halloween party you went to?" she asked.

Cassie nodded. "Yes, but we didn't do anything. We just talked and danced. I swear!"

Sydney chose to believe her, and as long as Cassie told her the truth, they could work through any situation together. "And were you going to meet him at the mall today?"

Cassie swallowed hard. "Yes. But I was going to be with Becky, too." Then, she buried her face in her hands. "Oh, God, you're going to ground me for life, aren't you?"

Holding back a smile at her daughter's dramatic display, Sydney pulled Cassie's hands away so she could look into her eyes. "Truly, if I had my way, I'd keep you my little girl forever, but that's just not going to happen, now is it?"

Cassie shook her head. "No. I'm fifteen years old, and you need to let me grow up."

"I know," Sydney admitted. "It's just hard for me to accept sometimes, but I promise to work on being better about it."

Cassie stared at Sydney, a humorous look changing her expression. "Who are you and what have you done with my *real* mother?"

Sydney laughed, knowing that this sudden change of hers must be a shock to her daughter. "I'm still your same old mom. I'm just trying to handle things differently, in a way that will hopefully strengthen our relationship."

Reaching out, she smoothed Cassie's auburn hair away from her beautiful face. A face that had matured over the years and would no doubt turn male heads one day—if it wasn't already. Cassie was a good kid, and Sydney's goal was to keep her that way as much as possible. "It's important that you talk to me and tell me the truth, always, and I promise to listen and give you the best advice that I can. But this doesn't mean you have free rein to run wild and do whatever you want. I still have final say, okay?"

Cassie rolled her eyes. "I'm not going to run wild, Mom. I just want to have fun, like the rest of my friends."

And Sydney had to trust that her daughter would make the right decisions and not be swayed by peer pressure when it came to all those issues that every teenager came up against at some point in their lives.

"Mom . . . what's going on with you and Mr. Barnett?"

Just as she'd thrown her daughter off kilter with her unexpected question about Ryan, Cassie had just done the same to her. "Why?" Sydney asked curiously, unsure what her daughter knew. "Did he say something to you?"

"No," she said, shaking her head. "But you've been crying the past few days, which you *never* do, and he wasn't in a great mood yesterday at school, so I thought that maybe the two of you had a fight or something."

If she expected Cassie to be truthful at all times, her daughter deserved the same respect. "Yeah, we had a fight."

A frown creased Cassie's brows. "Are you not dating any longer?"

"No, but I'm hoping to change that." Then a thought dawned on Sydney. "Does my seeing Daniel bother you?"

Cassie shrugged. "At first, I wasn't thrilled about it, but I really like Mr. Barnett and he seemed to make you happy. So even though it's not the coolest thing for my mom to be dating my math teacher, I guess I can live with it."

Sydney grinned. "Thanks." She'd always kept the men she'd dated in the past out of Cassie's life because it made no sense to bring a man into her daughter's life who was only going to be around for a few days or weeks at the most. But Daniel was Sydney's first real, serious relationship, and her daughter's acceptance and approval mattered to her.

Cassie bit her bottom lip again. "Ummm, you never did say if I could go to the mall today."

Sydney thought a moment before answering, letting her daughter sweat it out just a bit. "I'll tell you what. I'll make a deal with you. How about I drive you and Beck to the mall so I can meet Ryan for myself, and then the three of you can hang out for a few hours, and go to a movie."

A horrified look transformed Cassie's features. "Mom!" she wailed in protest. "Do I *have* to make Ryan meet you?"

Apparently, it wasn't so cool to have the boy you liked meet your mom so early in the game, but Sydney held firm, needing her daughter to realize that she was still setting boundaries for her. "Yeah, you do. That's the deal, and a damn good one, I'd say, considering what you've put me through the past few weeks." She gently chucked Cassie beneath the chin. "So take it or leave it. It's your choice."

"I'll take it," Cassie grumbled.

"That's what I thought." Sydney stood, and so did Cassie. But before her daughter could walk out of the bedroom, Sydney pulled her into a tight hug.

"I love you, Cass," she whispered into her ear. "You know that right?"

Cassie pulled back and grinned. "Of course I know you love me. You tell me every single day. And, I love you, too."

At that moment, Sydney felt more content and fulfilled than she had in a very long time. Like she'd finally come to terms with her past, her fears, and just maybe it wouldn't screw up her future. She'd resolved her dilemma with her daughter, now she had one more issue to go. Sydney just hoped that Daniel was as easy to sway as her daughter had been.

THE last person Daniel expected to find standing on his doorstep on a Saturday evening was Sydney. One, because he never thought he'd see her again after how they'd parted ways, and two, she normally worked at The Electric Blue on the weekends. So this was a surprise in many ways, though he was reserving judgment as to whether or not her visit was a good or bad thing until he found out why she was there.

"Can I come in?" she asked, a slight, hesitant smile curving her glossy lips.

No matter what happened between the two of them, he'd never turn her away. He also wanted to believe that if things didn't work out with them, they could at least be friends, and he extended that olive branch to her now.

"Sure." He stepped back and let her walk past him into the entryway, then shut the door behind her, wishing she didn't look and smell so damn good. He led the way into the living room, switched off the TV show he'd been watching, and turned back to Sydney.

"Would you like something to drink?" he asked pleasantly.

She shook her head, though he could tell that she wasn't

quite sure what to make of his amicable attitude. "No, thank you."

While it was cold outside, it was warm in the house, and she was wrapped up in a wool coat. "Can I take your coat?" he asked.

She shifted anxiously on her feet, which were encased in a pair of sexy red pumps, the kind that made him think of a dozen erotic scenarios that included her wearing those seductive heels. "I . . . ummm, sure," she said, and unbelted the sash.

Once the coat was off, she handed it to him, and he laid it over the back of a nearby recliner. When he turned around and glanced at Sydney again, his mouth went bone dry. She was wearing a red blouse to match her shoes, and a pair of jeans that showcased her phenomenal curves. The bright, cherry color suited her normal outrageous personality and take-charge attitude, yet at the moment that brash and bold female was nowhere to be seen. In her place was a woman with uncertainty in her eyes who was wringing her hands nervously.

He stood across from Sydney, fighting the urge to wrap her in the security of his arms and give her the reassurance she seemed to be searching for. He didn't, only because he had to know what she'd come here to say. "So, what brings you by?" he asked in his most casual tone.

"You. Us." She glanced away from him and let out a low, defeated groan. "God, I am so *not* good at this sort of thing," she muttered.

The first part of her reply gave him hope, and the second comment almost made him smile, because she just looked so adorable, like a young girl coming clean with her first crush. And in a lot of ways, he supposed he was exactly that for her.

Even though he had a pretty good indication of where she was heading with her emotional statement, he prompted her to finish what she'd just started. She needed to say the words as much as he needed to hear them. "What *thing* are you talking about, Sydney?"

She met his gaze, looking so sweet and vulnerable. So everything he wanted and needed in his life. "You know, that *thing* called a *relationship*?"

He tipped his head. "Is that why you're here?"

"Yeah," Sydney whispered achingly. "I don't know what to say or do to make up for the way I treated you the other night, and I wish I could take back some of the things I said. I never meant to hurt you."

The relief that Daniel felt in that moment was incredibly profound—that he hadn't lost this woman he'd come to love. "I know. You were scared, and that was your way of protecting your emotions, and I understand that, Sydney," he said, and slowly walked toward her. "I understand you more than you realize."

Because he cared. Because he hadn't allowed sex to get in the way of knowing her, *really* knowing *her* and who she was beneath the I-don't-give-a-damn facade she'd hidden behind for so long. Because he'd stayed around long after most men would have cut their losses and moved on.

"There's more I need to tell you," she said. "I talked to Cassie about her math and Ryan."

"And?" he asked curiously.

"I think we've come to an understanding." She smiled, obviously proud of what she'd accomplished with her daughter. "I'm going to try and lighten up with her and boys and being a teenager, and she promised to be open and honest with me, though I know she'll slip up from time to time."

He chuckled and folded his arms loosely over his chest. "Most teenagers do, but it's a fair compromise."

"I think so," Sydney said, and wished she still didn't feel so uncertain about where she stood with Daniel. He'd yet to touch her, or give her any sign that he still wanted her to be a part of his life, and it was making her insane not knowing.

"And it's a great start, Sydney," he said, his tone low and sincere. "I know you mean well with Cassie, but she'll be just fine out there in the big, bad world."

She laughed, the sound more nervous than humorous. "God, I hope so."

His features turned serious. "Now, back to you and me."

She steeled herself for the very worst—like the brush-off she deserved after everything she'd put him through.

He raised a blond brow. "So, what are we going to do about this *thing* that's a bone of contention between the two of us?"

She'd always been the one to deny any form of a relationship, and now it was up to her to acknowledge that she was ready and willing to give one a try. "I want a relationship with you, Daniel, and everything that goes with it. But as you know, I haven't had a whole lot of experience in that department, so you need to be patient with me, okay?" She laid all her insecurities bare, trusting him to help her along the way, and especially when those fears reared their ugly head.

Finally, *finally*, he reached out and caressed his fingers along her jaw, then cupped her cheek in his large, warm palm. "We'll do this together, every step of the way, I promise."

Her throat tightened with emotion, and she closed her eyes, absorbing the strength and tenderness of his hand framing her face. He was the first man who'd ever touched her so gently, and without sexual intent, and it stirred feelings like she'd never experienced before. She felt so safe with him, so protected and cared for, and she knew deep in her heart that this man would never, ever intentionally hurt her.

"I can't believe what a lucky man I am," he said huskily, and grazed his thumb along her bottom lip. "I'm even luckier to be your first."

She blinked her eyes back open and frowned, certain she'd misheard him. "My first?" She was far from being a virgin.

"Your first relationship," he clarified with a sexy, wicked grin. "And, I'm hoping, your last."

Her heart felt full enough to burst. "I like the sound of that."

With a sexy growl, he slid an arm around her waist and pulled her flush to his body, which was hard and hot against hers, despite their clothing. Then he lowered his head and kissed her, and she opened herself up to him— her heart, her soul, and everything else that had been locked up inside of her for much too long. He took her mouth with an added depth and intensity that eclipsed every kiss that had come before. This was magic, the kind that made her believe in the possibility of a happily ever after. She tasted the sweetness of a lifelong promise, the assurance that he'd always be there for her, and the patience to trust and believe in the future and everything it had to offer.

And underlying it all was all the heat and passion that always simmered between them . . . and the desire that had yet to be fulfilled.

He ended the kiss and pressed his forehead to hers, and she knew there was one more thing she had to say before she lost the nerve. "Daniel . . ." She swallowed hard and forced out the words. "I'm falling in love with you, and I have to admit that it scares the hell out of me."

"Ahhh, another first, huh?" he teased gently.

She shot him a mock glare. "Stop gloating already. You're going to get a big head."

He laughed, and his chest rumbled against hers, creating a delicious friction that made her breasts swell and her nipples harden. "I can't help myself," he said, then the mischievous sparkle in his gaze faded to something warmer and more intimate. "And just so you know, I'm a little ahead of you on this one, sweetheart. I'm already in love with you, and I'm more than willing to wait for you to catch up."

What an amazing man Daniel was, and she couldn't believe that he was all hers. Unable to help herself, she threw her arms around his neck and kissed him again, just because she could, but this time their embrace turned hot and hungry very quickly.

When they pulled back, they were both breathing hard.

Daniel skimmed a hand down her back and over the curve of her bottom, pulling her closer, if that was even possible. "God, Sydney, I want you so much," he groaned against her neck.

The evidence of his desire pressed against her, hard and thick and needy. The feel of him made her equally hot and bothered. "Well, I've devoted myself to you and this relationship thing we've got going on," she drawled teasingly. "So, how long are you going to make me wait until we make love?"

He lifted his head and stared into her eyes. "Make love, not have sex," he murmured, clearly pleased with her choice of words. "I think right now would be absolutely perfect."

Taking her hand in his, he led her down the hallway to his bedroom, and it didn't take long for the two of them to strip off each other's clothes. Seeing him naked for the first time, his gorgeous body made everything feminine in her respond like it truly was her first time, and she absorbed the breathtaking feeling, then locked it away in her heart like a rare treasure.

She reached out and flattened her hand on his chest, right over his rapidly beating heart. Then holding his gaze, she oh-so-slowly glided her palm downward, exploring hot skin and firm muscle, all the way down to his flat belly, then lower still. Eventually, she wrapped her fingers around his erection and stroked him once, twice, until he groaned deep in his throat and grasped her wrist to make her stop.

He shoved the bed covers out of the way and pressed her down onto the cool, crisp sheets. He joined her, his gaze dark and hot as he pushed her legs apart so he could kneel in between. But instead of moving over her and taking her as she'd come to expect from her own experience, he lifted her left leg and kissed her ankle . . . and from there, he started his slow, leisurely exploration of her body.

He nibbled on her calf and ran his tongue along the sensitive patch of skin at the back of her knee, where she discovered she was soooo sensitive, and very ticklish. She squirmed and tried not to giggle, then laughter became a moot point as he trailed hot, moist kisses along her inner thigh, making her moan, then gasp, when he pressed that incredible mouth of his against her sex.

The tip of his tongue teased the folds of flesh, and she closed her eyes, threaded her fingers through his hair, and languished in the pleasure he so selflessly gave her. He settled in and took his time, making her mindless with desire, making her beg for the release he held just out of her reach. Her orgasm, when he finally took her over that crest, hit her with the strength of a hurricane, sweeping her into another realm of ecstacy, far beyond any erotic fantasy she could have imagined.

Before she could touch back down to earth or catch her breath, he was easing his way up her body, trailing his lips across her abdomen, suckling her breasts, nibbling at the sensitive crook of her neck. Sighing, she ran her palms down his chest, wanting to reciprocate, but he gently pushed her hands away and murmured, "next time," then slanted his mouth across hers in another one of those slow, deep, bone-melting kisses.

He settled his hips against hers. She felt the tip of his shaft glide through the slick cleft between her legs, then fit its broad head against the opening that led to the core of her. Instinctively, she pulled her knees up until they were riding his waist, needing him inside her, to be part of her, with an ache that went soul deep.

And he knew. Knew what she needed, because he needed it, too.

With a thrust of his hips, he slid into her, and she arched to take all of him, until he was buried to the hilt. He groaned and shuddered, and gave them both what they wanted. With a hard, driving rhythm, he pumped into her body, deepening the contact, extending the pleasure that built and swelled with each endless stroke, until she felt him tense above her, then shudder with the force of his own orgasm.

After a short while, he lifted his head and glanced down at her face. Their gazes met and held in the soft lamplight, and the emotional intensity in his eyes, the heat and passion still glittering in the depths—all for her—was unlike anything she'd ever seen or felt before.

Tenderly, he brushed away a few wayward curls from her cheek and smiled at her. "You were so worth the wait," he said softly, reverently. "In every way."

She knew he wasn't just referring to the sex, and she was amazed at his ability to make her feel so much emotion, to make her heart so full.

In that moment, she knew it was this man who finally made her whole and complete. And no one else would ever come close.

"JEEZ, Wilde Man, you'd think by that dark look on your face we were heading to a funeral, instead of a strip club." Kevin gave Joel a firm shove in the arm. "Cheer up, will ya?"

Joel grunted in reply and pushed his hands into the front pockets of his jeans as they walked toward the entrance to Leather and Lace, a classy gentlemen's club where the guys had decided to spend the evening. Reluctantly, and after much ribbing, Joel had agreed to accompany his buddies, but now he was rethinking his decision. He wasn't great company these days, not since walking out on Lora three weeks ago, and he would have rather spent the evening alone, wallowing in his own misery.

"You'd think after that new three-week security case you just finished you'd be ready to appreciate some fine pieces of ass," Jon added with a lively grin. "And let me tell you, they've got nothing but the finest here."

"Oh, yeah," Kevin agreed with a cocky swagger. "We're about to see a bunch of naked women!"

Kevin and Jon glanced at each other and let out a jovial

"ooh-rah!" at the same time, using the Marine Corps war-rior cry to express their joint approval and enthusiasm.

Joel laughed and shook his head at his friends' ridicu-lous antics, then suddenly realized that Ben wasn't shar-ing in their enthusiasm. Oh, he'd definitely voted to hang out at the strip club, but it was apparent that Ben had something on his mind. That, and he was watching Joel too damn speculatively, which was starting to annoy the hell out of Joel.

Jon smirked. "I'm telling you, if Crimson Rose doesn't get a *rise* out of Joel, I'm writing him off as a lost cause."

Joel had heard enough about "Crimson Rose" to know that she was the star attraction at Leather and Lace on the weekends. He also knew the man who ran the establish-ment, a comrade from their time in Iraq, and since it had been a while since he'd seen him, he wondered if he might be there tonight.

As soon as the door opened to the club, they were greeted by a loud blast of music and a big hulk of a bouncer. Jon, Ben, and Kevin filtered inside the joint, and Joel stopped to talk to the bouncer.

"Would Nick Santori happen to be here tonight?" Joel asked.

"Sure thing," the guy replied with a nod. "He's around here somewhere. I'll let him know you're looking for him."

"Great, thanks."

Joel followed his buddies toward the bar, drawing stares from other patrons, which wasn't an unusual re-action when the four of them were together. Being ex-marines, they all possessed that military demeanor and confident attitude, and as a group in a male-dominated club, it was four times the intimidation factor.

"Semper fi, man."

Joel turned at the sound of the male voice, loud enough to be heard above the noise and music, and upon seeing his old friend, he extended his hand in greeting. "Hey, Nick."

The other man shook his hand in a firm grip. "Been a long time, Joel."

Joel nodded. "I figured I'd come in and see why this was so much better than coming to work with me at ESS."

As Nick acknowledged the other guys, Jon glanced toward the stage where a leggy redhead was stripped down to a rhinestone G-string and equally sparkly pasties. "I think I'm catching the vision," Jon said with a wolfish grin.

"What can I say?" Nick shrugged his wide shoulders. "I've settled down, become respectable." He grinned like the lucky man that he was. "And the little woman didn't want me doing anything as risky as working security with you guys."

Joel chuckled, but he could definitely understand the appeal of Nick's job.

His friend gestured to one of the hostesses and told her to get the four of them a good table. But just as the scantily clad woman started to lead them away, Nick stopped Joel one more time.

"Seriously, thanks for offering to let me in, but I'm pretty happy with what I'm doing."

"Got it," Joel said, though he wanted to make sure that the offer stood indefinitely. "Still, if you ever change your mind . . ." Pulling a crisp, white business card from the inside of his leather jacket, he handed it to Nick.

"Elite Security Specialists," he murmured, then glanced back at Joel and gave him a brief nod. "I'll keep it in mind."

Reaching out with his elbow bent and arm up, Joel grasped the other man's hand again in a brothers-of-the-field handshake, then went to join his group. He took the last vacant chair and ordered a bottle of Sam Adams from a cocktail waitress, who gave him a sultry once over, which did nothing to pique his interest or libido, despite her incredibly short shorts and tight white blouse that left little to the imagination.

Once she moved on to the next table, he slumped back in his seat, feeling oddly disconnected from everything around him. Or maybe it was more that he'd disconnected himself from everything but work, because the swank club not only catered to a customer's comfort and pleasure, but the women were centerfold gorgeous, and their barely there costumes should have gotten some kind of reaction out of him.

He watched a perky cheerleader strip off the seemingly innocent trappings of a schoolgirl, and sat through the performance of a cowgirl who knew how to straddle more than the brass pole in the middle of the stage. By the time a female cop ripped off her velcro uniform and pranced around in little more than her birthday suit, Joel was done with his beer, and done with the whole stripper gig. It just wasn't doing a thing for him.

"I'm outta here," he said, and started to stand.

Jon grabbed his forearm and yanked him back down into his seat. "You can't go anywhere until you've seen Crimson Rose perform, and she's up next. Trust me, this babe is hot, and well worth the wait."

Joel rolled his eyes, but reclined in his chair once more, just to be a good sport. The show began, and out strolled a curvaceous woman wearing red and pink rose petals all over her body, and a red velvet, rhinestone mask that only left her red lips and jaw visible, giving her an air of mystery, unlike all the other strippers, who'd bared all.

Jon and Kevin watched the show avidly, and while Ben seemed to enjoy the show, he was much more subdued and indifferent than their friends, which Joel found curious.

Within a few minutes, the woman's costume was down to a few rose petals and some colorful body art and a trailing vine. The mask remained in place, and Joel had to admit that she was definitely exotic and gorgeous and had a body that made a man think of every carnal sin, but the truth of the matter was that the only woman who filled his nightly dreams and haunted him during the day was Lora. Everything about her, from her smile to her scent to the way she understood him like no other, was embedded in his brain—and, he feared, his heart.

He'd spent three weeks working an on-site security case, thinking that the time away would clear his head and give him the space he needed to put everything back into perspective again after his time with Lora. No such luck. He used to be a carefree bachelor who would have thoroughly enjoyed a boys' night out like this, but all he was now was a miserable, moody son of a bitch.

The performance ended, and so did Joel's patience. This time when he stood, nobody tried to stop him. "I'm heading out," he said, and tossed down enough money to cover his beer and a generous tip. "I'll catch a cab back to my place, so you guys stay and enjoy the rest of the show."

Jon and Kevin stared at him as if he'd lost his mind for walking out on a bunch of naked women, and when Joel glanced at Ben, the other man was sitting very quietly in his seat with a knowing look on his face. Out of the three of them, Ben had a way of reading him the best, and Joel turned and walked toward the exit before Ben could call him on his pensive mood.

He stepped outside and dragged a much-needed deep breath of cool air into his lungs. Just as he reached into his jacket pocket to retrieve his cell phone and make a call for a cab, the main doors opened again and Ben started toward where he was walking along the side of the club.

"Hey, wait up," Ben said, picking up his pace to join him.

Joel stopped and groaned, seeing his moment of solitude, and his quick getaway, vanishing like the thin night air. "Yeah, what's up?"

The parking lot lights illuminated the concern in Ben's eyes. "I just want to make sure everything's okay. I don't think I've ever seen you walk out of a strip club before closing time," he added with a grin.

Joel sighed heavily and rubbed at the tension gathering at the back of his neck. "I'm fine. Just tired."

Ben raised a brow, clearly not believing the excuse. "It's Lora, isn't it?"

Just hearing her name aloud was enough to cause his stomach to clench, and he cut his gaze to Ben, unsure where this conversation was heading. And he certainly wasn't going to make any assumptions. "What are you talking about?"

"Oh, come off it, Joel," Ben said candidly, and braced his hands on his hips. "You know damn well what I'm talking about. You've been sulking around since we wrapped everything up with Zach and you ended things with Lora."

Joel glared at him. "I don't sulk."

"Yeah, whatever," the other man said with a wave of his hand. "The point is, you're being a stubborn ass about the whole thing."

"What do you know about it?" he asked, annoyed as hell at Ben's accusation.

Ben braced his legs apart and crossed his arms over his chest. "Remember that night you brought Lora to Nick's Sports Bar?"

There wasn't a moment that he'd spent with Lora that he'd forgotten, that night especially. "Yeah, I remember."

"It was so obvious that the two of you were attracted to one another. Are you telling me that nothing happened between you and Lora while you were protecting her?"

Joel stiffened, feeling way too transparent and not liking it one bit. "That's none of your fucking business."

His friend took his reply as an affirmative, and did nothing to disguise his smug look. "Yeah, I thought so."

Joel bit back another rude expletive telling Ben exactly where to go, and how to get there in blunt, precise terms.

Ben tipped his head and studied him reflectively. "Judging by what a prickly S.O.B. you've been lately, I'm going to take a wild guess and say that you fucked things up with her, didn't you?"

If Ben weren't such a good friend, Joel would have hauled off and decked him—as much to release some frustration as to get him to back off of the subject. "Leave it alone," he warned.

"Why? Because you can't handle the truth?" Ben laughed, clearly not afraid of Joel and his threat—and he had no reason to be, since they were pretty well matched in strength. "She's a great girl. You know it. I know it. Hell, even those two womanizers in there know it," he added, hooking a thumb back toward the club to indicate Jon and Kevin. "What the hell's holding you back?"

That was the question Joel dreaded, because it dug up issues he'd been running from his entire life. Painful, emotional issues he'd been too afraid to deal with, and instead had walked away from the one woman who'd cared enough to see beyond his reckless, military facade to the real man beneath.

She'd been so fearless in risking her heart for him, and even though he knew he felt the same for her, he hadn't been able to bring himself to say the words, or stay. No, he'd taken the coward's way out and bolted for the door in an attempt to put as much distance as possible between himself and those fears that were all but strangling him.

A man on the outside, always looking in. Truer words had never been spoken. Since his mother's death, keeping himself apart had become an automatic response for him, a way of protecting his emotions as a young boy, then later in life with women and relationships. Holding himself at a distance had even served him well in the military, and had become a way to insulate himself from the pain and anguish that came from being such a vital part of the war, and seeing good men die.

Yet as he looked at Ben, a man he'd served in the war with, a man who'd trusted with his life and more, Joel realized that the bond he shared with Ben, Jon, Kevin, and even Zach was stronger than the one he had with his own brothers. These men would do anything for him, and vice versa, but for as close as he was with them, the day had come when that comradery and friendship just wasn't enough.

And if he didn't act for himself now, one day each of these men would create lives of their own that would hopefully include wives and children, and he'd be all alone, once again on the outside looking in. Being the confirmed bachelor he'd always sworn he would be . . . with absolutely nothing to show for it.

No one to love, cherish, and care for.

And more than anything, he wanted that person to be Lora. She, out of all the women who'd come and gone throughout the years, had understood him like no other, and had given him that sense of belonging he'd craved, but that had eluded him for too long. Until her, there had never been another woman whom he thought was worth putting his heart and emotions on the line for.

He scrubbed a hand along his jaw and silently cursed himself for being such an idiot.

"Don't think about it anymore, Wilde Man, just do it," Ben urged, as if sensing Joel's hesitation and internal turmoil. "Beg, grovel, and do whatever it takes, but go get the girl already, before some other guy comes along and realizes what a catch she is."

The thought of another man so much as touching Lora spurred Joel to action, and he flipped open his cell phone and made the call for a cab, and was promised one would arrive within the next ten minutes. With his decision made, and now anxious to get to Lora as quickly as possible, he knew it would feel like ten hours.

He tucked the unit back onto his waistband and turned back to Ben, realizing his friend was still standing there when he should have been inside tucking dollar bills into G-strings and enjoying a lap dance or two. Yet here he was, keeping Joel company outside where it was cold and not nearly as entertaining. Which made him wonder, once again, what was up with Ben.

"I noticed you weren't all that into those strippers, either," Joel commented, just to see what kind of reaction he got out of his friend.

The other man shrugged. "I've got a lot on my mind."

Joel grinned. "A woman?"

"Maybe," Ben replied, not giving anything away.

Joel took that as a yes, but didn't press for details, because he of all people knew and understood how a woman could tie a guy up in a dozen different knots. Instead, he laughed, needing a dose of humor to help him get through the next few hours ahead. "What a sorry pair we make, huh?"

A slight smile curved Ben's mouth. "You're in sorrier shape than I am."

Joel grinned, and couldn't argue the truth. "Hopefully not for long."

Twenty

LORA cleared off her section of tables, more than a little relieved that Sydney had cut her loose for the night first, before any of the other bar waitresses. Even though it was a Saturday evening, the initial early rush had ebbed into a comfortable pace, one that the other employees could easily keep up with. And with one less waitress on board, it meant more tips for them.

She was exhausted, emotionally and physically, and she just wanted to go home and crash for the rest of the night and through tomorrow. Thank God Sunday was her day off from both the bar and spa, and she planned to take advantage of that fact and sleep in until noon. Maybe after she got up, she and Cassie could go and rent a movie, hang out together, and order in a pizza, which would also give Sydney some time alone with Daniel, which she knew her friend always appreciated.

As Lora headed back toward the bar with a tray full of dirty glasses and empty beer bottles, her gaze drifted to the opposite end of the counter and the chair that had become exclusively Daniel's on the weekends. Whenever Sydney worked a Saturday or Sunday, Daniel was always there, if only to support her with his presence and enjoy her seductive dancing on top of the bar, which she did just for him.

At the moment, Sydney was standing at the other side of the bar in front of Daniel, talking and laughing at something he said while she blended a frothy drink. It was so obvious that Daniel adored Sydney despite her tarnished past, and Lora couldn't remember ever seeing her friend so cheerful, upbeat, and genuinely content with her life. Not to mention being a much calmer and more understanding mother to Cassie. And Daniel was a huge part of the reason for all those positive changes, she knew.

But for as much as Lora was thrilled for Sydney, because she deserved every bit of happiness that had come her way, there were times when she experienced a pang of envy, too, because she could have had the same kind of close, intimate relationship with Joel if he'd just given them a chance.

Sighing, she sidled up to the bar and unloaded the glasses from her tray. It had been three long, lonely weeks since Joel had packed his bags and walked out of her life after she'd put her heart on the line for him, and while the saying went "time heals all wounds," she was pretty sure this was one ache that would take a lifetime to mend.

A few days after Joel had left her, she'd received a package from Wilde Designs, and was shocked to discover that he'd bought her the *Midsummer Dream* stained glass design she'd fallen in love with. He'd included a short note with the gift: *I wanted you to have this. Always, Joel.*

The message had been too brief and impersonal, and it only served to cement the fact that he'd shut down his emotions when it came to her, just like he had with everything else in his life. The realization hurt deeply, and she only wished that work, and lots of it, would take away or at least dull the pain. But so far, no such luck.

After wiping down her tray and putting it on a shelf behind the bar, she went and retrieved her coat and purse, then said good night to Sydney and Daniel and headed out the front door to go to her car. Except as she walked outside into the cool night air, she came to an abrupt stop when she caught sight of Joel, who was leaning casually against his big black motorcycle, dressed in his signature black jeans, T-shirt, and leather jacket.

Her breath seemed to leave her lungs in a whoosh. With his short hair mussed and his arms crossed loosely over his broad chest, he looked gorgeous and sexier than even she remembered. He watched her intently with those dark blue eyes that had the ability to make her melt, and her heart started pounding hard and fast in her chest.

"Hey there," he said, his voice low and a little gruff.

She searched his eyes and expression for some kind of indication of why he was there, but couldn't find the answer she was looking for. "Hi," she returned, and strolled closer, trying to keep everything casual and friendly between them. Considering what Joel had done for her brother, chances were they'd run into one another every now and then. And, there was no reason not to keep things amicable between them. "How are you?"

"Good." He inclined his dark head. "And you?"

"Tired," she replied honestly, and with a small smile. "It's been a long night." For that matter, it had been the longest three weeks of her life without him in it, but she kept that comment to herself. "Thank you again for the stained glass design you had sent to me. I truly love it, but you shouldn't have." She knew it hadn't been cheap, even with his sister's discount.

"You're welcome, and I wanted you to have it."

After receiving the gift, she'd left a message on his cell phone thanking him for the present, and when she never heard back from him she could only assume that had been his polite way of severing their relationship. But now, here he was, and she had no idea why.

She shifted on her sore feet and adjusted the strap of her purse over her shoulder, striving to maintain a sociable and cheerful attitude when she was feeling anything but. "So, what brings you by The Electric Blue?"

"I came to talk to you."

"Oh." Again, his features were completely unreadable, and while she wanted to believe he was there for *her*, she wasn't about to make any assumptions. Most likely, he just wanted to give her an update on Zach and how he was doing in rehab.

She wondered why he hadn't come inside the bar, especially since he had no idea when her shift ended. "Have you been waiting out here for me very long?" she asked curiously.

"Awhile. Doesn't matter. I would have waited all night for you if I had to."

His words held a double meaning, which threw her completely off kilter, because she wasn't sure what, exactly, to make of his reply.

He straightened, reached for the spare helmet hooked on his bike, and held it out to her. "Can I sway you into going on a ride with me so we can go somewhere quiet and private to talk?" Apprehensive hope shone in his eyes.

The smart thing to do was to tell him no, because she knew being alone with him and not being able to touch him the way she wanted to, would be pure torture. But she was merely a woman, and love made her weak. Her heart said to take whatever time she could get with him, and she followed that internal voice now.

"Sure." She put the helmet on, and just like the first time he'd taken her for a ride, he bundled her up in a scarf and gloves to help keep her warm.

Then he grinned down at her. "Fast and intense, or slow and easy?" he asked, a teasing light entering his gaze. "It's your choice."

More double entendres, and because she wanted to believe that his comment was about more than just how fast his motorcycle could go, she opted for a more intimate and lasting choice. "I think this time I'd like to take things slow and easy."

"That sounds perfect to me," he agreed, and within minutes they were on the road, taking a leisurely ride through the city.

Sitting behind Joel with her arms wrapped around his waist, she closed her eyes and absorbed everything about the man in front of her. The heat of his body, and the strength of his hips and legs between her thighs as she sat astride him. She relaxed and enjoyed the ride, and before long they were pulling off the main road and onto a familiar pathway that led to a private, secluded area.

He turned off the engine, and she slid off the seat and took off her helmet while Joel set the kickstand, then got off the motorcycle, too. All at once she was flooded with vivid and provocative memories of the last time they'd been in this exact spot, when she'd seduced him on the front seat of his bike.

She inhaled a deep breath and turned to face Joel. "Why did you bring me here?" she asked, needing to know what this was all about. And, especially, what was on his mind.

A tentative smile eased up the corners of his mouth. "It's a nice, quiet, makeout spot, don't you think?"

Remembering how she'd insinuated the same thing the first time he'd brought her here over a month ago, warmth spiraled straight to her stomach. "Seriously, Joel."

His smile faded, and his expression turned sincere. "I brought you here because it's *our* spot."

Her chest grew tight with a wealth of hope. "What do you mean?"

"Well, it's always been my spot, a place where I'd go when I wanted to be alone and think. But then I brought you here, and that changed everything," he said gently. "*You* changed everything."

She swallowed hard. "How?"

"God, where do I start?" he said with a laugh that sounded as rough as sandpaper. But somehow, he found a way to explain. "When I first agreed to protect you for Zach, you were just an assignment, even though I was very attracted to you. But right from the very beginning, you had a way of seeing through me like no one else ever has, and that scared the crap out of me."

He braced his hands on his hips and paused a moment, as if gathering his thoughts. "When my mother died, I just shut down emotionally, and that's how I coped with things, by keeping my distance and telling myself I didn't need anyone in my life." He tipped his head, a hint of that boyish smile of his making an appearance. "But you already know all this about me, don't you?"

She nodded. "Yes," she whispered.

"And you know why?" he asked as he slowly closed the distance between them. "Because you've cared more about me than any one else ever has. You're the only person who scratched deeper than the surface layers, and the things you exposed weren't always pleasant."

He stopped inches away from her, his eyes gleaming in the moonlit shadows as his gaze connected intimately with hers. "But, looking back, it was like cleaning out an infected wound in order for it to heal. And you did that for me, Lora. You coerced me to open up and purge the pain, even though I did everything to resist you and your attempts. You made me face the past and deal with it for the first time in my life. But mostly, you forced me to *feel* more than I have since I was a kid."

Reaching out, he skimmed his warm fingers along her jaw, then cupped her cheek in his warm palm. "How can I not love such a selfless, generous, caring woman like you? The thing is, I can't," he said, his deep voice raspy with emotion. "I can't *not* love you, and I can't live without you."

He loved her. Lora's breath caught in her throat, and tears of joy filled her eyes. "I knew you loved me," she said, her voice thick with those unshed tears. "It just took you a little longer to figure it out."

He laughed, the sound light and carefree, and ringing with undiluted happiness. "Yeah, you're a real know-it-all, aren't you?"

He swiped at a tear that had fallen while she gave him a sassy grin. "When it comes to you, yes."

Gently, he rubbed his thumb across her bottom lip, his eyes darkening with desire when she followed the touch with her tongue. "I don't want to be alone anymore, Lora," he said huskily, earnestly. "I don't want to be that man always standing on the outside. There's only one person I belong with, and that's you, because I can't function worth a damn without you in my life."

She'd never heard sweeter words, or such a heartfelt declaration, and she knew that Joel had finally stepped out of the shadows, and had finally stopped running. "So, are you saying that you're done playing it safe with your heart and relationships?"

"I'm done playing it safe with *you*," he said adamantly. "For you, I'm risking it all." He framed her face in his hands and stared so deeply into her eyes she felt as though he was a part of her soul. "I love you, Lora Marshall. Will you marry me?"

She didn't have to think twice, and she threw her arms around his neck and hugged him enthusiastically. "Yes, I'll marry you," she said, dizzy with elation. "Yes, yes, a hundred times, *yes!*"

He chuckled in her ear as he held on to her just as tight, the feel of him as solid and secure as the future ahead of them. "I'll take that as a yes," he teased.

Grinning, and deliriously happy, she pulled back and slanted her mouth across his, pouring every ounce of love and affection she felt for him into the depth and sweetness of their kiss. With a groan, he gave her just as much passion, a lifetime of devotion, and the promise of a happily ever after.

In time, they broke the heated kiss, and Joel pressed his forehead to hers. "Now, back to the reason why I brought you here," he said, and kissed her softly once more. "This used to be my spot, but now I want this to be *our* place, where we can go to when we want to talk or just be alone."

She liked the sound of that. A whole lot. "And to make out?" she added with a wicked grin.

"Yeah, that, too," he agreed, and slid his hands down to cup her bottom and lift her tighter against him so there was no mistaking how much he'd missed her over the past three weeks.

He glanced at the motorcycle, then back to her. "You know, there's an awful lot of different things we can try on that bike," he drawled in a deliciously sinful tone as those wonderful hands of his now found their way beneath her coat and shirt, and he filled his palm with her breast. "You up for a little bit of risk and adventure?"

Her entire body heated, and her nipple hardened against the sweep of his thumb. "Oh, yeah," she said, and knew that life with Joel would always include a whole lot of risk and adventure, and she wouldn't have it any other way.

Be sure to watch for
Janelle Denison's next novel,

Wild for Him

coming in the summer of 2008
from Berkley Sensation.

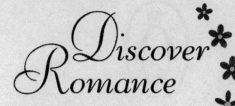